MW01514559

The Dragon's Lady

Scott Carman
and
Elizabeth Joy

© Copyright 2002 Elizabeth Joy and Scott Carman. All rights reserved.

No part of this publication may be reproduced, stored in a retrieval system, or transmitted, in any form or by any means, electronic, mechanical, photocopying, recording, or otherwise, without the written prior permission of the author.

Printed in Victoria, Canada

National Library of Canada Cataloguing in Publication

Joy, Elizabeth, 1966-
 The dragon's lady / Elizabeth Joy and Scott Carman.
ISBN 1-55369-541-0
 I. Carman, Scott II. Title.
PS3610.O9D73 2002   813'.6   C2002-902146-4

TRAFFORD

This book was published *on-demand* in cooperation with Trafford Publishing.
On-demand publishing is a unique process and service of making a book available for retail sale to the public taking advantage of on-demand manufacturing and Internet marketing.
On-demand publishing includes promotions, retail sales, manufacturing, order fulfilment, accounting and collecting royalties on behalf of the author.

Suite 6E, 2333 Government St., Victoria, B.C. V8T 4P4, CANADA
Phone   250-383-6864   Toll-free   1-888-232-4444 (Canada & US)
Fax   250-383-6804   E-mail   sales@trafford.com
Web site   www.trafford.com   TRAFFORD PUBLISHING IS A DIVISION OF TRAFFORD HOLDINGS LTD.
Trafford Catalogue #02-0354   www.trafford.com/robots/02-0354.html

10   9   8   7   6   5   4   3

Many people contributed to the telling of this tale. Our family and friends were incredibly patient and supportive. Without them, this would not have been possible.

First and foremost we thank God for our success and all with which he has blessed our lives. We'd also like to thank:

Our families: Bob & Sandy Carman, Joy and Carel Boots, Bill Irons, Brett Carman, and Eric Blanton

Our "support crew" who goaded us to finish the job faster: Kenny & Katie Hall, Kyle & Merritt Stokely, Chad Mirich, Bill Lechlitner, Eric Schnepp, Matt Chatlak, and Brian Bell

Our first readers, who helped us with the lengthy editing process: Eric Blanton, Rachel Spangler, and Adam, Jessica, and Ryan Zann

Wrestling technical advisor Joe Rules of the JWA Wrestling Alliance

Website host and giver of sound business advise, Tom Thomas of Inrgi.com

The Blanton Boys, who helped with the concept

Their continuing support has made this dream of ours so much sweeter, but all glory and praise goes to the Lord our God and his son Jesus Christ. We thank all of you from the bottoms of our hearts and God bless all of you.

This book is dedicated in loving memory to Judy Blanton and Walter Knapp.

Enjoy!

Scott and Elizabeth

Chapter 1

Robyn sat at her desk, wading through the day's paperwork. She was dressed in her green service dress uniform, and her short wavy blond hair fell softly around her face. It was already 0900 hours, and she hadn't gotten a thing done except sit through another boring meeting. Her door was shut, but she could still hear the phone ringing in the outer office, and there was a Private trimming the bushes with a noisy electric trimmer outside her window. She was grateful, however, to have a door to close. She'd been promoted to Major only three weeks before, and only then had she gotten her own office. It was small, but it was hers, and she'd spent an entire Saturday afternoon hanging pictures and arranging various souvenirs of her career. A cup of coffee sat steaming on her desk, and she sipped it gingerly as she reviewed the promotion package for one of her troops. She leaned back in her leather chair and propped her left foot on her right knee as she read.

The intercom buzzed and Robyn reached for it automatically. "Yes?"

"There's a Mr. Adkins on line two for you, ma'am."

"Thanks," she said and pressed the button. "Major Smith."

"I heard you got promoted. Congratulations!"

"Thanks! I figured Mama would have told everyone by now!"

"Yeah, she's awfully proud of you, but the Army is who really benefits. Listen, I have a job for you."

"For me? Chet, you know you have to go through DOD."

"Done. You are officially heading up a mission for CIA. The fax should be hitting your CO's desk shortly."

"What is it?"

"Can't tell you right now, just get three or four good guys and meet me in DC day after tomorrow."

"Who do you have on your end?"

"Me, Chad, Rachel, and Lilly. I'm working on either Matt or Doc, knowing them they'll arm wrestle for who gets to go."

"OK, see you there." She hung up the phone and called her Ranger counterpart.

"Major Hughes," was the answer.

"Major Hughes, Major Smith. I need a few good men."

He laughed. "I bet you do, you wild woman! What for?"

"Joint mission with CIA per the request of Mr. Adkins."

"Who do you want?"

"Rodriguez and Tomlin for sure. And Paxton."

"Paxton is out of the country on leave."

"Shit! Kenny, I really need a good sniper."

"Got you covered. I have a new guy, and he's good. His name is Ericson. Anyone else? What about a medic?"

"We're covered there."

"OK, I'll send those three over to you for briefing. Good luck if I don't talk to you before."

"Thanks!" She hung up the phone and it rang again.

"Major Smith," she answered.

"Smitty, did you get a call from the spooks?"

It was Colonel Benson, her commander. "Yes, sir, and I've begun assembling the team."

"Good. Any idea what it is?"

"None. Did he tell you?"

"No, but I'm itching to find out. He just said that he needed someone to help him with an operation, and he wanted you because you'd interned for him at CIA."

She laughed. "I'll let you know as soon as I find out, sir."

"You do that," he said, and hung up the phone.

She went to the filing cabinet and pulled out the paperwork she needed to go over before her mission. It was a standard packet of pre-deployment garbage, and she made photocopies for everyone on her team. Her current assignments were quickly organized so they could be finished or passed to someone else, and her team soon arrived. They were ushered into her office by a private and all three stood at attention before her desk.

"At ease, gentlemen. Have a seat."

"How's life been, Major?" She had worked with Rodriguez before, and he was both competent and companionable, but tended to be a little arrogant.

"Good, Rod. How about you?"

"Can't complain."

"Good. How about you, Tomlin?"

"Just fine, ma'am. Looking forward to a little action."

She smiled and extended her hand to the one man she didn't know. "You must be Ericson."

"Yes, ma'am," he answered, shaking her hand firmly.

"Welcome aboard. I have it on very good authority that you are an excellent sniper."

"I do my best. I'm a natural shot, must be genetic."

"How's that?"

"My father was in Army Intel, and my uncle was a tail gunner. We used to hunt together."

"And now you hunt for a living?"

"Yeah, and it's legal!" It didn't seem to bother him that part of his job could entail killing another human being solely on the orders of someone else. Snipers gave her the creeps, not because they killed people; everyone in the armed forces could be called on to do so. But she hadn't met a sniper yet who didn't love his job more than anything.

"Well, gentlemen, you've probably been told that we'll be doing a joint excursion with CIA. I don't know any of the details at this time, only that we need to be in DC day after tomorrow. I would suggest finishing your paperwork today, along with any loose ends you may have. Major Hughes will arrange with your companies to have any official appointments rescheduled, and I'll arrange for us to have transport tomorrow evening. I need phone numbers where you can be easily reached for the next 24-36 hours. Any questions?"

"What about hazard pay?" Tomlin asked.

"I'll get back to you, but I imagine it will be CIA standard."

There were no more questions, so she gave each of them the applicable paperwork, got phone and pager numbers, and dismissed them. The rest of the morning was spent clearing up the paperwork she had to finish, and the afternoon making arrangements for herself and the team to go.

Chapter 2

They arrived at CIA headquarters at 0915 hours on October 12. The guard called ahead, then ushered them to the office of Mr. Chet Adkins. He sat behind a large oak desk in front of a large computer. There were pictures of his wife and children on the desk and the credenza behind him. He hadn't changed much in the last six years, when she'd finished her last internship with him. She'd worked for him every summer while she was in college, due in part to the fact that he had known her parents for years, and in part because she was a Physics major with strong map reading skills. She'd spent a lot of time analyzing satellite reconnaissance and had found the knowledge invaluable in her military career. He was not a big man, only about 5'8" tall and 160 pounds, and he appeared to be in his late 30's. His black hair was neatly trimmed, and he wore a brown Armani suit with a white shirt and a matching tie.

Robyn always felt underdressed with him, and this was especially so as she entered his office in her black fatigues. Her team was similarly dressed, but it didn't seem to bother them.

Chet looked up from his computer and said, "Hi, Robyn!"

"Hi, Chet. What's up?"

"We'll go over that in just a minute. Everyone else is in the conference room. Is this your whole team?"

"Yes," she said, and introduced them individually. He shook their hands, and then led them all to the conference room down the hall. Inside sat a small group, all of whom Robyn knew well. They were friends of her parents and had been her neighbors during her teenage years. They all greeted her warmly as she entered, and she introduced her team. None of her men showed any sign of surprise that the other part of the team was comprised of more than half female members, but she knew she'd hear about it when they were in private.

Chet took his place at the head of the table as Robyn and her men seated themselves. To Chet's left was his younger brother Chad, who at 6'2" was six inches taller than his older brother. He had jet-black hair and a strong build, and he knew it. He was the vainest man Robyn knew, and also one of the most talented free-lance security specialists ever to work for the CIA.

Next to Chad sat Rachel Sanderson, a black-haired beauty in jeans and a black turtleneck sweater. She sat with an air of assurance that only came with years of experience with covert operations. Although she was ten years older, she was the closest thing Robyn had to a sister. She had met Robyn's father in the Army and later married a wrestling friend of his. She'd been Robyn's idol through high school, her mentor through college and Officer Candidate School, and her confidant and advisor above all.

In her Army days Rachel had been a helicopter pilot, dropping off and retrieving soldiers in hot landing zones during Operation Desert Storm and numerous other conflicts. As one of the few women in the pilot's seat, she'd had to endure discrimination and harassment. Many had dropped out of training because of it, but Rachel was toughened and strengthened by it and had been highly respected by those she worked with regularly. Her career was abruptly ended when she got into a fight started by an off-duty military police woman which escalated into an all-out brawl. Rachel was dismissed from the Army and escaped prosecution only because her father, a retired general, intervened on her behalf.

She met the others at a party Robyn's father threw years before. After a conversation with Chet she began free-lancing for the CIA occasionally. She was very selective about the jobs she accepted with him now; her main mission was to raise her three stepdaughters and provide stability for them while her husband was on the road.

Beside Rachel was Lilly Ryan, a very tall, statuesque Welsh woman. Her long brown hair hung loose around her shoulders, and her green eyes roamed the room, sizing up the newcomers. Her eyes passed over Robyn and moved to each man in turn. Robyn knew what she was doing: guessing what each man did and assessing his physical ability to do it. She had once been a member of the British Secret Service and had become accustomed to working with new people. Like the others, she occasionally free-lanced for operations that were considered highly covert. In real life, she was married to Mike, a full-time CIA agent, and owned an import/export business.

The last member of Chet's side of the team was Doctor Michaela Adkins, Chet and Chad's stepmother. She was very unassuming on the outside, shorter than everyone else at 5'5". Her build looked much more slight than it was, and her looks were deceiving. In reality, she was a true fighter. She could be ruthless when she had to be, and she'd needed to on more than one occasion having grown up in Tel Aviv, Israel. She was a medical doctor who had worked at a large hospital in Israel for a few years, treating small children for bullet wounds and soldiers who were stoning victims. When she began to burn out she accepted a position at the morgue and assisted the chief coroner with autopsies, but this too proved to be taxing. Eventually she immigrated to the United States and applied to the CIA Academy. She'd met her husband through his sons. After their marriage she resigned from the CIA and went back to practicing medicine. She was a strong willed woman and allowed only her husband to call her Michaela. To everyone else, she was just Doc. Whenever she was questioned about it, her standard reply was, "I was Michaela in Israel. When I left, part of me remained there. My name just doesn't fit me anymore."

"OK, guys," said Chet, "We have two people missing in action. Last contact with them was in the New Mexico desert, near Roswell, of all places. We had tracking devices on them, and they suddenly disappeared without a trace. We need to find out what happened to them and recover them if possible."

"Who is our official leader for this picnic?" asked Lilly with a thick accent.

"I'm handing the reins to Robyn. She knows more about this than I ever will; that's why I called her in."

"Do you have satellite reconnaissance yet?" asked Rachel.

Chad answered, "Not yet, Rachel, but Xenia is working on it. We should have some good stuff by the time we leave."

"And when will that be?" asked Doc, "I have to pick up a few more supplies for my medical bag."

"We're leaving at 10:00 PM tonight, or 0300 hours ZULU for you military types," answered Chet, looking at Robyn with a small grin. "See me after the meeting, Doc, and I'll help you with the supplies. Any other questions?"

There were none, so they got up to leave. Robyn took her time getting up, watching her team closely for reactions. Tomlin was the first to notice Lilly stand. She was a very noticeable woman. At six and a half feet tall, very muscular and toned, she was hard to miss. She turned heads wherever she went, and she paid very little attention to it. Today she wore black jeans and a gray turtleneck with a black denim vest, which was more clothing than Robyn had ever seen her in. Lilly normally tended to dress in more revealing clothing. Tomlin nudged Rodriguez and Ericson, who looked at her in amazement. Robyn stifled a grin, and ushered them out the door. She told them to go to the hotel and get some rest, and that she would join them later in the afternoon. Then she went back into the conference room to see Chad, Lilly and Rachel laughing, and Chet and Doc in deep conversation.

She went to stand by Chad and said, "I guess you saw my guys."

"Yeah, I thought their eyes would pop out," said Rachel, still chuckling.

"What can I say," said Lilly, "we grow big in that part of Wales. It's like the Welsh Texas!"

They all laughed, and Chad said, "So, kid, how's Uncle Sam treating you? Have you become all that you can be yet?"

"I'm still working on that. I'm told that when you become all you can be, they make you retire, so I'm milking it. I don't expect to reach full potential until I get to full bird colonel, at least!"

"Ah, the ambitions of a young Army officer," Rachel said, wistfully, "I used to be that way. Then that bitch MP had to pick a fight. Oh, well, it was the Army's loss."

"So what's the deal?" Robyn asked.

Lilly answered. "My darling Mike was out for a romp with two other agents. I don't know what they were doing, but they ran into a bit of trouble and Mike's testosterone level got the better of him. He escaped, but the other two were captured. We tracked them almost to Area 51 before their tracking devices were evidently discovered. Mike wanted to be here to fill us in on all of the details, but he was injured during their excursion, and they haven't released him from the hospital yet."

"Oh, goody, so we have to go to Area 51? I don't like the sound of that. It's like playing poker in a cemetery at midnight on Halloween."

"Exactly," Chet confirmed as he stepped up beside her, "which is why I called you. Your poker face is a lot better than mine."

"Wow, thanks, buddy. What am I up against?"

They spent the rest of the morning and the better part of the afternoon going over strategy, intelligence, and the logistics of getting the team from Washington to Roswell. When she was satisfied that she had all the information she needed, she went back to the hotel and took a hot shower to clear her head. Then she ordered dinner for herself and the team, and called them to her room. She gave them the details they needed and they formed a game plan. There were only a few hours left before it was time to get on the plane, so after the men left, she stretched out on the bed fully clothed and dozed. Her internal alarm went off automatically well before it was time to leave, and she moved about the room, preparing.

The flight was relatively short and uneventful as the CIA Lear jet skimmed through the clouds in the night sky. They arrived near midnight local time and set out immediately for the spot where the team had last been seen. They all dressed in black and wore the appropriate face paint, camouflaged with the desert night, in case there were still people with hostile intentions in the area. They tracked their missing colleagues to the spot where they had disappeared, and as anticipated, there was no sign of them. Just ahead loomed the fence, complete with concertina wire, which enclosed the infamous Area 51.

Her ear mike crackled, and she could hear Ericson, who was with Chad, checking out what lay ahead. Ericson had his spotter scope, and he said, "Major, I think there's something going on beyond the fence that you should come take a look at."

"Roger that," she answered, and moved to the front as Chad moved further ahead. Ericson handed her the spotter scope and she peered through it to the place he pointed out. It was a small building near the back of the complex. Very little of it was visible, the majority of it concealed by other buildings. But she could clearly see that a light was on, when the rest of the complex was dark. There were people moving back and forth past a window.

"Can you get a little more zoom on this thing?"

"Yes, ma'am." He took the scope and made an adjustment, then handed it back.

Suddenly her ear mike crackled, and Chad's voice informed her that they had company. She pressed her microphone to broadcast to her team and told them all to take cover. Simultaneously, they fell and lay flat on the sand. She gave the scope back to Ericson and told him to tell her what was out there.

"Looks like some sort of vehicle coming out of the complex. I've never seen one like it. Switching to ultraviolet. It's not a jeep, not a Hummer, not a truck."

"Well what the hell is it, corporal?" she hissed.

"I don't know ma'am, but it's headed this way."

She looked around. Their position couldn't have been much worse. There was no place to hide and very little cover. The cacti scattered around wouldn't stop bullets long if it came to that. She could see the vehicle now, and it was closing fast. Quickly she got the team together and moved to hide behind a relatively large clump of vegetation, hoping whomever it was driving that thing would pass right by. As she watched the vehicle closed on their position. She pulled her nine-millimeter side arm and quietly chambered a round. The others followed her lead. Beside her, Ericson pulled his sniper rifle off his back and aimed at the approaching vehicle. Her hand moved down to the left cargo pocket of her pants and she felt the extra clips that were tucked in there. As the vehicle approached, she undid the button for easy access in case she needed it. It looked as if it might go past, but suddenly it changed course slightly and stopped about thirty feet from their position. The only way she could think of to describe it was a pick-up truck the size of a Sherman tank. Whatever it was, it didn't have any wheels. It seemed to hover two to three feet over the ground, but sand underneath it was undisturbed. It made very little sound and seemed to be made of a flat black metal. A figure appeared from behind the enclosed area and ordered them to come out. She motioned to the others for silence, hoping whoever was out there would think they had been mistaken and look elsewhere. The order came again. Ericson looked at her, and she looked back at him and nodded. He aimed carefully, squeezed the trigger, and the round exploded from the end of the barrel. The figure fell, but five more popped up and returned fire. Robyn aimed at one and shot, and the others did the same. The five went down and there was silence. As she shifted slightly to look around, she heard the sound of the safety lever of a large rifle being clicked off. She froze, knowing the only large rifle in their group was Ericson's, and his safety was already off.

"Don't even think about moving," a strange voice said from behind them. There were steps as someone moved around to stand in front of her. The barrel of a large rifle was trained on the group. Whoever it was, he wasn't alone. She could hear other people moving into position to surround them.

"Put your weapons on the ground," said the voice. It was very deep and the accent was thick, rather like a Slavic language, but not one she could place. She put down her weapon, and the others followed suit. "Now put your hands up." As they did, she could hear her team being placed in handcuffs, and it was only a matter of seconds before she wore them herself.

They were ushered into the strange vehicle, which then returned to the building she'd seen earlier. Their handcuffs were removed and they were placed in a cell where they sat for almost an hour before a strange looking man came in. He was very big, nearly eight feet tall. He had very pale skin, crystal blue eyes, and short white hair. He was wearing what appeared to be a blue silk tunic that was belted around his waist, black leather pants, and black leather ankle boots. He had several tattoos on his neck, face, and hands, and there was no reason to believe that those weren't the only ones that he had. As he approached the cell, Robyn's heart pounded.

"Who is the leader of this group?"

She rose to her feet. "I am."

"A woman? Amusing. Please come with me." He opened the door, let her out, and locked it again. He took her to a small room with cinderblock walls. There were two plastic chairs, and he beckoned her to sit in one. She sat, taking a deep breath and willing herself into calmness.

"What is your name?"

"Robyn Smith."

"What are you doing here, Robyn Smith?" The accent was very thick, and she listened closely, as much to understand what he said as try to place the accent.

"I'm looking for some friends. They disappeared in this area."

"Why did you come at night?"

"It's when we arrived. We wanted to start right away."

"And you needed this to find them?" He walked to a corner and picked up Ericson's rifle.

"We considered doing a little hunting while we were out. I hear the jackrabbits in this area are particularly good this time of year."

He pulled the other chair closer to her and sat down, leaning forward until he was nose to nose with her. "Don't play games with me, little girl. You have no idea what you've gotten yourself into."

"Really? Why don't you tell me?"

He leaned back, a menacing smile on his face, and crossed his arms across his broad chest. "Who are your companions?"

"Friends of mine. They were helping me look for my other friends who disappeared."

He nodded, got up, picked up the rifle, and left the room. She watched in amazement, then got up and tried the handle. It was locked, as she knew it would be, and she looked quickly around the room. There was a very small window at the top of the wall opposite the door, near the ceiling. It was too high for her to get to, even with the chairs, and too small for her to get through even if she could. There was nothing else in the room. Sitting back down, she tried to think of a way to get everyone safely out. She didn't have to wait long. The man came back in and shut the door behind him.

"You will come with me, Robyn Smith."

"Look, I don't know what you have planned, but my friends don't need to be involved. Why don't you let them go and I'll do whatever needs to be done?"

He smiled and led her out of the room. They went back outside, and he put her in the back of another vehicle, very similar to the one she'd seen earlier, but fully enclosed. She got in and discovered that it was their version of a deuce and a half truck. She sat on the bench and noticed that her team was already there. The vehicle began to move. 'Well, so much for that attempt,' she thought.

Chet slid over to sit beside her. "Robyn, what did he say?"

"Nothing. He asked me who I was and what I was doing, then I tried to get him to let you guys go, and you see where we are."

They traveled in silence for a short time when suddenly a bright blue light appeared at the front of the truck, piercing the ceiling and moving back, as if they were driving through a curtain. As it passed over Robyn she felt dizzy and hot, and then the light passed out of the truck altogether. The noises from the outside of the vehicle had changed abruptly. The wind suddenly stopped blowing, crickets immediately ceased chirping, and it sounded as if they had entered a busy interstate. They all looked at each other nervously. The journey continued, and soon they stopped. The back of the vehicle opened and it was daylight. They were ushered out, taken into a large building, and placed in a room. There were other people who looked as if they'd been there several days.

They sat down on the dirt floor and talked quietly, trying to figure out where they were, why they were there, and what to do next. It was less than an hour, as far as Robyn could tell, when they were collected and taken to another room. They were checked for injuries and told to wash their face paint off, then fitted with shackles and chained together. The shackles were lined with thick leather on the inside, and when Robyn touched the outside of the metal ring around her ankle to adjust it, a shock traveled quickly up her arm. She cried out in pain and surprise. A nearby guard, who looked like he was part human, part ogre, and part ape, said, "Don't touch!"

Rachel, who was standing beside her, leaned over and said, "He must be a rocket scientist."

They were led onto a platform, and Robyn realized with a shock that they were about to be sold as slaves. Looking at her companions, she could see they had made the same realization. The crowd in front of them was very strange, and Robyn felt as if she had stepped off the face of the earth and landed in a bad science fiction movie. There were creatures that she had never even dreamed about, and they all spoke in some strange language. The auctioneer appeared to be the same race as the men who captured them. As she willed herself to wake up from this nightmare, a tall man in black cut through the crowded slave trading area. By-standers parted like the Red Sea. He wore black leather and a long hooded cloak, and he was the most gorgeous man Robyn had ever seen. As he moved through the crowd, Robyn heard a few people murmur 'Nyakas' in hushed tones of respect and awe. His companion was average height and well muscled, but he had tribal tattoos on his face and neck. His head was shaved except for a brown topknot, which was braided and still reached to his waist.

Nyakas stood beside his companion, his cloak blowing gently in the breeze, and intently surveyed the next group of humans for sale. The men seemed well built, always a good sign for manual labor. The women were attractive and well toned, and would make good servants and maids. When he saw the last of the females, he looked in amazement. 'She's beautiful,' he thought, and automatically began bidding. His companion looked at him with a bit of confusion when he heard his first bid. The dwarf-like man who had controlled the bidding previously stood up angrily and looked at his competition. Nyakas bid again before the dwarf could counter. The dwarf was furious, ranting in a strange language. He walked past Nyakas and left the arena. Nyakas' eyes were still locked on the woman with gorgeous blonde wavy hair and eyes as beautiful as the sky. Then, without warning his father was behind him.

"Quite a price to pay for just some humans, don't you think, Nyakas?"

"Father," Nyakas replied, "I had no idea you were here."

"Of course you did, my son. I'm always here on the third day of each new moon."

"Yes, yes, of course, I've just had a lot on my mind lately."

"Please, son, come to see me next week. There is something we need to discuss."

Nyakas replied, "Of course, Father. I'll see you soon." His father walked away, and Nyakas turned his companion with a confused look on his face. "Gravity, how much did I pay?"

Nonchalantly, Gravity replied, "One million gold." His eyes widened with a half smile at the look of shock on Nyakas' face and he said, "I tried to tell you."

Nyakas chuckled. "I guess we should go get our prize."

"Yes, my lord," Gravity replied.

They went to the holding area to meet the new help. Gravity studied them all, looking each of them deeply as if searching their souls. He briefly examined each of them, feeling their arms and shoulders for muscle and checking them over for any injuries that had not already been caught. Robyn observed, feeling very much like a newly acquired farm animal. Gravity looked at Nyakas and nodded, and Nyakas nodded back. As their servants escorted the new prisoners, Nyakas' father watched in silence.

A young man came to stand behind him. "Odd, isn't it, Father," the voice said.

"Yes, quite," Malitor replied, "I want you to keep a close eye on your brother for me."

The man stood behind his father, his handsome face broadening into a demonic smile underneath his neatly trimmed bleach blond hair. His tunic was white and immaculate, with buttons that looked like alligator teeth, and his loose black pants were held up with an elaborate gold belt. His neck and fingers were adorned with gold as well. His eyes were dark blue and mysterious, glittering in anticipation of what he had in store for his brother.

Robyn and her friends were led from the holding area to an archway. Gravity appeared to go into a trance and made some motions with his hands. The archway began to glow, and then crackle as if charged with electricity. Nyakas watched, his demeanor as if he was waiting for a bus. Without a word, he took Robyn's elbow and began walking to the archway. She resisted, and he pulled her along, her friends trailing behind, still shackled. They passed through the archway and they found themselves in a forest. The shackles had disappeared but were quickly replaced by rope. They were loaded into a wagon, and bumped through the forest for what seemed like hours, until a large castle appeared as they crested a hill. They passed through the castle wall gate, and Nyakas called to the guard at the portcullis.

"Creedan! Get some of the others and make our new guests at home!"

"Yes, my lord. Shall we accommodate them with the last ones?"

"Yes, that will do."

They were taken out of the wagon and led into a dungeon, where they were placed in a dark cell. The door clanged shut and the guards left. Robyn went to the far corner and sat down on the floor. Drawing her knees to her chest, she placed her arms on her knees and her face in her hands. She rubbed her temples with her fingertips, trying to make sense of it all. When she looked up, Tomlin, Rodriguez, and Ericson had taken their places around her.

Rodriguez spoke first. "Now what, Major?"

She dropped her hands and looked at him. "I don't know, Rod. I'm trying to figure that out."

They moved a few feet away, giving her space and time to think. She glanced around at the others and noticed Lilly sitting alone. Getting up, she walked over and sat down beside her, again drawing her knees up to her chest. "Are you all right, Lilly?"

"No, not really," Lilly answered slowly, "Not at all, really."

She placed her hand on Lilly's and squeezed her fingers lightly. It scared her that Lilly was afraid. Nothing ever seemed to frighten Lilly.

"There's something you don't know, Robyn, and I hadn't intended to tell anyone right now."

"What's that?"

"I'm pregnant."

Robyn stared in disbelief. "You're what? Oh, no, Lilly, please, tell me you're kidding."

"I'm afraid not. I only just found out myself. I thought all of this would be cut and dried and we'd be home in a day or two. I haven't even told Mike yet."

Robyn's eyes filled with tears and she placed her forehead on her knees and took a deep breath. This was all just too much. First the mission went badly, and then they were sold, now this. Just when she thought she'd hit bottom, Tomlin whispered to her that they had more company. Gravity was striding to the bars of their cell, and she stood to meet him.

He looked at her appraisingly, assessing this woman. "I'm sure you are wondering where you are."

"Yes, among other things."

"You are in the kingdom of King Nyakas. He is the man who bought all of you today. I am Gravity, his first knight and General of his army. You will remain here in the dungeon for a time, and then you will be given work assignments. When you see King Nyakas, you will bow to him. If you do not, you will die. If you try to escape, you will die. If you disobey, you will die. There is no way you can get back to your former life. It is in another dimension. If you cooperate and work well, you will be treated well. If you do not, you will die." He turned on his heel and walked away.

"Wait!" Robyn called after him. "Please wait!" He continued to walk away and was soon out of sight. "Damn it! Come on, I need to talk to someone here!" Nobody came, and she sat down, frustrated, beside the bars.

Chet sat beside her and put an arm around her shoulders. "It's OK, Robyn."

"No, it isn't, Chet. You were all my responsibility, and I let you down. I got us into this mess."

"There was no way you could have known what would happen."

"I should have known something, Chet."

"It was out of your control. All we can do is try to figure something out."

They sat for several hours when Gravity came back. This time two servants with trays accompanied him. The cell was opened, and the servants brought the trays in. They were filled with food, nothing fancy, but far better than any of them expected. Gravity came to stand directly in front of Robyn.

"The king wishes to see you."

"Me?"

"Yes, you are the leader, are you not?"

"Yes, I am. Does he want to see me now?"

"Yes. Follow me, please. You will eat with him."

She looked at the others and discovered they were watching her. She nodded, hoping to encourage them, and followed him from the cell. She shuddered as the door clanged shut and the lock slipped into place. She hated leaving them there, but she also knew that this could be the chance she was hoping for.

They walked up a flight of stairs and through a long hallway to a massive set of double doors. Gravity opened one and beckoned her in, then went in behind her and shut the door. She found herself in what appeared to be a throne room. Nyakas was sitting on a throne at the far end. She was nudged from behind, and began to walk forward. When she reached the far end, she stopped and bowed before the man on the throne. He was incredibly handsome, with long black hair and eyes so blue that they appeared almost black. Her heart skipped a beat, then lurched as she realized that she was attracted to the man who owned her. Gravity tapped the back of her knee, and she knelt on the floor, looking down, trying her best to be submissive so as to get on his good side.

"What is your name?" Although he didn't speak loudly, his voice resonated through the room.

"Robyn Smith."

Gravity whacked her back with the flat of his sword. "You will address him as 'my lord' or 'Majesty' when you speak to him."

She swallowed hard. "My name is Robyn Smith, my lord."

He whacked her again. "You will speak only when spoken to."

"That's enough, Gravity. Leave us and send in the servants."

"Yes, my lord." He turned and strode from the room. Robyn remained where she was, her eyes fixed on a spot on the marble floor, her breathing even as she sought to control her fear.

"You may rise." She stood up, but didn't take her eyes off the spot on the floor. "Are you frightened?"

"Yes, my lord."

"I see. Follow me." He walked to a nearby table and she followed. He indicated where she was to sit, and she stood beside the chair until he sat. Several servants entered from a nearby door, bringing food and drink. It smelled wonderful, and it woke Robyn's stomach up. She realized that she didn't know how long it had been since she'd last eaten. Still afraid of offending this man who obviously held their lives in his hand, she did not help herself to anything until he invited her to eat. She tried her best not to devour everything in front of her.

"Where are you from, Robyn?"

"Upstate New York, my lord. Gravity told us it was in another dimension."

"So it is. I've been there a couple of times." His voice was deep and seductive, and she wondered if he could sing. "How did you end up in the Romithian slave market?"

"I was in charge of a mission to find some people who were missing when we were captured, my lord. I guess the man who caught us must have taken us there."

"What did he look like?" She described the tall man, and he nodded. "Yes, it sounds like an Romithian slave trader. You are lucky that I happened to be at the market when I was. I don't go often. You'll be treated better here than you could have been elsewhere. I know the man I was bidding against. He would have been a cruel master."

She paused, gathering her courage. "May I speak, my lord?"

"Yes, I am sure you have questions."

"Yes, sir, I do, but I don't wish to offend you."

"Ask your questions."

"What do you intend to do with us?"

"I haven't decided yet, but it depends partly on you."

"On me, my lord?"

"Yes, I'm sure you don't want your friends to suffer."

"No, of course not. I'll do whatever is needed to make it easier for them."

"Anything that's needed?"

She met his eyes for the first time. "Yes, my lord. Please, I don't care what happens to me, but some of them are married and have families. I only just found out that one of the women is pregnant. I'll do whatever you want if only you'll have mercy on them."

He seemed to consider this, and then said, "I'll give it some thought. Is there anything you or your group needs?"

"No, my lord."

"We'll talk in the morning. Gravity, please escort the prisoner back to her cell."

"Yes, my lord." Gravity seemed to appear out of nowhere, and he seemed eager to return her to the dungeon. Again, she shuddered as the door clanged behind her. Immediately, the others clambered around her, asking her what had happened. She told them what was said, being sure to tell them the bits of protocol she'd learned. Finally, she made herself reasonably comfortable in a corner and went to sleep for what felt like the first time in a week.

Chapter 3

There was a loud clanging noise and it startled her awake. She sat up, looking around. Her companions seemed to be in a similar state. Gravity was at the door with the servants again. He looked at Robyn and said, "You will get your work assignments today. Be ready in half a candle." He drew his dagger gently across the candle that was providing light to the cell, scoring it but leaving it intact, to indicate the approximate time when he would return.

She got up and made sure everyone got part of the food that was brought before she took her own, paying special attention to Lilly. It was barely half a candle later when guards and servants began coming and collecting parts of her group. Soon she was the only one left.

Pacing nervously, she wondered why everyone else had gotten work assignments and she hadn't. The sounds of people training and fighting with swords drifted in through the small window. She began doing sit-ups and push-ups, trying to burn off nervous energy and keep her mind from wandering. There was a soft noise and she looked up to see Gravity watching her. She stopped and stood up.

He opened the door and said, "Follow me, please."

He led her back up the stairs, but this time they went to another room. It was very small and had a narrow bed against the far wall across from the door. To her right were a chair, a full-length mirror, and a washbasin. To her left was a small window. She stopped just inside the doorway, sure that the king had taken her at her word about doing whatever it took to save her friends. Surely she wouldn't be expected to sleep with Gravity!

He seemed to read her thoughts, and his mouth quirked into a half smile. "There is water in the basin. You will clean up and put this on." He reached behind the door and tossed a black velvet gown onto the bed. He left the room, closing the door behind him.

She stripped down to her bra and panties. There was a small cloth and a bar of what appeared to be soap, so she took a quick sponge bath. Slipping into the dress, she quickly discovered that her bra wouldn't work with it. The shoulders of the dress wouldn't cover the straps, and it seemed as if there was something like a bra already built into the dress. She took off her bra and tossed it onto the bed, then began trying to figure out how the dress fastened. It seemed like there were a thousand little hook and eye fasteners running down her back, but luckily most of them were easily accessible. It took a bit of work, but she managed to get even the ones in the middle of the dress. There were matching slippers and she put them on, sighing with relief to discover that both the dress and the shoes fit.

She looked in the mirror and was rather pleased with her appearance. The shoulders of the dress rested at the point where her collarbone connected with her shoulder, and the bodice was cut low enough that it showed cleavage. A small adjustment enhanced the effect. The bodice was fitted to the hips, accenting her narrow waist, and the skirt was full and reached the floor. The sleeves were long and hugged her arms. She smiled at her reflection. She'd never been one to use her body to get what she wanted, but in this case it seemed appropriate. More than anything she wanted to get her team safely home, and if she had to seduce her master to get that, that's what would be done. She was glad that they hadn't been sold to the little dwarfish man; she could actually enjoy seducing Nyakas. She primped a little, finger-combing her hair, pinching her cheeks and pressing her lips together put some color into her pale complexion.

She folded her own clothes neatly and placed them in a pile on the bed, then tried to open the door. It was locked, so she moved the chair to the small window and sat down. The view was beautiful. There was a large lake just outside the castle walls, and beyond that was a forest. A mountain loomed over all of it in the distance.

The door opened and Gravity came back in. Robyn stood up, and he looked at her, walking around her as if he wanted to see if her appearance was fit to be in the presence of the king. He nodded, then beckoned for her to follow him. He led her to another room. This one appeared to be an office with a very large desk and stuffed bookshelves. There were two wingback chairs before the fireplace on the right side of the room. Without a word, Gravity stepped back out and shut the door. She looked around cautiously only to discover that she was indeed alone. She crept about, looking around but not touching anything. The floor was covered with a thick red carpet and she resisted the urge to remove her shoes and curl her toes into it. The wall with the fireplace was largely elaborate stonework. There was a mantle over the fireplace that held a sword in a scabbard on a stand. Hanging over the sword was a red tapestry with two dragons, one gold and one black, poised to fight. The wall opposite the fireplace held built-in bookcases from the vaulted ceiling to the floor. Each shelf was completely full. She wondered how long it had taken to collect his library; he didn't seem to be much older than she was. Maybe some of the books had been passed down to him. As she stood perusing the books, the large desk was to her right, the door to her left. Behind the desk was a large picture window with a view similar to the one in the room she'd just left.

Suddenly the door opened. She spun instinctively toward the door, her right hand reaching automatically for the side arm that wasn't there as the king walked in. Startled, she bowed then went immediately to her knees. He walked past her to the desk and she wondered if he'd seen her, until he said, "Good morning, Robyn."

"Good morning, my lord."

He shuffled some papers, seemingly distracted by something, and then he looked up and chuckled. "You can get up, Robyn."

"Thank you, my lord." She stood up but didn't move from the spot. Nervous, she tried not to fidget and contented herself with brushing a bit of lint off her dress and wiggling her toes. The dress was long enough that he wouldn't notice that.

"Why don't you have a seat in front of the fireplace," he said, "I have a few things to take care of, and I'll be with you momentarily." She took a chair as she was directed to do, and he watched her covertly. The black velvet contrasted with her pale skin and she looked beautiful. Her wavy blonde hair fell around her face. It was too short to touch her shoulders, but it seemed to caress her neck. He could tell she was still frightened, but he admired the way she tried to hide it. He grinned slightly as he wondered how she would react if she saw him as he truly was.

He put his papers down and went to sit in the other chair. "I've given some thought to your question last night. If you were in control, what would become of you and your friends?"

She looked at her hands, which were folded neatly in her lap, took a deep breath, and said, "We'd be released and returned home, my lord."

"I see. I paid a substantial amount of money to buy all of you. I'm sorry, I can't justify that."

She nodded. "Would you be willing to release any of them? I'm a very hard worker, my lord. I can work for you until I earn enough to buy the freedom of the others."

"And what of yourself?"

"I was the leader. It doesn't matter what happens to me. They wouldn't be in this situation if I'd done my job properly, so my top priority is to secure the release of the others on my team before I think about my own."

"How could you have done your job properly and avoided the situation?"

"Well, for starters, when that strange vehicle approached, I could have laid low and not had Ericson fire at the man in the back. I'm certain that's what gave away our position. If we'd just been quiet, maybe they would have gone away."

"Obviously you know nothing about Romithian slave traders. They don't just go away. They knew exactly where you were, why you were there, and what price you'd fetch as a group. You were ambushed." He paused and let her think about that for a moment. "I'll release two. You choose which ones."

"Lilly, the tall woman, and Chet, the shortest of the men."

He nodded and left the room. Gravity stood outside, and Nyakas told him to get the two she'd indicated and have them brought to the office. Gravity's eyes were questioning, but he turned and left to do as he was told. Nyakas went back into the office and sat back down. Moments later, Lilly and Chet were escorted into the room. Robyn stood up and went to them.

"Are you guys OK?" They nodded and looked past her. Looking back over her shoulder, she saw that Nyakas was watching them. "Bow, quick!" she whispered. They did and he approached them.

"Your leader has negotiated the release of two of your party. She chose the two of you. Is there anything you wish to tell them before they leave, Robyn?"

"Yes, my lord, and thank you. OK, guys. Go home and tell CIA and DOD to nuke Area 51. I don't care what they have to do, but the slave traders are probably still there, and they may capture more people. They'll have to come up with a way to kill them. Prosecution and imprisonment won't work for these folks. Do not, under any circumstances, send anybody after us. I'm going to work that from this end. Oh, and one other thing. Tell my parents not to worry and that I love them."

"Robyn, don't send me," Chet said, "send one of the other women. I'll be fine here."

"Chet, I need you to go. You're the only one who can convince the government to do what needs to be done. Besides, Joyce and the kids need you. Trust me, this is for the best. You don't have to like it, but you put me in charge and I'm making a command decision. Lilly, you take care of yourself. Tell Mike about the baby as soon as you get home, and no more missions! Period! And I won't mind if you name the baby after me, although Robyn Ryan sounds a little silly." She hugged them both and watched as Gravity escorted them from the room. "Thank you, my lord." She turned to face him again. "Now, what can I do to earn the release of the others?"

"Sit down and tell me about yourself, Robyn, and I'll make a decision."

She sat down. "I'm a Major in the United States Army. I just assumed command of a company, and I'm a qualified chopper pilot. My parents live in New York."

"Are you married?"

"No, I'm not even dating anyone. I don't have a lot of time to date. I don't have any commitments, even my house plants are fake."

He smiled. "What else can you do?"

"Well, I can cook, I can sew a little, I'm great at fishing, and I can fight hand to hand, although I've never picked up a sword. What do you need?"

He got up and went to stand in front of the window. From where he stood he could see one of her companions standing guard on the battlements with Creedan. He turned to face her. "How badly do you want your friends to be released?"

"I told you, my lord, my top priority is to secure the release of my team."

"How quickly would your priorities change? I have a proposition for you, but it will require great personal sacrifice on your part."

"Great personal sacrifice? You aren't going to feed me to a dragon or anything, are you?"

He laughed out loud, thinking, 'If you only knew, my dear.' He picked up his quill and began to twirl it casually. "We do have dragons here, but that wasn't what I was thinking of. I will release all of your companions and see that they are delivered safely home, just as I did your other friends, on one condition: That you stay here and be my wife."

"Excuse me?"

"My wife, my partner, my Queen. Someone who can bear and raise children."

"Oh. I see." Her face was suddenly pale. "Well, as far as bearing children, I don't know. I've never even thought I was pregnant. Well, OK, once I did, but it was years ago in college and I was only two days late. Those were the longest two days of my life, up to this point. I think I can raise children; I did quite a bit of babysitting, so how hard could it be?" She rambled on, in shock. He wanted her to marry him in return for the release of her team. 'This is too strange,' she thought, 'It has to be a dream. It can't be real. Wake up, Robyn!'

"I can see you need some time to think it over. I'll have someone take you to the Great Hall. The rest of your team will be in there soon." He opened the door and motioned for a servant.

She stood up quickly. "I accept, my lord."

He turned to look at her. "You accept? You are willing to stay here and be my wife in exchange for the release of the others?"

"Yes, my lord, as long as I have your assurance that they will be returned home unharmed."

"You have my word. Go with Evan, he will see to it that everything is prepared for tonight."

"Tonight?"

"For our wedding. We'll get married tonight, and tomorrow I'll have your friends sent home. That will be my gift to you."

"Thank you. It's, um, been a pleasure doing business with you, my lord."

"You can call me Nyakas. After all, you'll be the Queen in a matter of hours. I'll see you soon, my dear." He sat down behind the desk as the door opened. Evan opened the door and indicated that she was to follow him. He led her to the Great Hall, where her team was waiting for her.

"Whoa, Ma'am! You look dynamite!" Rodriguez was the first to see her, and Tomlin and Ericson quickly agreed. Doc walked over quickly, looking closely at her face.

"I can tell something is wrong, Robyn," she said, "Tell me what it is."

Robyn looked at the older woman. "Nothing is wrong, Doc. You're going home tomorrow."

"I am, or we are?" The others drew closer as they heard what Robyn said.

"All of you. I've negotiated your release."

Chad put his hands on her shoulders. "What about you?"

She shrugged casually and said, "I'm going to hang out here for a while. They don't take government charge cards here, so I'm working off your ransom."

Rodriguez stepped up. "No way, Major. If you ain't going, neither am I. I don't know about the rest of you, but I ain't leaving her here alone."

She straightened her back and stood nose to nose with him. He meant well, but she was going to get all of her team home, and that was that. "Listen to me, Rod. If I hadn't given away our position we wouldn't be in the mess we're in. I had a chance to get all of you out of here, and I took it. There will be no exceptions! You are all leaving. I will stay behind and get back as soon as I can. If I have to order you, that's what I'll do." She stepped back to look at all of them. "I mean it. I'm still in charge of this mission, and it's not over until you are all safe and sound in your snug little beds. Don't try to cross me, because I can still kick your butts if I need to."

"Robyn, what are you going to do to work off our ransom?" asked Rachel.

"Don't worry about that. Suffice it to say that I've secured my position here. I'll be well treated, don't worry."

"Now what are you not telling us?" asked Tomlin.

"Nothing! Look, I got in good with Nyakas, he thinks I'm the cat's meow, and I talked him into letting all of you go. I'll be fine here, I'm going to be frigging royalty." She stopped short and bit her tongue. She hadn't intended to tell them about the details of her deal quite so soon.

"Whoa, there, Trigger!" exclaimed Chad, "The only way I can think of for you to become royalty is to marry into it!"

"Very observant, Chad. Can't put anything past you. Would you like to give me away before you leave?"

"You can't do that!" he countered, "It's not right for you to marry him so we can go free!"

She grabbed the front of his shirt and pulled his face down to her level. "Now you listen to me! The decision is made! I'm going to do it because I love all of you too much to let you stay away from your families for the rest of your lives! I'm doing this for you because it is exactly the right thing to do! Now either work with me or I'll have you put back down in the damn dungeon until it's time for you to go!" She shoved him away and strode angrily to the nearest window. She hated having to order them away. She didn't want them to go, but the needs of the many outweighed the needs of the few, and right now there were a lot more lives affected than the ones in the room. Rachel, Chad and Doc were all married, and she knew that Tomlin was due to be soon. Rachel had three stepdaughters, Chad had two daughters, Doc had several stepchildren and step-grandchildren, and Rodriguez had a son. There was no way she would allow those children to grow up without their parents. She'd been there, having been raised only by her mother during her early years.

There was a hand on her shoulder, and she turned to see to whom it belonged. It was Rachel. "Don't worry, Robyn. We'll go if that's what you really want. I don't think it is, I think you're just trying to do what you think is right, but I've talked to them and we'll cooperate. I admire what you're doing, honey, I really do. But for the record, I don't see how any of this could have been avoided."

"I know, Rachel, and between us, you're right. I'm scared to death and I don't want you guys to leave. But I won't be able to live with myself knowing that all those kids back home are growing up without the parents they need."

"What about your parents?"

"It will be hard on them, I know. But there isn't much I can do about it. Maybe somehow, someday, I'll get home to see them again. They'll help each other through this. Just make sure you tell them that I love them."

"I will, sweetie. Don't you worry about a thing, OK?"

"Thanks." They walked back over to the group and Chad took her hand.

"Are you sure about this?"

"Absolutely. This is something I have to do."

"OK."

Chapter 4

Lars Jorgensson sat at the window, looking at the lake. He was a young man, only 18, far younger than his colleagues at the university, and also considerably bigger. He was six and a half feet tall and easily 250 pounds with sandy blond hair and the tattoo of a cross on the left side of his face. The horizontal piece above his left eye intersected the vertical portion just to the left of his left eye from his temple to his jawbone.

He sensed a great evil in the land. It had come recently into this world from afar, that much he could tell. He couldn't put a face to it or fathom the reason it was there, but he could tell that it was looking for something. He had recently started having these feelings when he traveled around the city. He chalked it up to a side benefit of being a Priest of the Light.

He still wasn't sure what happened the day Tom showed up on his doorstep and challenged him to what he'd called a scavenger hunt. Tom was a chess buddy of his and liked to play games, all types of them, and frequently challenged him in games of strategy and tactics, so Lars hadn't thought much about it until Tom took him to the ruins of an abandoned church and led him under ground. There was a group of people standing around a pool and chanting in Latin. He knew Latin and realized that, in present-day America, only scholars spoke it. This hypothesis led him to the conclusion that he was among friends. They all were dressed in monk's habits with the cowls pulled down so Lars couldn't see their faces.

The room looked like it had come out of the middle ages. Frescoes all around the room showed angelic beings smiting down demons and devils and other ugly looking things. A pulpit stood in the nave at the front of the sanctuary behind which a large cross hung, What was unusual about this church was there weren't any of the more traditional trappings, such as a choir loft, seating for more than thirty people, an organ or even a piano. This place had the feel of being very old. The only sources of light were torches in iron wall sconces every fifteen feet. Except for the frescoes and paintings, it had an austere look. There was a man in the middle of the crowd, and he broke away from his companions to approach Lars.

"Greetings, Lars Son of Jorgen. We remember the old days when your name was handed down from your Viking ancestors. You are among friends here. Everyone here has a deep and reverent faith for the forces of good. We have watched you from afar and recognize a kindred soul. If you are willing, we will welcome you with open arms into the Brotherhood of Light. Before you say yeah or nay, be forewarned as to some of the risks. Forever your faith will be tested. No longer will you have any doubt as to what is evil and what is good. You will forever be marked a warrior in the brotherhood. You will always have brothers in arms. Even though the forces of evil be legion, the forces of light have always trusted in the quality of their brothers, not the endless legions of bumbling incompetents that the forces of evil use. Are there any questions that you might ask us?"

"Yes. What have you been doing here in this old church, instead of being out fighting all of the world's evils? There is widespread famine, disease, and drug use out there and yet you sit here in this ancient run down church and do nothing. What have you done against that evil, huh? And you claim to be warriors for the Light? Yeah, right."

"My son, that is man-made evil, a by-product of our God-given free will. We are talking about an evil greater than that: the evils that come from the nether regions. These evils are but shadows of the Evil One, but they are great when they get here to our dimension. It is our sworn duty to vanquish all of them wherever they might be found. The Evil one also has priests here and their name is the 'The Dark Brotherhood'. This brotherhood has been in existence since the fall of Lucifer from Heaven. They have one purpose in mind and one only. They are trying to bring their master here to this realm, so they can amass an army and bring about Armageddon before its time. They would enslave the entire human race to do their bidding. There has been a war on this planet since The Fall. Our forces are always in constant battle with the forces of Evil. The main question that you have to ask yourself is, do you believe? For if you do then you know that you can never rest until evil has been vanquished here on earth. Brother Thomas has been watching you and testing you to see if your faith is as deep as it needs to be. Based upon his recommendations we feel that you would benefit from the initiation into our brotherhood. There are no background checks, no hidden fees, and no secret passwords. All you have to do is read a paragraph from a book. The Most Holy One will decide if you are to be accepted. We do only the recruiting. He does all of the deciding. If you choose, you may become one of the Order, or you can walk back outside of this church and not remember a single thing. You will never be approached again. If you are ready then please step up to the podium and read the portion of text that has been marked. Once you have started reading you can't change your mind, so be sure in your heart that you are ready."

Lars looked into his heart and saw only his desire to best evil, so he started to walk to the podium. As he walked the short distance to it he noticed that things were starting to come to an unnatural refinement. He saw the individual dust motes as they danced in the air and heard the fire crackling all around him. The scent of incense, once subtle, was becoming more pronounced. He reached the pulpit and the men started that chant again, only this time it was in Hebrew. He looked down at the book and several more things came into focus. It was a black leather bound book. He couldn't see what was on the cover as the pages were open. This book had been written in a variety of languages. He recognized Hebrew, Latin, and Greek, but there were a couple of others he couldn't recognize. One particular passage drew his attention more than any other. It seemed to radiate with a bright light. As he started to read the passage, he tried to decipher it, but an unseen force compelled him to press on with his reading. Everything else in the room seemed to darken and grow dim. Even the voices of the monks grew faint as he heard what seemed like harp music. A ray of light appeared and centered on Lars. It seemed to be looking for something in his very soul. After what seemed an eternity the ray of light winked out and he felt a faint heat wash across his face. He opened his eyes, although he had not been aware of closing them. He looked back at the book could now read the passage before him. It said, 'You have been accepted into the Brotherhood of the Light. Be welcome and rejoice in your choice!'

He looked at the monks and realized that sometime while he was at the pulpit all of them had thrown back their cowls to show their faces. Another thing that struck him as odd was that there were a couple of women among the 'brethren'. Lars didn't know how to react to that.

The man in the middle spoke up and said, "Be welcome into our sanctuary, Brother Lars. We have awaited you and the fulfillment of the Holy One's prophecy, which He laid down me almost two thousand years ago. I was a young man and He said I would see it come true." The old man continued to speak as he came up to Lars and gently led him to a fountain in the back corner where Lars had missed it and motioned that he was to drink from it. He said, "My name is Saul, and I am a follower of the Most Holy. I was not a devout man when I first had a visitation from the Most Holy. He appeared to me in a vision and said, 'You have been chosen to be set apart from common man, Saul. Will you obey me? Walk for three days and you will find a spring. At this spring you will build a fountain; and after you have done as I wish, I will be back.' I passed from what is modern day Iraq into Jordan and built my fountain there. When I placed the last stone into the mortar and looked upon my handiwork a spark even brighter than the sunlight fell from the heavens and landed in the fountain. The water boiled and sizzled but was icy cold when I touched it. Then a voice from above and all around me said, 'Saul, drink, for you are to be the first of a new type of priest. Upon you and your new brethren will fall the task of fighting all of the evil that is in the world. In the fullness of time a man will come in your darkest hour to be entered into your brotherhood. Upon him will rest all of your hopes and he will be the one who will lead the Knights out of the wasteland that was their downfall. Have all of your brothers and no others drink from this fountain. It will grant them eternal life until I personally call them from this earth. They need not fear death through old age or sickness. You and the ones who come after you are my warriors in this battle. Rejoice for you have been truly blessed.' You are that man, Brother Lars."

There were some quiet whispers in the back. One of them was a little louder than the rest and said, "He really is the chosen one! His mark is different than the rest of ours. His is right side up, where ours are upside down. The Most Holy has blessed us beyond belief. Who would have thought that we would be here when he is among us?" The last of the sentence was said with such wonder and awe that Lars wondered if they were going to get down on their knees right then and give thanks to Him!

"Be warned, brother," said Saul, "you are entering troubled times. There is one close to you who will require your protection. This lost soul is sought after and knows it not. Mind your heart, Lars. You will know what to do and when."

He spent the rest of the evening learning about the rich history of the Brotherhood of Light and the Knights, as they were called, and his personal role in the group. He decided to do some more research in the morning, or perhaps the next day after he got some rest, so he took his leave of his new family and went home.

When he arrived, he found a message on his answering machine from his friend and colleague, Mike Ryan. He'd left the university suddenly to go on a sabbatical, and when he came back several days later he looked like he'd been through the wringer. Mike's message was to invite Lars to dinner since Lilly had been called out of town. He accepted the invitation, and during dinner realized that it was no routine business meeting that had called Lilly away. He decided to stay with Mike until she returned and took up residence in one of the many guest rooms in their home.

The next day, Mike told him that he and Lilly occasionally did free-lance work for the CIA. He told him the basics of his aborted mission and Lilly's current involvement without revealing too many details. For that, Lars was grateful.

It had been two days since anyone had heard from Lilly or anyone on the team. From his spot at the window he could see Mike, fidgeting on the couch. He had eight stitches over his right eye and four more in his shoulder where he'd been grazed by a bullet during his mission in New Mexico. His brown hair hadn't been combed; his jeans and sweatshirt looked like they'd been slept in, and his brown eyes were worried. The bay window through which Lars stared looked onto a lake, which Mike owned.

Suddenly, he saw a white gleam of light and squinted to make out what caused it. He saw a man walk through the bright white light. He wore a black cloak, and his head was bald except for a topknot that reached the middle of his back and was bound by a silver ball. The man wore a white tunic and black pants with black boots. His face bore tribal tattoos that ran down his neck and surely around his arms and chest. He looked menacing, intimidating, and worst of all Lars could sense great evil in his presence. As Lars stared at the figure that had only just arrived, he had an eerie feeling that the man knew exactly where Lars was. He stood aside as if to let another pass, and Lilly had walked out of the light. Lars' jaw hit the floor, and suddenly, the man in black was gone, the light vanished, and Lilly was alone.

Mike looked up to see his friend staring out the window with his jaw resting on top of his sneakers and said, "Lars, what is it?"

"Mike come look, quickly, please," Lars stammered, his face pale.

Mike went to the window to see his wife making her way to the mansion. He leaped away from the window and bolted for the door, flung it open, and ran to his wife. Lilly saw Mike as the door flew wide open and she ran to meet him halfway. Within moments they were in each other's arms.

Mike quickly stepped away and assessed his wife for obvious injuries; he looked her over thoroughly and then put his hands to her cheeks as to make sure it was she.

She looked deeply into his eyes. "Mike, it is me. I love you so much."

He quickly responded by holding her tightly and caressing her hair; he was now complete. "Are you all right?" he asked, looking very concerned. "Where is everyone else?"

"He only allowed Chet and I to go. Robyn was in charge and she requested we be released. She agreed to work off our debts for us," Lilly replied.

"Who released you? What happened?" demanded Mike.

"We were captured by Romithian slave traders, probably the same ones who got your team. A man bought our whole group. Robyn was able to negotiate my release and Chet's."

"So the others are still there?" Mike asked.

"Yes," she said quietly.

Mike's face turned red with anger and he led Lilly back into the house. When he entered, he called, "Lars, we must get to the place Lilly just left and get the others out by whatever means possible. Money is no problem for me, but I need to get them set free."

"Mike," answered Lars evenly, "my Master doesn't just grant passage to whatever plane I wish. It may take a few minutes of meditation and even then it might not work. Hello, Lilly."

"I don't care. We have to try," Mike replied.

"I'm going, too! I don't care what you have to say Mike but I'm going and there is no way you can stop me! Hello, Lars." Lilly said.

"Lilly, you just got back from this hell. Why would you want to go back?" Mike asked.

"Because I'm not going to live without you. If something happens to you I'll never forgive myself for letting you go."

Mike didn't like her logic but it was sound and he felt the same about her. He looked at Lars, and Lars knew what had to be done. He went outside, a few feet away, and sat Indian style on the manicured lawn. He laid his hands on his legs with the palms facing up, closed his eyes, and began to chant.

Chapter 5

Nyakas sat in his bedroom alone. In his left hand he loosely held a large goblet made of silver adorned with two entwined dragons with gems for eyes. In his right hand was a small book that he seemed to be reading intently. He wore a black robe with gold embroidery like a large necklace from the neck to the waist. He sat in a large oak throne-like chair with his right foot on his left knee behind a large desk. He could see himself out of the corner of his eye in the elaborate gold and ivory mirror. Next to the mirror was a water basin, and his washcloth and towel lay neatly on the edge. His queen-size bed was neatly made, but it seemed that it was only slept in on one side. Putting down his book and goblet, he stared at the large bed. Tears filled his eyes as he smiled and looked upward as though he had been given some advice from his god.

At that moment, Gravity walked in. "Lord, do you understand what you have done?"

"Yes, of course I do," Nyakas replied.

"Nyakas, you are to take your father's throne in a short time. Why have you chosen to take a human bride with whom you are infatuated?"

Nyakas stood angrily. "No! A woman I'm in love with. I know the meaning of love, Gravity, thank you."

"Friend, all I want is for you to be happy, and if she makes you happy, that's great. Nyakas, your father knows what you've done, and you know he'll try to break this up. Making her your concubine would be safer."

"He has no choice in this matter."

"He doesn't? Have your father's abilities slipped your mind?"

"No, they haven't!" Nyakas said angrily.

Gravity was frustrated and shook his head in disbelief. "Friend, I'll fight beside you if he comes, just do me one favor."

"Your loyalty never came with conditions before, Gravity. What is the favor?"

"Just answer a question. Is she worth it? Are you sure in your heart that you love her?"

He smiled and said, "With every moment of every day."

Gravity smiled. "I'm behind you one hundred percent."

Nyakas relaxed visibly. "I'm glad. Do you know she was in the military?"

"I suspected as much. She'll probably ask you if she can train with the men. She could really cause a stir here, my lord."

"True. Can you think of a reason why she can't train?"

"None, but if you don't want her to, I can come up with something."

Nyakas laughed out loud. "If she is going to train, I think it needs to be with you. The Queen shouldn't be practicing warfare with common soldiers."

"I don't think she'll go along with it when she finds out I'm the teacher."

"Actually, she might surprise you. You have been hard on her, but then again, you're not exactly a people person!"

Gravity smiled and opened the door to leave. "It must be the hair."

Nyakas laughed. "It's about time for me to get ready for my wedding. I'll see you later, Grav."

"I hope so, my lord."

Chapter 6

Nyakas allowed Robyn's group to stay with her for the remainder of the day. When the time drew near to prepare for the wedding, they were shown to a lavish chamber. The room was dominated by a large four-poster bed on the far side of the room opposite the door. As she stood in the doorway, Robyn could see that to the right were French doors leading onto a balcony overlooking the lake. To her immediate left was a large stone fireplace with a small couch and table in front of it. To the left of that was a very large wardrobe, and across the room from the wardrobe was a small dressing table with a bench and a mirror. The far left wall had another, smaller window which overlooked the castle wall. A delicate looking writing desk and chair sat in front of it. Near the corner between the wardrobe and the window, a screen was set up, and behind it was a gown, similar to the style she wore, but made of white satin. Small buttons ran from the neck to the waist. A lace overlay formed a short flowing train. The lace on the sleeves went past the satin to end in a peak over the tops of her hands and buttoned around her wrist, preventing them from getting in the way. There were matching shoes and a long lace veil to go with the dress.

The men were sent out onto the balcony while Doc and Rachel helped her change into the gown. When she was dressed, the men were allowed back in, and she emerged from behind the screen. All four men stared, almost in disbelief.

"Well?"

Ericson was the first to speak. "Wow, Major, you look outstanding! If I knew you looked this good in a wedding gown I would have proposed to you myself!" The others nodded in agreement. Soon there was a knock at the door, and Gravity escorted them to the throne room. He ushered her friends in first, while Chad stood outside with her. She froze as she peeked through the door and saw that the large room was full. She wondered where all the people had come from, and suddenly she couldn't decide whether she wanted to cry or vomit. She took a few steps away from the door and took several deep breaths. Then the doors opened, and Gravity held them so they could enter.

She took Chad's arm and clung to it, willing herself with each step both to look calm and to wake up. He walked her all the way to the end of the long aisle, and then took his seat with the others. The ceremony was brief, and she felt as if she was in a haze as she promised service and fidelity a man she knew so little about. When it was over, Nyakas lifted her veil and kissed her lightly, and suddenly she felt drunk. She opened her eyes and looked into his; they looked suspiciously like those of a man in love.

He placed her arm on his, and they walked back up the aisle. There was a large feast in the Great Hall, and Robyn stood beside her new husband to accept best wishes from hundreds of strangers. The party lasted far into the night, and when she didn't think she could stay awake any longer, Nyakas leaned toward her. He took her hand, looked into her eyes, and said, "Shall I have Gravity take you to your chamber?"

She nodded. "I am tired. Um, what are wedding night customs here?"

"We'll dispense with those for a time. You have many adjustments to make." He motioned to Gravity, and he stepped forward. "Take the Queen to her chamber, please, Gravity." He kissed her cheek lightly as she rose to follow her escort.

Gravity took her from the Great Hall to chamber where she had gotten dressed for the wedding. He motioned her in and said, "The maid will be here in the morning. Good night, my queen." With that he turned and silently left the room. Robyn shut the door lightly and surveyed the room. She saw that the bed was turned down and there was a fire banked in the fireplace. A muslin nightgown lay on the foot of the bed. She got out of the beautiful satin gown carefully, put on the muslin, and hung the dress up. She sat in front of the fire for a while, staring at the ring on her finger. Then she got up and climbed into the large bed. She shut her eyes for a moment, and when she opened them, the fire was out and the sun was coming up over the lake.

Unable to stay in bed, she went to the French doors that led onto the balcony. She opened one, then quickly closed it again as the cold air hit her warm body. Looking around, she noticed a robe hanging on the bedpost, and a pair of slippers on the floor. She wondered how she'd missed them earlier, and then realized it was because she'd rolled out of the bed on the other side.

The wind didn't seem as cold with the additional clothing, and she partially closed the door so the room wouldn't get cold. As she watched the remainder of the sunrise, the light glinted off her new ring. Looking down at it, she thought, 'So, it's not a dream. Yesterday really happened, I really am married, and I really am a Queen. Well, it could be worse. Hey, if you have to be stuck in a strange place far from home, you might as well get as many fringe benefits as you can. I have a really nice room, the people here are cordial, and even though I really don't know the first thing about him, my husband is a good-looking guy! It beats taking up a permanent residence in the dungeon. All in all, I got off pretty lucky.' As she mused over her situation, she heard a feminine voice behind her.

"Good morning, Majesty."

Robyn turned and went back into the room to see a young woman enter the room with a small tray. She was a little shorter than Robyn and quite slender, with long red hair pulled back in a French braid and a smattering of freckles over her attractive face. She wore a brown muslin dress with a white apron. The tray held what appeared to be a fine bone china cup and saucer, and a small pitcher. Robyn heartily hoped that whatever was in that pitcher had lots of caffeine. The woman placed the tray on a low table near the fireplace and turned to see Robyn as she came through the door.

"Majesty," she exclaimed, "what were you doing outside in your night clothes?"

"I wanted to watch the sun rise. I'm sorry, I didn't think I was doing anything wrong."

"It's not that you were doing anything wrong, milady," the woman said in a softer tone, "it's just that you could catch your death of a cold out there dressed like that. The mornings here are very damp and chilly, one must dress properly."

"I'll keep that in mind. Thank you."

"Very well, then, milady. My name in Gwyneth, and I'll be your lady in waiting. If there is anything you need, please let me know. The king has risen already and is requesting your presence at breakfast, so we should get you dressed without delay." She poured some of the contents of the pitcher into the cup, adjusted it precisely on the saucer, and handed it to Robyn with a shallow curtsy.

"OK, Gwyneth. What does one wear to have breakfast with the king?" She sniffed at the cup surreptitiously and was overjoyed to smell coffee. It smelled stronger than what she usually brewed for herself, but she'd lived through military gut rot many times. She sipped tentatively as Gwyneth went to the wardrobe and selected a silk gown. The coffee was strong and tasted wonderful, especially since she wasn't entirely sure how long it had been since she'd had coffee. The gown Gwyneth chose was midnight blue, with long sleeves and a full skirt. It had a high collar with choker that closed at the center of the throat with a mother of pearl button. The bodice had a large scoop opening which she was sure would reveal at least a bit of cleavage, and there were buttons from the bottom of the scoop to the waist. Gwyneth shook the gown out gently to remove any small wrinkles, and held it up for her approval.

"It's beautiful," Robyn said, "but it's not too formal, is it?"

"Oh, no, milady!"

"Well, then I guess I should get into it." She put her coffee cup on the tray with a bit of regret and removed her robe and nightgown. Gwyneth handed her the appropriate undergarments and soon Robyn was buttoning her gown, feeling very much like a child who needed help dressing.

When she was dressed, Gwyneth led her to the dressing table. Robyn sat down on the bench and Gwyneth began brushing her hair.

"Are you from very far away, milady?"

Robyn laughed. "Oh, yes! Very far. It is that obvious?"

"Well," said Gwyneth tentatively, "Actually, yes, milady. You've never had a servant before, have you?"

"Not really. Not a personal servant, anyway. The closest I ever came were the privates under my command."

"Privates, milady?"

"Yes, low ranking soldiers. I guess you would call them squires here, or maybe foot soldiers."

"You had squires under your command? They allow women to be knights in your home land?"

"I wasn't a knight. I was an army officer. You have those here, don't you?"

"Oh, yes, milady! My husband is in the king's army."

"Really? Is he an officer or a regular soldier?"

"He's one of the King's Undercaptains."

"So, in Nyakas' army, where does that put him?"

"Well, Lord Gravity is the General of the Army, and he takes orders only from the King. He has two Captains, and they each have two Undercaptains. The Undercaptains have Sergeants, who pass orders to the foot soldiers." She finished brushing Robyn's hair. "Are you ready, milady?"

"Yes."

"Well, then, you have a short journey. You'll be dining with the king in his chamber, just across the hall. Would you like me to accompany you?"

"That won't be necessary. Thank you, Gwyneth."

Gwyneth curtsied, and Robyn went to the room across the hall. She knocked tentatively and heard his voice tell her to enter. She opened the door and saw Nyakas sitting in front of the fireplace, reading a book. The room looked similar to hers, with the large four-poster bed, wardrobe, and desk. It seemed to lack personal possessions, and she thought that a little odd. There was a small table and two chairs in front of the French doors. He looked up to see her enter. His face lit up for a second, only to be replaced by a calmer, more dignified expression.

"Good morning, my lady," he said.

"Good morning, my lord," she responded.

"You look lovely this morning. I trust you slept well?"

"Yes, thank you. And you?"

"Very well." This wasn't entirely true. He'd spent a good portion of the night trying ignore the fact that she was directly across the hall in what was actually his bed. This hampered his ability to go to sleep, and when he did, he dreamed only of her. He'd woken early and made it very clear to his chamberlain, Jerome, that he wanted his wife to join him for breakfast. He'd dressed quickly and fidgeted, waiting for her, until he finally forced himself to calm down and read. When she knocked at the door his heart skipped a beat, and when she entered looking lovelier than the moonlit sky he thought it would stop altogether.

He stood and led her to a small table. As if on cue, a servant entered with a large silver tray. He placed the tray on the table and removed the cover to reveal warm crusty rolls and coffee. They talked about nothing in particular as they ate together, and Robyn felt as if she was on a first date. This was very strange, considering she was married to the man.

"We'll be sending your friends back in a couple of hours, my dear. I thought perhaps you'd like to spend some time with them before they go. I will arrange for you to meet them in the Great Hall. I would prefer that you remain within the castle walls unless you have an escort."

"That's very kind of you, my lord. I appreciate your help in this matter."

"I know that you'll have a period of adjustment, and that it probably will be quite difficult for you. If there is anything I can do to make things easier for you, please don't hesitate to ask."

They finished breakfast and walked to the Great Hall together. Her friends were waiting inside, and they all seemed to be better rested than they had been since the entire ordeal began. They sat and talked for a while, then went to walk in the courtyard. She felt as if everyone was afraid to say what they were really thinking.

When the time came, Nyakas and Gravity came to collect them. They went to an archway just outside the castle walls. As Gravity began his spell, Robyn hugged Rachel, Doc, and Chad and asked all of them not to worry about her. She returned the salutes of Ericson, Rodriguez, and Tomlin, thanked them for their hard work, and asked them to tell her commander what had happened, no matter how bizarre it sounded. The spell took effect and the archway began to glow with a blue light. Gravity opened his eyes, and then escorted her friends through the archway. She watched as they walked through, one by one. She was relieved to have them going back to safety, but at the same time she was saddened to see them go.

The light faded and she was alone with Nyakas. Without a word he led her back to the castle, and she excused herself to her room. She lay on the bed and wept quietly as the full effect of the situation took hold. She realized for the first time that she was in a strange place with no friends, married to a man she didn't know, and would probably never go home again. At dusk there was a tap on her door, and Gwyneth entered. She had a covered tray with her, and placed it on the table in front of the fireplace. As she started the fire, she said, "King Nyakas thought perhaps you would prefer to be alone tonight, but if you would like to have dinner with the court I can easily return this to the kitchen."

"No, thank you, Gwyneth. I would prefer to stay here. Is there anything else in that wardrobe besides these gowns?"

"Yes, milady." She opened the wardrobe and removed a pair of loose leather pants and a tunic, which she carried to the bed. "Are these more to your liking?"

"Yes. Are there any more?"

"Yes, and I can arrange to have more made if you like."

"They're so soft. What are they made of?"

"They are deer skin, my lady."

"Well, I'm not usually one to wear deer skin, but they look more comfortable than this gown." She got up, removed the gown, and put the clothes on as Gwyneth hung the gown in the wardrobe.

"Would you like some made from cloth, milady?"

"Is it possible? That would be wonderful."

"Yes, milady. I'll speak to the tailor straight away. Is there anything else you need?"

"How about some boots? I assume they would be made out of leather here. Are they made with left and right feet? These slippers are making my feet hurt."

"Of course milady, I will speak to the tanner tomorrow morning first thing. Is there anything else that you require?"

"No, Gwyneth, but thank you."

Gwyneth left the room, and Robyn sat down on her couch, feeling a little better in the pants and tunic. She peeked under the cover of the tray to find a bowl of stew, a big chunk of bread, and a mug of what looked like beer. She tasted all of it, but discovered she really wasn't hungry, so she picked at it for a while, then replaced the cover on the off chance that maybe she would be later.

She went out on the balcony. It was dark now, and the stars shone brightly. She looked for familiar constellations, but couldn't see any.

Feeling restless, she went back into her room and out the door. A bit of exploration revealed a staircase leading up, and she soon found herself on the battlements. Further wandering revealed the perfect spot to watch the stars reflecting off the lake. The wind on the battlements was stronger and colder than it had been on her balcony, and she wrapped her arms around herself in an attempt to ward off the chill. Suddenly she was surrounded by warmth, and she found that someone had draped a cloak around her shoulders. She looked around to see Nyakas standing behind her.

"Lovely, aren't they?"

"Yes. Thank you for the cloak."

"A page told me that you had been seen coming up, and I didn't think you would realize how much colder it is up here."

"No, I didn't. Won't you get cold?"

"Don't worry about me, my lady. I'm accustomed to it." He sat down beside her. "Gravity returned. He asked me to tell you that your friends all arrived safely. The one called Rachel sent this back for you." He handed her a silver cross on a thick silver chain.

As she took it, tears sprang unbidden to her eyes. She put it on and tried not to cry. The necklace had once belonged to Rachel's mother, and before she died she told Rachel to keep it until she found someone who needed it more. Robyn had long thought of Rachel as an older sister, and often called her when Army life got a little too hard to handle alone. Rachel always knew when to be sympathetic, when to kick Robyn in the tail, and when to inject a little humor. Once again, she had known just what to do.

She swallowed hard and turned to Nyakas. "OK, now what do I do?"

"Pardon me?"

"I'm the queen, but I don't have any clue what I'm supposed to do. What are my duties? Do I make state visits? Sit and knit all day? Concentrate on being an attractive showpiece? Help me out here, I've never done this before."

Nyakas smiled. "The attractive show piece sounds like it has potential, but it's not what I had in mind. What do you want to do?"

"I don't know what needs to be done. If I had my choice, I'd work out with the soldiers and learn about sword fighting in the morning and fish all afternoon, but I'm pretty sure there's more to being a queen than fighting and fishing."

"Not necessarily. We've been so long without a queen that there aren't any duties set aside for that position. If you want to learn swordplay and fish, that sounds like as good a place to start as any."

"How long has it been since you've had a queen?"

"Well, never, actually. I established this kingdom, and you are my first wife."

"I am? Wow, everything around here must look a lot older than it is. I assumed that you'd inherited it."

"Some things here are not what they seem. I'm a bit older than you may think."

"Not much older. If you're over 35, I'd be surprised."

He laughed out loud. "You'd be surprised."

"Really? How old are you?"

"Robyn, I think you've got enough to deal with right now. I don't want to overwhelm you."

"How bad could it be? OK, you're 40? It's cool, I like older guys."

He laughed again and kissed the back of her hand. "You are so innocent, Robyn."

She shivered involuntarily at the touch of his warm hand. "Me? Innocent? I guess I'm not the only one who would be surprised!"

"Why is that?"

"You can't be a female Army officer, live through flight school, jump school, and survival training, and come out innocent. I may be naïve about the customs here, Nyakas, but I am not innocent."

"There is much you will discover about this place. The first is that there are creatures and dangers here that you know nothing about. If you wish to venture outside the castle walls, please tell Gravity or me first and we will accompany you. To coin a phrase from your time, you're not in Kansas anymore!"

Robyn laughed to hear those words from him. "OK, so I'm grounded for the time being. What about these creatures? Do you have a troll living in the lake?"

"No, but there is a dragon who frequents it quite often." He laughed at the look of shock on her face.

Cautiously, she said, "You are kidding, right?"

"No, I'm not kidding. He can usually be seen around dawn. Don't worry. He won't hurt you. He has seen fit to keep an eye on my kingdom and has become something of a protector. In fact, if he happened to be down there when you go to fish, he might even help you."

"Help me fish? How, by letting me use him as a boat?"

"No, I believe you would call it a swan dive. He frequently dives into the middle of the lake, and the water drives the big fish closer to the shore, increasing the probability that you would catch one."

"Hmm, I guess that would pretty much eliminate the need for a lure. Maybe my worms would last longer. I'll have to give it a shot! Want to go fishing tomorrow morning?"

He laughed out loud. "I'm afraid I can't! You are braver than I gave you credit for. I'll have Gravity take you to the lake tomorrow morning if that is what you would like to do."

"If there is one thing I know I can do here, it's fish. Why am I brave?"

"You have just jumped wholeheartedly at going fishing with a dragon in the lake. Have you ever seen a dragon?"

"A real, live dragon? No, we don't have them at home. I've seen pictures of real dragons, and I saw a live Komodo dragon in a zoo once. Does that count?"

"No, real dragons are much larger. This particular one is longer than one of your football fields."

She thought about that for a minute. "That's pretty big. You know, I bet he'll displace a lot of water. Do you have any wet weather gear here? I'd hate to soak this leather."

He laughed again, amused at her logic. He had expected her to be frightened enough to stay away from the lake. It wasn't that he minded her going fishing. If fishing helped her to adjust to her new surroundings, he would encourage her to do so often. She was full of surprises, and he found that highly intriguing.

"I'll tell Gravity to meet you in the courtyard with the appropriate gear at dawn. How does that sound?"

"Sounds fine to me," she said. Actually it sounded all right, but not quite fine.

"Is that a hesitation I hear in your voice?"

"No, well, yes, kind of. It's just that I don't think Gravity likes me very much."

"Gravity is very quiet and reserved. He doesn't dislike you; he just chooses not to get close to many people. He'll protect you without hesitation. I trust him with my back; you can trust him with yours."

"If you say so. Well, if I'm going fishing in the morning, I'd better go get some sleep. Here, you might want your cloak back."

"Keep it. You'll need it in the morning, and I have another one. Good night, Robyn."

"Good night, Nyakas." She went back to her room, changed into her muslin nightgown, and climbed into bed. Gwyneth had been back; the fire was banked and the tray removed. She curled up under the thick quilt, and after tossing and turning for a while, finally cried herself to sleep.

Chapter 7

Her internal alarm went off shortly before false dawn, and she got up to dress. She had just pulled the tunic over her head when there was a gentle tap at the door and Gwyneth came in. She had the tray with her and looked up in surprise as she saw Robyn was already up.

"Good morning, milady. I might have known you'd be awake."

"Why?"

"Word travels quickly here, milady. I heard you were going to the lake with Lord Gravity this morning, so I brought you a bit of breakfast. I called in a favor with the tanner and got you some boots."

"Thank you."

Gwyneth stoked the fire to take the chill out of the air, then opened the curtains and made the bed. After seeing that Robyn had everything she needed, she excused herself to attend to other duties. Robyn ate quickly and pulled on her new boots. They were soft, like her pants and tunic, but more solidly constructed. She estimated that these new boots would serve her for several years, and what made them better was that they didn't need to be broken in like her combat boots had.

She carefully banked the fire the way she had seen Gwyneth do, put on her borrowed cloak, and went down to the courtyard. It wasn't quite dawn, but she wasn't there more than a few minutes when Gravity appeared, seemingly from nowhere. He had a fishing pole and two cloaks over his arm.

"Good morning, my Queen."

"Good morning, my lord."

"I'm not your lord now. I'm only Gravity."

"Forgive me, I don't know all the customs yet."

"Understandable. Under the circumstances, I'd say you are doing well."

She thanked him, and they walked in silence to the lake. The cloaks he carried seemed to be thick leather treated with something to make to them water resistant. He placed one gently over her shoulders, on top of Nyakas' cloak, and it was very heavy. She sat down on the dewy grass and cast her line in. He stood nearby, and seemed to be looking for something in the sky. Unsure of what to say, Robyn decided to say nothing and merely observed. The sun rose over the mountain, casting a long shadow over the lake. It was early fall, and the leaves were just changing colors. The view was glorious, but Robyn was glad to have the extra cloak. It encumbered her movement, but she knew she'd be shivering without it.

Suddenly there was a dark spot in the sky. It appeared to be something flying, and dread curled in her stomach. She looked at Gravity and he didn't seem to be disturbed by it. He merely watched as the spot came closer, loomed larger. As it drew nearer she could see it was a very large black dragon. Instinct told her to drop the fishing pole and run, but she sat frozen to the spot as it came closer. It was more graceful then she ever would have thought something that large could be. It looked like it was heading straight for them, but it turned and dove into the lake. There was an amazingly small splash considering the size of the beast, but she had to scramble out of the way to avoid being drenched by the waves it caused. Gravity calmly took two large steps backward as a large wave came crashing toward the shore, and when the waves receded there were a half dozen large fish gasping on the bank.

Gravity looked at the fish, then at Robyn and said, "Nice catch, my lady."

The dragon flew out of the water as gracefully as it dove in, causing more waves. Robyn and Gravity had to move quickly to get the fish and put them on stringers before they were washed back into the lake. The dragon circled the castle twice, and then flew back over the mountain. She watched in fascination until it was gone, then turned to follow Gravity back to the castle. They had just taken the fish to the kitchen when they ran into Nyakas.

"Good morning, Robyn, Gravity."

"Good morning, my lord," answered Gravity, "If you will excuse me I have some other duties to attend to." With a half bow, he swept back down the hall.

"How were the fish biting this morning?" he asked.

"They weren't until your dragon came around."

"He did come? What did you think?"

"I was scared at first. You weren't exaggerating when you said he was big. But it was so cool! He dove into the lake with hardly any splash, and come out the same way! It must really be deep out there in the middle to accommodate something that big!"

"You weren't too frightened by him then? I'm impressed."

"Oh, I'm sure I would have been if he'd come any closer. He was big enough to eat me in one bite like a cocktail sausage! But he kept his distance, and I got a really good look at him. He was gorgeous! Are they all that beautiful?"

"No, not all. They tend to get more attractive as they age. Hatchlings are actually quite homely."

"Really? How old is he?"

"About twelve hundred years old."

"Whoa!! How long do they live?"

"If they die of natural causes, several thousand years. Of course, most don't live that long. Villagers hunt them down and so forth. Dragon hide makes excellent armor, and mages use their blood. Their teeth are considered good luck charms, and of course they usually have a lair that is loaded with gold. The one you saw today is far from a youngster, but he isn't very old by dragon standards, and he'll probably live longer than most dragons because of the non-aggression pact between him and my kingdom."

"I see. So he's our ally?"

"Yes. Would you like a full tour of the castle?"

"Sounds good! I guess I should learn my way around."

"This way, then." As he showed her around, he thought about their conversation. The reference she made to 'our ally' didn't fly past him, as he'd let her think it had. It made quite an impact on him; it told him she was serious about making their arrangement work. Also, the fact that she wasn't terrified of the dragon was very good news to him. She seemed to be making quite a good adjustment, especially since she'd only been there a few days.

He ended the tour in the salle. It had been a barn in a former life, before he'd had it converted into a training center so that weather would never be an excuse for not practicing. The stalls at the far end had been converted into supply rooms where weapons, both real and wooden, and armor were stored. The rest of the stalls had been removed, and only the supports that were needed remained. There were large shuttered windows added for ventilation in the summer and wide benches around the walls, leaving plenty of space for classes and private instruction. The dirt floor was neatly raked and sprinkled with sawdust to cushion falls. There was a young man in the middle with a group of boys, and he seemed to be instructing them on the proper way to hold a sword.

Gravity stood nearby, watching the class as if he were assessing the young teacher. He walked over as Nyakas and Robyn entered. The men talked momentarily about how best to instruct the Queen and it was quickly decided that she should be in private tutelage under Gravity. This decided, Nyakas took his leave and returned to his office, and Robyn was soon armed with a wooden sword.

Chapter 8

Lars chanted for the better part of an hour. As luck would have it, a white gleam of light came from above and placed itself in front of them, glowing brightly. Lars opened his eyes to see his prayers had been answered. He stood up and put his hands out to Mike and Lilly and they walked through the light to find what looked to be a field. The wind blew through the tall grass and the sun gleamed through the trees. Animals ran free among the forest in front of them, and through the foliage of trees stood an enormous castle. Its white and gray stone walls seemed to shimmer. Behind the castle and to the right they could also see a lake with rolling hills and snow-capped mountains behind it. It seemed to be out of a picture back home. Mike and Lilly looked at each other in amazement, then at Lars, who seemed to be unruffled at what had just taken place.

"You do this often, Lars?" Mike asked facetiously.

"No, not really," Lars replied without expression.

Lilly just sighed and moved toward the castle, and Mike and Lars quickly followed. As they approached the castle gate there were three men at the top of the wall and two on the ground manning the castle doors. They walked until the pole arms of the two men at the castle doors clanged together, and watched as one of the men on the wall made a gesture to the others.

"Dalen," he said, "I've seen the female. She was one of the prisoners I took to the dungeon for Lord Nyakas."

"Art thou certain, Creedan? I would hate to disturb the king or Lord Gravity if it is not," Dalen replied.

"I'm sure of it! How could you mistake a woman that size?" he replied a little more softly than before.

Dalen left the wall and went directly to the salle, where he knew Gravity had been working with Robyn for several hours. He approached quickly and said, "Lord Gravity, a small group seeks admittance."

Gravity answered, "Who is it?"

"That is not certain, my lord. There are two men and the tall woman the King ordered set free earlier."

Robyn looked at Dalen. "What do the men look like? Is one of them a little taller than me with dark hair and a pair of swords?"

"Yes, my lady. How didst thou know?"

"His name is Mike Ryan. He's Lilly's husband. Watch him, Gravity. He's got quite an attitude, and he's probably on some self-imposed mission to get the rest of my people and me out."

"And how would he do that?"

"He's a formidable swordsman, almost as good as you, and a martial artist. He's arrogant enough to think that he can take on Nyakas' army single-handedly."

"Stay here with Dalen, please. Creedan, go get the king. I'll see if I can resolve it in the meantime." He turned on his heel and left the salle.

Meanwhile, Mike was beginning to get very impatient. "Excuse me, up there!" he called, "Is the man or boy of the house at home? I need to speak with him. Or, if he's busy, you can just release those you have in the dungeon and we can be on our way," Mike said scornfully.

Gravity arrived on the wall just in time to hear what Mike said and was far from amused. "What is it I can do for you, sir?"

Lars looked up at him and remembered the face of the man who had brought Lilly back. He nudged Mike and said, "Mike, that's the guy who brought Lilly back."

"Hey, why don't you come down here so we can talk?" Mike said.

"What do we have to discuss?" Gravity replied. He was irritated, but he decided to descend anyway. Within moments he was stalking towards them. "What is it? I have a very busy schedule."

"I want the release of all others you have taken prisoner. You know the ones. They were in there with my wife and the other man you set free with her. The others will be released to me."

Gravity was irritated with the man's insolence, and answered, "I don't understand. They have been set free already, except for one."

"Then set the last one free as well, and we'll be out of what's left of your hair," Mike cut in.

"That will not be done. She bought the freedom of everyone else."

Mike was irritated that this man was not riled, at least not that he could see. "Are you the king? I want to talk to the person who is solely in charge of running this kingdom or castle or whatever it is."

"Sorry, but the king is busy at the moment. You can come back tomorrow, and I'll see if he can see you then," Gravity replied. He began to walk away and Mike grabbed his cloak and got in his face. A cold feeling passed through Mike's body. Gravity's eyes seemed to change color and Mike could hear thousands of screams in his head. He quickly let go of Gravity and took a few steps away from him, staring at him in shock. Mike had just made an enemy for life.

Gravity backed away as Robyn approached with another man. He was easily a foot taller than Robyn with finely braided black hair, and eyes like diamonds, beautiful and blue. His cloak was black, his white tunic gleamed and his loose silk pants were tucked into black boots.

Mike eyed the man coming toward him; Lars quickly took a few steps back as he realized this so-called man wasn't a man but something much worse. The man possessed many abilities that normal humans did not, and he shuddered to think about what was there that he could not see.

"Yes? What is it I can do for you, my friend?" Nyakas said calmly and politely.

"You can give us back our friend, or we can destroy everything here until we get her back. Your choice."

Nyakas looked at Mike closely and then let his eyes wander to Lilly, and then to Lars, who had backed up a few more steps to assess the situation. "Your friend has bought the freedom of the others with her marriage to me. I set the others free," Nyakas said.

"I don't think so, oh pal of mine. See, I don't think you get it. You give me my friend or I gut you like a Thanksgiving goose. Got it?"

"No, I don't think you understand. You get off my land and fast, or my army and I will have you for dinner. Or, at least I will," Nyakas retorted.

Lars quickly said, "Mike, I believe him. He'll literally have us for dinner. There's more to him than meets the eye."

"Take some advice from your friend. He's wiser than you appear. Leave now and no one will get hurt. Stay, and all three of you will suffer the consequences."

Mike reached for his sword slowly and Gravity for his. "I wouldn't do that, my friend," Gravity said, "you don't want this and neither do we."

"Mike," said Robyn, stepping forward, "I've taken care of it. I appreciate your efforts, really, I do, but it's a done deal, and I'm staying."

"Like hell you are! You're going back with me, young lady, and that's final!"

Anger at his words and tone flared in her eyes, but her voice was calm. "No, I'm not, and I'll thank you to stop talking to me that way!"

"Oh, sorry," Mike said sarcastically, "I respectfully request that you reconsider your decision, Captain, and accompany us home, or I will be forced to vivisect your alleged husband and his little playmate."

Robyn strode angrily toward him as Nyakas drew his sword. She stopped two paces away from him and said quietly, "First of all, Mr. Ryan, I'm a Major now. Second, you are stepping on my operation. You have no jurisdiction here. Third, I gave my oath on my word of honor that I would stay in this place to obtain the freedom of the rest of my team. I am staying of my own free will."

"You gave him your oath?" Mike said incredulously. "Why the hell did you do that? Did I not teach you that your oath was binding, and that you have to abide by what you say when you give it? Didn't you listen to a word I said during the years you trained with me?"

"Yes, that's why I did it! Please, Sensei, I know what I'm doing. It may not seem like it, but I do. Now, please, just take your wife, go home, and enjoy your family."

"What about your family?"

"They are going to be fine. They have all of you to worry about them. It's not as if I'm never going to see them again, and you don't need to worry about it. Trust me, I'm not sixteen anymore, and I know what I'm doing."

"You know nothing of the sort!"

Nyakas moved to stand beside Robyn. "She told you to leave. She will remain here."

"Get away from me, pretty boy. You're not involved in this."

"Yes, I am! I paid a substantial amount of money for the group, and I negotiated with Robyn to set them free on the condition that she remains here. The deal is final."

"Oh, I see. How much did you pay? I'll give you your money back."

"The money is no longer an issue."

"It sounds like it is the issue."

"It's not. The issue is the deal that Robyn and I negotiated. She wants to stay."

"She has prior urgent commitments."

"Mike, I'm a woman of my word," Robyn said.

"Your oath as an Army officer forbids you from entering into any other oaths."

"It's because of that oath that I made this oath. I bought the freedom of my team so they wouldn't be prisoners. Besides, it's a matter of interpretation."

"Whatever happened to Article Six of the Code of Conduct?"

"I haven't given up hope, and the time for escape is not now!"

"It's always now. There is no later. When do you propose to carry out that Article?"

"When the time is right. I can't go back on my word."

"Excuse me, Major?"

"The decision is final, Mr. Ryan," Robyn replied firmly.

"If you won't take her word for it, Mr. Ryan," said Gravity, "maybe you'll take theirs." He gestured over his shoulder to indicate the archers standing on the wall, bows drawn.

Mike saw there was no point in trying to convince her. "Fine, Robyn, we'll go. I just hope you know as much as you think you do."

"I hate to point this out, but I'm a grown-up now. I know you hate to admit it, but it's true. My life is here now. Please tell my parents I love them, and thank you for your concern. Now, why don't you let Gravity open a portal, and he can get you safely back."

"Let him? Yeah, right. We'll probably end back up in Romith. Don't worry, we can manage on our own."

Mike turned slowly and walked away toward the woods. Lars waited as Lilly stepped forward to hug Robyn. Quietly, she said in Robyn's ear, "I admire your courage. Be strong, and don't attempt to escape until they least expect you to."

Robyn nodded, and Lars and Lilly followed Mike as he walked to the forest. They retraced their steps into the field, and the portal opened as if it knew they would be going back. Mike stopped and took one final look back, his face filled with mixed emotions, and walked through the light.

The crisis averted, Robyn returned to her chamber to find Gwyneth having just prepared a hot bath. A large copper tub had been moved into her chamber and was filled with steaming water. It looked so inviting that Robyn wanted to hug her lady-in-waiting. Gwyneth helped her out of her clothing and into the tub, then left with Robyn's very dirty clothes. Robyn lay back in the tub. The water was very hot, and although Robyn felt like a lobster, it leeched much of the stiffness from her muscles rather quickly. A short time later, Gwyneth returned.

"Milady? Are you nearly ready to dress?"

"Dress? Dress for what?"

"For dinner, of course."

"Dress for dinner?" Robyn knew she sounded stupid, but she'd had no idea that she'd be expected to have dinner with Nyakas after working so hard. She was surprised he hadn't said anything.

"Of course, milady. You're the Queen now."

"Oh, all right. Duty calls." She grudgingly pulled herself from the tub and accepted the towel that Gwyneth was holding for her. She dried off and put on her undergarments while Gwyneth chose her gown. This one was dark blue silk with long sleeves and a deep scoop neck. As with most of her gowns, the bodice was fitted, but this skirt was not as full as some of the others and clung lightly to her slender hips. Gwyneth helped her into the gown and buttoned it up the back, then placed a necklace around her neck. When Robyn looked in the mirror as Gwyneth brushed her hair, she saw it was a thick gold chain with a large sapphire pendant. She'd never seen one so big; it was nearly the size of a walnut.

When Gwyneth was finished Robyn went as quickly as she could to the Great Hall. Although still quite stiff from her workout, she managed to conceal it. A page caught her as she started in the main door and escorted her to a side entrance. This one was very close to the head table, and Nyakas saw her enter and motioned her over. Nyakas' chamberlain, Jerome, announced her presence, and to her astonishment, everyone in the room stood until she was seated. She looked at Nyakas as he sat beside her, and he winked, causing her to blush. Her seat was to Nyakas' left, and Gravity sat on his right. There were several other people at the head table, but Robyn had no idea who they were. She found out quickly enough that they the council members who happened to be at court, and she soon found herself trying to follow conversations dealing with local politics and agriculture.

Dinner seemed to drag on for hours. When she didn't think she could stay awake any longer, she felt a hand on her shoulder. She turned to see Gravity leaning back to talk to her without interfering with Nyakas' conversation.

"How are you feeling, my Queen?"

"Stiff, sore, and tired, thanks to you."

"I'll have something sent to your chamber to help with that. How is your sword hand?"

"Just one blister."

"I can help with that as well. Are you ready to go?"

"Are you kidding? I was ready to go half a hour ago!"

Nyakas turned to her. "Leaving so soon? Well, you did work hard today. Are you ready to start again in the morning?"

"Yes, I think so."

"Well, then, have a good rest, my dear, and I'll see you tomorrow." He motioned to the chamberlain as Robyn stood, and again the room rose collectively as she left the Great Hall. Gravity followed her out.

She turned to him as they went to her chamber. "Can I expect that every night?"

"Dinner? Yes."

"No!   I mean the announcement and the standing and all that pomp and circumstance!"

"Yes. They are so glad to finally have a Queen that you might as well get used to being treated like that. Don't worry, it won't be long before the moral majority sees fit to protest your training."

"Well, they can get over it. The training was my idea to start with. I have to be able to defend myself if I ever get caught alone, and the best I can do right now is hand to hand fighting. That's all well and good if that's all my opponent has!"

"This is true enough. Of course, the chances of you being in such a situation are slim, but it's always good to be prepared. If you want to keep training, Nyakas will come up with an excuse for you to appease them. His main concern right now is helping you get settled."

"Well, I wish he'd quit walking on eggshells. It makes me nervous."

They stopped at the door of her chamber. "I'll pass it on to him. I shall have Gwyneth bring you some tea to ease your discomfort and help you sleep. May I see your hand?"

She showed him her hand. There was a blister in the webbing between her thumb and forefinger. He held her hand with his left hand and placed his right index and middle fingers lightly over the blister. The area of the blister warmed, and when he removed his fingers a few seconds, the blister had been replaced by a callous.

"Don't tell the squires I did that," he said gravely, "I'd have every whining noble son at court pounding on my door. I make them work for their calluses. I toughen their spirits as I toughen their hands."

"I won't say a word. Does this mean my spirit is tough?"

"I can tell you are a brave fighter, my lady, but untaught. Tomorrow your education will begin, and I can assure you that by this time tomorrow you will not think highly of me. Good night, my Queen."

Robyn watched as he swept down the hall, and then went into her room. Knowing that it would be nearly impossible to get out of her gown by herself, she went out on the balcony to wait for Gwyneth. It was chilly, but her balcony was protected from the worst of the wind. It was cloudy and looked as if it wanted to rain. She wondered what the next day would hold, but for a change she didn't worry about it. She was glad to have something to do, and Gravity couldn't be any worse than some of her survival instructors. Some of them had been brutal, but she had been tougher than some of the men to begin with, and only one of many had even made her think of quitting. If she could handle them, she could handle Gravity.

She smiled as she realized that some of her survival instructors weren't as tough as Mike had been. She'd done martial arts training with him from an early age, and he never took it easy on her because of her gender. She hoped he understood why she was doing this. She'd wanted to leave with them, but he'd taught her that honor was the most important thing anyone possessed, and she would never have been able to face herself in the mirror if she'd taken advantage of the opportunity.

There was a tap at the door and Gwyneth came in with a steaming mug. Robyn went back into the room as Gwyneth placed the mug on the table and added a small log to the banked coals. The fire blazed hungrily, and the room warmed quickly. Gwyneth unbuttoned Robyn's gown, and while she hung it up, Robyn put on her muslin night gown, which had been hanging in front of the fire to get warm, and sat stiffly on the couch to drink her tea. It was sweet and she drank it quickly, letting the warmth seep through her. She began to feel very relaxed as she drank the last of it, and Gwyneth took the mug and helped her into bed. Robyn curled underneath the covers and was asleep before Gwyneth left the room.

Chapter 9

A noise cut through her sleep. Instinct told her that someone was in the room. She intentionally kept her breathing even and did not open her eyes. Listening carefully, she heard the door shut quietly and almost imperceptible footsteps approaching her bed. She waited until the footsteps stopped, and then slowly opened her eyes. There was a hand coming toward her, and her adrenaline surged. She quickly grabbed the wrist, and then simultaneously jerked the arm down while rolling out of the way. She rolled off the end of the bed and shoved the already off-balance cloaked figure, sending him onto the bed. Leaping onto his back, she grabbed his chin in her left hand and the back of his shaved head with her right and twisted quickly. As his head jerked, the long brown topknot whipped against her face and the body disappeared. She looked around quickly, not understanding what had just happened but sure nothing good would come of it. She saw nothing out of the ordinary until she heard hands slowly clapping in a dark corner. She looked up and saw Gravity leaning casually against the wall.

"Well done, my lady. You have had training."

"What the hell are you doing?"

"Testing you, majesty. I wanted to see how you would react to a sudden, unexpected attack."

"Were you testing me, Gravity, or were you trying to eliminate me?"

"Why would I want to eliminate you, my lady?"

He sounded smug, and it made her angry, but she controlled it as she had learned to do years before. "Maybe I'm infringing on your turf. Maybe you and Nyakas have been buddies for so long that you think I'm not good enough for him and you're going to put me out of his misery."

"With whom he chooses to consort is none of my concern. I have no 'turf' that you could infringe on, at least not yet. And if I'd wanted to eliminate you, I could have used magic, or I could have used my sword before you had a chance to move. Now, my lady, I shall leave you momentarily. I would suggest that you dress warmly. If you still have Nyakas' cloak, wear it. If not, I will get one for you before we begin." He left the room, closing the door quietly behind him.

She quickly pulled off her muslin gown and tossed it on the bed, then jerked open the wardrobe to see what was in there. She quickly wiggled into the culture's version of undergarments, then pulled on a pair of breeches, a tunic, a pair of thick wool socks, and her boots. Closer examination of the wardrobe revealed something similar to a wool

sweater, so she put it on and topped it all off with Nyakas' cloak. She caught a glimpse
of her reflection as she turned toward the door and saw a hood on the cloak that she
hadn't noticed before. She pulled it up as she cautiously opened the door. She looked
down the long hall in both directions before stepping out and closing the door quietly
behind her. She couldn't see Gravity, but that didn't necessarily mean anything. Rather
than stand around waiting for him, she decided to head for the courtyard. The knights
and squires sometimes trained down there and logic told her she'd probably be spending
a fair amount of time there. She strode quickly down the hall and realized that she had
instinctively slipped into training mode. Fear had been pushed out of her conscious
mind, and training and heightened instinct took over.

She arrived in the courtyard to find Gravity and Nyakas. They seemed to be in deep
conversation and didn't appear to notice her, so she flattened her back to the stone wall
and slid noiselessly behind the shrubbery. She looked around, getting a feel for her
surroundings and formulating a plan. She knew she didn't have much time; Gravity
would be looking for her soon.

A stone wall about six feet high surrounded the courtyard. The shrubs she hid
behind were about four feet tall and lined the entire courtyard wall. There was one
entrance besides the one from the castle that she had just come out, and it was directly
across from her on the far wall. If she could get out that door, the salle was within
running distance, and that happened to be the most direct route. There were some stones
nearby that were about the size of golf balls, so she picked a couple up, testing their
weight in her hand. They were heavy enough to cause a loud noise when they hit
something, but light enough to travel a fair distance. She looked at the two men and saw
they were still talking, but Gravity had begun watching the door. She waited until he
looked back at Nyakas, then quickly stood, lobbed a stone at the far left wall, and ducked
back down. It had the desired effect. The stone hit the wall with a loud crack, and both
men jumped and immediately went to see what it was. She moved quickly between the
shrubs and the wall, making as little noise as possible and watching to see that they were
still distracted. She was almost to the last corner when they found her stone and began
looking around, so she stopped and watched. As they tried to figure out which direction
it had come from, she edged quietly to the corner, another rock in her hand if she needed
a distraction. They found the spot where she'd been hiding and she knew it was only a
matter of seconds before they saw her footprints in the dirt, so she lobbed her rock at the
wall above them. As it hit the wall and bounced off, they both looked up. She was only

a few feet from the courtyard gate that, thankfully, was open. She leaped for the gate and sprinted to the salle.

A small group of knights who were fencing together looked up in alarm when the door opened suddenly, then slammed shut behind the Queen. She was as shocked to see them as they were to see her, and she stopped in her tracks.

She smiled brightly and tried to be regal. "Good morning, gentlemen! Don't mind me, carry on, and if anyone asks you, I strolled in casually several minutes ago." She walked to the left side of the building, and they watched her closely. "Really, it's fine. Go right ahead with what you were doing. I'll just sit right over here and observe." She chose a spot about halfway down the wall and sat down as one of the knights spoke quietly to a young squire. They began fencing again, and Robyn watched, trying to learn the technique.

The squire approached her and knelt before her. "Beg your pardon, Majesty. Is there something you need?"

She started to say no, but then grinned and said, "Yes, actually there is. What is your name, young man?"

"William, my lady."

"William, Lord Gravity was supposed to meet me, and I'm wondering if he's been delayed for some reason. Would you see if you could find him? We have a lot of work to do today, and I'd like to get started as soon as possible."

"As you wish, my lady." William stood, bowed, and walked to the door. He was nearly there when the door opened and Gravity strode in. He looked around and saw her on the bench. William wisely moved out of the way and went back to his duties.

Gravity strolled over and stood before her. He dropped her rocks into her lap and said, "My lady, I believe these are yours. Shall we begin?"

She stood and followed him outside. The morning was spent in physical training. When he finally allowed her to stop after her third cycle of running, push-ups, sit-ups, and pull-ups, Robyn estimated that it was about noon. She sank to the ground and leaned against a tree, hot, tired, and hungry. He handed her a bag and a water skin. She drank cautiously to determine what was in it. It was just water, so she sipped at it, careful not to get waterlogged. The bag contained bread, meat, and cheese, and she ate every bit. He sat nearby and did the same, but he didn't seem to be fatigued, even though he had done the same things she had. By the time she finished her lunch she was feeling like her old self. Gravity produced a pair of wooden swords and moved into position to fence with her. He allowed her to make a few mistakes, correcting her verbally as they reviewed what she'd learned the previous day. She learned quickly to watch his practice blade to anticipate his next move, but soon miscalculated his motion and left her side open. He corrected her with a smack in the ribs with the flat of his blade. She yelped in surprise, but he didn't stop and she clumsily got back into the rhythm. Soon she had the few new moves down, and the process was repeated with a few additional ones. By the time he stopped, she felt as though she had been run over by a herd of elephants.

He took her wooden blade and said, "Not bad, my lady. You're a fast learner, but you still have much to learn. We have dinner in two hours. We shall begin again at dawn tomorrow." He turned and strolled casually back to the salle as if he'd been lounging by the lake all day.

Robyn managed to maintain some semblance of dignity as she went to her room, but as soon as her door shut, she limped to the bed and fell face first onto it, exhausted. She had no idea how she was going to manage to live through dinner, and she wondered if anyone would believe it if she sent word that she was on her death bed and to go on without her. The bathtub was back, and she got up gingerly to see if it had anything in it yet. It was full and steaming, and she stripped her clothing off and dropped it on the floor. She was so stiff that by the time she slipped into the tub she was weeping, and she wondered how long it would be before anyone discovered her body if she went ahead and drowned herself in this hot heaven.

She didn't have long enough to try. Gwyneth came in and began choosing her clothing for dinner. She took one look at Robyn weeping in the tub and said, "I have someone who can help you, milady. I'll be back." She left the room and came back a short time later with another young woman. She was petite with short brown hair and big brown eyes. She looked like a little brown wren in her muslin dress and white apron.

"Milady," said Gwyneth, "This is Tess. She can help with your stiffness if you will get out of the tub."

Robyn gingerly got out, and Gwyneth handed her a towel. She dried off and wrapped the towel around her, and Tess directed her to lie down on her stomach on the bed. It wasn't long before Robyn discovered that Gwyneth was correct. Tess was a wonderful masseuse, and when she was finished Robyn felt like a new woman. Gwyneth gently rubbed a funny smelling salve into her new bruises, then helped her dress. She thanked the two women and asked Tess to return every day at the same time until Robyn told her otherwise.

Feeling refreshed, Robyn went to dinner. Tonight's dress was mauve silk and the same style as the night before. She entered the Great Hall looking as though she had spent the day strolling with her ladies, and got great satisfaction from the look of surprise on Gravity's face as she sat gracefully beside Nyakas.

"Good evening, my lady," Nyakas said, leaning toward her to kiss her cheek. "Did you not train with Gravity today?"

"Yes, I did. We had a splendid time, didn't we Gravity?"

"Indeed, my lady," answered Gravity, who looked slightly dumbfounded and not at all amused.

She smiled brightly as Nyakas and Gravity exchanged looks of confusion and made a mental note to do something nice for Gwyneth and Tess. Dinner seemed to pass much more quickly than it had the night before, and Robyn chatted with the nobles around her.

Soon she began to tire, so she bade goodnight to those at her table, excused herself, and left the Great Hall. She was nearly to her room when she heard someone call her name. She turned and saw Nyakas strolling toward her, so she stopped and waited for him to catch up. He was wearing black, as usual. His silk tunic was open at the neck and she could see dark hairs curling lightly. It clung to his body and she could see that he was well muscled as well as broad shouldered. He moved with a grace possessed only by the most agile people, and his black cloak billowed in his wake. She found herself mesmerized as she watched him approach, and desire curled in her stomach.

"Would you like to have a drink with me before you retire, my lady?"

"Well, maybe a small one. I have to be up early in the morning, you know."

"Yes, I know. But there is a small matter I wish to discuss with you." He took her hand and led her to his office. It looked a little different. It was dark outside, so it was lit dimly with candles, and a fire crackled in the fireplace. He led her to the chairs and she sat down while he poured two glasses of wine. On one hand, she heartily hoped this was when they would discuss taking care of the delayed wedding night customs. The setting was certainly romantic enough. The only thing missing was the soft music, but she decided she'd rather not have that, since any music would have to be provided by somebody in the room, and she preferred for romantic situations to be private. On the other hand, she hoped he'd changed his mind and would send her home. As much as she wanted to be fully committed to fulfilling her promise, she missed her family and friends, and even missed her work.

He handed her a wine glass and sat in the other chair. "So, tell me about how today went."

"It was fine. We worked hard, and to tell the truth I was a little tired when we finished, but I took a hot bath and felt as good as new."

"That's good. It was rather amusing; Gravity is trying to figure out how you recovered so quickly. I don't think he expected to see you at dinner."

"Really? Well, it's part of my duty to show up for dinner, right? You don't ask much of me, so I feel I have to do that much. Maybe I'm just a little tougher than he's giving me credit for."

"Perhaps. Just be prepared for him to test your full strength, my dear. He will do his best to push you to your limits. He's very good at what he does, and he'll want to see just how much you can endure. Don't try to push yourself too hard; he'll do that for you."

"Thanks for the advice. I expected as much. I'll get through it just fine, and I'll keep showing up for dinner for as long as I'm able just to see that look on his face!"

"It was funny, wasn't it? I'd never seen it before, and we've been friends for a very long time."

"Really? How long?"

"Years. He helped me establish this kingdom. When we found this castle it was pretty run-down, but we recruited some help and got it running, and you see where it is today."

"Yes. How long have you been here?"

"Longer than I care to admit."

"Still not telling? You know I'll get it out of you sooner or later."

"Yes, I know. You just have more important things to concentrate on."

She sipped her wine thoughtfully. "Yes, I suppose I do. I just like to know everything up front so I can weigh my odds. Many Army officers are compulsive planners. So, what was it that you wanted to discuss?"

"That was it. I just wanted to hear about your day. Will you answer one more question?"

"Sure."

"Are you happy here so far?"

"Mostly, yes. I miss my home and my family and friends, but I like it here. It's a simple life, and I think I needed that more than I realized. If you're worried about me trying to leave, don't. Even if I knew how to leave, I made a promise and I'll stand by it. I won't leave until you get tired of me and kick me out!"

"Fair enough. But if you should become unhappy, please tell me. I want you to be happy with me, Robyn."

He sounded almost vulnerable, and Robyn's heart skipped a beat. She took his hand and said, "Don't worry. I was raised to see the bright side of everything, and I don't stay sad long. I'll be fine. Now, I'd better go get some sleep before your friend decides to wake me up again."

"Have a good rest, my dear. By the way, why did you use the distraction techniques to get past us this morning?"

"I wanted you to see what I could do."

"Well, it was impressive, but not necessary."

Robyn shrugged her shoulders and said, "I was just showing off. You've seen it, so there's no need for me to do it again. Good night, Nyakas." She placed her glass on the table and stood up to leave.

He took her hand, looked up into her eyes, and kissed her hand lightly. Butterflies began to flutter in her stomach, and she her pulse quickened in anticipation, but he simply let her hand go and said, "I'll let you in on a little secret. Gravity is telepathic; you got past me, but not past him. He just let you go to see what you'd do. Good night, Robyn."

She smiled at him and left the room. She floated back to her room to find Gwyneth waiting for her. She got out of her dress and into her nightgown, then curled into bed. Gwyneth banked the coals in the fireplace and left, and Robyn suddenly remembered how she had woken up that morning. She went to the door and locked it, checked the security of the French doors to the balcony, then got back into bed. She drifted off to sleep and dreamed that Nyakas came to her and held her through the cold night.

Chapter 10

The next several days were similar to the first. They trained all day and Robyn progressed steadily, but Gravity pushed harder every day. After a week he gave her an afternoon off, and Robyn announced that she was going fishing. Tired and emotionally drained, she went to collect her fishing pole and headed to the lake. Nyakas was already there.

"Good afternoon, my lady. I understand you have some time off."

She smiled and said, "Yes. It's about time. I really need some. Too bad it's not dawn."

"Why?"

"Because then I could really relax and your dragon friend could do all the work!"

He laughed. "How is your training coming?"

"Better than I expected. We've been working really hard, but it's coming along."

"If I ask you a question, will you answer truthfully?"

"Of course! I've found it's always best to be truthful because then I don't have to remember what I said."

"I know you've been working very hard, and yet you always look so beautiful when you come for dinner. How is it that you are managing this?"

"I don't know if I should answer that one," she replied with a smile.

"Why not?"

"Well, you are Gravity's best friend and I wouldn't want you to have to keep secrets from him."

"All I know is that yesterday Gravity had to resort to a hot bath when he finished with you, and I have never seen him do that before. Yet you came down looking as fresh as a daisy. I've never seen him look more irritated; I found it amusing! How are you doing it?"

"If I tell you, will you promise not to tell Gravity?"

"Yes, I promise, because I'm dying to know myself."

"Well, just suffice it to say that you have a wonderful masseuse on your staff."

"I have a masseuse?"

"Well that's not really her job, she's just really good at it. She's one of the maids. Her name is Tess."

"Tess? How did you find out about Tess?"

"Gwyneth brought her to me."

"Perhaps I should have a chat with Gwyneth."

"Why is that?"

"Let's just say that if Tess decided to further her advancement in this household by sleeping with the royalty, I'd have more competition than you would."

Robyn thought about that for moment and then said, "Well that explains why she is so thorough." She laughed at the look of shock on his face and said, "No, she hasn't tried anything! She's just a very good masseuse! Besides, Gwyneth is always in the room, so I don't think she'd try anything if she wanted to. My goodness, from the look on your face I'd say you were jealous for a moment!"

"Of course I'd be jealous! Besides, how would it look if the Queen was having a relationship with a maid?"

"I'm not that kind of woman! I like men, so don't worry about that! I'm just surprised to hear that you would be jealous of another woman."

"I'd be jealous of another man, too. You're my wife."

"Yes, I know, but we haven't exactly had a real marriage yet, have we?"

"What do you mean? We had a ceremony."

"Come on, don't play dumb with me. Yes, we had a ceremony, but since then you've treated me like a guest. We don't do anything that married couples do except have dinner together. I hardly know anything about you!"

"I'll tell you everything in due time. You've got enough to deal with right now." He turned around to see a page trotting toward him. "Yes, lad?"

"Majesty," the boy said breathlessly bowing, "You have a visitor in your office."

"Thank you, I shall be up straight away. Will you please fetch Lord Gravity and ask him to come to the lake?"

"Yes, my lord." The page turned and trotted back up to the castle.

"Duty calls, my dear. Will you be all right here until Gravity comes?"

"Yes, of course, my lord, I'm not totally helpless," she answered with a hard edge in her voice.

He kissed her hand, then stood and left. Robyn fumed. Every time she tried to get to know him, he left. She was beginning to think that he was hiding something big from her. Maybe he and Gravity were really 'best friends' and she was just a showpiece. One of the other female officers in her company swore that all the good men were married or gay. Was Nyakas both? The thought made her even angrier, and she decided that she didn't want to fish anymore. She stalked to the castle and met Gravity in the courtyard as he was coming out.

"My lady! I thought you were fishing."

"I was, but they're not biting. Go back to what you were doing."

"Are you all right?"

"Fine! Just fine!" Stalking past him, she dropped her fishing pole off in her room, then headed for the battlements. On her way up she way-laid a page and said, "Please tell Gwyneth that I have the afternoon off, so the usual routine won't be necessary today, but that the Queen wishes to wear black for dinner tonight."

He looked at her as if she might kill him if he didn't do as he was asked and said, "Yes, Majesty! Right away!" Then he turned and ran back down the hall.

She sat on the battlements and tried to figure out why he would not tell her anything about himself, and before long her anger faded to irritation. Her attitude began to slowly improve until Gravity came up a couple of hours later and plopped down unceremoniously beside her.

"Would you like to discuss it now, my lady?"

"No, it's between Nyakas and me. I don't think it's appropriate for me to discuss it with you. And quit calling me that when no one is around! I have a name. It's Robyn. I promise, I'm still just a person!"

"I think it is very appropriate for you to discuss it with me if it involves him."

"Well, I don't! You are my teacher and his best friend and you don't need to be caught in the middle of it!"

"Is it because you feel he's not telling you something?"

"Are you reading my mind?"

"Yes, actually I am. It's a talent I have."

"Well, quit! And no, it's not that I feel he's not telling me something. It's that he's not telling me anything at all. That's all I'm going to say on the subject."

"He will tell you, Robyn. He just wants you to be ready."

"Ready for what? For pity sake, I'm an adult! I can take it! Look, I said I'm not going to discuss it with you, and I'm not. End of subject."

"Well, all I can say is that he's looking out for your best interests. I know him better than anyone except maybe his sister."

"His sister? Maybe she'd tell me something."

"Yes, Lady Stephan. Would you like to talk to her? She is here, I can have her meet you in your chamber."

Robyn looked at him in surprise. "Yes, that would be lovely. Thank you."

"You're welcome. I'll go find her straight away."

Robyn watched him go, and then went back to her chamber. A few minutes later there was a tap at the door and Nyakas' sister entered. Her hair was a sparkling shade of gold, and her eyes reminded Robyn of the ocean on a calm day. She had a tanned, athletic physique, which was nicely accented by a cream gown. It was fitted from bodice to waist with a flared skirt and long fitted sleeves.

She floated into the room with a cheery, "Good afternoon, Robyn!"

"Lady Stephan, thank you for coming to see me."

"The pleasure is mine, and just call me Stephan. We are sisters, now, after all. I don't know about you, but I've never had a sister before."

Robyn smiled as Stephan sat beside her on the couch. "Neither have I."

"Good! Then we have something in common besides Nyakas already! Is he what you wanted to discuss with me?"

"Yes. I have been trying to get to know him, and I'm getting the feeling that there is something he doesn't want me to know. I was hoping perhaps you could shed some light on it for me."

"Actually, that's one of the reasons I came to see him. I know outwardly we appear to be as you are, but there is more to us than that. I had a feeling perhaps he would be putting off telling you, and from what he and Gravity have told me about you, I thought that would be a mistake."

"Oh, yes! I really hate being treated like a mushroom!"

"A mushroom?"

"Yes, kept in the dark and fed manure, if you know what I mean."

Stephan laughed and touched Robyn's hand. "I've never heard that one! In any case, I've already spoken to Nyakas and told him that if he hasn't explained things to you in the next two days, I shall do it myself. He wasn't happy with me, but that's all right!"

"So you won't just tell me now?"

"I think it's best coming from him. I told him so, but if necessary I will tell you myself."

"Would you consider answering a question?"

"That depends upon the question."

"Does Nyakas prefer to keep company with women in his bedroom, or men?"

Stephan laughed loudly. "I've never caught Nyakas in bed with anyone, male or female, but I've seen the way he looks at you. I don't think you will have any competition with the squires."

"I guess that's acceptable."

"Good! Now, I will leave you to prepare for dinner. Nyakas has insisted that I have dinner with his court before I go home."

"I'll see you there, then."

Stephan hugged Robyn's shoulders and swept gracefully from the room. Gwyneth came in a few minutes later. It didn't take her long to talk Robyn out of the black gown when she came up with a lovely gown that was such a deep shade of crimson that it appeared almost black. Like her black one, this one had a scoop neck, a fitted embroidered bodice that just graced her shoulders, long sleeves, and a full skirt. A dazzling ruby necklace was added, jeweled combs pulled her hair back, and the ensemble was complete. She arrived for dinner precisely on time and was soon seated beside Nyakas.

"Good evening, my dear. You look lovely tonight."

"Thank you, my lord."

"What did you do after I left? Did you catch anything?"

"No. I went to the battlements, and then I had a nice chat with Stephan."

He looked suspiciously at Stephan, who sat on Robyn's left. Stephan smiled brightly at him as he asked, "Really? What did you talk about?"

"Why, you, of course, dear brother!" said Stephan. Robyn couldn't help but smile.

"I see," said Nyakas sourly, "Robyn, would you like to take a walk after dinner?"

"That sounds lovely, my lord. I'd be delighted." She thought she'd handled it very well, then Stephan kicked her foot and Robyn laughed. Nyakas looked at her, and both she and Stephan looked back at him innocently. He grunted in displeasure and turned to Gravity.

As she ate dinner the maid placed a mug of what appeared to be beer before her. Gravity leaned back and said, "I thought you'd like to try that, my lady. It's my own brew."

"Thank you, Gravity," she said. She picked up the mug and looked at Stephan questioningly. Stephan shrugged, and Robyn sipped tentatively. It was the worst beer she'd ever had and she forced herself to swallow it. Gravity was looking at her expectantly, and she smiled weakly at him.

"Well," he asked, "what do you think?"

"It's, umm, quite unlike anything I've ever had, Gravity."

"But do you like it?"

"Honestly, it's not exactly my taste, Gravity, but I'm not much of a beer drinker."

He seemed to accept her answer and turned to a noble who had just asked him a question. Stephan leaned toward her and said, "How is it, really?"

Robyn whispered, "Terrible!"

After dinner she and Nyakas left together for the first time. All eyes followed them as they left the Great Hall, and Robyn was glad to get outside. They went through the courtyard to the lake, and he spread his cloak on the ground for her to sit on.

"There are a few things you don't know about me, Robyn, and you will need to know sooner or later. It's quite significant, so if you need more time to deal with other things, I won't tell you right now."

"Nyakas, I would rather know everything up front. Just tell me everything and I'll sort it out and deal with different pieces at a time."

"I just don't want you to be frightened of me, that's all."

"Why would I be frightened of you? You've never been anything but kind to me."

He nodded and took a deep breath. "Do you remember the dragon you saw when you were fishing?"

"Yes, you have a beautiful dragon."

"I am that dragon."

"Pardon?"

"I was the one who dove into the lake. I'm a dragon. In this realm, dragons often take on human form. It makes it easier to interact with other races and tends to increase our life expectancy."

"You're a dragon? Come on, you're kidding, right?"

He stood up and said, "Watch. Don't be afraid, OK?" He walked away, then stopped and turned to face her. He began to shimmer. His skin darkened and began to form hard scales, his body grew up and became reptilian at the same time. In less than a minute he had turned to a dragon before her eyes. He'd been big when she saw him before. Now, being so close, he was enormous. Robyn sat on the cloak and stared incredulously. He lowered his head to look at her and said, "Now do you see what I was keeping from you?" She nodded, and he seemed to smile. "Put on the cloak, Robyn, and climb onto my neck. I promise I won't hurt you." She did as she was told, and soon he was soaring over the lake with Robyn clinging to his neck for dear life. He flew gently and steadily, making no sharp turns or fancy moves, and gradually she began to relax. It was nothing like flying her chopper. It felt more like she was riding a motorcycle hundreds of feet off the ground, and before she knew it, she was enjoying herself.

He flew for a while, then landed and changed back to his human form. She felt exhilarated, and he smiled to see her so happy.

"If I had known it would make you that happy, I would have told you sooner," he said.

"I wish you had. It would have saved me a lot of frustration! You have no idea the thoughts that came to my mind!"

"Did you ever consider that I was a dragon?"

Robyn blushed lightly. "Never crossed my mind! So, I guess this means Stephan is a dragon, too."

"Yes, but she's more gold. Unlike most animals, the females of our race tend to be more colorful than the males."

"So what else is there?"

"Well, you should know that my father doesn't approve of my choice of mates."

"Why? He'd rather you married another dragon?"

"He'd rather I didn't marry at all. Among some of the more power hungry dragons, like my father, the custom is to take a concubine, and after she bears you one child, you kill her."

"Kill her? Why?"

"Because then the male dragon has full authority over how the hatchling is raised, and there are no female influences. This tends to produce more power hungry dragons. In his case, it only worked with one of his three offspring. Stephan and I have been somewhat of a disappointment to him. My brother, Vaytawn, is the one who is most like him. Unfortunately for my father, I am stronger than Vaytawn is."

"Well, if you think I'm going to let you kill me after I bear you one child, think again!"

He laughed and said, "I wouldn't think of it."

"Does this mean that you are actually 1,200 years old?"

"Yes. Stephan is just under 1,000."

"Wow. I like older guys, but you take the cake! Gosh, 1,200 years old. How old is that in dog years?"

He laughed loudly, put his arm around her shoulder, and pulled her to his side. She put her arms around his waist and they laughed together, then sat by the lake and watched the stars. Before she knew it she was falling asleep, and he escorted her to her room. As usual, she went to bed alone.

Chapter 11

The next day was business as usual. Robyn was up with the sun, and she and Gravity worked and practiced all day. Then she went back to her chamber for her bath and massage and to change for dinner. Everyone was assembled in the Great Hall and she took her seat to beside Nyakas.

"You look lovely tonight," he said.

"Thank you," she said, blushing slightly.

The food was served and Gravity offered her a beer.

"No, thank you, Gravity," she said, "I think tonight I'll try the wine, or did you make that as well?"

"No," he said looking slightly confused, "only the beer."

"Well then," she said "wine it is!" He gave her a very black look and she laughed.

She drank more wine than she intended to with dinner, but she didn't realize it until she rose from her seat. She barely managed a graceful exit, and went back to her chamber. Rather than reading in front of the fire, as was her custom, she changed into her deerskin breeches and tunic, ascended the steps to the battlements, and sat looking at the stars. The guards patrolled regularly, and soon one approached her to make sure everything was all right. She assured him that everything was fine, and he resumed his rounds.

As she sat gazing at the stars, a song from her childhood entered her mind from no place in particular. She began humming, and switched to singing as the alcohol took a stronger hold. It had been quite a long time since she had more than one drink, and the wine was particularly strong. Each song reminded her of another, and soon she was singing anything they came to her mind, and not very well. Suddenly, Nyakas was standing in front of her.

"What are you doing, Robyn?" he asked.

"Why, I'm singing! What does it look like?"

He chuckled and sat down beside her. "What are you singing about?"

"Whatever comes to mind," she answered, "What are you doing up here?"

"One of the guards came and told me that the Queen was singing on the battlements, so I thought I'd better come up and check it out for myself."

"Well, he was right!" she said.

"It's chilly up here," he said, "Aren't you getting cold?"

As soon as he said it, she realized she was. "As a matter of fact, I am. Perhaps I should go to my room now." She stood up intending to go back downstairs but her legs suddenly felt rubbery and she wobbled. He stood up quickly and caught her, lifting her easily. He turned and carried her back down the stairs. She leaned her head against his chest and sighed. It felt good to be in a man's arms, even if it was only to carry her drunken derriere to bed.

"You have very strong arms," she said, closing her eyes.

"I have to, my dear."

She smiled slightly. "Why? Am I that heavy?"

"Not at all. It's rather like carrying a piece of fine porcelain."

"I guess the porcelain must be bigger here." She immediately wished she hadn't said such a ridiculous thing. He chuckled and it seemed as though it thundered through his chest. He opened the door to her room and carried her to the bed, placed her gently upon the heavy quilt and sat down beside her.

"Is there anything I can do for you, my lady?" he asked gently.

She sat up and leaned against the pillows. "You can stay and keep me company for a while. I hate being drunk alone. I always start to wish for things that never would have been in the first place, and I get sad. I really hate being sad."

"What kinds of things do you wish for?"

"Right now, or when I've been drunk and alone in the past?"

"In the past."

"Well, mostly I wish that my father had come into my life sooner. By the time Mama discovered she was pregnant, my father had left the Army and they'd lost touch. It wasn't until I was eight and Mama saw Dad wrestling on TV that she was able to get in touch with him to tell him. He came to see us in Tulsa, and a year later he and Mama got married and we moved to New York."

"How did they loose touch?"

"Mama says it was her fault. They were both stationed at Fort Hood when they met and Mama has always been one to play hard to get. They started dating, and Mama didn't tell him how she felt, so when his date of separation from the Army came around, he left and went back to New York. Somehow they both managed to lose each other's addresses. When Mama found out she was pregnant with me and she couldn't find him, she got out of the Army and moved back to Tulsa so at least she'd have her parents nearby. So I guess if I could change one thing, it would be that my dad would have been part of my life from the beginning. He missed a lot in my first eight years, and so did I."

There was a gentle tap at the door, and they both looked to see a squire peeking in the door. "Yes, boy," Nyakas said, and the boy entered and bowed.

"Majesty, your sister is here to see you."

"Is she? Have her wait in my office, tell her I'm having a discussion with my wife and if she cannot wait I will come and see her tomorrow."

"Yes, my lord."

Nyakas turned his attention back to Robyn and caught her studying him. The look in her eyes spoke of an emotion that he knew she was not yet ready to admit to. "What would you wish for if you were alone now?"

"I don't know," she lied. She knew she'd be wishing that he'd kissed her after he left to see Stephan. She had never wanted anything more in her life, but she couldn't bring herself to say the words. He smiled softly and ran the back of his right index finger down her left cheek. Slowly he leaned toward her and entwined his hand in her hair. She involuntarily closed her eyes as his face moved toward hers. The touch on her lips might have been a butterfly at first, or a rose petal, but it deepened slightly and Robyn felt as though her heart was being swept away with a receding tide. She didn't realize at first when it stopped, but when she opened her eyes his face was still very near hers. She wrapped her arms around his neck and he held her. Never in her life had she felt such contentment.

"Nyakas?" she said to his shoulder.

"Yes?"

"When can I start being your wife?"

He drew back and looked at her, smiling. "Silly drunkard! You are my wife!"

"I mean, when can I start really being your wife? It's been almost two weeks, and that's the first time you've kissed me since the wedding."

He looked away and seemed genuinely embarrassed. "Is that really what you want, Robyn?"

"I agreed to stay and be your wife, and I feel like I'm not upholding my end of the bargain. But if staying in separate rooms will make you happy, I'll live with that. It will complicate things a little, though, if I'm supposed to bear your children."

"I'd planned on waiting for a while."

"We have; almost two weeks."

He smiled at her logic and looked at her. "No, I'd planned on waiting until you feel for me as I do for you."

"And how is that?"

"I've been in love with you since the first time I saw you."

She did her best to hide her surprise, but he saw it and said, "I know it will take time, and given the circumstances which brought us together, it may never happen. All I know is that when we do come together as husband and wife, I want it to be because we love each other, not out of contractual obligation." She looked like a little girl who was being chastised, and when she looked at him her lovely blue eyes had tears in them.

"As you wish, my lord."

He hugged her again, holding her close. She breathed deeply, willing herself not to cry. 'It's the alcohol, Robyn,' she thought, 'that's all it is. It will be much better after the buzz and the hangover wear off. Note to me: Take it easy on that wine the next time! It's stronger than you think!'

He pulled away, looked at her, and said, "I hope I haven't frightened you away."

She smiled slightly. "Of course not."

"I need to go see what Stephan wants. Will you be all right if I leave you?"

"Yes, I'll be fine."

"Shall I come back and sit with you after I finish, if it isn't late?"

"Sure."

He kissed her cheek and left the room. She slid gingerly off the bed and tested her legs. They seemed better, so she walked to the fireplace and added a log to the flames, then sat on the couch and watched it burn. There was a tap at the door, and she automatically bade whomever it was to enter. Gravity came in and plopped down on the hearth.

"I saw Nyakas in the hall. He said you might want some company."

She smiled. "Is that the only reason you come to see me?"

He looked at her as if he didn't understand, and she smiled sadly and added, "Sorry, I forgot. As your best friend's wife, my good looks and charm don't affect you the way they do mortal men."

"Well, drunkenness hasn't improved your humor at all."

She smiled and let the comment pass without retort.

"OK," he said, "what is it?"

"What is what?"

"You've never let a comment like that slide past before. Do you want to talk about what's on your mind?"

"Thanks, Gravity, but it's between Nyakas and me."

"It's the consummation of the marriage?"

She looked at him, shocked, and he laughed loudly. She silently cursed herself for forgetting that he could read her thoughts.

"I know him better than anybody. He is just biding his time until it's right."

"Yeah, well, he'll live another five or ten thousand years. I won't."

"It will not take that long. How do you feel about him?"

"I'm not really sure. I can safely say that I'm in like, and I'm in lust. I can't honestly say I'm in love yet because I don't know him well enough yet."

"Are you sure you aren't in love with him because you don't know him well enough, or because you're still holding on to the fact that you're stuck here?"

"I've accepted that I'm going to be here, Gravity. The fact that he bought me isn't even an issue for me anymore. It's not his fault I was captured by Romithian slave traders and sold. I could have had it a lot worse!"

"Yes, you could. But if you asked him, he'd let you go."

Robyn realized that with Gravity's telepathy, any attempt to escape would be futile, even if she were willing to go back on her word. Although she missed her friends and family, she didn't have much tying her to Earth. She'd spent her life seeking out adventure, never content with what others accepted as normal. Such was the life Nyakas offered her as his queen. "I can't do that. I have to keep my word."

"If you want to be a stubborn little nit and keep your word to him, then let yourself fall in love with him. That's all he really wants."

There was a knock at the door, and Nyakas entered. "Gravity, good, you are here. Now I can tell both of you at once. Stephan is having a little trouble on her northern border. She asked if we, Gravity and I, could come help her. It seems that there are some bandits coming in and harassing the farming villages on the border. We've had this problem before, and it's nothing a big black dragon and a few rune spells won't fix. We'll only be gone a few days." He turned to Gravity. "While we're in that area, we may want to pay our respects to King Talledrin. It's been a while since we have done anything diplomatic in that region."

"Good idea. I'll go tell the stable hands to have the horses ready early."

"Thank you, Gravity."

"Good night, Nyakas." He turned and bowed to her. "Good night, my Queen." Turning on his heel, he left the room and shut the door.

Robyn watched the flames as she wrapped her mind around Nyakas' imminent departure, then turned to him and said, "Well, I suppose you should get some sleep. It's getting late, and you'll have to be up early. Do you need any help packing or anything?"

"No," he answered, "Are you trying to get rid of me so soon?"

She could tell he was teasing, but it still hurt to hear the words. "No, I'm not trying to get rid of you. I'm trying to be a good wife."

"I'll be fine. Will you be all right here for a few days?"

"Yes, of course. Don't worry about me, I'll be just peachy."

He sat beside her and put an arm around her shoulders. She leaned against him and watched the flames, content for the moment but heartily wishing he would stay. She put her arms around his waist, as if she could hold him there, at least for the night. His heartbeat was steady, and the flames mesmerizing, and before she could stop herself, she fell asleep.

Chapter 12

Robyn opened her eyes and found herself in bed. Gwyneth was opening the heavy curtains and the sun was just beginning to rise. She sat up in bed and ran her hands over her face, trying to remember how she'd gotten there and why her head was pounding.

Gwyneth handed her a cup of coffee. "Good morning, milady. I heard that the king and Lord Gravity would be leaving early this morning and I thought you'd want to see them off."

"Yes, Gwyneth, thank you." She didn't bother sipping the coffee. She drank the whole scalding cup at once and got out of bed. The sudden shot of caffeine spread through her quickly, waking her up and doing no small part in relieving her headache. She had no other hangover symptoms, which surprised her. The last time she'd gotten drunk on wine, most of the following day had been spent in the bathroom, and the headache had been blinding. When night had finally rolled around, her head throbbed, her ribs ached, she still had dry heaves, and she came very close to dispatching herself with her service automatic out of sheer desperation.

She poured herself another cup of coffee and sat down on the couch. She noticed she was still wearing her deerskin clothing. Gwyneth went to the wardrobe and opened it, and Robyn said, "Don't bother, Gwyneth. I'll be getting dirty today, and they won't be here much longer, so there's no point in dressing up. Although it would be fantastic to have a hot bath waiting about two hours before dinner."

"Yes, milady. Is there anything else you need right now?"

"No, thank you. You might check with the tailor, though, and see if he has my new work clothes ready yet. This deer skin has got to be difficult to clean, especially as dirty as I get."

Gwyneth smiled. "You do at that, milady. What are your plans for the day?"

"The same as they usually are. After Nyakas and Gravity leave, I'll go work out and practice with the squires. Although between us, I think I'll show up a little late and sit by the lake for a while."

"Very good, milady. I'll check with the tailor straight away. Send a page after me if you need anything else."

"Thank you, Gwyneth."

She took the coffee cup and sat down at the dressing table. In a matter of minutes her hair was brushed and face washed. She gulped the last of her coffee, and then strode briskly to the courtyard.

Nyakas and Gravity were checking the security of their saddles when she came out. She walked quietly forward, trying to see how close she could get without being noticed. As Nyakas turned so his back was to her, Gravity looked up and saw her approaching. She placed one finger over her lips to silence him, and he looked away and moved to the other side of his horse with a smirk. She snuck up behind Nyakas, but prudence prevented her from startling him outright. This man was a fighter, and fighters often had violent reactions to being startled. Experience had taught her that when sneaking up on someone with lightning fast reflexes, it was best to be more than an arm length away, or very close. There were no other people in the vicinity, so she chose the latter. Walking up very quietly, she slipped her arms around his waist from behind. Even with his cloak on, his stomach felt like a steel washboard.

It didn't have the desired reaction. Without stopping what he was doing, her rubbed her hands and said, "Good morning, my lady. What brings you out here so early?"

She dropped her arms, pouting that he hadn't at least jumped. Gravity, seeing her expression, laughed out loud and walked into the stable.

"I came to see you off," she said simply, "Isn't that what a good queen does when the king is going somewhere without her?"

He turned, smiling at her. "Indeed it is. You're learning quickly." He caught the hint that she wanted to go with him, but this was not a pleasure trip. He'd be working, and he didn't want to take the chance of her getting caught in crossfire. He also hoped that their time apart would give her a chance to sort out her feelings.

Their eyes locked and she felt as if she were being drawn into his. She wished he wouldn't leave with things between them as they were. She wanted him to stay and spend every minute with her and nobody else. Without breaking his gaze, he said, "Is there anything you need before I leave?"

"Will you kiss me, just once?"

His answer was a soft kiss, and the butterflies fluttered in her stomach. The stable door banged, warning them of Gravity's imminent return. Nyakas was gazing at her as she opened her eyes, and he whispered, "I love you, Robyn."

"Have a safe journey, my lord," was all she could say.

"I shall. Look at what I'll have waiting for me when I get back." He caressed her cheek, and then mounted his horse. She watched them ride off and stood in the courtyard until she couldn't see them any more.

"My lady?"

She turned to see William standing behind her. He bowed, and then offered her a small cloth bag. "I wasn't sure you'd want company for breakfast, so I brought you something from the kitchen."

She looked inside to see a thick slice of bread, some cheese, and an orange. "That's very kind of you, William. Thank you."

He bowed and went back inside the castle, and she took her small picnic down to the lake. He was right; she wasn't really in the mood for company right now. She nibbled at her breakfast, trying not to think about anything except banishing her headache. She finished the cheese and the orange, but the bread was a bit dry for her liking. She broke it into small pieces and tossed it into the lake for the fish, hoping superstitiously that they would know she was feeding them, be lulled into a false sense of security, and bite her hook when she managed to get around to fishing again. She heard someone approaching and turned to see Stephan.

"Good morning, Robyn!" she called cheerily.

"And to you, Stephan."

"Shall I ask how you are?"

"Hung over, but otherwise fine. You just missed your brother. He and Gravity left a while ago for your northern border."

"I know. I was going to ride back with them, but I thought perhaps you could use some company this morning. What did you drink last night?"

"A very fruity wine. I didn't realize I had too much until I stood up!"

"Ah, yes. Nyakas and I call it Ambush. It smiles in your face, but it creeps up on you from behind."

Robin laughed. "Yes, it does! What's in it?"

"A combination of local berries and a touch of mint. Did you have a positively hellish headache when you woke up this morning?"

"Not hellish, but close. It's mostly gone now. It's nowhere close to last wine hangover I had."

Stephan laughed sympathetically. "So, how are things with you and my brother?"

"Not bad, now that I'm getting to know him."

"Has he told you yet how he feels?"

"Yes, last night."

"Only just last night? He never listens to me. What did you think?"

"I was a little shocked, but it made some things fall into place."

"Like what?"

"The way he looks at me, the way he studies me when he thinks I'm not looking, stuff like that."

"And how you feel about him?"

"I'm not sure exactly. I like him; he's very kind and strong, and he's so good looking. I was thinking right after I married him that it could be much worse. I could be stuck with a short ugly tyrant."

"Instead, you're stuck with a dragon."

Robin laughed. "Yes, that was a bit of shock at first. I had no idea that dragons could actually take on human form. What I haven't been able to understand is why he would want a human. He's got to know that I've only got eighty to one hundred years left, maximum."

"He does. It's partly that he thinks you're exotic and fragile, but also because you're smart and strong. He came to see me when you first started training with Gravity. He was so excited. I understand you're catching on quickly."

"I'm trying. It's keeping me busy and giving me something to focus on that I'm a little familiar with."

"Good! Do you think you'll ever love him?"

"I think so. Now, if you'll excuse me, I have to get to work. I can't stop practicing just because my teacher abandoned me! Will you be staying?"

"No, I'm afraid I can't. But if you need me for anything while Nyakas is away, tell Gwyneth and she will send a messenger. I will be glad to come straight way."

"Thank you, Stephan. I appreciate your thoughtfulness."

Stephan smiled. "What are sisters for? I'll talk to you soon."

Robyn watched as Stephan walked back up to the castle, then got up and went to the salle.

Chapter 13

Robyn was returning to her room a few days later when a page trotted up from behind her. "Majesty! I have a message for you!"

She stopped and waited for the boy to catch up with her. She'd seen him around the castle and was fairly certain that he was the youngest son of one of the nobles. As he drew closer, Robyn marveled at the ages at which people began work here. The lad was no more than eight, yet he worked from dawn to dusk, as did many of the other children. He stopped two paces in front of her, bowed, and handed her a scroll. Then he turned and ran back the way he had come.

Laughing quietly, she broke the seal and read the message. The writing was beautiful, almost like calligraphy, and it turned out to be a message from Stephan telling her that Nyakas and Gravity would be returning the following afternoon. She smiled and proceeded to her room, a little surprised that they'd be back so soon. They'd only been gone four days; she'd been expecting them to be gone more than a week.

As usual, her bath was waiting. She dropped Stephan's message on the desk, then took off her clothes and climbed into the tub. It wasn't necessary to soak today. She hadn't worked as hard as she usually did. The day Nyakas and Gravity left, she had gone to the salle, and two of the knights offered to let her train with them while Gravity was gone. While they were excellent fighters and teachers, they weren't slave drivers of Gravity's caliber, and Robyn had taken to running an extra mile or two each day so she wouldn't get soft in her teacher's absence. Today she had jokingly shamed them into running with her, and they had barely kept up with her the extra distance, which she found quite amusing.

She leisurely washed off the sweat and dirt from the day's work and got out of the tub. She dried off and put on her dressing robe, then went to the wardrobe. She took out the blue silk gown that she'd worn to dinner the first day of her training and hung it on the outside of the wardrobe so the wrinkles could fall out. There was still plenty of time before she had to dress, so she sat at the desk and read Stephan's note again.

'So, he'll be home tomorrow,' she thought, 'I wonder what will happen next. It's so strange, he's a dragon, and he's in love with me. Why? I know I'm not ugly, but Stephan is much more beautiful than I am. If she's more beautiful than me, then other female dragons must be as well. So why would he choose a woman from a different race altogether, a race that is much more short-lived than his own, for his wife? What's really blowing my mind is that his father disapproves so strongly, and yet he defied him to marry me. It's just not logical. What is it about me that would cause him to risk such trouble?'

Gwyneth tapped on the door and entered. "Good afternoon, milady. How was your practice today?"

"Fine, Gwyneth, thank you. I took out the blue silk for dinner."

"Very good, milady."

"Gwyneth, how quickly can we get a message to Lady Stephan? I'd like to discuss something with her before my husband returns tomorrow, if possible."

"It would take a rider until nearly midnight to carry her a message, but she could arrive by breakfast. Her mode of travel is much more efficient. Shall I make the arrangements?"

Robyn smiled. "That's not necessary, but thank you. It's not really that important. I guess I should get dressed."

"Yes, milady." Gwyneth helped her into the gown, and Robyn went to dinner as usual. She'd discovered that, in the Nyakas' absence, everyone looked to her for guidance. This seemed highly unusual to her; it wasn't until that point that she realized that she had some political power. While it was strange, it felt good, almost like her old Army position.

The nobles greeted her as she took her usual spot. Dinner wasn't quite as formal in the absence of the King, and good-hearted banter was tossed about more liberally than usual, especially when it became apparent to the nobles that the Queen could take a joke without taking offense.

One of the minor nobles had joined the table, and Robyn had discovered the night before that he was the older brother of one of the knights she'd been training with. He happened to be sitting nearby, and she leaned over and said, "Tristan, are you aware that your brother Cristof has been working with me this week?"

"Yes, my lady. He's enjoyed it very much."

"As have I. He's been a great help to me. Tell me again, please, what region are you from?"

"The east, my lady."

"Ah, yes, the nobles of the sea. How is the fishing there?"

"Excellent, but our peak season has passed for the year. It's better in the summer. I understand you enjoy a bit of fishing yourself."

"Indeed I do! I hope to visit your province soon for that very purpose! By the way, when you get a chance, ask Cristof about our training today. Tell him I said that the score is one to zero in the Queen's favor!"

"Pardon me, my lady?"

She grinned and said, "He'll understand. It's a joke that he can explain to you."

A short time later, she excused herself and went to sit on the battlements after making a quick stop in her chamber to change back to her pants, tunic, and Nyakas' cloak. The tailor had made one for her in the same style that fit her properly, but it didn't smell like him. His also had the added benefit of being far too big, which gave extra fabric to wrap around herself when she went to the battlements.

"Good evening, my lady," said a voice from nearby.

She looked around, saw the source of the voice, and said, "Good evening, Cristof."

"What brings you up here tonight?"

"I come up here often. It's a good place to think, and the view is wonderful."

"That it is, my lady. Might I ask what you're here to think about? I hope it isn't how to get Dalen and I to run with you every day!"

"No," she said laughing, "but it does warrant some thought! I was surprised that I outran both of you, but I figured you just let me win because I'm the queen!"

He laughed and said, "Yes! That's it exactly!"

"I'm sure it is! Be nice to me, or I'll tell Gravity when he comes back!"

"Please don't do that, Majesty!"

She laughed again, and then fell silent. He sat quietly beside her for a moment, and then said, "My lady, if you have something on your mind, I'd be happy to listen."

"I just have some personal stuff to sort out. The king and Gravity are due back tomorrow afternoon, and I've put off thinking about this for too long."

"I understand. Your adjustment to our culture seems to be going well. You have fulfilled your role very well thus far, and you seem to be a good influence on the king."

"Thank you. It's nice to hear such kind words."

"They are more than kind words, my lady. I mean them sincerely. I can see that the king cares for you a great deal, and it's not difficult to see why, if you don't mind my saying."

"I don't mind at all if you'll explain why."

"You're strong and intelligent, my lady. You've learned more than any of us expected you would in such a short time, and you've trained very hard without compromising your grace or position. Already you have a strong following among the knights and squires."

"I do? Why? All I've done is learned to use the weapons available. I've done that for years."

"That's obvious, and that's why you are admired. A lesser woman would have retreated to her chamber and only come out when ordered to do so. You chose to make the best of your situation and do something productive."

"Well, I've never been a timid wallflower, and I've never liked being unhappy any longer than necessary. What's the point of sitting around doing nothing when I can do something about it?"

"Exactly. If I tell you something, will you keep my confidence?"

"Sure."

"One of the squires was overheard talking about you this afternoon. He'll be a fine knight one day, and my advice would be to have him kept close to you and the king when that time comes. You have a very loyal admirer."

"Who is it?"

"William. He's a tenacious lad, and will make an excellent protector. He doesn't come from a highborn family, and in his case, it's all the better. He works harder than any three of the other squires."

"I'll mention it to the king and keep an eye on him. I know him, and you're right. He will be a good knight, once he's fully trained and developed. Now I have a question for you: What is your opinion of the king?"

"He's an excellent leader, my lady. He's never been anything but fair and just. He deals harshly with those who deserve it, a bit too harshly sometimes, but I suppose that's his nature, considering he is a dragon. He's much less ruthless than some I've dealt with."

"You've had dealings with other dragons?"

"Oh, yes, many, my lady. I came here from his father's court."

"Really? Tell me, in their human forms, are they all so beautiful?"

"Most are. Some are not because they don't wish to attract other races. Of course, if I were able to change my form to that of another being, I'd choose to change to one of the more beautiful of the race. If one is going to change form, one might as well look good!"

Robyn laughed at his logic, but it was sound. "So is he a typical dragon, then?"

"I wouldn't say typical. Dragons are inherently highly intelligent, observant, and charismatic. He does possess these qualities, but there's more to him, and between us, I think that's why his father fears him. Lord Malitor would never admit to such a thing, of course, but he is. King Nyakas has an uncanny way of being able to judge one's character very quickly. He can see things in people that would normally take a lot of time for others to see. I think that's why he brought you here. I think he sensed your strength and courage and knew that you'd make a good queen."

"I see. Do you think that's the only reason he bought me?"

"I can't say, my lady. He doesn't confide in me."

"It sounds as if you admire him."

"I do, very much. Often, I'd trust his judgment before my own. He's a very noble man and I can think of no one who deserves loyalty and happiness more than him."

"What does it take make him happy?"

"I think he is happy now, my lady, and I believe he will continue to be happy as long as he has you."

Robyn smiled and stood up. "Thank you, Cristof. Now, if you'll excuse me, I believe I'll retire. I'll need to be up early if I'm going to finish my work before he comes back."

"Of course, my lady. I'll see you in the salle tomorrow morning."

She touched his shoulder as she walked past and went back to her chamber. A short time later there was a large fire crackling merrily in her fireplace and she curled up on the couch, thinking about her conversation with Cristof. As the words replayed in her mind, she toyed absently with the necklace Rachel had sent back to her. She hadn't taken it off since she got it, and she often played with it when she was concentrating. As her finger traced the shape of the cross, she remembered a conversation she'd had with Rachel a few years before. Rachel had called to tell her that she had finally met the man of her dreams, and in the course of the discussion, she said she knew he was the one when she realized she was 'in like' and 'in lust' at the same time with the same man. With a jolt, Robyn realized that was exactly how she described her feelings toward Nyakas in her conversation with Gravity. She nibbled pensively on a hangnail as she pondered the thought.

'So, I'm in love with a dragon,' she thought. 'I can't say I ever thought that would happen, but that's been the norm here lately. Now what? Well, he's due home tomorrow, I'm going to have to tell him. I wonder what he'll say. I guess there's really nothing to worry about. The first time will be the hardest, but I'm going to have to do it or I'll be making the same mistake Mama did.'

She got up, smiling, and banked the fire, then got undressed, put on her nightgown, and went to bed. She was asleep before she realized it, and when she woke up the next morning she felt energized. Dressing quickly, she headed for the salle and met Gwyneth in the hallway.

"Milady! You are up early!"

"Yes, I have a lot to do this morning. I'll need a hot bath at lunchtime. I'm going to cram a full day's work into half a day, and then I'll need to get ready. Nyakas will be home this afternoon. Pick out a really pretty gown, OK? I'll be up at noon to get cleaned up, so it would be great to have something to eat and some coffee here too. Thanks a lot, Gwyneth, you're the best! See ya'!" She strode quickly down the hall passed through the kitchen and swiped a chunk of fresh bread and some water, then went outside into the courtyard. She quickly ate her breakfast, then stretched out and began running. She ran her regular circuit twice, and then met Cristof and Dalen, both still looking sleepy, in the salle. She woke them both up with energetic fencing and good-natured goading, and before long, they both went on the offensive against her. They had switched to practice foils, and the salle rang with the sounds of laughter and metal striking metal. She fought them both valiantly before she realized she'd made a tactical error and found herself backed into a corner. She surrendered just in time for the squires to arrive for their first training session of the day, and Cristof and Dalen were victorious once again, their reputations saved for another day.

Chapter 14

When she heard they had returned, she went to Nyakas' office to find him speaking with his council. He saw her appear in the open door and stopped, entranced. She wore a gown of green velvet, quite a change from the tunic and breeches she had taken to wearing since she began her training. Nyakas stared at her, and she at him. His advisors all looked at Nyakas, then turned to see what he was looking at, and after a few seconds Gravity rose from his chair, walked over, and bowed before her.

"Majesty, how good of you to join us. We were just telling the council that our trip was successful."

She looked at him and said, "Good. I'm glad. I'm sorry; I didn't realize you were working. I just came to welcome you home. I'll leave you to your meeting."

She turned and fled up the large winding staircase. The day was sunny and relatively warm, so she stopped in her chamber and got Nyakas' cloak, then went to the battlements. There was already snow on the top of the mountain and the colors of the fall foliage were spectacular. The air was crisp and she realized that it had been a long time since she'd felt so good about life. She only wished her parents could be here. She heard someone approach and looked up. Nyakas was still wearing black riding leathers, but not his cloak. His long black hair hung loose around his shoulders, and his tanned face was still rosy from riding in the wind. She didn't think she'd ever seen a better looking man and her heart began to race.

"I'm glad to see you've arrived safely, my lord."

"Are you? That's good, I'm glad to have finally brought you some happiness. Here, I brought this for you. I found it when I went to see King Talledrin." He reached into his belt and handed her a small leather pouch. She opened it to find a wide silver ring. It was buffed and shiny, and engraved with twining leaves around its entire circumference. A little experimentation revealed that it fit on her right middle finger.

"Thank you for thinking of me, Nyakas. It's lovely."

Before he could stop himself, he said, "Not as lovely as you."

"Thank you, my lord."

"Is there something wrong? You seem nervous."

"No, nothing is wrong. I just missed you while you were gone."

"Did you? Why? I left instructions that you were to be given whatever you needed while I was away. Did you not have companionship? Was there a problem with the staff?"

"No, there weren't any problems, the staff was fine. I just had time to think, and I realized how accustomed I've become to seeing you."

"Is that all there is to it?"

She was quiet, studying the ring. "I came to realize while you were gone that I've developed certain feelings for you. I can tell you that it was rather a shock at first to realize that I had fallen in love with a dragon, but it seems as though that's what has happened."

"Robyn, what are you saying?"

She looked at her hands folded neatly in her lap, then at him. "I love you."

She sat still, studying his face, wondering what would happen next. He placed his arms around her waist and kissed her hair, and she leaned against his chest. They sat that way, saying nothing more, until a page came to inform them that dinner was nearly ready. He took her hand and they left the battlements. He made a brief stop in his chamber to change to black pants and a black silk tunic while she went to hers to put away the cloak, brush her hair and freshen up, then they went down to dinner together. Although nothing had changed in their outward appearances, Gravity and those close to Nyakas could tell that there was something different. Robyn took her usual place to his left at the table, and it seemed as if there was an electricity between them that hadn't been there before. She sat through dinner impatiently, not wanting to eat. She was nervous and excited, and she hoped that she wouldn't be going to bed alone.

She retired to her chamber shortly after dinner, and a short time later there was a tap on her door. She jumped, startled, and called for whomever it was to come in. It was Nyakas and her heart skipped a beat. He came to sit beside her on the couch, and he seemed nervous.

"So," he said, taking her hand, "how did things go while I was gone?"

"Fine! Everything went just fine. A couple of the knights worked with me while Gravity was gone, but they were a little intimidated I think, and they weren't very hard on me. That part was almost like a vacation!" She rambled on at length, detailing whom she had worked with and what they had done, and how she learned some new things with which to surprise Gravity. Non-stop talking was a nervous habit that she'd tried very hard to conquer, but it sometimes got the better of her, and this was one of those times.

He watched her, captivated. Her voice was music to him, and although she appeared to be talking out of nervousness, he did not attempt to stop her. He just listened as her voice soothed his travel-worn nerves. Suddenly, he realized she'd asked him something.

"I'm sorry, what did you say?"

She smiled and touched his face. "I asked if you missed me."

He smiled gently, as much at her touch as the question. "Yes, very much. I knew I would, but I had no idea how much."

"Will you stay with me tonight?"

He seemed to blush in the firelight. "Do you want me to?"

She laughed. "I must be losing my touch! I've wanted you to stay with me for weeks! I was hoping that when I said I loved you this afternoon that you'd want to skip dinner!"

He smiled and said, "Don't think I wasn't tempted!"

"Why didn't you?"

"There's one other thing I haven't told you, and I am tempted not to because I know your culture. I don't want to shock you."

"I'm hard to shock. Tell me."

"I've never been with a woman."

She shrugged her shoulders. "That's all right, I've never been with a dragon."

He laughed. "No, Robyn, I've never been with a woman or a dragon."

"You're a virgin?"

He blushed again, and she said, "I'm sorry, that didn't come out right. I didn't mean for it to sound like that. It's OK, really. I just hope you don't mind that I'm not a virgin."

"I don't care, Robyn, I love you. That's why I'm hesitant to stay. I want it to be good for you, and I really don't know what I'm doing."

"The way you kiss me, I don't think you have a thing to worry about. Besides, the first time isn't supposed to be great. There has to be something to work up to, or there's no point in doing it again!"

He laughed and the tension broke. She slipped her arms around his waist and laid her head on his shoulder. He kissed her, lightly at first, then more deeply. His back muscles rippled as he shifted to pull her closer, and she ran her hands up his back. Without thinking, she ran one hand across his shoulders while the other found its way to his hair. He was holding her tightly now, and she could feel the heat of his skin through his tunic. He seemed to hesitate as if unsure of what to do next, so she started kissing his neck lightly. He shivered and ran his hands down her back, discovering the buttons. She waited for him to start undoing them, and when he didn't, she tucked her hands under his tunic and felt his bare chest for the first time. His skin was warm and she ran her hands over the hard muscles while still kissing his neck. She breathed deeply, enjoying his scent and the feel of his hands as he explored her body. He undid the top few buttons of her dress, and she thought about the chemise she'd discovered earlier in the week. She'd been looking for something in the wardrobe, found it in a drawer, and tucked it away for her 'wedding night.'

Pulling away gently, she said, "Stay right there. I found something I wanted to wear when we got to this point. Don't move, OK?"

"OK," he said, smiling lazily.

She went to the wardrobe to get it, and then quickly ducked behind the screen. He'd gotten the worst of the buttons for her, so she wiggled out of the dress and put it quickly on a hanger, kicked off her slippers, and put the chemise on. It was white and opaque with no sleeves and light pink embroidered flowers around the edge of the scoop bodice. It reached almost to her knees and clung to her curves lightly. In the firelight she knew it would be quite enticing. She stepped from behind the screen and he stared.

"Well, do you like it? It's not exactly what I thought I'd be wearing, but they don't make teddies here." He didn't say anything, but the look on his face told her that she'd made the right choice. She sat back down beside him and began kissing his face lightly. It seemed as if he was afraid to touch her, so she moved from her spot into his lap to kiss the side of his neck that she couldn't get to before.

"Robyn," he said softly, "I'm not worthy of this."

"Of course you are," she whispered in his ear.

"No, I'm not. I don't deserve to be loved by such a strong, beautiful woman."

She pulled away enough to look at him. "You should have thought of that earlier, my love. You're stuck with me now!" She touched his face and smiled softly. "Nyakas, I'm your wife in name and heart. Now it's time to make me your wife in body and soul. Don't worry about what you're doing. Trust me, everything will be fine." She kissed him deeply before he had a chance to protest again.

He hesitated for a second, and then began his exploration anew. She pushed his tunic up to kiss his chest. Hunger and desire overrode any remaining fear. He scooped her up and carried her to the bed, and laid her gently on top of the quilt. Impatiently, he kicked off his boots and stretched out beside her. She wrapped one arm around his neck, the other around his waist, and kissed him passionately, pressing her body against his. She wanted him more than she'd ever wanted anyone before, and she was determined to show him how much. They kissed and caressed each other, removing clothing slowly, one piece at a time. She ran her hands over his body, and he soon felt encouraged enough to do the same. Robyn waited patiently for Nyakas to finish his exploration and move to the next stage, and he seemed to be moving in that direction at a steady pace when he hesitated.

"What's wrong?" she asked, stroking his face.

"It's, ah, nothing," he stammered.

She could see the desire and confusion intermingled in his eyes. "It's all right. Shall I show you?"

"Please?"

Smiling, she ran her hand over his cheek and down his neck. His pulse was racing, so she kissed him gently. "Don't worry," she said with a soft smile. "I promise I won't hurt you." She rolled on top of him, proceeding slowly. She knew that the longer she took, the more desire would push fear out of the way, so she took her time, kissing and nibbling. She sighed when they finally joined, and their bodies moved in tandem, as if they had been together for years. He reached his pinnacle and called out her name, and she followed two heartbeats later.

The marriage was consummated, and they lay in each other's arms, warm and content. Long after she'd fallen asleep, he stayed awake, watching her in the dying firelight, amazed that he could feel about one person the way he did for her. It was nearly false dawn before he allowed himself to fall asleep.

Chapter 15

Someone was tapping at her door. Nyakas lay asleep beside her, so she slipped out of bed, shrugged on her robe, and answered the door before it woke him up, too. It was Gravity, and he looked puzzled. Behind him, the door to Nyakas' room was open.

"Did I wake you?" he asked sarcastically.

"Why, yes, you did," she answered, grinning smugly.

"Is Nyakas with you?"

"Yes, and he's still sleeping."

Gravity grunted as if it were more than he wanted to know, then turned to the open door behind him and said, "I've found him. He's with the queen." He turned back to Robyn. "I came up here to see what was taking you so long and found his servants in a lather because they couldn't find him and the bed hadn't been slept in. Apparently, they thought it was more likely that he was kidnapped than with you. Has he been with you all night?"

Leaning against the doorframe, she grinned lazily said, "All night. Don't worry, he's perfectly safe."

Gravity looked at her as if she were a jezebel, and said, "Take the day off and go back to bed." Turning on his heel, he strode back down the hall without waiting for an answer.

Grinning, Robyn shut the door lightly and said softly to herself, "Try and stop me!" Hanging her robe back up, she got back into bed and snuggled up to Nyakas.

He stirred, put his arm around her, and pulled her closer. "What was that all about?"

"Nothing you need to worry about. Your servants thought you'd been kidnapped. Rather amusing that they didn't think to check here before going off the deep end!"

He chuckled and kissed her hair. "Jerome knows me too well! Is there something I need to attend to?"

"Yes, actually there is, but it's right here."

He smiled sleepily, and they dozed off again. A short time later, Robyn heard the door open again and looked to see Gwyneth entering. Instead of her customary tray, she carried a large covered platter which she balanced carefully as she shut the door behind her. Robyn reached for her robe and put it on quickly, then went to help her, but Gwyneth was putting the tray on the table by the time Robyn approached.

"Good morning, milady," Gwyneth whispered.

"That it is, Gwyneth!"

Smiling, Gwyneth stoked the fire and added wood, softly saying, "I brought enough food for two meals if you stretch it. Between us girls, I'm glad to finally see this. If you need anything, send a page after me. Otherwise, I'll be back late this afternoon to help you dress for dinner."

"Thank you, Gwyneth."

Robyn sat on the couch as Gwyneth quietly left. Peeking under the lid, she found a pot of coffee and two cups, bread, cheese, grapes, and strawberries. Plucking a small bunch of grapes, she replaced the lid and sat back, wondering where they had gotten fresh fruit so late in the fall. There was a noise behind her as she nibbled.

"What are you doing way over there?"

"Eating," she said, smiling but not turning around, "would you like some?"

"Only if you bring it here."

She rose slowly, walking to the far side of the bed before climbing in to sit beside him. "Did you sleep well, my lord?"

"Very well. It's good to be back in my own bed. Did you?"

She fed him a grape and said, "Yes. I had no idea this was your bed, but I should have known."

"Why?"

"It took me the better part of a week to get the lumps arranged to my liking. They were far too big for my small body." She ate another grape, and then tickled his lips with one before she let him have it.

"Poor thing," he said, "I hope you can remember how to sleep on one side, because you'll be sharing it now."

"I think I can manage that. So tell me, was last night satisfactory?"

He grinned widely. "It was all right."

"All right? Just all right?" She fed him the last grape, and as soon as he stopped chewing she began tickling him. It was the perfect sneak attack, but it didn't go unchallenged long and within seconds both were squirming on the bed, trying to stay away from the other's hands without losing the advantage. Finally, when it appeared to have come to a stalemate, Nyakas grabbed Robyn's shoulders and pinned her to the bed. He tossed a leg over hers, effectively immobilizing her, and kissed her.

When she stopped squirming, he pulled back a bit and said, "How was it for you?"

Looking deeply into his eyes, she said, "Magic."

He smiled and rolled off of her, but held her close. Listening to his heartbeat, she watched the fire. She chuckled as she remembered her mother singing 'Puff the Magic Dragon' to her when she'd been little.

"What are you laughing about?"

"Nothing, really. Just remembering a song my mother used to sing to me."

"Being here with me reminds you of a song your mother used to sing? What kind of songs did she sing to you?"

"It's a children's song, silly about a really nice dragon who plays with a little boy. It's called 'Puff the Magic Dragon.' "

"Dare I ask why it reminds you of me?"

"It's logical, isn't it? You're a dragon, and we made magic."

"I should have guessed. You aren't thinking what I think you're thinking, are you?"

"Yes, Puff."

"Don't go there, darling, or I'll have to come up with a nickname for you."

"That's fine. Just keep in mind that Puff is a nice nickname, and I wouldn't use it with other people around."

"I won't use yours around other people either, Buzz."

"Buzz? Do I even want to know?"

"A robin is a type of bird in your home, isn't it?"

"Yes," she answered warily.

"I'm just going along with the bird theme."

"The bird theme, huh? Nyakas, I do hope you're not thinking of a buzzard!"

He laughed and said, "That's one of the reasons I love you. You're so smart!"

"A buzzard?!" She punched him in the stomach and was rewarded by a small 'Oof' as he continued to laugh. She pulled out of his arms and got out of the bed.

"Robyn," he said, "come back."

"No," she said, pretending to be hurt, "I'm hungry. I'm just going to sit over here and eat a little road kill!" She plopped indignantly on the couch and helped herself to some strawberries.

"Robyn, please. Come back to bed." She ignored him, and he called her name again, softly and slowly. She looked at him inquiringly over her shoulder as she licked then slowly bit her strawberry.

"Come back, please," he said, and she turned her back to him. She heard him get out of the bed and come to the back of the couch. He knelt down and put his arms around her shoulders. She didn't move as he kissed her neck.

"What's wrong, Robyn?"

"A buzzard? Apparently the buzzards you have here aren't like the ones we have. Ours are ugly, nasty creatures that eat dead animals. I've seen them. They're filthy and they smell really bad."

He chuckled and licked her earlobe. "All is fair in love and war, my darling."

"Hey, all I can say is that you're the one coming out on the short end of the stick with that one! I might be stuck with a dragon, but you're stuck with a buzzard, and you chose me first!"

He laughed and said, "That may be true, but you started this!"

"Maybe," she pouted, "but at least Puff was nice. Buzzards are nasty."

"They're also tough, tenacious, and difficult to kill without a weapon."

"Yes, because you don't want to get close enough to them to wring their stinky necks."

"Did you know that some buzzards can fly as far as a dragon? In the air they're remarkably graceful."

"That little factoid is supposed to impress me?"

He moved around kneel in front of her. He'd put a robe on, and Robyn wondered where he'd gotten it.

"I love you," he said.

"Mm hmm," she said, trying not to laugh. Being called Buzz really didn't upset her; she'd been called worse, and she actually thought it was rather funny. She just wanted to see what he'd do next. He took a strawberry off the tray and let her bite the end off. Then he slowly trailed it across her jaw, down the side of her neck, and across tops of her breasts. He fed her the rest of the strawberry, and then licked off the juice he'd put on her. By the time he got to the end of the trail she was clinging to him, her robe half open. He scooped her up and took her back to bed to make up to her for the first time.

Chapter 16

Days melted into weeks. Robyn spent her days training with Gravity, and Nyakas spent his attending to the matters of state. Late in the afternoon, they would meet back in their chamber and talk while Robyn took her bath, and then they would go to dinner together. By day, they were the hard-working leaders of a flourishing kingdom; by night, they were passionate lovers. Their contentment spread through the court, and it was a prosperous time for Nyakas' kingdom.

One afternoon, Robyn got back to their chamber to find Nyakas packing a small bag. He looked up as she entered and said, "I'm glad you're back. My father summoned me, so I have to go see what he wants."

"Oh. How long will that take?"

"A couple of days, no more than that. I may be back by tomorrow evening."

"Why don't you give me an hour and I'll go with you?"

"Not this time, my darling. He's been out of sorts lately, and I think it's best that I deal with him alone. I'll appease him, and then get him to come here to meet you. We can have a formal banquet and you can receive your first dignitary." He cupped her face in his hands and kissed her. "Trust me, love, it's better this way."

"I do trust you. I just don't want you to leave."

"I know," he said, hugging her. "I don't want to go, but I promise it won't take long. I'll be back before you know it."

"I doubt that," she said to his chest. "When will you leave?"

"Early tomorrow morning. You have me for the whole night. I've sent word that we won't be joining the court for dinner tonight. Gwyneth will be bringing it to us soon. Your bath is ready, and I have a couple details to wrap up, and then we'll have a quiet evening together."

"Not too quiet, I hope," Robyn said. She took off her clothes and slid into the bath.

"Of course not," he said, grinning as he finished his packing. "How was your day?"

"Fine. I finally beat Emerit."

"Did you? Well done, my love."

"I think even Gravity was marginally impressed. Emerit lunged, and I dove out of the way and rolled up behind him. It's a good thing I had a practice sword because I had a little more momentum than I thought. If it had been a real blade I would have gotten his right kidney and left lung. As it is, I may have broken a couple of ribs."

"You broke his ribs?"

"Well, I don't know yet. At best they're bruised. I got him pretty hard. He wasn't too happy."

Nyakas laughed and came to rub her shoulders. "I bet not! Who is next on your list?"

"I don't know. It's not my list; it's Gravity's. It doesn't really matter to me who I go against tomorrow, as long as it isn't Cristof, Dalen, or William. I don't think I'm ready for them yet."

"He'll make you work up to them."

"I know, the operative word being 'work.' I swear I'd love to take him home and let him get a hold of some of the privates in my company. Of course, he'd probably scare the hell out of them. It would be funny!" She paused for a moment as if she were thinking about something, and then said, "I wonder what my status is right now."

"Status? For what?"

"I wonder if the Army is considering me missing-in-action or AWOL."

"A wall?"

She laughed. "No, not 'a wall'! A-W-O-L, 'absent without leave.' It's a big no-no."

"I see. Does it make a difference?"

"No, not really, except that if I'm AWOL, the Army is probably giving my parents a hard time, and Mama's probably having fun telling them to go to hell. On the other hand, if I'm MIA, they might still be getting my paychecks, which would be good. Either option could make a visit home a little dicey. I'll have a tough time explaining where I've been all this time!"

"Very true. Before we send you home, I'll send Gravity ahead to find out what your status is." Nyakas looked closely at Robyn, feeling at peace in her presence. He knew she wanted to see her family, and he was bound and determined to do whatever was necessary to see she did. He took her hand and looked deep into her eyes. "You'll see your family very soon, I give you my word," Nyakas said with a smile.

She smiled back. "I believe you."

He cupped his hands around her face, and she wrapped her arms around his neck. They kissed and she felt her knees shake. She wondered absently why she felt almost dizzy and faint every time he kissed her. She stopped and looked at his dark blue eyes, and suddenly she understood. He was everything she ever wanted and nobody could love her any more, with the possible exception of her own parents.

"I have to go check something with Gravity. I won't be gone long, OK?"

"OK," she answered, and sank into the hot water up to her chin. Nyakas smiled, then headed for the salle. Gravity was coming out as Nyakas approached.

"Glorious day, is it not, my friend?" Nyakas said with a large smile.

"Yes," Gravity replied cautiously, "and so I see the king got lucky again. I asked if you would not discuss that certain subject around me. Please, would you both keep it where it belongs, in the bedroom, locked up? I need not hear about your romps."

"I know. I just love seeing you get all flustered about it. Your non-expressions are priceless!" Nyakas replied chuckling as they walked.

"I'm very happy for you, my lord. No one deserves it anymore than you," Gravity replied with a small smile. "What is it you need?"

"Robyn and I were discussing the possibility of her visiting home for a little while, but she's worried about the military thinking she was absent without leave, whatever that means," Nyakas replied, shaking his head. He clearly conveyed that he had no idea what that meant.

Gravity laughed. "I believe that means she is not at their post presently and hasn't been for a while, so she's in big trouble."

"Shut up," Nyakas laughed. "Sorry, I'm not from her home, I don't understand why they shorten everything. People who don't know have no idea what you're talking about. Damn soldiers."

Gravity shoved him lightly. "Careful on the soldiers there, old friend," Gravity said, chuckling. "I'll go to her plane and see what is going on at the moment. I'm sure her family is safe. Your father has her here and if he sends someone after her he'll do it here," Gravity replied.

"Do you really think my father will go to such extremes to take her away from me?"

"Your father wishes you to succeed him. Of course if he knows it will only enrage you and make you more evil than you are toward him and your brother he'll do whatever it takes," Gravity replied.

"I wish I knew for sure, though."

"My lord, we have something your father doesn't know about. She has been training for some time, and she is very good. She could best probably any one of my knights," Gravity replied.

"Can she best you, Gravity?"

"No, she can't, but there is probably no one who could. I don't mean that arrogantly but no one has trained harder at this than I have, I can assure you. I would have met him by now, considering all the dimensions that we have traveled," Gravity replied.

"All right. Go and find her family and assure them that she is safe, and find out what she is to the military, AWOL, MIA, ABA, whatever," Nyakas chuckled. He turned and went back to his chamber to find Robyn still in her bath. He sat at the desk to finish the last of his paperwork.

When she'd scrubbed off the dirt from the day, she climbed out and dried off. She didn't bother dressing, reaching instead for her robe and settling down on the bed with a book. A short time later, Gwyneth arrived with dinner.

The night passed too quickly for Robyn's taste. They ate dinner and made love all night, and she did her best to keep him from noticing when the sun began to rise. Unfortunately, he noticed, and an hour later he kissed her good-bye with a promise to return home as quickly as he could.

As he left their chamber she reached for his spare cloak and put it on, then went to the battlements. She reached the spot where she'd be sure to see him and watched as he walked a half mile from the castle walls, then changed to his dragon form and flew north toward his father's domain. It still amazed her as she watched the transformation: She was the wife of a dragon.

"Hurry home, Puff," she said softly to herself, then turned and went to the salle to start her day's work.

Gravity was waiting for her and seemed intent on taking her mind off of her troubles. He pushed her to the brink of her endurance, and she was grateful when the day was over. As usual, she took a bath and dressed for dinner. She ate quietly and didn't engage in the conversation around her unless she was asked a question. She knew that it looked like she was depressed and sulky; in reality, she was exhausted. She excused herself as soon as it was proper and went up to bed.

The next day was much the same. She rose early, worked hard, and retired early. When she woke up, she wasn't alone. Nyakas had come in during the night and lay sleeping beside her. She snuggled up to him and kissed his neck, but he didn't stir, and she knew he must have been exhausted. Slipping quietly out of bed, she dressed and slipped from the room, making her customary stop in the kitchen. She did her run and went to the salle.

"Well, good morning, Majesty," said Gravity.

"Good morning," she answered, "you seem surprised to see me."

"I am. Nyakas is back, after all. I thought you'd take the day off."

"He's sound asleep. I figured I might as well get some work done."

"Well, then I guess we can work for a while. Have you talked to him?"

"No."

"Oh. Well, come then."

"Oh? What does that mean? Have you talked to him?"

"Yes, actually. I was on the battlements when he flew in last night."

"What did he say?"

"I think it's better that you hear it from him."

"Why? What happened?"

"Let's just say that he and his father have a difference of opinion and leave it at that for now. He can explain it to you. Now, shall we?"

"No, we shan't. What did their opinions differ about? It was about me, wasn't it?"

"Robyn, talk to him please. He can explain it far better than I can, and he'll want to tell you about it himself anyway. Come on, let's get to work."

They began their usual workout, but Robyn's heart was far from it, and she made mistake after mistake. Her mind kept wandering as she imagined scenes between Nyakas and his father. She didn't know why, but she couldn't help but be afraid that his father was going to somehow come between them. She'd grown to love him so much that the thought of living without him turned her stomach to a mass of knots.

Finally, out of sheer exasperation, Gravity told her to stop and take the rest of the day off. She protested weakly, then turned and left the salle. Her strides were long as she walked through the courtyard and into the castle. By the time she reached the winding staircase she was almost running, and she took the steps two at a time, much to the surprise of the servants and nobles she passed.

As she neared her chamber, she realized that she really hadn't been gone very long and he might still be sleeping, so she slowed down, took a deep breath, and opened the door quietly. He was still asleep, but he'd shifted positions. She kicked off her boots and went to lie beside him. It was less than a minute before he stirred and pulled her closer. His sleepy kiss told her that he'd missed her, and that was encouraging, but it did little to slow her heartbeat or banish the butterflies in her stomach.

"Good morning," he said with a soft smile.

"Good morning," she answered, returning his smile. "How was your trip?"

He sighed deeply. "Suffice it to say that I'm glad to be home."

"I'm glad, too. Did you and your father have a nice discussion?"

This time he laughed ruefully. "My father is a stubborn old man who sees things far differently than I do."

She could tell he was being evasive, so she cut to the chase. "It was about me, wasn't it?"

He held her closer and said, "Yes. He doesn't approve of what I've done."

"What would make him approve?"

"He wants me to put you aside and take a concubine. He even has one picked out."

Her heart skipped a beat and tears pricked her eyes as her fears were confirmed. She started to move away, but he held her tightly and said, "I listened respectfully to what he had to say, thanked him and told him to give the concubine to Vaytawn, and then I left. I don't care what he wants, Robyn. I need you, and I won't give you up."

"You won't?"

"No. He's just going to have to accept it."

"What if he won't?"

"Then I won't succeed him. He can either give the throne to Vaytawn, or he can accept the fact that the next Dragon Lord will have a human wife. He won't like either choice, but I don't much care."

"Are you sure it wouldn't be easier if I went home? You can always come to see me."

He drew back to look at her face. "Is that what you want? Do you want to go home?"

"No! No, I don't want to go anywhere that's away from you. But I don't want to cause trouble for you."

"Robyn, you don't know my father. He has never been satisfied with my choices in life. He had me imprisoned and tortured for five hundred years so that I would become like him out of anger, and it worked for a long time. In fact, it's only been since I've met you that I've become more like my old self and put the anger aside. He blames you for undoing what he did."

"Is he really that bad?"

"He is evil, pure and simple. I fought for centuries to bring peace to all the dimensions, and as I fought for good, my strength and power increased. He saw it, and decided that I would be a formidable Dragon Lord, but he had to turn me away from what I was, or all of his work would be undone with mine. He is ambitious and power hungry, and he typically takes what he wants without regard to what is best for others. He can't stand the fact that I've fallen in love, because he knows that the good he repressed will come out again."

"What if I wasn't human?"

"It wouldn't matter much. It's the love that is changing me back. You could be a dragon, human, harpy, or troll, and it wouldn't matter in the end."

"Oh. Now what?"

"We go on as we have been. Don't worry, love, everything will be fine. I'm not going to let anything happen." He held her and soon fell asleep again. When his breathing became even, she pulled out of his arms enough to look at this incredible man who loved her so much that he would defy his father. She watched him sleep for a while, then got up to look for Gravity. He was in the middle of a class, so she asked a squire to let him know she needed to talk to him when he finished.

It was a clear day, and relatively warm for mid-winter, so she walked down to the lake. Ice was forming around the edge, and she stood on the shore and tossed small rocks in to break it up. After an hour or so, she started to get cold and decided to go in. When she turned around, a strange man walked up to her. He wore a tight red tunic and loose black pants with a long gray cloak. His face was rough, and his dark blue eyes were hard in spite of his amicable smile. His beach blonde hair was short and it reminded her of one of her Army training instructors.

The strange man extended his hand to her and said, "Good morning, Queen Robyn."

"Good morning," she answered, warily shaking his hand.

"I was in the neighborhood and I thought I'd stop by and introduce myself. I am Lord Vaytawn."

Bells went off in Robyn's head. "I'm honored to make your acquaintance, Lord Vaytawn. I'm sorry, but your brother is not available just now. Would you like me to send a servant to see when he will be?"

"Oh, no, that's not necessary. Actually, I came to see how you are fairing in this dreary little corner of the cosmos. How do you like your new home?"

"I'm very happy here, my lord. Thank you for asking."

"You are welcome, although I am a bit surprised. I've visited your dimension, and I've found it to be infinitely more interesting than this one. Are you not bored?"

"No, I find amusements to wile away my time."

"I see. You must be very easy to please."

"Well, in the Army they teach us to adapt and overcome. I can't go to a movie, but we don't have bards at home. I adapted, I overcame, and I'm happy." This man was beginning to get on her nerves, and she fought to hide her irritation.

"So you don't miss your home?"

"I miss my parents, but other than that I'm content here. Your brother is an incredibly strong man, and I find him to be very interesting. I think I could happily live out my days with him, and I hope to get to know his family as well." A movement nearby attracted her attention, and she glanced quickly to see Gravity strolling toward them.

"Vaytawn," said Gravity as he approached, "How nice of you to drop by. We saw your approach and King Nyakas is awaiting your visit in his office."

"Thank you, Gravity," Vaytawn said dryly. "Actually, I came to visit the Queen."

"Well, I was asked to fetch the Queen. Something important has arisen that requires her attention, and it can be difficult to get her away from the lake. You know how strong women are."

"Yes, that's why I tend to avoid them. I prefer my women to warm my bed and do as they are told. I trust my brother is in his office?"

"Yes."

"Well, then I shall go and say hello. Good day, Majesty." He bowed to her, then turned on his heel and walked up to the castle.

Robyn started to follow, but Gravity caught her arm and held her back. When Vaytawn turned the corner to enter the courtyard, he turned to her and said, "What did he say?"

"We talked about how much nicer my home is than here. I think he was trying to convince me to leave on my own. He's his father's favorite toady, isn't he?"

Gravity chuckled. "How could you tell?"

"He oozed arrogance. He couldn't be any more different from Nyakas."

"That is correct. What did you want to see me about?"

"I had some questions about Nyakas' father. It seems Nyakas is out of favor because of me."

"You've talked to him. Good. I told him he should tell you right away. Walk with me while you ask your questions." He turned and walked back toward the salle.

She walked beside him and asked, "What am I up against, besides a strong-willed demigod?"

"He's unpredictable. Be prepared for him to take matters into his own hands if he doesn't get his own way."

"What can I expect him to do?"

"Whatever he feels is necessary to accomplish his goal. I wouldn't rule out assassination."

"Of me?"

"Well, Nyakas can't succeed him if he's dead, and it wouldn't do him much good to kill me! I'm sure he'd rather enjoy that, actually, but it wouldn't serve the current purpose. I think we need to step up your training."

"I agree. Shall we begin in the morning?"

"Yes. I'll get Dalen to take over my morning classes so I can devote all of my time to you."

"That doesn't bode well for me!"

They entered the salle and he led her to the equipment room. Rather than asking the arms-master for what he wanted, he went in and entered a room in the back corner that Robyn had never noticed. It was very small, only about eight by ten feet from Robyn's estimation. The walls were lined with weapons of various types.

"This is my personal equipment. I have accumulated it through the years, although I rarely need it now." He walked to the west wall and took down a sheathed sword. As he walked back toward Robyn, he turned it in his hands, examining it. "Here," he said, handing it to her. "Try this one."

Robyn removed it from its sheath and tested the grip. It fit her hand perfectly. A few practice strokes confirmed that the weight was right. It seemed to move with her and almost anticipated her actions. "It's great, Gravity! Where can I get one?"

"Right here," he answered. "Keep it."

"What? Gravity, I can't take your sword."

"It's not my sword. It's yours. When I acquired it, I kept it only because I knew that it would pass through my hands to its rightful owner. You have progressed sufficiently to have need of your own blade, so you may have that one."

"Are you sure? I'm sure Nyakas has one in the armory that will do just as well."

"Take it, Robyn. It was made for you, and it's too light for me."

Robyn smiled and belted the sheath around her waist. "Thank you, Gravity."

"You are welcome, my lady. Come, your husband awaits us."

As they left the salle, a large shadow passed over them and Robyn looked up to see a crimson dragon fly over the lake. Gravity smirked. "Goodbye, Vaytawn."

They walked back to the castle and went to Nyakas' office. They found him sitting at his desk, twirling his quill between his hands. The set of his face told Robyn that he was more than a little irritated. He looked up to see them enter and said curtly, "Come in. Close the door."

They did as they were told, and he turned to Robyn. "What did my brother say to you?" His voice was hard and angry.

"Polite small talk laced with hints that I would be happier at home. Don't worry, it didn't work."

"I didn't think it had. I don't think I need to tell you that if he ever approaches you again, you need to tell me immediately."

"I assumed as much. It looks as if you dislike him as much as I do."

"More. I have plenty of reasons to hate my brother. He is not a nice man."

"Technically, Nyakas, neither are you," interjected Gravity.

"That's changing, and that is the burr under Father's saddle. We'll need to tighten security."

"Agreed," said Gravity. "Robyn is going to become my only pupil for a time."

"Good. Sorry, darling, but I want you able to defend yourself without thought."

"Me too! I'm not at all thrilled with the thought of being skewered!"

Both men laughed, and the tension broke.

"I'm going back to work," said Gravity. "I'll see you both at dinner."

After he left and closed the door behind him, Robyn went around the desk to sit on Nyakas' lap. She quickly found that, with the sword belted to her side, she couldn't just plop down as she was accustomed to doing. She adjusted the sword and sat gently. "I have an idea," she said quietly. "Since my torture is to begin in the morning, I propose that we leave the hall right after dinner, go up to a nice dark place on the battlements and make out for a while, and adjourn to our chamber. What do you say?"

"I say it's a great idea."

"Good. I'm going to let you get your work done, and I'll see you later, OK?"

Nyakas sighed. "OK. Go get used to your new toy."

Chapter 17

Snow drifted lazily through the bare branches as the morning sun came over the mountains. Malitor stood in the forest near the edge of a clearing, his black cloak not quite touching the ground. His hair, lush and black, hung loosely at his shoulders, and he was clad comfortably in white boots and tunic with brown deerskin pants. He watched as a man on a pale horse crested the hill on the far side of the clearing and rode toward the edge of the forest. The man and the horse were an intimidating pair. The man was easily seven feet tall and at least 300 pounds, and his horse had red eyes and the build of a strong stallion. The man dismounted, his beautiful clothes embroidered and studded with gems. His eyes were pink and mysterious, and his bald head steamed lightly as the cold air met warm skin. His steps were slow and methodical as though he knew where each step would land. He stopped and bowed before Malitor.

"Hello, my lord, a pleasure to see you," he said with a smile of assurance.

"Greetings, Kerrigan, so happy you could make it here with such short notice."

"Anything for you, my lord. Why is it you have summoned me? It must be important."

"I have a problem I need remedied and it's something I think you will enjoy," Malitor said with a large smile.

"What is the problem, my lord? I'll take care of it right away."

"I was hoping you would be excited. I need you to go to the Kingdom of Nyakas and kill his queen."

With a look of confusion on his face Kerrigan asked, "My lord, do you know you're asking me to kill the wife of your son, Nyakas?"

"Of course I know! You do as I ask! Don't ever question me!"

"Correct me if I'm wrong, my lord, but aren't most people happy when their children marry?"

"She's a human woman," he snapped, "She don't deserve my son. One day Nyakas will be a god and she doesn't deserve him."

"The heart is blind when it comes to such things, my lord," Kerrigan answered.

"I don't care! You destroy her very soon or I shall destroy you very soon, understood?" Malitor's voice shook with anger.

"Yes, my lord, I understand," Kerrigan replied.

"Now leave me," Malitor ordered.

Kerrigan mounted his steed and rode back in the direction from which he had come. Malitor watched the sun as it crept toward its zenith and waited as though his business had yet to be completed.

As he waited, he thought about how to bring Nyakas back into line. He had always known that Nyakas was powerful. Once, his son had fought on the side of good. He was known as Protector of the Realms, a general of armies that defeated a clan of beasts that had tried to take over all dimensions. Nyakas and his armies had stopped them dead in their tracks after three hundred years of war, and the dimensions were safe.

He once lived in a place known as the Gate, the gateway to all other dimensions, past and present. He stayed there until there was anarchy in another plane and then he went and disposed of it. Malitor knew that if he could turn Nyakas to the side of evil that he would be the most feared Dragon Lord ever. So he asked Nyakas to travel with him, and the young dragon, wanting to spend time with his father and find out what made him the way he was, readily agreed.

Malitor lured his son into a trap, which resulted in Nyakas' imprisonment in another dimension where dragons were highly prized for medical experimentation. The dragons were never placed in a situation where they might die, but the processes to which they were exposed were lengthy and painful. Their captors tried to duplicate the dragon traits that were highly prized, such as their scales and blood, to be sold for profit. It was thought that if altering common items could duplicate these things, market share would be increased and profits would rise dramatically.

Nyakas' rage and anger built during his centuries of imprisonment. Vaytawn, Nyakas' brother, was Malitor's obedient follower and delighted visiting his brother to torment and anger him. Slowly, Nyakas became no better than Malitor. When he escaped from his imprisonment, he was the evilest of beings with bad intentions not only toward his father, but also toward his brother. After escaping, he searched for his brother, but never found him. Malitor apologized to Nyakas, telling him that what happened had been an accident over which he had no control. Nyakas did not believe his father, but he took his words to heart and promised him that sooner or later he would be short one son. His father was happy to hear that news, knowing the stronger of the two would someday take his place on the throne of the Dragon Lord.

Malitor's thoughts were interrupted as a large winged creature eclipsed the sun. The crimson dragon made a wide turn and glided into the clearing. His scales shimmered in the bright sunlight, reflecting an array of colors like a prism. Knowing his father was nearby, he changed back to his human form. His tight tunic did little to hide the hard muscle underneath, and even though his pants were loose, they didn't mask his powerful legs. His face was rough with stubble, his beach blonde hair short, and his eyes a dark shade of blue. He was a handsome man, yet his eyes warned those who were observant not to trust him. He walked quickly to his father's side and extended his hand.

"Good to see you, my son," Malitor said.

"Always good to see you, father," his son replied.

"So, have you found out any more of what your brother is up to, as far as he and the woman are concerned?"

Vaytawn chuckled, knowing his father's dislike and outrage for the situation. "I've come to find out that they are living well and happily inside and outside the castle walls."

Malitor's face turned red with anger, and his fists clenched. "This is an outrage! How could he do something like this?"

"I don't know, father, but something must be done soon or we'll face him."

Malitor's angry expression turned to one of confusion. "What do you mean?"

"The longer they are together, the more likely it is that Nyakas will decide that good is better than evil and then we will have real problems."

"How's that?"

"Father, even the other Dragon Lords think it is Nyakas who can bring worlds together and help them to live as one in peace and harmony, all other dimensions living as one and coexisting together," his son replied with contempt in his voice. "While it's appealing to the lower creatures, it could be disastrous for Dragon Lord. If all the people are happy, why do they need you? Foolish peasants!"

Malitor's face paled at the news he already knew. Slowly, he said, "I will give you some help. I don't trust Kerrigan, although he is a good servant."

"Father, I will take care of it," Vaytawn assured him.

"Don't underestimate your brother or the friend who stands beside him."

"Gravity? Why should I worry about Gravity? He's a witch and makes deals with demons. He's of no concern to us, I can assure you, father."

"He's much more than he appears. He's also the best swordsman in the land, possibly in all dimensions. He's a tortured soul, and if I could get my hands on him I may be able to turn him against Nyakas and the girl."

"I don't think he's worth the trouble. I'll handle Nyakas' pretty little human wife." Vaytawn walked away. The grotesque transformation from human to dragon took place and he flew off into the morning sky. Malitor watched as his son took off and said to himself, "I'm sure you will, son. I'm sure you will."

Chapter 18

"Majesty!" A page trotted toward Robyn and Gravity as they practiced in the courtyard. "The King requests your presence in his office as soon as possible."

Robyn looked at Gravity and he nodded toward the door. Without a word, she sheathed her sword and went to Nyakas' office. He was reading a scroll when she arrived. She sauntered in, shut the door behind her, and crossed the room to plant herself firmly in his lap.

"What's up, dear?"

"I've received word from Stephan that she's facing an uprising. I can't imagine why; she's one of the kindest landowners in this dimension. In any case, she needs my help."

"Of course! Go! Do you want Gravity and me to come along?"

"I may take Gravity, but I need you to stay here. One of us needs to be here."

"OK. When do you leave?"

"As soon as I can."

"Do you want me to send for Gravity?"

"Yes, please."

She pulled the bell cord and went to the door. When a page arrived, she asked him to fetch Gravity, then went back to the desk. Sitting back on his lap, she said, "Be careful out there, Puff. I need you."

"Don't worry," he answered, "you can't loose me." He kissed her just in time for Gravity to open the door.

"So this is what you needed me for?" asked Gravity.

Nyakas chuckled and said, "No, you and I are going to Stephan's. When can you be ready?"

"Oh, about ten minutes. Why?"

"Now she's having a problem with some of her serfs. She's got a possible uprising on her hands."

"Why? Are they mad because they can only keep eighty-five percent of their crops? I'd hate to see what they'd do if they came to work here!"

"I know," Nyakas said. "It doesn't sound right. Maybe it's something else and she just couldn't tell me. Sometimes I think my sister is too soft. First it's bandits on the northern border and now this. She needs to look into hiring a better mage. In any case, we'll need to get there as soon as possible."

"I'll make the arrangements with Dalen and meet you in the courtyard. I trust you plan to fly?"

"Yes. It will be faster."

Gravity nodded and left the office. Nyakas kissed his wife again and held her for a few minutes. Since they were flying there was no need for him to pack anything, and he didn't intend to be gone long.

"I'll miss you, my love," he said.

"I'll miss you more," she answered, and he laughed softly.

"I don't plan to be gone more than a couple days at the most. If it's going to be longer, I'll send word."

"OK. Do what you need to do, then hurry home to me."

"Done! Walk with me to the courtyard?"

"Try to stop me."

He kissed her again, and then they walked to the courtyard together. A few minutes later Gravity joined them.

"It's all arranged," Gravity said, "Dalen will take my classes, and Cristof will take my star pupil."

Robyn feigned innocence. "Are you sure he'll be able to teach William anything?"

Nyakas laughed and Gravity gave her a black look. "Are you ready, Nyakas?"

"Yes, let's get this over with so we can come back home." He kissed Robyn chastely on the cheek, and then he and Gravity left the courtyard. A quarter of an hour later, she sat on the battlements and watched a black dragon with a rider flying north toward Stephan's kingdom.

Robyn went back down to the courtyard and worked with Cristof. He released her early, and since she still had two hours before dinner, she walked down to the lake. She strolled along the edge for a little while, and then turned back toward the castle. Suddenly she heard a horse approaching at a gallop. She turned toward the sound to see a bald man on a pale horse approaching quickly.

The enormous man dismounted. She estimated that he was at least seven feet tall and weighed at least three hundred pounds. He was wearing a white robe with crimson markings on the back. From what she could see, he had his palms up and in front of him as though he was just wandering helplessly. She started around the lake at a slow to jog to keep the person in her sight and caught up with him quickly. When she was about forty yards away she slowed down. He walked another fifty yards, and she continued to follow. He stopped just out of view of the guards behind some high shrubbery, which

Nyakas had been meaning to have trimmed in order to give the guards a better view. She watched him stop and put his arms down to his sides. He stood silently with his back turned to Robyn. When she got to about twenty yards away she stopped and waited.

The stranger turned around slowly. His face was the first thing Robyn saw. His pink eyes sent shivers up Robyn's spine. He was a well-muscled man with a cleanly shaved head. His robe, now open, uncovered what looked to be the same type of swords Gravity used. She was suddenly afraid without knowing why.

"Hello," said the stranger, his voice deep and raspy.

"Hello, may I help you sir?" Robyn asked politely, masking the fear in her voice.

He took off his robe to reveal a full suit of chain mail. "I've been looking for you, Robyn. I see you have a sword. Do you like to swordplay, my dear?" he asked nicely.

"Why, yes. I like swordplay. Do you?"

"Yes, I enjoy it immensely," he replied, smiling demonically. "You are the human that married Nyakas, are you not?"

"Yes, I am King Nyakas' wife. Why do you ask?"

"I want to make sure I'm taking care of the right person. I would hate to disappoint Lord Malitor," he replied, the demonic smile slowly getting bigger.

Robyn stared at her opponent knowing full well what she was in for.

"Kerrigan is the name, my beauty. I want to share it with you because it will be the last name your lovely ears will have the pleasure of hearing before I destroy you."

Robyn jerked her sword quickly from its sheath and moved to a defensive position.

In an instant he swung his sword toward her right side to cleave her in half. She brought her sword to meet his and stepped away from the velocity it brought. The power behind his blows was strong and direct. She moved to the side and began her work, making quick advances from left to right with her sword. He parried each blow as though they were nothing, grinning widely in an attempt to enrage her. She had learned well enough from previous training and from Gravity that rage could be her downfall and not to let it take effect no matter what the circumstances were.

She brought her sword toward his head to take it off his shoulders, but his sword was much quicker. As his sword caught hers, he kicked her side with his right leg. She doubled over as air was forced from her lungs and his left foot caught her temple, sending her to the hard forest ground. His sword came down toward her head and she quickly rolled out of the way. As his sword hit the ground she recalled her father's teaching and swept his legs out from under him. Kerrigan fell to his back and kicked up almost as fast as he went down. Robyn quickly got to her feet and moved away, putting a small distance between herself and Kerrigan. They glared at one another as if they were the only two people on the planet.

With no warning, Kerrigan's blade sliced Robyn's left thigh, leaving a gash in her quadricep, and Robyn went to the ground. She began to crawl away to a safer distance so she could get back to her feet. As she did Kerrigan kicked her in the ribs, sending her into the air. She hit the ground.

Kerrigan paused momentarily to gloat. Robyn rolled from her side to her knees. Her ribs throbbed painfully. She wrapped her arms around them and put her forehead on the ground, trying to breath. Nyakas came into her mind, and she felt a surge of adrenaline, knowing she could not die. He needed her as much as she needed him.

Kerrigan looked in amazement as she got back to her feet. Her leg was partially numb, and the pain seemed to disappear. She pulled her sword back into position, ready to start a round two. Kerrigan watched and smiled slightly.

"Robyn, please lie down and this can just end. I would hate to mess up that pretty face and most gorgeous body," Kerrigan said arrogantly.

"You lie down and I won't tell anyone that you were beaten by a girl. When was the last time you got laid by a queen, Kerrigan?" Robyn asked, smiling grimly at her pun.

He ignored it. "You can't win, my child. You can barely walk. How do you expect to fight?"

Robyn glared at him with a look that could kill. "Heart, that's how," she replied. She advanced as quickly as she could, wielding her sword left to right. Sparks flew as the swords met each other time after time, and it looked like Fourth of July fireworks. Kerrigan backed up, trying to keep his distance and rethink his strategy, and Robyn advanced. She saw an opening and delivered a solid front kick to the abdomen. He doubled over and her free fist met his face. His head went to the side and he staggered further back. Her roundhouse kick connected with the back of his head and he still stayed on his feet. The spinning heel kick took him off his feet and drew blood from the corner of his mouth. He hit the ground hard, then slowly made his way to his feet tried to regain his balance. As he did, Robyn quickly set herself up for one final blow. As he tried to steady himself, his sword dropped from his hand and he looked at Robyn.

She returned the look and said, "The name is Robyn. Remember it. It's the last name you'll hear."

With her final words her blade made contact with his neck and cleaved his head off of his shoulders. His head hit the ground seconds before his body, and both dissipated into mist.

Robyn looked around, shocked. He appeared to be gone, but she'd trained with Gravity long enough to know that appearances didn't matter. Her adrenaline began to wear off and the pain in her leg and her ribs returned.

She sheathed her sword, clutched at her ribs and staggered toward the castle. Cristof ran down toward her as blood ran freely down her leg. "My lady! What happened?"

"I don't know," answered Robyn, her voice husky with pain. "A man named Kerrigan attacked without provocation. I'm going inside."

"Of course! Come, my lady."

"I can get there on my own!" She limped toward the castle and he followed in her wake. "Go and find a messenger. I want word sent to Lord Malitor that he failed, and a message sent to the king at his sister's estate. Have a small squad patrol this area. The body disappeared when I killed him; I want to be sure he's gone."

Cristof followed closely until she got to the courtyard. Suddenly irritated, she turned quickly and barked, "Now, Cristof!" He turned and sprinted away, but Robyn didn't watch as he turned toward the healers' quarters.

Dalen met her as she entered the foyer. "Majesty! Thou art wounded!"

"It's a flesh wound, Dalen, I'll be fine. I'll just go upstairs; have one of the healers come up, will you?" Even as the words left her mouth, her legs trembled and gave way. Dalen caught her just before she hit the ground and scooped her up effortlessly. Robyn gasped as the wound in her thigh seared, and Dalen carried her up the stairs, yelling for a healer. As he took her to her chamber and laid her gently on the bed, she muttered curses under her breath. Her wounds throbbed, and although Dalen tried not to jostle her, the slightest motion intensified the pain. A healer in a green robe followed him closely, and he began to assess her condition. He took Dalen aside and whispered something to him, and Dalen left the room and shut the door.

"Quite a nice wound you've there, Majesty," he said. Deftly, he cut off her pant leg and put a clean towel on the wound, holding it tightly with one hand to staunch the bleeding.

"Thank you. The scar should be cool," she answered, her jaws clenched.

He smiled placidly and opened his bag with his free hand, laying out bandages and jars. He slipped several folded towels under her bleeding leg to elevate it and to absorb the blood. The door opened a few moments later and Gwyneth came in with a steaming cup. "Here it is, Shaylon."

"Good. You need to drink that, my lady."

"Drink what? What is it?" Robyn knew she was being difficult, but she just couldn't help it. Pain made her irritable. The more she hurt, the worse she was as a patient, and the pain was intense.

"It's tea, my lady," answered Gwyneth. She held the cup to Robyn's lips. She managed to gag down the first sip and shoved the cup away, coughing. "Please, my lady, you must drink it all."

"Gwyneth, I don't know what you've been smoking, but I do know you haven't been sharing!"

"Now, now, my lady. Be reasonable," Gwyneth cajoled. Robyn opened her mouth to protest and Gwyneth quickly poured the contents of the cup down her throat. The choices available were to swallow or choke, so Robyn gagged down the vile liquid. The language that resulted from Gwyneth's deftness came from years of military training, and what she had been muttering she began yelling in a tone that would have made her survival school instructors cringe. Shaylon actually blushed to hear such verbiage from the queen.

Robyn continued her tirade as the edges of her vision began to turn black. As the tea began to take effect, the door slammed open and Nyakas walked in purposefully. Gwyneth and Shaylon backed away and Nyakas moved forward to kneel beside the bed.

"Robyn?" His voice was shaking, and Robyn noted somewhat absently that there were tears in his eyes.

She stopped yelling and said, "How did you get here so fast? I'm fine, Nyakas. It's just a flesh wound. Got a Band-Aid?"

Her blood soaked the towels, although Nyakas took no notice. He moved to look at the wound on her leg and as he did, his tears fell on it. As if his tears were a magic tonic, the wound on her leg began closing and healing. As his tears began to slow down, he laid his head on her stomach, holding her as though he was already losing her. As she lost consciousness, she twined her fingers into his thick black hair.

It took a few minutes for him to realize that she was only asleep and that Shaylon was still in the room. He moved back and let Shaylon examine Robyn and put bandages around her ribs. While Shaylon put his things back in his bag, Gwyneth moved in quietly to remove the bloody clothing and linens and replace them with clean ones. Gravity came in to stand beside Nyakas as Shaylon was leaving.

"She'll be fine, my lord. She is exhausted and will need rest. She fought valiantly from the heart and won," Gravity said proudly.

"I know, Gravity. I just wonder if it was my father's doing and if it is over," Nyakas replied, wiping the tears from his eyes.

"I spoke with Cristof. He said she told him that Kerrigan attacked her. The last time I heard his name was when it was rumored that he'd aligned himself with your father. Regardless of Malitor's involvement, I'm behind you. It won't matter what he tries. You said it yourself, you love her every minute of every day."

"Thank you, Gravity. I know we'll make it. I just wish my father would leave us alone and try to understand."

"He's set in his ways. Although that is no excuse for his actions, if he is behind this, he will next time think before he does something. Maybe he now sees just how much you do care for her. I'm going to take my leave, my lord. You try and get some rest. She'll awake soon enough, I'm certain," Gravity said putting his hand on Nyakas' shoulder.

Nyakas put his hand on Gravity's and said, "Thank you, my friend. You know she considers you a friend even though you are harsh."

Gravity looked at Nyakas, and then at Robyn, who was still unconscious, and smiled. "I know, my lord, and I consider her the same."

Nyakas smiled and Gravity silently left the room. As he walked down the hall he saw some of the guards who had informed Nyakas and him of what had happened.

"You guards keep watch on this door. If anyone wishes to enter you have them come and see me first," Gravity commanded.

"Yes, General," they all said in unison.

Gravity walked briskly past them and they took position with their weapons and stood at attention. Gravity walked down the stairs and yelled to the others to take their positions, keep watch, and to double guard on the towers. He made it abundantly clear that if anyone got in, the soldier who let it happen would answer to Gravity himself. Finally, he took his own position outside the front of the castle. He stood silently through what was to be a quiet night, watchful for any sign of retaliation from Malitor.

Nyakas sat silently beside Robyn on the bed, waiting for her to awaken. He held her hand, waiting for the first signs of her consciousness and thinking about this strange turn of events.

When he and Gravity had arrived at Stephan's, she was happy to see him, but curious about why Gravity was with him and not Robyn. He'd had the foresight to bring the scroll with her message; he took it from his tunic and handed it to her, and her face became a mask of anger and confusion. It had taken mere minutes to determine that someone other than Stephan had written the message and signed her name.

Fear made the journey home faster than normal, and he landed just outside the castle wall just in time to see Cristof sprinting from the healer's quarters. Gravity slid off his neck and ran to catch up with Cristof as Nyakas quickly changed back to his human form. He met Gravity in the courtyard and was told to go directly to his chamber because Robyn had been wounded. Nyakas' heart had skipped a beat, and then he sprinted to his chamber, where he'd found Robyn bleeding on the bed. All he could think was that he couldn't bear to lose her. Now he sat staring at the floor trying not to think about it.

He was sure it was a few hours later when he felt her hand squeeze. The movement jerked him out of his reverie. She was lazily smiling at him, her head slightly turned as if she had been watching him.

Nyakas brushed her cheek softly, feeling her soft skin under his touch. She lifted her hand to his face and ran her fingers over the soft stubble on his chin. They stared into each other's eyes, and their lips met. She twined her arms around his broad shoulders, pulled him down, and began slowly unbuttoning his tunic. She ran her hands across his chest. His lips wandered to her neck, and then to her ears. He nibbled on them and she began to laugh, making a feeble attempt to escape. She pulled away to look at his face and he smiled, softly brushing her hair away from her face.

"I love you, Robyn, and I'll never let anyone come between us. I can't afford to lose you, I love you too much to have you away from me."

She returned the smile. "You can't lose me, babe. I love you and I'm not to going to let anything happen to you either."

She looked deeply into his eyes and he went back to the task at hand. She arched her neck, enjoying his soft lips. He moved slowly down her neck to her chest and her breathing became heavier.

As midnight passed, Gravity passed his watch to Cristof and came to check in with the guards, who stood silently at the door. "Has everything been all right?" he asked.

"Everything has been silent my lord, at least outside the door," one of the guards replied somewhat evasively.

"You all are relieved from your post. Good work. I'll see you in the morning."

The men left the door and walked briskly down the hall and down the stairs. Gravity quietly reached for the doorknob, but a familiar sound from the other side made him stop. He smiled and walked to his chamber. As he opened his door, he looked back at their door and shook his head.

Chapter 19

Vaytawn tapped on the door to his father's office and entered. Malitor was sitting at his desk and looked up when Vaytawn walked quietly in.

"What is it, son?" he asked impatiently.

"Kerrigan failed," Vaytawn answered angrily. "You sent him to do a simple job, and the imbecile failed!"

"What do you mean, he failed?"

"He's dead, Father. The little wench has been trained by Gravity. She killed him."

"She what? How do you know this?"

"My spy reported the details to me, and she also sent a cowering, simpering messenger. I was tempted to kill him, but I just sent him away. She beheaded him, the oaf. Don't worry, Father. I can take care of her."

"No. You'll do as I say and stay out of the way until I tell you otherwise. It's time to consider drastic measures."

"What do you plan to do?"

"I don't know yet! Leave me! I have to think about this! Your brother will be shown the error of his ways, and he will be brought back into line, or he will die! Mark my words, Vaytawn!"

"As you wish, Father," answered Vaytawn. He backed out of the room, away from his father's rage, and quietly shut the door. He grinned as he walked back down the hall, savoring Nyakas' dishonor and reveling in the fact that one day he, not Nyakas, would succeed Malitor.

He opened the door to his own chamber. A beautiful woman sat on the cold hearth. Her long black hair was in disarray, and her lovely face swollen and bruised. The dress she wore appeared to have once been a fine satin gown but was now torn. She looked up, saw Vaytawn, and cringed as if she were trying to become part of the wall. Her skin began to change to the scales of a green dragon as she shook in fear.

"Hello, Delaria," he said. "Oh, come now, don't be afraid. If you cooperate I won't have to hurt you. Now, come, play with me." He stretched out on the bed and patted the side. Delaria forced back her fear as she moved to the bed to do her master's bidding.

Chapter 20

As the morning sun crested the mountains, Robyn awoke. Nyakas lay asleep at her side. She brushed his hair away from his eyes, intently watching him for a few moments, and then silently got out of bed and tiptoed across the room. Her ribs, still bandaged, felt a little tender, and her thigh bore an angry red scar where she'd been cut only the day before. She pulled on her deerskin pants and her white tunic, and laced her boots. She added another log to the fire so it wouldn't go out, then grabbed Nyakas' cloak and her sword and silently crept to the door. As she reached for the handle she heard a voice from behind her.

"Leaving so soon, my love?" Nyakas asked softly. Robyn could hear just a touch of sorrow in his voice.

She smiled and then turned to see him slowly sit up. "Yes, love. I have some work to do if I'm going to best Gravity, the little bastard."

Nyakas laughed and replied, "Oh, so you think you can best my first knight and general of my armies, do you? Don't underestimate Gravity, not for a second."

"I won't, trust me. If there's something I've learned from Gravity, that is definitely it!" Robyn replied, reaching for the door. "I love you. Go back to sleep. You need your rest."

"Me? What about you? I'm not the one who had a sword fight to the death yesterday."

"I know, but I just feel absolutely wonderful today for some reason. I can't explain it. When I went to sleep after our 'quality time,' I was dead to the world! But I woke up a little while ago, and I'm just filled with energy." She walked back to the bed to kiss him lightly. "I'll be back before lunch. I love you, Nyakas."

"And I love you, Robyn," Nyakas said, his voice deepened with emotion.

Robyn went as quickly as her tender ribs would allow to the salle. She could see Gravity through the crack in the door and stopped from opening it. He was wielding his paired swords like they were toys. It seemed as though he knew where they would land each time. She wondered how it was he could do all of this. He stepped into the sunlight, which streamed in the windows. She could finally see that the markings he wore on his face did, in fact, run down his chest and arms. She could see many scars on his back, arms, and neck.

She stepped back, surprised, as the door opened itself. "Come in, Robyn," Gravity replied with no expression, as if he knew she was there the whole time.

Robyn slowly walked in, remembering his earlier lesson about knowing where everything was and to never enter a room unprepared.

"Robyn, please, I am alone," Gravity said as he turned around and slipped his tunic on over his head.

As he did Robyn saw the perfect opportunity to get one over on her teacher. She grabbed for her sword but he was gone, and she felt the tip of something pointed at her back.

"Don't think about it. When you have the opportunity to do something, you just do it," Gravity said.

Robyn held her sword and quickly whipped around to go on the offensive. She lunged and swung at every possible opening and still she could not get inside of him. She then made a crucial mistake. She tried for a backward sweep and Gravity saw the attack and jumped. While he was in the air his foot shot out to stop a few inches away from her face. She flinched, and then looked back at him. His face bore an expression of open confusion. It was not uncommon for him to pull punches and kicks when he practiced with her, but he had stopped completely and studied her closely.

"What is it, Gravity? You look like you have seen a ghost."

"Robyn, come with me," Gravity said, quickly sheathing his sword.

"Gravity, what's wrong? Tell me! I want to know," Robyn replied, sheathing her sword.

Gravity quickly opened the door and held it for Robyn. "Quickly, come now," Gravity replied sounding very serious.

Robyn slowly followed, wondering what had just happened. She walked behind Gravity as he strode to the royal chamber. He knocked on the door almost hard enough to knock it off of its hinges.

"Come in," said a voice from inside the room. Nyakas sat at the desk. He'd dressed in his silk pants, and black deerskin boots with a white tunic, which was open at the chest. He was writing something in a large book and continued as Gravity and Robyn entered. Gravity stood motionless in front of the desk with Robyn beside him, wondering what she had done. Nyakas looked up from his book and slowly closed it.

"What is it, Gravity? Is something wrong?" He still sounded tired and Robyn wondered why he'd gotten up.

"Not exactly wrong, my lord; I think Robyn should sit down first," Gravity replied.

Robyn quickly looked at Gravity and then at Nyakas. "What the hell is wrong with you today, Gravity? Are you feeling all right?" Confused and slightly irritated, she perched on the dressing table bench.

"I'm fine. Thank you for asking," Gravity said. He turned to Nyakas. "My lord, I request that Robyn be instructed to stay out of the salle and slow her exercise regiment down."

"What? I can't believe this! What is going on? OK, so I was wounded in a sword fight less than twenty-four hours ago. I feel fine and I want to go back to work!" Robyn exclaimed angrily.

"What is it, Gravity? This is rather sudden," Nyakas answered sounding concerned and confused.

"Indeed. I'd just hate to see anything happen to your heir."

"What are you saying, Gravity?" asked Nyakas.

"My lord, Robyn is pregnant," Gravity replied with a small grin.

Robyn stared in disbelief, positive that she hadn't heard what Gravity had just said properly. Nyakas' face bore the same expression.

Slowly their eyes met. Their disbelief turned to joy. Seconds later Nyakas held her close and kissed her deeply, and she felt almost limp in his arms. He lifted her and twirled her around in excitement, then turned to Gravity.

"Is it true? Are you sure?" Nyakas asked excitedly.

"Yes, my friend. When we were practicing I could feel another life inside of her," Gravity replied.

"Well, maybe she's just possessed. She did kill Kerrigan yesterday," Nyakas replied laughing.

"My lord, with all due respect I think the only time she was possessed was last night, and I don't mean out on the battlefield! That's all I have to say and I don't want any details either way, thank you. I must go. Congratulations to both of you." Gravity went out the door and closed it softly.

Nyakas held Robyn and kissed her, and then, no longer able to contain himself, he quickly went to the balcony. He could see the people of his kingdom outside setting up their shops and walking briskly to get the day's work done. People walking by slowed down and he called out, "People of my kingdom! You shall have a prince or princess come the first moon of autumn! We will have a glorious celebration tonight!"

As the people cheered the joyous news Nyakas then went inside to his wife. "We will celebrate this joyous event, and I love you, Robyn. You have made me the happiest dragon in all dimensions far and wide," he said as he put his arms around her waist and pulled her close.

She pulled her head back and looked into his eyes. "You know, you just said there's going to be a great celebration, and we only just found out. Now you have to go prepare for it."

"No, I don't! Gravity, come in," Nyakas replied.

The door opened and Gravity entered, shutting the door behind him quietly. "Yes, my lord, a party for the newest member of the royal family," he replied.

Nyakas looked at Robyn with a large grin. "It's good to be king," he said with mock arrogance.

Robyn laughed and punched him gently in the stomach. "Well, it's better to be the queen. We all know you do as I wish!"

Nyakas' mock arrogance changed to surprise and Robyn laughed again. She walked out of Nyakas' arms to the bed, maintaining eye contact and silently challenging him to deny it.

"Is that all, my lord?" Gravity asked as began to leave.

"Yes, thank you, Gravity. I appreciate everything," Nyakas said as he turned to look at Gravity.

"It is nothing, my lord," Gravity replied and left the room closing the door behind him. Nyakas stood on the other side of the bed. Robyn had made herself comfortable. She lay on the bed innocently trailing her fingers around the collar of her tunic. Nyakas stared and slowly grinned, and she smiled. He lay beside her and she turned her back to him. He put his arms around her waist and she laid her hands on his arms. They lay that way until there was a light tap at the door. Gwyneth came in softly and placed a tray on the table, then left quietly. They moved to cuddle on the couch and feed each other the bread, meat, and fruit that Gwyneth had brought.

"Everything is going to be fine now, my love, I promise," Nyakas said, smiling at Robyn.

"I know. I'm so excited that we're having a baby, I just wish that the rest of your family would enjoy it with us," Robyn replied, a little sadly.

"Stephan is already being brought the news of our soon to be newborn. Don't worry, she'll be here tonight," Nyakas replied.

"I mean your father and brother. I wish they could just be happy for you," Robyn said laying her head sideways looking at Nyakas with a small smile.

"I wish they could too, but they're not. I have got everything I've ever wanted and that's what's important," Nyakas said.

She smiled and laid her head on his chest with her arms around his waist and his arms around on her shoulders. He held her close until it was time to get ready for their celebration. Gwyneth came to help Robyn into her favorite green velvet gown, and Nyakas changed into dark blue silk pants and a green tunic.

They strolled hand in hand to the courtyard for their party. They walked out the doors to find that the knights had formed a gauntlet and crossed their swords above their heads. The king and queen walked together through the gauntlet to meet with the nobles and Stephan, who were waiting at the end. Robyn smiled as she saw the woman she considered her sister, and Stephan returned the smile. As they got to the end the nobles extended their hands to Nyakas and Robyn and congratulated them. She made her way through the nobles to Stephan and embraced her.

Stephan pulled away to assess her sister-in-law. "You don't look pregnant," Stephan said with a smile.

"Well, I just found out today. They say when you're pregnant your supposed to glow, but I thought morning sickness and fatness came first! I guess here it's the other way around!"

"Well, I'm not sure. I've never been pregnant. Most impregnated female dragons don't bother to get married. My brother broke the mold as far as that's concerned, but that's not unusual for Nyakas. I can see he's happy and so are you, so that means I am, too," Stephan replied, embracing Robyn once again.

"Well come, let's celebrate. I want one more glass of wine before she's born," Robyn said as she and Stephan began walking arm in arm.

"A girl? How do you know?" Stephan asked sounding confused.

"Well, it's wishful thinking, actually. I'm hoping it's a girl because Nyakas has enough testosterone for the whole kingdom! We don't need anymore for this family!"

"Touché!"

Nyakas watched as they walked together, looking back at him and smiling as though they knew something he didn't. He laughed as they walked, looking back periodically until they were out of sight.

Nyakas grinned and shook his head as he turned back around to talk to the other nobles.

The festival began as the sun crept down behind the mountains. Knights, nobles, and common folk all drank and danced together. Robyn and Stephan stood and talked as people went by, giving congratulations to the Queen. Gwyneth approached Robyn and said, "Your majesty, this is my husband, Creedan."

Robyn tried to hide her surprise. "Gwyneth, you never told me that you were married to Creedan!"

Creedan grinned and said, "Your majesty, my sincere congratulations to you and the king. May your son or daughter be as admirable as you are."

"Thank you. I must say your wife is a great woman. She has helped me through some rough times. I couldn't have done it without her," Robyn replied smiling. As Gwyneth and her husband moved along with their two small sons trailing behind, Robyn smiled. A minute later, Robyn saw young William making his way to her.

"Hello, William," Robyn said amazed at the way the young lad was dressed. He wore dark blue silk pants with fine lacing around his waist, and his bright white tunic was loosely laced. His boots were polished and decorated with intricate lacing. His sandy brown hair was pulled into a ponytail.

"Your majesty," he said awkwardly, "I congratulate you on your soon to be born child."

"Thank you, William. How are you this evening?" Robyn replied, smiling brightly at the young lad.

William stuffed his hands into his pants pockets and shifted uncomfortably. He looked slowly up at Robyn, swallowed hard, and said with fear in his voice, "Would you like to dance, your majesty?" Tears slowly came to his eyes as he visibly braced himself to be sent away.

Robyn's heart went out to the boy, and she replied, "I would be honored."

They walked to the dance floor and William began to lead her awkwardly. Robyn could tell that although he was still learning, he tried so hard. "Relax, William," she said softly and began to help him. William let his eyes wander, as if he could not bring himself to look at her eyes. He seemed scared and Robyn could feel the nervousness in the boy as he shook.

Gravity was a few steps away, standing beside a guard. The guard saw what was happening, and he started to move toward Robyn, but Gravity put his hand in front of him to stop him.

"My lord, we can't allow this," the guard said hesitantly.

"The boy's not going to hurt her. If he was he would have been taken care of, and if there was a problem the king would have already done something," Gravity replied without expression.

The guard went back to his position. Gravity looked over at Nyakas, who smiled, and Gravity knew what he was looking at. Gravity smiled a little and Nyakas laughed. As the music ended, Nyakas went to the dance floor.

William stepped back from Robyn, laid his right hand across his waist and bowed. She curtsied and William walked away. She stared at the young boy and smiled. She could see he was proud and at that moment she couldn't wait to have her first child.

Realizing that she stood alone on the dance floor, she quickly looked around to see where everyone had gone and saw Nyakas walking slowly toward her. She looked at his eyes as she took his hand. Nyakas put his right hand on her waist and kept her right hand in his left. The music began and Nyakas led her slowly and softly. She stared into his eyes as they danced into the night. Slowly, others began to join in. Everyone danced until late in the evening, and soon Robyn and Nyakas stopped dancing to make their way to where Stephan was standing.

"Hello, little sister," Nyakas said, and leaned to kiss his sister on the cheek.

"Hello, big brother. I can see you're not jealous anymore," Stephan said with a slight grin.

"No, no, I'm not, although I should be. William is quite the dancer," Nyakas said wiping the sweat from his brow.

Robyn laughed. "He's got promise. A few years from now he'll be great."

"Don't think I didn't notice! You're lucky! If he had asked me, I wouldn't have let go," Stephan replied laughing as well.

"Remember, little sister, he's still a young squire and has a curfew," Nyakas said.

"He wouldn't with me! If he comes up missing tomorrow, I didn't take him!" Stephan said with a broad grin.

As they laughed, a guard from one of the towers yelled down, "There are riders coming from the north!"

Nyakas quickly ran to the front gate, and Gravity was already standing by them.

"Do you know who it is Gravity?" Nyakas asked.

Gravity's face looked serious as he looked at Nyakas eyes. "Yes. It's Malitor and Vaytawn."

They walked under the partially open portcullis to meet the two men who were approaching. Malitor and Vaytawn got down from their horses. Everyone stood motionless. Vaytawn removed his helm. His eyes were black and he glared at Nyakas. He whipped his black cloak to his side and moved to stand closer to Nyakas, but Nyakas stood steadfast and didn't move. Gravity glared at Vaytawn, and Vaytawn moved stand in front of Gravity. Their eyes locked, and Gravity didn't budge. Malitor looked intensely at his son and behind him at Robyn and Stephan, who stepped through the portcullis to stand behind Nyakas and Gravity.

"So, my son, I see you're having a party. What's the occasion?" Malitor said as though he had forgotten the look he had just given his son.

"It's for my unborn child and you weren't invited," Nyakas replied without expression.

Malitor's face became confused. "You're going to be a father? Well, that does call for a celebration," Malitor replied as though he was happy.

Nyakas stood without expression. He'd played his father's games before and lost horribly. "Yes, I'm going to be a father and Robyn a mother. We found out today," Nyakas replied.

"Well, I'm happy for you," Malitor replied extending his hand to his son. He looked at Nyakas as though he meant it.

Nyakas glanced at Gravity. Gravity's eyes said not to shake it, but Nyakas' eyes hardened and he extended his hand to his father's and shook it firmly.

Malitor smiled as his son's hand meet his, and everyone watching trembled in fear. Gravity's eyes closed as he watched his friend shake hands with the man who, at one time, had made Nyakas' life a living hell for not bending to his father's will. The people watched as Malitor and Vaytawn moved to walk past Nyakas to join the party.

Suddenly, Nyakas put his hand on his father's chest. Vaytawn looked at his brother and Gravity, his eyes questioning. Gravity realized what Nyakas was doing, and he stood tall and proud, glaring at Vaytawn.

"Father, I am sorry but I'm still not going to let you in. I respect your position, but you still will not pass," Nyakas said fearlessly.

"Nyakas, what do you think are you doing? You don't tell me where I can and can't go! I am one of the Dragon Lords! No one tells me where I'm not allowed!" Malitor replied angrily.

"Well, father, this is my kingdom, and as long as you are in my kingdom, I will tell you where you are allowed," Nyakas replied.

Malitor glared at his son, his face a mask of disgust and anger. Nyakas stood his ground and glared back, which enraged Malitor even more. Vaytawn and Gravity, the two right-hand men, glared at each other.

Those who watched began to back away. As Malitor glared at his son, his face began to change color and contort into the shape of a demonic dragon. Nyakas stood motionless and undisturbed by his father's anger. Robyn moved closer to Nyakas' back and took his hand, wishing she'd strapped on her sword. He sensed her fear and gripped her hand tighter in reassurance.

Malitor regained his composure as he realized that his son was not disturbed by his anger. Vaytawn had even backed up when his father began to become enraged; yet Nyakas and Gravity stood tall, proud, and motionless.

"You'll regret this my son, I promise you. You have made the last mistake you'll ever dream of making," Malitor said with irritation still in his voice.

"No, father, my mistake was trusting you. It's a mistake I'll never make again."

"You are insolent and weak, and that will be your downfall, like it was your sister's."

"No, father, my sister is strong and kind, as I wish to be. She is my only blood family now, and I'll do whatever is necessary to keep it that way," Nyakas said, still undisturbed by his father's presence.

Malitor sneered. "You didn't make a mistake, Nyakas. You are the mistake. I should have kept your mother and crushed your egg before you hatched! After this night you'll realize the consequences of your actions. I promise you that." Malitor climbed up onto his horse, pulling the reigns to his chest. His eyes found his son's for the last time and glared. Vaytawn got onto his horse as well, giving Gravity one final look before pulling his reigns and leading his horse out.

"I give you one last chance to join my side, son," Malitor said as he began to lead his horse toward the gate.

Nyakas turned enough to grab Robyn's other hand and glared at his father. "Never."

Malitor angrily pulled the reigns hard and led his horse through the gate, galloping away into the night with Vaytawn following behind. As they rode away Malitor and Vaytawn changed to their dragon forms and people scattered as if they were afraid they would come back. Nyakas watched as the enormous beasts flew into the night sky and the pale horses disappeared in the dark.

Robyn put her arms around Nyakas' waist and laid her head on his chest. She could feel his heartbeat, and though she thought it would be rapid, it was slow and steady. He put his arms around her and held her tightly. The people came out of their hiding places, looking in amazement at their king, who had just stood up to one of the most feared dragons in all the kingdoms. They were astonished at his courage and began to chant his name. Robyn looked up from his chest and they smiled at each other.

"It looks as though you're famous now," she said.

Stephan looked at her brother Nyakas' eyes met hers. They grinned at each other as she whispered, "I love you."

Nyakas quietly replied, "And I, you."

Stephan stepped closer and put her arms around Nyakas and Robyn. "So, this is family. I must admit I've waited a long time to say that I had one of these." She smiled and leaned her head touched theirs.

"We will always be family, no matter where we are. No place is too far to keep us apart, and no one will tear us apart as long as I am alive and breathing."

Nyakas looked over at Gravity as he ordered the knights and soldiers to new posts and watched them scatter quickly to their assignments.

"Gravity, come, you are as much a part of this family as the rest," Nyakas said with a smile.

Gravity's face was blank except for a hint of amusement as he replied, "Sorry, my lord, I'm not a hugger. I have some things to take care of before night's end, and since the festival is dying down I'm going to take care of them now." With a half bow, he swept away.

Robyn watched Gravity walk away, a little hurt at his apparent snub. Then she saw him turn around, smile and nod his head at her, and in her heart she knew he was speaking to her and that he really did care. She felt proud to be his student and felt that he was finally proud of her as well. She hugged Nyakas and Stephan tighter and they began walking into the castle and up the stairs, laughing and talking. Stephan walked them to their chamber and hugged them both and then walked back down the stairs. They watched her leave, still holding on to one another until she was out of sight. Nyakas opened the door to their chamber and Robyn walked in looking even happier than before. Nyakas looked confused but only smiled and watched as she went to the balcony.

Stephan walked back through the courtyard and watched, as Gravity was gave orders and helped the others tear down what was left of the party. She walked over to him as he was putting some wooden poles in a bundle and tying them with string.

"Gravity," she said with a smile as he turned around.

"Yes, my lady," replied Gravity with a small smile.

"I wanted to thank you for everything. I know how hard it is for you." Stephan touched his hand.

Gravity looked confused. "What is it that you have to thank me for, Lady Stephan?"

Stephan smiled and looked at the balcony and then at him, and Gravity turned to look at what she was looking at. Robyn stood on the balcony looking down at where

Gravity was standing. He looked back, and she felt that finally the animosity had died and she finally was his friend as he nodded again. He let his right hand fall in front of him and bowed to the queen. She saw his smile, which was so rare. Robyn knew even with their newfound connection that he wasn't going to take it any easier on her, though that's what she was hoping for. She was fine working hard for him, especially now knowing that he was proud of her and finally her friend.

As Gravity turned away and continued to walk through the courtyard yelling out orders, Nyakas came to the balcony and put his arms around her waist. She put her hands on his arms and laid her head back on his chest. Her fear of Nyakas' father was non-existent now and she felt at peace with all that was around her. They stood that way for some time and finally Nyakas led her back into their chamber.

"Is everything all right, Robyn?"

"Wonderful now," she answered, putting her arms around his waist and deeply kissing him.

"Well, I'm glad," he said, still looked somewhat confused. He led her to the bed and they made love like they never had before. When it was over they lay in each other's arms until they both fell fast asleep.

Chapter 21

Malitor sat on his throne with his cheek on his hand, deep in thought. His son stood at his right side. It had been a week since Nyakas had sent him away, and his anger still seethed.

He looked up as seven figures came down the long hall toward him and stood up to greet the seven Dragon Lords who entered. Malitor and Vaytawn moved away from the throne and Malitor dismissed his son. Vaytawn half bowed and walked past the other Dragon Lords. They all walked into a huge circular room. There was a large round marble table with a flame that burned in the middle. Eight wingback chairs ornately detailed with gold, gems, and dragon heads carved into the centers surrounded the table. They all took their seats and began to look around at one another and then at Malitor, since he was the one who had called the meeting.

"Friends, I have gathered you all to speak of outrage from one of our brethren who could very well someday sit in this very seat," Malitor said with disgust.

"Speak of this upstart and we will set him straight in his ways," said Lord Althan.

Malitor looked at all the members and then sat back and said, "It is my son, Nyakas."

They all looked at one another. They had heard of prophecies of the great protector of the gateway. There were rumors that Nyakas was the key to peace in all dimensions. His father's plots during Nyakas' younger years were thought to have negated the ancient prophecy. The prospect of all-encompassing peace disturbed all the Dragon Lords, good and evil alike. They felt there needed to be some form of enemy to keep their followers loyal. A dragon that strayed from the ways of the Dragon Lords could pose a serious threat; their followers could turn to him if they thought their Lord was not worthy of being worshipped.

"What has he done? We should put a stop to it as soon as possible!" exclaimed Rodor.

"My son has taken a human bride," Malitor replied.

The others looked at Malitor oddly. Although Nyakas was the first to take a human bride, it didn't seem to be a threat.

"Malitor," said Treylan, "it is known that we take no wives because we have enough to do being Dragon Lords. However, I'm struggling to see why you are so worried. I'm sure she'll keep him occupied."

"If she were an ignorant human interested only in satisfying his carnal urges, it would be one thing. This bride could make Nyakas remember why it is better to be on the side of good than evil," Malitor replied. "His heart is dark for the moment, but with her it could change. Don't underestimate the power of love, because I'm seeing first hand the hold it has on my son. Furthermore she could establish a hold on Gravity as well, and that could be very detrimental to our plans in the future."

They all thought about what Malitor had said. His theory was sound, and if it did happen, they all risked being overthrown by Malitor's son. This was a cause for concern. A few minutes went by as they all sat silently pondering the situation.

Treylan leaned forward and said, "If this is true, then how can we separate them without hurting them, and keep them apart?"

"I don't know how, but if we are able to separate them and keep them apart long enough, Nyakas will give up search. Or better yet, when he finds her gone he might just think she was kidnapped and killed and will forget and then stay on the same path he is on now," said Althan.

"Maybe not. He might become enraged and spend the rest of his days searching and destroying everything in his wake to find her. You said it yourself, Malitor, this mortal has quite the hold on your son," Rodor replied.

Malitor turned red with anger, gritting his teeth and swallowing hard. "Then again, maybe if we banish her and wipe her memory clean it won't really matter if he ever finds her."

Rodor looked confused. "Are you suggesting the ancient spell of banishment? The mere existence of that spell is questionable."

"Yes, why not? It can't hurt and if it fails we lose nothing," Malitor replied.

"We lose nothing? It is said that it takes a lot of power to do it and a personal sacrifice by one of the participants," remarked Denzan, who sat said a few seats down from Malitor.

"I'll take the personal sacrifice. The rest of you will just help with the power. Or we can settle for the alternative and wait to see if she turns him, in which case it will be too late for us to do anything about it."

They all sat back in silence, wondering about the wisdom of casting a spell that, even if it really existed was not proven to work, and what the affects would be.

Finally, Rodor stood up. "It will take some time to research the spell. We will meet in six moons to discuss this further. Malitor, be ready, because if this doesn't work then you'll be the one at fault. This will only be tried once. If it doesn't work, it will never be spoken of again."

They all nodded their heads and Malitor smiled. As the others left, he got up and left to find Vaytawn outside of the cathedral.

"Well, father, what did they say to your plan?" Vaytawn asked.

"They said we shall do it, but only once. Don't worry, once will be all it takes," Malitor replied with a self-assured smile.

Chapter 22

Delaria sat in her lair, shifting in her gold. She was glad to be back, away from that horrid castle, away from Vaytawn. She contemplated the egg in the corner, wondering if the hatchling inside was male or female. She had considered crushing it to avoid Vaytawn's seed being carried on, but it was also her progeny in there. It was not the hatchling's fault that Vaytawn was its father, and she could not bring herself to kill her own offspring.

Her position was precarious. As Vaytawn's concubine, she was expected to do his bidding and bring forth male offspring. As soon as a male hatchling was produced, Vaytawn would kill her. If she failed to produce offspring, he would also kill her; this was a contributing factor to her decision not to crush the egg. A female hatchling could lengthen her life by as much as a year, having proved that she could indeed produce offspring. He would most likely impregnate her again at the earliest opportunity, but it would be another nine months before she could produce another viable egg.

Her only real hope was for the hatchling to be female. While it didn't guarantee her survival, it did increase it somewhat. A female hatchling was not what Vaytawn wanted, of course, so he'd try again to prove his masculinity, and that would buy her some time. She could appeal to another of the Dragon Lords for refuge, or maybe flee to the Kingdom of Nyakas.

She snorted in contempt. 'Nyakas,' she thought, 'what a fool! He has no idea what he gave up when he refused me. I wouldn't have made him give up his human toy, even if I am more beautiful and better suited to be queen than she! What do humans know about running a kingdom in a dragon realm? Nothing! He should know that, and yet he put me aside without a thought or even a look! Perhaps Stephan would be sympathetic to my plight. Everyone knows how rebellious and passionate she is. I won't pretend to understand it, but I will use it to my advantage if it will protect my hatchling and me. Yes, that is what I shall do. The other Dragon Lords will not listen to a concubine, but Stephan might.'

There was little she could do right away. She couldn't leave the egg for very long, and there were no servants to carry a message to Stephan. She would have to wait for the egg to hatch. With luck, it would hatch and she could carry the hatchling to Stephan's domain before Vaytawn discovered that he was a father. Her window of opportunity for escape would be marginally longer than it would have been. She had waited nearly a week to notify Vaytawn that the egg had been laid and appeared to be viable. She expected the egg would hatch within three weeks, but Vaytawn would not send a servant for the hatchling for four.

Would Stephan's domain be safe? It was no secret that although they were siblings, there was no love lost between Stephan and Vaytawn. If he discovered she had gone to his sister, he would probably attempt to destroy her domain. Of course, Nyakas and his merry little band of humans would come to her rescue; between them, Vaytawn could be messily destroyed. She smiled, cheered by the thought of Vaytawn being ripped to shreds in mid-air by Nyakas and Stephan.

'He is an evil, horrid dragon,' she thought with a shudder, 'and the sooner someone destroys him, the better off we'll all be.'

She sifted around in her gold, turned to face the mouth of her lair, and slept.

Chapter 23

Robyn sat by the lake, wrapped in Nyakas' arms. She leaned her head lazily against his chest and closed her eyes. The sun was warm, and flowers scented the summer morning. It had been four moons since the party, and they still had yet to hear anything from Malitor or Vaytawn. Naturally, the guards were still alert to trouble, but a tentative peace settled over Nyakas' kingdom as everyone awaited the birth of the heir.

Nyakas rubbed the slight swell of Robyn's belly, and the baby she carried shifted under his father's hands. Robyn smiled as Nyakas jumped.

"What was that?" he asked incredulously.

"That was your son, rolling over," she answered calmly.

"Human babies move before birth?"

"So I'm told. I've only ever felt them from the outside. Pretty amazing, isn't it?"

"Incredible! What else do they do?"

"I'm not really sure. My friend Kara said her baby got the hiccups every day at the same time. You should have seen her husband when he came out of delivery room. He looked like he'd seen an angel!"

"What's a delivery room?"

"That's where human babies are born."

"They have a special room?"

"Of course they do! Don't you here?"

"Not that I know of. Dragons are hatched, remember?"

"I remember. OK, here's the scoop. If I were at home, I'd be pretty much doing what I'm doing now until I start labor, at which time you would take me to the hospital; that's where the healers hang out. You'd stay with me all through my labor and see your son's birth."

"I see. How long does this 'labor' take?"

"It varies. The shortest I ever heard of was two hours, and the longest was three days."

"Three days? Isn't that an awfully long time?"

"Yeah, sounds like hell, doesn't it? I can't imagine being in that much pain for that long."

"The process is painful?"

Robyn laughed. "So I'm told! It's logical, isn't it? Human babies weigh an average of six pounds at birth, and you know first hand the size of the opening from which he'll emerge! You'd better hope that my labor isn't that long or you might be in trouble! You know how I am with pain!"

Nyakas shuddered. "I love you, Robyn. It's an amazing thing you are doing!"

"I'm not doing anything any woman wouldn't do for the man she loves. I'm thrilled to be giving you a baby. You will, however, be with me when this baby is born!"

Chapter 24

Vaytawn woke early. For some reason, he had an urge to visit Delaria nagging him. He dressed and left the castle grounds on a warhorse he'd borrowed from the stable. He had, at first, intended to ride his own steed, but decided against it. He knew that Delaria would recognize the sound of his horse, and he didn't want to give her too much warning. It was a short ride through the woods to Delaria's lair, and he wanted his visit to be a surprise. The morning was warm and humid and promised to be hot before it ended.

He rode to the edge of the clearing where her cave was, dismounted, and picketed the warhorse. He walked the last hundred feet to the mouth of her lair and peeked inside. To his amazement, he saw Delaria moving about as if she were going somewhere. She had taken great pains to hide most of her gold; her lair looked almost dismal. Vaytawn's eyes widened in surprise and anger surged through him when he saw Delaria move aside to reveal a small hatchling. It was too early to discern the gender from a distance; apparently it hadn't hatched very long ago, but according to what she'd told him, he hadn't expected it for another week. He stepped back to think for a moment. He could hear her talking to the hatchling and crept closer to eavesdrop.

"All right, my darling. I'll get us some food. We'll have a lovely meal together, and then we'll fly to visit your Auntie Stephan! Doesn't that sound lovely? She'll be so happy to see you! You stay right there, snug and cozy, and I'll be right back."

Vaytawn turned and ran back to the woods when he heard her moving toward the mouth of the lair. A plan formed quickly in his head. Glad he'd borrowed a horse from the stable, he untied the picket, led it to the edge of the woods, and slapped its rump. The horse bolted into the clearing. It was easy prey and excellent bait for the green dragon now circling overhead.

Vaytawn watched the horse run to the far end of the meadow and noted that Delaria had seen it and was moving in. When he was sure she was distracted, he stepped into the clearing, quickly changed to his dragon form, and launched in pursuit.

He closed the distance quickly but Delaria saw him coming. She forgot about the horse she'd been about to kill and turned to get away, but Vaytawn had momentum on his side. He chased her through the sky, blowing flames ahead of him. He gloated as his fire scorched her tail and she screamed. She flew faster but he overtook her quickly and swatted her wing with his tail. She fell several yards before recovering and turning to breath her own fire back at him. Vaytawn dodged quickly, annoyed that she'd thought to fight back. He dove at her, claws open, aiming for her eyes. She ducked just in time, and

Vaytawn's efforts won him a deep gash from the horn he caught instead. She flew quickly toward the lair, then seemed to change her mind and headed toward Stephan's realm. He started to let her go, but decided that she might become a problem under his sister's influence. He overtook her again, and this time bit her wing. She screamed and tried to get away, but he held on until a piece of her wing tore off. She screamed again and barely avoided a crash landing in the woods. She tried to run to her lair, but he landed on top of her. His claws met with resistance at first, but as he damaged the scales they sank into flesh.

Delaria screamed again, still trying to get away. She knew she was going to die, but it wasn't too far to her lair. If she could get close, she could use her final breath to torch the inside of the lair and kill the hatchling before she died. If Vaytawn was going to kill her he would have no part of the hatchling!

She staggered toward the lair as Vaytawn ripped her scales off. She tried to swat at him with her tail and wings to no avail. She stumbled weakly as Vaytawn continued his attack, her vision becoming veiled in red. From the corner of her eye she could see his head moving toward hers. She tried to jump away but wasn't fast enough. She felt the immense pressure of his jaws on her neck before everything went black.

Delaria slumped to the earth as Vaytawn bathed in the blood that spurted from her throat. He roared in triumph, breathing flames high into the air as her blood sprayed over his body. He bit her again and again to increase the bleeding from her now still body, and seemed to derive an almost erotic pleasure from it.

When she bled no more he flew quickly to a nearby lake and washed her blood off, then flew back to the lair. The hatchling was asleep inside and he went to it. He observed it closely for a few minutes before picking it up and leaving the lair. He flew back to his castle and landed on the battlements, oblivious to the distress he was causing his servants. He put the hatchling down and it stared back at him as he changed back to his human form. The hatchling regarded him seriously for a moment and then slowly changed to the form of a small girl. She was the size of a human toddler with long black hair and green eyes with red pupils.

Vaytawn picked up his daughter and walked downstairs. "Come, Parek," he said to the child, "and meet the rest of your family. We'll have a grand feast, just for you." He informed the chamberlain to prepare a feast in his daughter's honor and made it clear that attendance was mandatory. Next he took her to his father's office to allow them to get acquainted. Finally he had her ensconced in the chamber beside his for a nap before the ceremony of formally presenting his daughter to his court.

Chapter 25

The days passed quickly, and Robyn's condition progressed. Since she could no longer work, she spent her days strolling by the lake when weather permitted, and reading when it did not. She remained as active as she could in the politics of the kingdom, and Nyakas came to rely on her advice.

As the summer melted into autumn, Robyn found herself inside more often than not. Reading soon lost some of its appeal, and one day she found herself in Nyakas' office, looking out the window. It was raining, and the landscape was an oddly appealing mixture of gray and blue. The baby she carried kicked and she smiled and rubbed her hands over her swollen belly.

"Hello, Marcus," she said to her abdomen. "I was wondering when you'd wake up."

The door opened and Nyakas came in. He carried a scroll which he read while he walked. Robyn turned back toward the door, and the noise got his attention. He stopped short, then smiled and said, "Hello, love. What brings you here?"

"The view is best here today. I can look out and not get wet. The last time I walked in the rain, you and Gwyneth both fussed at me."

"Very true," he answered, walking to the desk. He sat on the edge of the desk and placed his hand on her belly. "How are you today, little one?"

"Oh, please, don't get him started! He's been quiet for a change!"

"Perhaps we should take advantage of it, then," said Nyakas, leaning to kiss Robyn's neck.

"Hmm, sounds promising. Do we have time before dinner?"

"Yes, actually."

"Well, OK, but you'll have to help me up. I'm stuck again."

Nyakas laughed and offered his hand. Robyn grasped his wrist, and he pulled her out of the chair. They walked sedately up the stairs and down the hall. Robyn had abandoned walking normally months before and now waddled, usually with one hand at the small of her back. Recently she'd begun placing her other hand on her belly, which had caused Gravity to laugh out loud the first time he saw her.

They got to their chamber and he picked her up and placed her softly on the bed. Nyakas kissed her gently, lightly stroking her belly. Robyn put her arms around his neck and pulled him closer, deepening the kiss. The baby shifted, but she ignored it. She twined her fingers into Nyakas' hair, unbraiding it until it fell in dark waves around her face. The baby shifted again as her belly contracted suddenly, and she gasped involuntarily.

Nyakas pulled back quickly. "What? What's wrong?"

Robyn put her hands on her belly. "Nothing, I think. He moved, maybe he just hit me wrong. It's OK now," she answered as her belly contracted again. "Then again," she said, clutching her midsection, "maybe not."

She sat up and rubbed her abdomen. "What are you doing in there, bud? Putting up drywall? Feel this, Nyakas, my belly is hard."

Nyakas rubbed her stomach and it tightened under his hand. Robyn gasped and said, "Marcus, come on! Cut it out!"

"Do you think he's in a hurry?" Nyakas asked, his voice concerned.

"Oh, I bet I know what it is," Robyn answered, getting off the bed. "We thought Kara had gone into labor one day at work. It turned out to be false labor. It can start weeks before the baby is due."

"What do you do about it?"

"Her doctor told her to walk it off and practice her Lamaze breathing," she answered, waddling around the room.

Nyakas watched her pace back and forth for a minute, then said, "Well, is it working?"

"Yeah, I think it is! Oh, shit!" She grabbed the post of the bed with one hand and her belly with the other as another contraction began.

Nyakas leaped off the bed. In two long steps he was at her side, supporting her weight and guiding her to sit on the end of the bed. Robyn did her best to remember how she was supposed to breath. As the contraction subsided, she said, "OK, I think it's all right now. Wow, that was a doozy."

"Robyn, are you sure this is false labor?"

"I don't know! I've never done this before! Besides, what little I do know about giving birth may or may not apply, given the fact that this baby is half dragon!"

"OK, love, I'm sorry. I've never done this before either."

"I know, I'm sorry. It's just a little scary. I like to know what to expect." She put her arms around his waist and laid her head on his chest as he pulled her close. A few minutes later they lay down together, holding each other until it was time to go to dinner.

Robyn waddled into the Great Hall beside Nyakas. She started to relax a little, since she hadn't had any more contractions, and she'd almost convinced herself that it was false labor. Dinner was served, but she wasn't very hungry and only picked at her food.

Gravity looked at her and said, "Are you feeling all right, my lady?"

"Fine," Robyn answered. "Why do you ask?"

"You aren't eating. Usually there isn't anything on the table that's safe when you're with us."

"Hush, now! I'm just not really hungry tonight."

"Really? That's highly unusual. Are you sure all is well? I seem to sense something different with the child."

"I'm fine, Gravity, really."

"If you say so," Gravity said, sounding unconvinced. He knew better than to press the issue, but that didn't stop him from keeping a close eye on her.

Dinner wound down and Robyn leaned over to Nyakas. "I'm a little tired, honey. I think I'm going to go up to bed."

"Very well, love. Shall I walk with you?"

"No, I'll be fine. Besides, I think Lord Trellan needs to have a word with you."

"I'll be along soon."

"OK," she said, trying to rise gracefully. She didn't notice the look exchanged between Gravity and Nyakas, but she did notice Gravity stand. As she waddled to the door, he walked behind her. She glanced at him and said, "I don't really need an escort, Gravity."

"Don't argue, my lady," he answered quietly.

They left the Great Hall. As they approached the staircase Robyn felt another contraction beginning and she took a deep breath, determined to conceal it if possible. She casually placed her free hand on her abdomen, glad she'd begun doing so weeks before, and breathed through the contraction. Gravity said nothing and she wondered if he noticed. The contraction began to subside, then suddenly intensified. She stopped walking and put her hand on the wall for support. As the pain subsided again, she realized her feet were wet.

"Ah, hell," she said.

"My lady? What is it?"

"My water broke, Gravity. Marcus is on his way."

"It's about time you realized that," Gravity said calmly. "Come, you should change your clothes."

He escorted her to her chamber. She began unbuttoning her gown as she went behind the screen, and Gravity pulled the bell cord to summon a servant. Robyn heard a tap at the door, the door open, and Gravity ask the page to summon Gwyneth. She let her gown drop to the floor and put on a dry muslin nightgown, dry underwear, and her robe before coming out to sit on the couch.

"My lady, your discomfort will be eased if you walk."

She got up without asking how he knew and began pacing the room. Gwyneth came in a few minutes later and said, "How are you feeling, my lady?"

"Fine, at least for now. I hope you know something about giving birth."

"Aye, my lady. I've had two, and I'll stay with you until you've had yours."

"Thank you. Has anyone told Nyakas yet?"

"No, my lady," said Gravity.

"Good, just let him stay downstairs for a while longer. It's going to be a long night; there's not much point in worrying him this early."

"Are you sure, my lady?" asked Gravity. "He'd want to be here with you."

"Gravity, you didn't see him earlier when a had a contraction. It scared him as much as it did me. I'll have plenty more contractions for him to experience with me."

"Well, perhaps I should go sit with him then."

"As you think best, friend."

"My lord," said Gwyneth, "could I trouble you for something?"

"What is it, Gwyneth?"

"If you are going back to the Great Hall, could you pass through the kitchen and inform Cook that the Queen will have need of a particular tea tonight, and that I shall send someone to let him know when to begin brewing?"

"Certainly," Gravity answered. He touched Robyn's shoulder and left the room. Gwyneth poured her a cup of tea and pressed it into her hand. Robyn sat on the couch and sipped it, breathing through the occasional contractions.

Gravity passed through the kitchen and spoke to the cook, then went back to the Great Hall. He took his seat beside Nyakas wordlessly. Nyakas was deep in conversation with Lord Trellan, and for the moment Gravity had to agree with Robyn's logic.

His conversation was rather lengthy, but as it wound down, Nyakas noticed that Gravity was again sitting beside him.

"Gravity," Nyakas said, "did you get my wife settled?"

"Yes, my lord, she is comfortably ensconced in your chamber, and Gwyneth is with her."

"Gwyneth? Why? I thought Robyn was going to bed."

"I'm sure she will eventually, my lord."

"Eventually? What are you keeping from me?"

Gravity leaned toward Nyakas and lowered his voice. "She asked me to let you stay down here a bit longer. I hope you slept well last night, my lord, because I doubt you'll be sleeping much tonight."

Nyakas' expression was blank, and then realization gave way to terror. He stood suddenly, knocking his chair over, and strode briskly from the room, brushing past confused servants as he made his way quickly to his chamber.

Robyn and Gwyneth looked up sedately as Nyakas burst into the room.

"Robyn?" He looked around and saw her sitting on couch with a mug in one hand and a book in the other. Gwyneth sat nearby with her knitting. "Robyn, are you all right?" He rushed to her side.

She put down her mug and took his hand. "I'm fine, love, really. Hopefully by the end of the night you'll be a daddy."

"How long have you known that?"

"Since just after dinner."

"You didn't summon me? Robyn, why? I would have come right up to be with you!"

"I know that, darling, but there hasn't been anything for you to do. You'd have only made me nervous. Really, it's been quite boring. I've only had eight contractions in the last hour and a half."

"Eight? Robyn, you should have sent someone to get me!"

"Nyakas, please, give me a break. It's going to be a really long night if you keep hovering over me, and I'm already a horrible patient as it is! Trust me, you'll have plenty of time to keep me company through the coming agony."

"But I'm supposed to be here with you! I'm supposed to help you! Isn't that what humans do?"

"My lord, if I may," interrupted Gwyneth, "it would be most helpful if you could ask the cook to brew some more tea."

"Tea? Right! I'll summon a page."

"No, my lord, I think, in this case, that you should ask him yourself. You see, it's the time when he usually inspects the kitchen, and he hates to be interrupted. However, if you asked him, and told him the tea is for the queen, mayhap he would be more receptive."

"I see. Robyn, will you be all right if I step out for a moment?"

"Yes, darling," Robyn answered with a gentle smile. "I promise I won't have the baby without you."

"I'll be right back then," Nyakas said, kissing Robyn's cheek and leaving the room.

"Thank you, Gwyneth," said Robyn. "I really don't need any more tea, but he really needed something to do."

"True, my lady, but my purpose was two-fold. Cook has a special tea, which will help ease the pain as your labor progresses, but it does take a bit of time to brew properly. He shall keep the king occupied for a time, and when your tea arrives, I think you'll be ready for it. Now, if you will excuse me momentarily, I have some preparations to attend to."

"Of course, I'll be fine."

"I'll be in the next room, my lady, setting up for the birthing. I've already sent word to Creedan that I'll not be home. It will not hurt him to attend to the boys for one night."

Robyn smiled as she imagined Creedan reading to the little boys and tucking them in. Another contraction started, and she breathed through it. Gwyneth left the room and returned a short time later to her knitting. As Robyn's contractions became more frequent and intense, she got up and began to walk, and that seemed to help. She'd paced and breathed through four contractions when the door opened and Nyakas came in with a tray.

"Robyn? Here's your tea, love. Here, sit down and drink it."

"Thanks, honey, but I think I'll walk and drink, at least for right now."

"Walk? Why?"

"Because, Nyakas, this is really starting to hurt, and it hurts marginally less if I walk. Care to join me?"

"Umm, sure. Whatever you need, love."

He paced with her, taking her mug when necessary, encouraging her to drink when possible. Within an hour, Robyn could no longer walk, and Nyakas and Gwyneth helped her to the room beside their chamber and settled her in the bed. He held her hand as she tried to breath through her contractions. Suddenly, in the midst of the pain, Robyn felt the need to bear down. Gwyneth recognized the sign and immediately summoned the midwife.

"My lady," she said, "do not push if you can help it."

"Don't push? You're kidding, right? I have to push!"

"Do, if you must, but try not to. The midwife will be here momentarily, and she will tell you if it's time."

"Oh, it's time, Gwyneth. Trust me, it's time!"

The door opened a few moments later, and a middle-aged woman entered. "Good evening, my lady. I understand you're ready to give birth."

"Oh, you have no idea how ready I am. Come on; let's get this show on the road! Nyakas, this is it! I'm not doing this again! You can have the next one!"

Gwyneth chuckled as Nyakas looked at her, puzzled. "Not to worry, my lord. This is normal."

The contraction subsided and the midwife did a quick assessment of Robyn's condition. "Aye, my lady. Push to your heart's content. The prince or princess should be here soon."

"Prince. It's a prince. And he'd better be here soon!"

There was a tap at the door and Gwyneth answered it. A moment later Gravity came in.

"Oh, great," said Robyn, "thanks for stopping in, Grav, but this isn't really the best time."

"Actually it is the best time, majesty," answered Gravity evenly.

"No, it's really not. The last thing I need right now is an audience."

"What you do need is this," said Gravity, placing his hand on her head. Immediately, the pain lessened. Although she could still feel what was happening, the pain was suddenly bearable.

"Whoa, thanks Gravity. I don't know what that was, but don't go anywhere, OK?"

"I would not think of it, my lady," said Gravity, sitting in a chair nearby.

It was nearly an hour later when the midwife announced that the end was in sight; she could see the baby's head. Robyn's adrenaline surged and she pushed harder. Nyakas moved to sit behind her on the bed, supporting her in a reclining position. A few minutes later, the baby emerged with a lusty wail, and Robyn collapsed against Nyakas' chest, weeping with relief. A minute later, the crying baby was wrapped and placed in her arms. For a moment, Robyn's world contracted to the child in her arms and the man at her side. She wept with happiness as she and Nyakas counted their son's fingers and toes. He had the customary ten of each, fuzzy black hair, and his mother's blue eyes. Nyakas noted with surprise that Marcus bore no outward sign of his dragon heritage, although he could sense its presence.

A moment later, Gravity stood beside them. Wordlessly, he placed a hand on Nyakas' and Robyn's shoulders then left the room.

Nyakas put his arms around Robyn and Marcus, and kissed Robyn's hair. The midwife busied herself cleaning up the aftermath, and then nodded to Gwyneth.

"My lord," said Gwyneth, "I think that the queen would be more comfortable in her own bed."

"True," said Nyakas. "Darling, give Marcus to Gwyneth for a moment and let's get you to bed."

Robyn kissed the top of Marcus' head, and then handed him to Gwyneth. Nyakas stood up carefully, and gently lifted her. He carried her to their chamber and tucked her into bed. Gwyneth brought in Marcus, who was beginning to fuss.

As she placed the baby in his mother's arms, Gwyneth smiled gently and said, "I believe he's hungry, my lady."

"What's wrong, buddy? Did you miss dinner? OK, I've never done this before, but neither have you, so I guess we'll learn together." Robyn took the baby and held him to her breast. As he began to feed, Robyn jumped in surprise. "Whoa, Hoover! Easy!"

Gwyneth chuckled and said, "It is a bit strange the first time, my lady. Have no fears, you'll both get used to it."

Robyn settled back with the baby as he hungrily suckled, and Nyakas sat beside them, savoring the moment. When the baby was done, Robyn gingerly burped him and Gwyneth laughed.

"My lady, try it this way." She took Marcus and held him to her own shoulder, and began vigorously patting and rubbing Marcus' back. Within seconds he produced a hearty belch that made Nyakas' eyes widen in surprise. As Gwyneth handed the baby back, she said, "You'll not hurt him, my lady, I assure you. I've not hurt either of mine yet!"

Robyn smiled as she held her son. Within moments the baby had dozed off, warm, full, and content. Robyn's adrenaline suddenly wore off and she felt as if she couldn't stay awake another minute. Nyakas took Marcus and put him into the cradle he'd had made for him, which was near their bed. When he turned back around, Robyn was fast asleep, so he sat on the edge of the bed and watched his sleeping child until the fire began to die down. He put on another log so Marcus wouldn't catch a chill, and then lay down beside his wife to sleep.

Chapter 26

The sun rose.   The castle seemed quiet as guards stood watch at their posts. The people went about their business as usual, and the knights and squires made their way to the salle.

Nyakas sat in front of the fireplace cradling his newborn son in his arms. As he brushed the small amount of black hair away from the baby's eyes, Robyn woke up and watched silently for a moment. Then she got up from the bed and walked stiffly to the couch to sit beside Nyakas.

"Good morning, my lady, how are you feeling this morning?"

"Much better! You?"

"Great! Marcus woke up early, so we sat here and talked about when he will succeed me, and about the birds and the bees, you know guy stuff," Nyakas replied with a large grin.

Robyn laughed and punched him lightly in the ribs. "He doesn't need to know about the birds and the bees quite this early!"

"No, we were just sitting enjoying the morning sun. It is a beautiful day. Not quite as beautiful as you, but beautiful." He kissed her gently and she wrapped her arms around him, mindful of the fact that he was holding Marcus. As they talked, Marcus seemed to sense his mother's presence and began to fuss. She took him and quickly realized that he was hungry. She offered her breast awkwardly, not quite sure of what she was doing, and smiled when he began to nurse enthusiastically. When he finished feeding, they all dressed and went to the Great Hall. Normally they did not take breakfast with the court, but special occasions were the exception, and today was definitely a special occasion.

Nyakas and Robyn entered the Great Hall to find everyone standing and smiling. As they took their seats, Gravity greeted them. Everyone talked among themselves until arrival of Lady Stephan was announced. Everyone stood once again and waited as she came into the Great Hall.

Stephan swept in, radiant as always in white. Her cloak and tunic were embroidered with the same pattern Nyakas wore on his cloak, her pants had gold lacings down the outside of each leg.

The other nobles made a place for her to sit beside Robyn. She took the proffered seat and looked at her new nephew.

"You're an aunt now, little sister," Nyakas said with a smile.

"Yes, I know." Tears filled her eyes as she and Robyn put their arms around each other.

Gravity smiled, and Nyakas looked at his friend. "Is he not beautiful?"

"As long as he takes after his mother, yes," Gravity replied without expression.

Everyone in the vicinity laughed. Nyakas' face was expressionless at first, but quickly turned to a smile with a small chuckle.

"He will break a lot of hearts, I'm sure, my lord. He has some good teachers," Gravity said.

"You will teach him the ways of the blade, will you not?" Nyakas asked.

"I think since I've taught everyone else in the household, what could one more hurt?" Gravity replied as he began to eat.

"Just one? He is only the first of many, my friend," Nyakas laughed.

Gravity stopped chewing, and he looked as though he had been shot just as he was beginning to swallow his food. He swallowed hard and took a breath as Nyakas laughed.

"One of many, you say?" said Gravity. "Well, you had better hire some more help, because if they're all boys I'll have more than even I can handle. If I'm lucky there will be a girl or two. Hold on, what am I talking about? Your wife is as stubborn as you! Guess I'm out of luck anyway I look at it!"

Robyn laughed and made a feeble attempt to look hurt. Gravity gave her a black look, daring her to challenge him. As they laughed, they continued to eat their breakfast and talk about the days to come.

Chapter 27

Robyn began training again a month after Marcus' birth. She began slowly, deliberately starting with a short run and a light workout, and adding a little each day. As her physical condition began to improve, she started fencing again. Under Gravity's watchful eye, she worked her way through the squires, then the knights, defeating each before moving on to the next. After each bout, Gravity would critique the performance.

One day, after she had defeated the first of the knights, Gravity took her aside. "Robyn, you've done well, and I have no doubt that before the year is out, there is will be no knight among our ranks who will defeat you. There is a challenge upon which you should focus."

"What is that, Gravity? Defeating you?"

Gravity stared blankly at her. "No, my lady. As well as you have done, you are still years from defeating me. You should focus on defeating Nyakas."

"Nyakas?"

"Yes. He's better than anyone here except me. If you can defeat him, you will defeat anyone. The key is to not tell him all of what you have been doing."

"You want me to lie to my husband?"

"No, my lady, just don't volunteer the fact that you are working your way through his best fighters. If he asks, simply tell him, as I will, that you are working hard and coming along. As much as Nyakas cares for you, he still knows that you are female and therefore, in the dragon culture, a little inferior. He'll take it easy on you to begin with and will be in for quite a shock when he realizes that he should not have underestimated you."

"You know, Grav, I like your idea. How long do you think it will be before I can challenge him?"

"If you continue at the pace you are now, in about three moons. After you defeat Cristof and Dalen, you'll be ready for Nyakas."

Chapter 28

Days turned into weeks and weeks into months. With the birth of the prince, the kingdom flourished and people could see a change in their King. He seemed more gentle and more kind, as though his wife and child had changed him somehow. There were more festivals. Crops flourished, and the farmers got to keep a larger percentage. The businesses inside the castle walls flourished as well.

Even as much as the people loved Nyakas, they still feared Gravity. As the peace progressed, the people began to wonder how long it would be before the king released Gravity. They all knew the friendship between Gravity, and the king and queen, yet the people still feared his intentions. During the second moon of the summer Robyn began hearing of the people of her kingdom talking about Nyakas regaining his morality. They wondered why he still aligned himself with Gravity, who was known to be evil. They speculated that Gravity was a spy for Malitor, and that sooner or later, he would betray his friends.

She stood in the courtyard one beautiful sunny day when one of the guards came running toward her. "Your majesty, I have news!" he said, winded.

"What is it?"

"Lord Gravity just walked out of the kingdom into the forest with his swords, uniform, and a sack filled with something, with what I don't know," the guard replied catching his breath. "We believe it may contain something he is taking to Lord Malitor."

"Slow down! I'll go and see. Don't worry, just go back to your post."

"No, your majesty! You can't leave without the king or someone else to guard you!"

Robyn bristled, annoyed that he thought she needed a bodyguard when she'd worked so hard. "I am the queen and I can assure you that I can defend myself. If you wish, you may tell the king where I'm going."

He bowed quickly and ran into the castle. Robyn turned on her heel and quickly walked to see where Gravity had gone. She walked about a quarter of a mile when she saw Gravity in front of a fenced in graveyard with two headstones. She watched from a distance to see Gravity pull flowers out of the bag and lay them on the graves. Robyn smiled slightly; the man everyone feared must have not wanted anyone to know that even he had a gentler side.

Robyn walked up behind him and waited for him to say something, knowing he knew where she was before she got there. Gravity just sat inside the gates.

"Hi, Gravity," she said softly.

"Hello, your majesty," he answered. He stood and bowed, and then looked back at the graves one last time before coming out and closing the gate. "Is there something I can do for you?"

"Nothing. They said you had left with a sack and I just wondered where you had run off to."

"You think as your people think. I can understand," Gravity said with a bit of loss in his voice.

"No, Gravity, I don't. It's just that I'm afraid they'll revolt if Nyakas doesn't banish you," she replied, sounding more concerned.

"Robyn, let me tell you something. I would carve out my own black heart before aligning myself with Malitor and Vaytawn. I would never turn my back on you and Nyakas."

"I know. I'm sorry."

"Don't be sorry. All of this I brought upon myself a long time ago. There is nothing that can be done about it now. I care for you, Nyakas, Marcus, and Stephan. I won't hurt any of you, I give you my word."

"I know, Gravity," said a voice from behind Robyn, "and you need not fear." Nyakas walked to them, carrying Marcus.

"Hello, friend. Good to see you."

"You too, Gravity. Visiting, I presume?"

"Yes," Gravity replied beginning to laugh.

Nyakas smiled. "Friend, I'm not getting rid of you no matter what happens. If the people don't like it, they can leave. They don't have to like all my decisions, they just have to live with them."

Robyn put her arm around Nyakas' waist and they all walked back to the castle in amicable silence. When they returned, the guards stood their posts without a word, but seeing them come back made them all nervous. They knew what they had said about Gravity and now awaited the General's backlash. He surprised them all when he merely surveyed his soldiers and gave them a small smile to assure them that he was content with their work. They all stood their posts, wondering if it was a sign that he was proud, or of something worse to come.

Chapter 29

Robyn sat in the nursery, feeding Marcus his cereal. He sat on her lap, fussing because she wasn't feeding him his breakfast fast enough. She spooned the gooey food into his waiting mouth as quickly as she could, talking to him about what she was going to do that day.

The day before, she had defeated Cristof, and Gravity pronounced her ready to challenge Nyakas. It had been all she could do not to tell Nyakas outright, but she knew she'd have more fun if she kept it to herself. She also knew that Nyakas would be in to join them soon, and so she talked to Marcus, even though she knew he really didn't care as long as she kept feeding him.

She heard Nyakas enter the room, but pretended she hadn't heard him. She fed Marcus another spoonful of food as she said, "So Uncle Gravity said that I had a really long way to go, and that if I kept working hard, maybe someday I could defeat you! Can you believe that? I bet he's just grumpy. I bet I could beat your Daddy if I really wanted to." Nyakas chuckled softly and she turned to see him standing in the doorway. She pretended to be surprised as she said, "Oh, hi, honey! Gosh, how long have you been standing there?"

"Long enough to hear that you could beat me in a sword fight if you really wanted to."

"Oh, that. I was just talking to Marcus."

"Do you always just say things like that? One day he'll believe you, you know."

"Why shouldn't he believe me now?"

"Well, dear, because if Gravity doesn't think you can beat Marcus, what makes you think you can beat me?"

"I probably could beat you if I really tried. I defeated Delamore!"

"Delamore is a first year knight, Robyn!"

"Well, hey, if you choose not to believe me, that's fine. There's only one way to find out for sure."

"Is that a challenge, my love?"

She paused as if she were thinking about it, and then answered with false bravado, "Yes. Yes it is."

"I see. Well, then, I guess I'll just have to come down to the salle later and prove my point. Would you like to place a small wager on our contest?"

"What did you have in mind?" she asked as she fed Marcus the last bite of cereal, then settled back in the rocking chair to let him nurse.

"Loser has to serve the winner for a full day."

Robyn hesitated. "I don't know. How about we just wager a gold piece?"

Nyakas laughed. "One gold? Is that how confident you are?"

"OK, two gold and the loser serves the winner for one evening."

Nyakas laughed. "Looks like this will be an easy win for me!"

"Oh, all right!" Robyn exclaimed. "A full day of service and five gold! That's my final offer!"

"Fine, dear. Bring the gold with you to the salle."

"Hey, you'd best bring yours, too."

Nyakas laughed and kissed her, then left the room. She smiled as he left and finished with Marcus. When the nanny arrived, she went to find Gravity. He nearly laughed when she told him about their conversation, and word quickly spread that the King would be answering the queen's 'tentative' challenge.

They all proceeded as they normally did, looking forward to the show they would witness. They all knew that the queen loved a good joke, and they also knew that she was the biggest jokester in the group, with the possible exception of a couple of the squires and Delamore, the son of the court bard. It was also common knowledge that the king and nobles heard about very few of the queen's pranks.

Robyn did her best to look as if she was terribly nervous but trying to hide it. When Nyakas came into the salle dressed in his old riding leathers, she allowed a look of stark terror to cross her face but replaced it quickly with a look of false bravado. He walked up to her jauntily, grinning broadly, and kissed her cheek.

"Did you bring your gold?" he asked quietly.

"Yes," she answered, "but I doubt I'll need it. Do you have yours?"

He took a small pouch out of his belt, shook it, and tossed it to a nearby squire. "Hold that for me for a moment, boy."

"Yes, your majesty," said the boy and quickly retreated out of range.

Gravity walked over and said, "Ah, Nyakas, thank you for joining us. I think you'll be surprised at the Queen's progress."

"Yes," Nyakas answered, still looking at Robyn. "She told me she beat Delamore."

Gravity shot a look of surprise at Robyn; she'd defeated Delamore several months before.

"Well, I did!" exclaimed Robyn emphatically. A few of the knights chuckled, and Dalen coughed and walked away to avoid laughing. Robyn looked around as if challenging anyone who dared to say a word.

Delamore stood nearby, and said dramatically, "My lady, please, must we relive that painful memory yet again?"

"Sorry, Delamore, I was just so excited I couldn't help but tell him. Can we get on with this, please?"

"We don't have to do this yet if you don't want to," Nyakas replied. "I can just take my gold and go back to work."

"No, I have to do it now. If I back out, Gravity will have my hide."

"Very true," interjected Gravity, thinking that he'd have to stand in line to get to her hide if she disappointed all of these men by canceling her performance. "Are you ready, my lady?"

"Yes," Robyn said as if resigned to her fate. She moved into position, and Nyakas drew his sword and followed suit. Gravity gave the signal, and she quickly gave a tentative offensive stroke. Nyakas quickly countered it and returned the stroke, which she parried sloppily. They traded a dozen strokes before Robyn got serious.

Gravity was watching her carefully, and a chill ran down his spine as her expression changed from controlled fear to the look of stony determination he'd come to know so well.

She quickly went on the offensive with several powerful strikes, which were barely countered. She quickened her pace and advanced before he had a chance to recover from the shock. His face was expressionless and he began to trade her stroke for stroke. She parried each stroke until she saw his pattern develop. A well-timed leg-sweep sent him tumbling to the ground. Before he could get back up, she kicked him just hard enough in the shoulder to keep him down, then placed her foot in the middle of his chest and the point of her blade at his heart. She kept enough of her weight on his chest that he wouldn't stick himself with her sword before he realized he'd been beaten.

The salle erupted with applause and cheering as the on-lookers saw Nyakas look from the blade to his wife's triumphant face. She sheathed her sword and held out her hand to help him up. He accepted her hand, but pulled her down on top of him. Her yelp of surprise quickly changed to laughter as he held her with one arm and tickled her with the other. She wiggled out of his grasp, but instead of moving away, she straddled his chest with a knee on each of his arms.

Laughing, she said, "Be nice and I'll let you up."

"I won't tickle you, but you're going to have to take the rest of the day off and be nice to me!"

Robyn laughed again and stood up, moving far enough away to give Nyakas room to roll gracefully to his feet. Robyn's audience had broken up, but there was still laughter as they went back to work. The squire holding his gold approached shyly and offered the small bag to him. Nyakas took it gently from his hand with a word of thanks, and shoved it unceremoniously at Robyn.

"I can't believe you did that to me," he said with mock anger in his voice. "Gravity, I bet you were in on that from the start, weren't you?"

Gravity's eyes opened wide in surprise, "Me, my lord? Why would you think such a thing of a man who has been your faithful friend and loyal compatriot for so long?"

"Because I know you, that's why! I should have known when the only straight answer I could get from you about her training was, 'Oh, she's coming along. You know how stubborn she is!' Stubborn, indeed, and devious!"

Gravity chuckled, and Robyn was near tears of hysteria.

"Well," Gravity said slowly, "I guess I may have encouraged her a bit, but you must admit that she set and attained a lofty goal!"

Nyakas grunted in disapproval, turned on his heel, and walked to the door. Robyn watched in surprise, wondering if their joke had gone a bit too far, but Gravity knew well enough that he would have his pay-back.

"My lady," said Gravity, "you did well. Take the rest of the day off." He nodded to the door, which was closing behind Nyakas. "Go make up, or whatever it is you do." He turned to the few men who had yet to return to their training and said loudly, "As for the rest of you, back to work! You'll not see any time off until you defeat the King!"

Chapter 30

The first moon of autumn brought Marcus' first birthday. Nyakas and Robyn spent a quiet day with Marcus, Gravity, and Stephan. It was raining, so they sat in the throne room together, telling of long forgotten battles from Nyakas' realm, and jokes from Robyn's time. They enjoyed an early dinner and cake alone with Marcus before the public celebration. The highlight of the day for Robyn came when Gravity gingerly took the young boy in his arms and held him as though he were a fine piece of porcelain. He looked at Marcus with a grimace as though he wondered about the young boy's intention. Marcus replied with a dribble of drool on Gravity's cloak and a wide grin as he wet his diaper. Everyone laughed as Gravity looked gravely at the child in his arms and said, "This won't happen in my salle, I don't care whose kid you are."

Gravity smiled and gave the baby back to Nyakas. "He's your son; you'd better remedy that problem before sending him back to me."

Nyakas laughed. "That's a sign he likes you Gravity! Didn't you know?"

"Robyn, what is it you say? 'I was born in the dark, but it wasn't last night.' Is that accurate?"

Everyone laughed, and Robyn did her best to hide a surge of homesickness, but Nyakas noticed. He passed the baby to Stephan and quietly asked, "Robyn, what is it?"

"It's nothing. I just miss home, that's all."

"How's this? We'll go to your home first thing in the morning."

Robyn's face lit up. She leaned into his arms and kissed him deeply. "Thank you, Nyakas. I love you so much."

They all continued to laugh and talk, but it wasn't long before Marcus decided he'd had enough fun and went to sleep in Robyn's arms. Gwyneth came to take him upstairs to bed, promising to stay with him until they returned.

As if on cue some bards made their way to the Great Hall and began to play a soft melody. Nyakas took Robyn's hand and led her to the dance floor. Stephan watched, smiling, and didn't notice the expression on Gravity's face as the warrior worked up the courage to ask her to dance. When he did, Stephan agreed politely and he took her right hand in his and led her into the dance. Robyn noticed that Gravity was a magnificent dancer and wondered where he'd learned. She realized that there were a lot of things she wanted to know about her friend but was fearful of asking. She said nothing as he caught her eye and smiled slightly. They all danced until it began to get late, and Stephan announced that it was time for her to leave.

Stephan took one final glance back at the castle as she walked to the woods, where she would change to her dragon form.   She felt uneasy about leaving but did not understand why; she chalked it up to maybe a bad piece of fish.

Gravity stood on the battlements, watching as Stephan walked to the forest and silently wished for her safe return to her castle.

Nyakas sat in front of the fireplace in the Great Hall, enjoying a few minutes alone to reflect on the joy in his life.

Robyn went to Marcus' crib and brushed away his black hair and kissed his head lightly.   She knew where Nyakas was, and she got into bed to wait for him, but quickly fell asleep.

Chapter 31

Malitor and the other Dragon Lords met at the Cathedral. They had gathered the necessary components for the banishment spell and met briefly in the throne room while the sacrifices of choice for each Dragon Lord were gathered. Some preferred virgins with blonde hair and blue eyes, others favored animals. Still others took mortal men and women who were accomplished warriors and considered it an honor to give themselves to their Dragon Lord.

When the sacrifices were assembled, they moved into the chamber where the spell would be performed. The room had the feel of antiquity. In the center of the room was a pit of fire, which was started during the reign of the first Dragon Lord. It burned constantly, never dying. Although the room was clean and free of dust, it had the feel of not having been used in several centuries, as if the only beings to enter the room were those who tended it.

The individual Dragon Lords instructed their sacrifices to line up around the edge of the fire pit and to remain motionless while the spell was being cast. At Malitor's signal all of the Dragon Lords joined hands and began speaking in a language that was written on the walls of forgotten tombs. Mortals hadn't heard this language since ancient times. Their hands moved in circles, and rips in their plane of existence began to appear as they continued to chant. They drew the strength from their sacrifices, and one by one, the victims began to fall. The portal crackled with thunder and sparked with lightning as it opened. Some of the virgins began to scream and cower in fear, and the warriors gave final battle cries as their souls were ripped from their bodies.

Lights of all colors began to shoot out of the portal. They watched as it got bigger and bigger. A strong wind began to blow and Malitor began to yell. "Robyn, wife of Nyakas, you are banished to the life which you wish you had led! Never again will you interfere in my son's life! Kerrigan, rise! You have a job that has not yet been completed, and you may not rest until it is! Havoc, fear, trepidation, rain down upon the Kingdom of Nyakas!"

Suddenly there was a surge of power, which knocked them all over. As the one who was controlling the spell, Malitor was thrown against the far wall. The spell took effect, and the portal disappeared. As the Dragon Lords watched, the spell seemed to end. The only thing left to do was wait to hear if it had, indeed, worked.

****

As Gravity watched from the battlements, a wave of uneasiness swept over him. He quickly looked around behind him when the ground fell almost completely out from underneath him. He fell hard to the ground and found that it had, in fact, fallen a few feet as if the castle had sunk into the ground.

Nyakas fell from his seat and quickly got to his feet. He tried to move quickly to his chamber but found there was something in his way. He tried to move past it when a bolt of energy flung his body into the wall. As he lost consciousness he slid to the floor.

Vaytawn appeared in the royal family's chamber. He had been waiting invisibly on the balcony for the spell to take affect. As he entered through the French doors, he saw his sleeping sister-in-law disappear in a flash of light. He quickly grabbed the baby and disappeared into the night.

Nyakas regained consciousness a few minutes later to see Gravity standing in front of him. Gravity helped him to his feet.

"Thank you, Gravity," said Nyakas, dusting himself off. "What happened?"

"My lord," Gravity said with concern and loss in his voice, "they are gone."

Nyakas' body froze, knowing exactly what that meant. He ran to their chamber, calling out for Robyn and Marcus and hoping for a reply. There was none. He began running through the castle yelling their names. Gravity let him go, but waited for him in the throne room, where he was sure Nyakas would go after he finished.

"Where are they, Gravity?" Nyakas demanded when he arrived.

"I don't know, my lord."

Nyakas' voice was deep with sorrow as his eyes filled with tears. "Please help me find her."

"We will find her Nyakas, I give you my word." His eyes were red and his muscles tense; whoever took Robyn would suffer a great deal when they were found.

Gravity walked briskly through the castle checking everywhere, but he found nothing. He went to the throne room to find Nyakas at the foot of his throne holding a necklace. Gravity came to his side and placed his hand upon his shoulder.

"Nyakas, we have searched everywhere. We can't find them," Gravity replied swallowing hard to prevent the tears from falling.

"You see this, Gravity?" Nyakas lifted a thick chain with a silver cross on it. "This was Robyn's. Her friend gave it to you to give her. It was to help her get through the time she would have to spend here, so she would be able to bear all of this. She wore it every day. This necklace got her through the days she had to be without her family and friends. Now she's gone and wherever she is, she won't have it. How will she be able to deal with everything?"

"Nyakas, it's all right. We will find her and get her back."

Nyakas' face began to get red as tears came running down it, but the tears quickly disappeared as his face and body began to change to his true form. Gravity backed away, knowing what was happening. Nyakas changed from human to dragon in record time. His enormous body was too big for the throne room. Rocks and stones crashed from the ceiling to the beautiful marble floor, cracking the floor as they hit. Nyakas' wings expanded and the walls were the next to go. Gravity had already moved quickly to get out of the way of the crashing rocks and stones. Nyakas shot like a rocket through the already falling ceiling and breathed fire. His people, having been awakened by the apparent earthquake and the commotion to find the queen and the prince, saw that their king was torn apart. They all took cover in their homes.

He flew in the darkness and breathed long streaks of fire at the sky as if to blame it for his loss. In his heart he already knew who was to blame for the atrocity and vowed to find her wherever she was.

As Nyakas flew, Gravity sat in the empty throne room, looking at the carnage that Nyakas had left. As he sat silently, he caught a glimpse of one of the nobles walking by the throne room. He wondered why that particular man, who was not known for extraordinary courage, would be this close to such devastation. Gravity rose from his place on the marble floor and silently followed him to Nyakas' chambers. When he got to the door, he saw the noble standing in the middle of the room looking at the bed and the crib where Robyn and Marcus slept.

Lord Vermeer was one of the minor nobles and had a great dislike for Gravity. He stood there with a smug grin on his face. Gravity searched Vermeer's soul to find that there was a spy in their midst, and he was thinking smugly about how much he would be paid for his betrayal. Gravity walked in behind him, making no effort to be quiet. Vermeer turned around to find Gravity behind him and froze.

"Gravity, what are you doing here?" Vermeer asked with an edge of fear in his voice.

"I was just going to ask you the same thing, Vermeer, but I guess I already know the answer to that."

"I was looking for Nyakas. I was going to tell him I found out who the spy was," he replied, sounding a bit more confident now.

"I'm surprised. I didn't expect you to turn yourself in. I must say you have earned my respect."

"No, you're the spy, Gravity, you soul-less beast from hell!"

"I'm going to enjoy this."

As Gravity stared into his eyes, Vermeer reached behind his back, pulling the back of his tunic out of his pants to expose the dagger he had hidden there. He acted as though he was scratching his back as he replied, "Gravity, see you in hell."

Vermeer quickly drew the dagger from his back and swung for Gravity's neck, but he wasn't fast enough. Gravity pulled his katana and drew it up the length a Vermeer's body with both hands in one fluid motion. He split Vermeer's body from waist to shoulder. The skin split like butter. Vermeer's nerves held him up for a few seconds, and it was long enough for Gravity to grab the hand that bore the dagger and drive it directly through Vermeer's neck. Vermeer found himself pinned against the solid stone wall, gasping for air that never reached his lungs. Gravity looked deep into his eyes as Vermeer's blood spurted onto him. Vermeer's eyes were still open, watching Gravity stare at him as he struggled to take his last breath.

"Vermeer, you're not saying much. Dagger got your tongue? You go to hell, and when you get there, tell them Gravity sent you." He twisted Vermeer's head, and his neck snapped. He allowed Vermeer's body to fall to the ground, and then went to the battlements, where Nyakas had landed and now rested. Gravity approached and stood in front of his master's huge face. "Nyakas, I found the spy. It was Vermeer. Your father had them banished, Robyn as well as Marcus."

"Where is Vermeer now?"

"I'm sorry, my Lord, but I disposed of the traitor already."

"Why are you sorry?"

"I'm sure you had something in mind for him as well. Sorry I didn't come and get you when I found out the news, but he made a feeble attempt to kill me."

"It's all right, Gravity. I'll have his body sent to my father. As long as we find them, that's all I care about. It's only been a few hours and my heart is already lost without them."

"Nyakas, I promise, even if it takes us centuries, we'll find them. I know how much they mean to you."

Nyakas changed back to his human form and sat down on the battlements with his arms on his knees and his head in his hands. He lifted his head slowly and saw Gravity looking at him.

Gravity put his hand on Nyakas' shoulder and nodded. "No place will be too far to search."

Nyakas looked out at the dark forest. "You're right, Gravity, we will find her. But my father erased her memory, I'm sure of it. If he used the banishment spell, it is so powerful I can't see how I will be able to find her and if she will even remember me."

"Your love was strong for both of you. You have to believe in your heart that it will lead you to her."

"I know my father placed her someplace where she doesn't know anything or anybody."

"The spell doesn't have that control, and neither does the caster. That's what makes it so dangerous. She could be anywhere. I know that's not what you want to hear, but we will find them both."

They sat on the battlements for a while longer, and then Nyakas got to his feet and walked back into the castle. The people said nothing as Nyakas and Gravity gathered their weapons, armor, clothes, and provisions for what would be a long journey. A messenger was sent to Stephan to tell her of the situation, and another messenger was dispatched to take Vermeer's body to Malitor's castle. Nyakas informed the Seneschal that he was in charge until Stephan came, and no matter what happened he was to keep the castle together and keep it running. The noble agreed and Nyakas and Gravity walked into the forest and the journey began.

****

Robyn woke up and stretched contentedly. She was disoriented, as if she'd woken up in a place different from where she'd fallen asleep. After a few minutes, she realized it was the first day of her last summer vacation. She'd graduated from high school the night before, and now she had ten weeks before she went off to college.

She rolled over onto her stomach, remembering the dream she'd been having. She was dancing with a man in a black cloak. She tried to remember his name, but couldn't.

Finally, she rolled out of bed, pulled on a pair of shorts and a tank top, and went downstairs. Her mother, Gina, was sitting at the kitchen table with a cup of coffee and the morning newspaper.

"Morning, Mom."

"Good morning, sweetie. Did you sleep well?"

"Yes, but I had the strangest dream. I was dancing with a tall handsome man."

"Really? That sounds nice. Was it your dad?"

"No. He seemed familiar, but I can't remember his name."

"You know what they say. If you dream about a man every night for a week, you're destined to be with him always."

"Well, then I'll get back to you."

Gina laughed. "No need for that just yet, and there isn't any need to tell your father either! Listen, babe, your dad and I were talking. What do you think about going to Florida for your 18th birthday? Your dad has to be in Orlando the following week, so we thought we'd take one more family vacation."

"That sounds great! I'd love to spend my birthday on the beach. Can we go fishing?"

"Of course! Why would we go to Florida and not go fishing? I think this will be the year we get a barracuda!"

"Isn't it going to be awfully hot in July, though?"

"Yes, probably, but that's why the hotels have swimming pools."

"Good point. Can Kathy and I go to the mall to shop for bikinis?"

"As long as you buy something decent. Your father will be there."

"I know, Mom. No thong. Daddy always tells me he's too young to be a grandpa."

"Yes, but some of his wrestling buddies will be there too."

"Oh. Better go for the tank suit."

"Good choice. Have fun shopping, OK?"

Chapter 32

The sunset was orange and yellow as far as the eye could see. Nyakas stood on a ridge, and in the dying light he could see what remained of a battle that had ensued earlier that day. Men, women, and children lay in pools of blood, having tried to fight an unstoppable force. The commoners, villagers, and farmers who defended their land were no match against the insurmountable force and lost. One old man who survived said a great evil had ravaged through and destroyed everything in its wake.

"What did this evil look like?" Nyakas asked the old man.

He answered with fear in his voice as though they still were on the battlefield. "They wore crimson red cloaks over their charcoal black armor. The armor looked as though it was living and breathing the way it moved with them. One of the evil men wore an emblem upon his cloak. It was a diamond where two swords met and crossed one another, and in the middle was a dragon's head breathing fire. That one had to be their leader. He was a giant, at least seven feet tall. He seemed to be a chiseled sculpture. He was the most evil of them all. He scared everyone; half our people ran in fear when he and his pale horse came to our village. His helm was an alligator's skull stripped of skin, open jaws ready to snap!" He collapsed to the ground with nothing but his tears to accompany his lonely state. Nyakas watched as the old man's tears mixed with the blood of his family and friends.

After a few minutes the man composed himself enough to say, "He was bald and his eyes changed color, blue one minute and pitch black the next. His voice was distinct and demanding. He made me tremble with every word. His face seemed to change with every moment, and I don't just don't mean his expressions, I mean his whole face changed. He used two swords, a long one and a short one of a type that I had never seen before. He butchered my entire village like he knew no one would be able to stop him, and he was enjoying himself. He played and toyed with them as though he were only practicing. He knew where they would be every moment; he could have destroyed us by himself. He would pick up some of the half dead victims and gloat to them about how he had just destroyed their family, bite their lower lips just to taste their blood. He could have finished our village quickly but instead he let his soldiers rape our women and pillage our village first."

Nyakas turned away from what was destroyed and walked because he knew the symbol on the crimson cloak and would catch the evil man soon enough. He only felt hatred and anger as he looked at the carnage that had been left. As he climbed up on his black horse and pulled the reigns close, he saw Gravity standing at the edge of the forest waiting for his arrival.

"You're late," he said as he approached his friend.

"A group of bandits held me up. Sorry for the delay, Nyakas."

As Gravity and Nyakas looked at the blood soaked battlefield, all Nyakas could think of was his one true love. In his mind's eye, he could see her at the lake. He would sit with her for hours at a time while she fished. She would sit at the lake at sunset, and the dark blue water shimmered in the dimming light. He could see her looking back at him with her striking blue eyes. They were like diamonds, mysterious yet warm, and they melted his heart. Her short hair was the most glorious shade of blonde. Her touch was soft and warm; he could feel her hand against his cheek, her head coming his, her eyes closing as they came together.

"Nyakas? Nyakas! Wake up! Are you all right?" Gravity asked. "You zoned out on me for a minute."

Nyakas looked at Gravity, his eyes lonely. "Yes. I need to find her, Gravity. My heart is lost without her."

"We'll find her, my friend, I promise." They turned back toward Nyakas' castle, passing by the carnage caused by Kerrigan and his followers.

"Do you think we can win?" asked Nyakas.

"Of course, my friend. Don't worry, we'll find her and destroy the evil which lurks in this land."

"Thanks, Gravity. I wish I could have your optimism."

Chapter 33

Robyn was almost home. She'd finished her last exam and had her first year of college behind her. The plane made its final approach and landed. After the bulk of the passengers got off, she stepped off the plane, walked down the ramp, and entered the terminal. She paused, looking around. Her father stood near the wall; he would have been hard to miss. At six and a half feet tall and nearly 275 pounds, Kevin Smith dwarfed the people standing near him. She waved, grinning broadly. He returned her smile and his long strides took him to her. He engulfed his daughter in a bear hug.

"Hi, Squirt! Welcome home! How was the flight?"

"Fine, Dad! I'm glad to be back. Here, you'll want to see this." She extricated herself from her father's arms and reached for the paper in her back pocket. Grinning, she handed it to him, and he unfolded it.

"Straight A's! Good for you, Robyn! I knew you could do it! Didn't I tell you that you'd live through Chemistry?"

"Yeah, but it was hard."

"Well, you aced it, and that's all that matters. Come on; let's get your stuff. Mom is waiting at home for you, and the guys have been counting the days until you come back to the school."

"If Mom is waiting at home, does that mean she's making lasagna?"

"She's been in the kitchen all morning. She made me go to Harrigan's for extra ricotta, and then I had to go to three fruit stands to look for fresh strawberries for her cheesecake!"

"Yes!! What are we standing around for?" She took her father's arm and dragged him to the baggage pick-up area. As they stood waiting, a man approached.

"Excuse me," the man said to Kevin, "but aren't you Brick Barabas?"

Kevin smiled. "Yeah, that's me!"

"Wow! Can I have your autograph?"

"Sure," said Kevin. He and the man both began searching their pockets for something to write on.

Robyn smiled and tore a piece of paper out of her planner. "Here, Dad."

Kevin took the paper, signed it, and offered it to the man who stared at Robyn.

"Is that your daughter?" he asked.

"Yeah," answered Kevin with a smile, "that's my little girl. Not so little anymore!"

"This is the oldest one, right?"

"She's the only one!" Kevin said, laughing.

The man shook his head slowly. "Boy, do I feel old! I was at the autograph session in Philly when you kicked the Reaper!"

Robyn laughed. "I'm never going to live that down! Dad, did you pay him to bring that up again?"

"Not me!"

"I never will forget it," said the man. "I was standing in line and I could see Reaper's face when this little bitty girl in pigtails and a frilly dress came marching out of the crowd. The look on his face was, 'Oh, look, a little fan. I could step on her and be done with it, but I'll let her live today.' Then you walked right up to him and said, 'You meanie! You choke slammed my Daddy!' And you kicked him right in the shin! It was priceless! You were so little, I'm surprised you remember it!"

"I can't forget it! What you don't know is what happened later! My mother took me back to the hotel after the show and when Reaper came back, she made me apologize to him."

"What do you say to a man that big when you embarrass him like that? Weren't you afraid?"

"Heck no! I'd just turned four; I wasn't afraid of anything then! I just walked over and looked WAY up at him, and said, 'I'm sorry I kicked you, Uncle Mark, but it's just business!' That was all it took. He picked me and told me not to do it again."

"That's amazing! Well, I've got to run," said the man. "Thanks! It was nice meeting you." He turned and walked away.

Robyn put her arm around Kevin's waist. "I wonder what Mom did with those shoes after I outgrew them."

Kevin stepped forward to pull one of Robyn's bags off the conveyor belt. "She gave them to Mark."

"You're kidding! Why?"

"He asked for them. They're still on his mantle, bronzed and mounted on a plaque that says, 'Yea, though I walk through the valley of the shadow of death, I will fear no evil, because Little Robyn Smith is on MY side!' Do you know he had a bruise on his shin for the better part of two weeks?"

"Really? I didn't know I kicked him that hard!"

"It wasn't so much that it was that hard; it's just that your foot was so little. Is this all?"

"That's it! Let's go home!"

Chapter 34

Lars was puzzled about some signs he'd been receiving. There were definite signs that something around him wasn't right, but he couldn't seem to put his finger on what it was. He'd just finished teaching his last class of the day, and it was still early. His schedule was much lighter during the summer semester.

He decided to pray for a while on it. He went back into his modest Victorian two-story home near the University and closed the door behind him. As he turned around he saw an apparition clothed all in white, floating about six inches off of the floor. It was dressed in regal fashion with wings that sprang from his back and nearly reached the top of his ten-foot ceiling.

"My son, there will be no need to spend time in prayer. Your thoughts have been heard and He has sent me to you with some information. You must remember that the treaties forbid His direct intervention in this matter. However, He can offer information to His servants. His Order of the Light is a major player in this world in the fight for what is right and all that is holy. You already know this, having been inducted into this order.

"You are the first in a new style of priest. The tattoo that has appeared on your face is the symbol of this, but what you don't know is that it serves several purposes. One, it identifies you as a servant of Him. Two, it enables you to carry more magical power in your system than the rest of your brethren. And three, it has a special power that He will determine when you are in greatest need. You and your friend Mike Ryan are entering a time of crisis, for there are two evils battling for one prize. If the lesser of two evils finds the object of their search, then the greater evil will be destroyed. If the greater of two evils finds it first then evil will reign supreme, not only in a land far removed from this plane of existence, but here as well.

"Your new task is to find the object of their search and protect it with all of your powers and the formidable resources that Mr. Ryan commands. Continue to teach and learn more of your special kind of magic, for the object of your search is both nearer and farther than you think. Remember what I have said and we will help when we can. Put your trust in Him and you shall prevail."

With that the apparition disappeared and Lars looked at his surroundings again. His house was the same as it had been before the visit, but it was now morning and time for him to get to his first class. The students would be a little miffed if he was late.

Being a teenager had its benefits, like being able to stay up all night with no repercussions except a few hours of extra sleep the following night. He changed clothes and went into the bathroom to brush his teeth, studying his tattoo as he did so.

Noting the time he ran out of the house slid into his Porsche. He barely kept to the speed limit as he drove to the university. There, he would fill some minds with knowledge and wit, while the others used his class as an exercise in futility to get the course that they needed to graduate in their chosen major. He hadn't passed any of those other people and wasn't sure why they thought he would.

He parked in the faculty parking area and jogged to his classroom. He made it with barely a minute to spare. A couple of students filed in after him and found their way to seats near the back. He motioned to them and said, "Come, come people, the price of arriving after the teacher is to sit in the front of the class, where it is guaranteed that you will not fall asleep. Now, let's see who did their homework over the last two days. Who can tell me what the weight of an anti-quark is? What is the theoretical dimension of a brown dwarf star and what is gravity in relation to the other stellar objects within 15 Astronomical Units of its epicenter? Any takers?"

The only response that he got was a groan from the class, as they were anticipating easy questions. These were the easy questions. The hard questions were the ones he was seeking the answers to. He was still trying to find the actual mass of one cubic centimeter of a neutron star. His one burning question, the one he vowed to answer at some point during his life, was if the theorized pathways in the middle of a black hole actually existed, could they really be, in essence, a door to another plane of existence? The class dragged on as anticipated. Nobody wanted to take him up on his questions.

Between classes he wandered over to Mike's classroom. Rumor had it that on the very first day of class he asked everyone why they were there in his classroom. Didn't they know that he was going to fail each and every one in his class? Some of the students had shocked looks on their faces and said, "You're kidding, right, Doctor Ryan?" They saw with utter dismay the look on his face that said he wasn't kidding. Lars decided that he also would have freaked out at the age of ten when he was earning his first doctorate.

He arrived at Mike's classroom and found a few stragglers of the last class just leaving. A young woman was looking at Mike over her shoulder, and Lars smiled slightly. It wasn't the sort of look that girls had when they were sizing a guy up, and Lars surmised that she had just heard the rumor that Mike was, before he began teaching, an agent for the British Secret Service. This rumor had been circulating for quite a while, and nobody wanted to come out and ask him if it was true, just on the off-chance that it was. As far as Lars knew, he and Lilly were the only ones who knew it was true.

Mike Ryan was the epitome of bland. He was the kind of guy that nobody would think about looking at twice. His was the nondescript face that would blend into a crowd. The only thing that gave any credit at all to the rumor of Mike's having been some sort of secret agent was the fact that the man had a feline sort of grace to his movements and an assurance to his walk. When he walked by, something caused people to unconsciously get out of his way. Well, that and a six and a half foot Welsh woman who could break the spine of any of the football players if she so desired. Lilly had a way of drawing the attention away from him to herself, not only because of her sheer mass but also because she had the beauty that people expected to see in a model, not the manager of a retail import/export shop. She also had a tendency to dress exotically. She seemed to dislike clothing, and so wore as little of it as possible. Lars approached his colleague's desk.

"Hey, Mike," Lars said, "what's happening?"

"Just the usual," he replied with almost no trace of an accent from anywhere, "What's up with you, Lars?"

"Not much. What are you doing for dinner?"

"Staying in tonight for a small meal with the wife. Why?"

Lars chuckled inwardly at the thought of Lilly eating a small meal. What would that be, a side of beef? "I was wondering if you would let me take the two of you to dinner. I have some questions that I think you would be singularly qualified to answer."

"Let me check with Lilly and make sure that is all right with her. Where did you want to go?"

"I was thinking of that little steak joint down on 6th and 42nd street. I have been meaning to go there and just haven't made it that far. I think it is called O'Malley's or O'Reilly's or some thing like that. I was thinking around seven."

"Sure, we could do that, I will let you know by the end of the class day one way or the other. How about that?"

"Sure, talk to you later."

Lars turned on his heel and left the classroom just as some students started to file in for the next class. His next two classes went by quickly since one of his favorite students had paid attention and had a clue about the answers. Grace was one of the few bright spots in his whole class load. A very bright star, he smiled inwardly at the pun, who would go far in this field. She was well on her way to making something of a spectacle of herself, especially at the old age of nineteen.

It was a major bummer to be eighteen and teaching "young adult women." At least that was how they were described in the faculty handbook. He still wanted to date some of his students. Of course that would get him fired on the spot. Even his three Ph.D.s wouldn't save him, and that was a colossal blunder that he could ill afford to make. A man had to eat, didn't he? His mind wandered for the rest of the day as he graded the quizzes that he had given earlier.

"Oh, this one is good, the weight of an anti-quark is the exact opposite of a quark," he said aloud to the empty classroom.

"And why is that one good, Doctor?"

Lars looked up, startled at the sound of the voice, and saw the dean of the University. Dean Evans was a short man, around five feet, two inches tall (with his platform shoes on). He wore a three-piece suit, complete with red power tie, and gold rimmed oval spectacles on his lined weather beaten face. He always had a faint smile, as if he were enjoying a private joke that no one else was privy to. As always, he was the epitome of a New England Dean.

"Well, Dean Evans," Lars answered, trying to sound respectful, "this student will have a career in comedy because he obviously doesn't have the necessary study and research skills to pass my class. If he did, he would have indicated that he needed to know which kind of anti-quark to which I was referring. I am looking for thinkers, not people who do nothing but memorize the work and assignments and then 'brain dump' everything at the end of the semester. I am looking for people who will further the field of science with genuine thought, not candy covered horse manure!" Regurgitation education was Lars' pet peeve, and he spoke with a little more heat than he intended.

"Well, Dr. Jorgensson, judging by the pass/fail statistics of your classes, I can believe this. In fact, that is the very thing which has precipitated my arrival today."

"Really?" he said, "Is there something wrong with the way I teach? Or is it something more basic and fundamental, like the majority of the kids that come through my class don't have an original thought in their heads? The only thing that they think about is how to get drunk, skip class, and invent new ways to get into the good graces of the opposite sex. Am I the only Professor that sees this?"

"No, Dr. Jorgensson, you are not the only one who sees this. You are, however, one of the few with a highly technical course of study. Yours is the most intense of all our curriculum classes. You might pass fifteen percent of your entire class load. This is unacceptable. We are a University, Dr. Jorgensson, not a research laboratory! You will do either of two things: Either you will either make you curriculum easier, or you will start passing more of your students with D's. Frankly I like option one as it will hopefully ease your reputation as a fail Professor," Dean Evans said a little testily.

"And if I don't choose either of those two options?"

"Then you will find yourself relieved of all academic teaching responsibilities in the coming semester. Do I make myself clear, Doctor?"

"Yes, Dean Evans, you have made yourself crystal clear. I will look at the course curriculum and decide what needs to be cut. I will have a copy for you by the end of the week for your review. Is that acceptable?"

"Perfectly acceptable, Doctor Jorgensson. I am looking forward to your revisions. Hopefully they will allow your students to pass. I am relying on your discretion." He turned on his heel and exited the classroom.

After the door was safely closed Lars muttered to himself, "That ungrateful, unlettered, uneducated, misbegotten excuse for a human being thinks he can push me around?" He finished grading papers and decided to do the course corrections that the Dean had requested. It was fairly easy; he decided to take out almost all of the higher learning that he considered important. If any of his brighter students decided that they wanted to pursue the original course of study, then he would offer more instruction on a private basis. Einstein's theories were very deep work and required a good basis if one was to do any good work in the sciences. Just then there was a knock at the door and in strode Mike Ryan.

"Hey Lars, how's it going?"

"It's going," Lars replied, "Dean Evans was just in here a little while ago and asked me to revise course content and basically gave me an ultimatum. Either I revise my curriculum and make my classes easier or my contract with the university wouldn't be renewed next semester. I mean, the only things that would be open to me then would be the business sector and the research sector. Both of those sectors appeal to me for different reasons, but I really enjoy filling young heads with knowledge and learning. Listen to me, here I am saying 'young heads' and I am not even old enough to drink!"

Mike laughed and said, "Dinner is fine with us and the time is also good. We will see you there. By the way is this place formal, casual or someplace in between?"

"I don't know, I haven't been there before. I have only heard that their bourbon steak is excellent. It was described to me as a cross between Irish and Cajun. It should be interesting. The only problem is that I won't be able to drink and tonight I feel the need to get roaring drunk. I want to get the taste of the Dean's instructions out of my mouth. Just thinking of that mealy mouthed insignificant, miniscule minded imbecile just makes my blood boil!"

"Hah, too right you know! The Dean is nothing more than an educated boor. Well, I must go home and get Lilly into some decent clothes. Are there any plans such as dancing afterwards?"

"Not unless I can find a date in an hour and a half. I don't think that will happen so you might want to count me out on dancing. Don't let that stop you and your beautiful wife from going out. If I show up with a girl on my arm, then most certainly let's go out for dancing."

They turned left to exit the building when suddenly they heard a commotion. Both turned around quickly, and Lars noticed that Mike turned around more quickly and much more gracefully than he had. He wondered what kind of martial arts training that Mike had received, because nobody was that graceful naturally.

They noticed that, farther down the hallway, a group of football players had managed to stuff one of the freshmen into a trashcan. The biggest of them was doing most of the stuffing, and the freshman was fighting a losing battle. In the time it took for Lars to catalog all of the players, Mike had closed the distance between him and the football players and stopped three inches away from the biggest. Mike said to him in the most condescending and frosty tone that Lars had ever heard, "Mr. Armstrong, just what do you think you are doing?"

"I am stuffing a freshman geek into the trashcan. What does it look like I'm doing, and why does it matter to you?"

Lars had quietly walked up, extricated the freshman from the trash can and said to him, "You might want to stay out of Mr. Armstrong's way for a while, if you know what is good for you, son."

Mike had seen what he was doing out of the corner of his eye but his attention never wavered from Mr. Armstrong. "Mr. Armstrong, if I ever see or hear that you have done this kind of bone headed, irresponsible, immature stunt I will cause three things to happen. First I will have you suspended. Second I will have your scholarship revoked, and third I will see to it that you are put on academic probation. The last has the added side benefit of benching you for the rest of the season. Do I make myself clear?" Mike's tone had gotten increasingly colder.

Mr. Armstrong's face had been turning red as Mike was berating him and at the mere mention of being benched he turned an amazing shade of reddish white. His hands and were clenched into fists and he looked like he wanted to kill something, and this teacher had just volunteered to be the punching bag. The other football players, taking their cues from Mr. Armstrong, were looking like they were going to spread out to encircle Mike to prevent him escaping.

"You might want to rethink those actions, boys." Lars pitched his voice as low as it would go and they looked at him in surprise. Not many people took him seriously, perhaps because the usual perception of him was a geek teacher, not as the six foot six, two hundred fifty pound man that he was, nor would they expect him to have had any martial arts training. It was a common mistake, which was usually quickly corrected. It normally came as a surprise to his opponents after they had beaten and were lying in various heaps on the floor.

Mr. Armstrong was oblivious to his companions' dilemma; all he wanted to do was smash this arrogant professor who dared to get in the way of his fun and then to threaten him in front of his friends. Just then two of the campus security guards 'happened' to come over.

"Is there a problem, Doctor Ryan?" the taller of the two asked.

Mike turned his head slightly to answer, but his eyes never left the angry man who stood before him. "No, there isn't a problem. Is there, Mr. Armstrong?"

"No. There will be next time, though, Professor Ryan. Count on it," he said in a sullen tone, then turned on his heel and huffily left the building through the other exit with his cohorts trailing after him like puppies.

The first guard said, "You might want to watch yourself around that one, Doctor Ryan. He's just plain mean and spoiled rotten except when he is with his lady friends. Then he is perfect gentleman jock, no brains and all brawn."

"Thanks, I will," Mike said.

"Well, that was exciting wasn't it?" Lars said as they resumed their short walk to their respective cars. Mike noticed that Lars was driving a Porsche and said, "How in the name of all that is holy can you afford a Porsche? You are just a little whelp of a kid; well you know what I mean. Even our seniors who are getting cars for graduation aren't getting that kind of car. Yet here you are, driving around a fifty thousand dollar car! What model is it?"

"It's a ~911 Cabrio. I had it fully loaded at a really good Porsche dealership in Antwerp and moved the wheel over for American driving, then had it shipped here from Belgium. They had some other cool stuff there, too, but they didn't have what I was looking for. I visited several dealers in Belgium and finally found a topless car. I normally leave the top in the garage on nice days and put it on when there is a threat of rain or anything. I don't want the leather to get ruined. As to how I afforded it, well, I designed a new type of program that would make it easier for a telescope in space to track celestial bodies by using the variable in the weak nuclear force and the effects of electromagnetism. A side benefit was that it also had subroutines in it that would allow it to track Soviet ballistic missile submarines by noting the interference in the earth's magnetic field. Big chunks of metal that move have a tendency to do that. After the patent came through, one of the agencies over in the beltway saw what it was and decided to buy up all of the rights to it. I believe the defense department wanted it, but the space agency got first dibs on it and they were going to sell copies to them. Anyway, they bought it and all of the rights to it for a cool two and half million dollars. Not bad for two months worth of work, is it? I invested most of it in the stock market. The rest went to buy the car and my house. I don't mean to brag, but I am a self-made millionaire before the age of twenty. I only have to work if I want to. There is so much to learn and to teach. I want to do it all."

"Really," Mike said. He really hadn't expected the dissertation, but it didn't surprise him.

"Well, I will see you at the restaurant at 7:00." Lars drove back to his house to take a power nap before he had to get ready for dinner. He got inside and heard a small pop. He turned around and saw the same apparition that had visited him the night before.

"Beware the Greater Evil. He is stronger than anticipated. He has already run into several of your brethren and defeated them with ease. The Holy One has sent me to give you a gift. This Book is called the Liber Vitae or The Book of Life. Use it wisely, my son. This book replaces the other one your friends gave you. Keep it with you at all times, as you might have need of it sooner than you think."

The apparition stopped and cocked his head as if listening to something very far away. Suddenly he looked at Lars and said, "I must go! Another of your brethren has been wiped from the face of the earth and I must investigate. Remember to keep the book near! It must not fall into evil hands!" The last was said in a small voice as the apparition faded from view.

Lars picked up the book and immediately noticed several things. The first was that it was warm; he felt like he was warming his hands in front of a fire. It was not uncomfortable to hold it but noticeably warm in his cool house. The second was that the book had the look and feel of leather, but not the smell of leather. The third was that it was a loose collection of paper that with three leather thongs woven through the book. It had the "feel" of something very old and very new at the same time. He opened the book expecting to see English, but it was printed in some unintelligible language that he couldn't decipher. He knew several languages and this didn't appear to be any of them. He looked at the root words of some of the phrases but they still didn't make any sense. He said in exasperation, "Cool! An ancient spiral notebook! I like it already! Now, how in Hell am I supposed to read this?"

With a puff of smoke and the burning stench of brimstone another apparition appeared and said in a voice that sounded like the cross between fingernails on a blackboard and a train wreck, "Why, you have to learn faith, you dumb jerk!"

This apparition was nothing like the other one. It had the classic devil features out of some nightmare. He had a goat-like lower body that had been attached to a well-muscled man's torso. He carried several bandoleers across his torso that had several holsters and ammunition clips on them. This apparition's face was the most horrendous that Lars had ever had the displeasure to put his eyes upon. His face looked like a normal man's face with one important exception: He had no eyes. The picture was made complete with the addition of small vestigial horns on the top of his head. Lars was stunned and shocked that one of the Evil Ones minions had been called to him!

The apparition spoke and his voice sounded like he was gargling with gravel in his throat. "Of course you can't read it, you jerk. You haven't studied it yet! Only after you have studied can you learn how to read it. You might try sleeping on it tonight. You might be able to understand it then. You know, the osmosis theory!" He started laughing with glee.

Lars decided he didn't have the patience or the time for this. "Why you miserable little excuse for a nightmare. I'm gonna..."

With astonishing speed the man pulled one of the guns from his bandoleer and had trained it unerringly at Lars' head with the safety off. He said, "Your gonna what, mortal? Just because I have no eyes doesn't mean that I can't see you."

"I thought all of you guys carried pitchforks and things like that," Lars said.

"Get real, youngster. I used to carry a pitchfork several hundred of your years ago but that was then and this is the new millennium. We all carry enough guns and ammunition to start a small war. And that is just what is needed in this day and age. Of course it isn't time for that yet, but it will be one day."

"So why are you here? To tempt me?" Lars asked haughtily.

"Hell no! We already know that you are bound to Him. Why bother? Besides, you goody-two-shoes types are too boring to hang around with us! I just have some scuttlebutt to pass along, tattoo boy. This force that has arrived here, both of our bosses very badly underestimated it. It is being backed from outside of this plane by a very powerful force. It is doing its level best to destroy both of our agents in this world. For what purpose we aren't sure but rest assured that both sides have just signed a contract on this jerk and both sides want him removed from this plane. For some reason he has taken particular pleasure in doing in our agents in very messy fashion. He also seems to like sword-work or knife-work. All of our agents that appeared before His Nastiness have been carved up like a Thanksgiving turkey, while all of the agents of His Pureness have just been terminated with a simple beheading. We aren't sure of the significance of that yet."

With a clap of out-rushing air the first apparition appeared and said in a voice of outrage, "What are you doing here? Get thee hence!"

The second apparition just looked at him and said, "You can't make me, featherhead!" He pointed an outstretched hand at Lars. "He summoned me, so only he can make me leave. The Lord Below felt it was important to make sure that this Greater Evil is removed from this plane so that the fight can go on here. A third party just throws a monkey wrench into the works. So relax, we won't do anything to your priest. The Greater Evil, oh to hell with it, Kerrigan is decimating our forces with ease. The Lord Below is not happy. So for the time being the Lord Below has talked to your boss and called for a temporary truce, just until Kerrigan is removed from this plane. After that, well, all bets are off. Besides, the only forces left in a two hundred mile radius are yours, so we are left with the only game in town. Help the other side or allow Kerrigan to get the object he seeks. That option stinks as it will put Kerrigan on par with the Lord Below, and if there is one thing the boss doesn't need, it is competition. Well that's about it, jerky boy. If you need any more information, don't hesitate to ask." With another puff of smoke and smell of burning brimstone the second apparition disappeared.

The first apparition turned to Lars and said, "You have fallen!" He peered at Lars as if he were trying to read his soul and said, "I was mistaken. You have not fallen; you merely lack experience, for now. Remember what your brethren told you in the past, that words have power! Now more than ever you must be careful what you say. Your brother has been eliminated and appeared at the Court of the Most Holy. Just before he was beheaded he was given a rather unusual message. It said 'I will decimate all who stand between me and the prize.' This was very unusual since this individual was systematically destroying both of our agents. Always be on your toes, Lars. You never know when something might appear in a puff of smoke." The apparition slowly faded from view.

"Why do these people always appear when I am in the process of getting ready to go somewhere?" Lars wondered aloud. He still had a couple of hours before he had to go so he decided to sit down and spend a couple of minutes in intense study of his newfound book. Lars bent all of his will and concentration on the book and he could only translate two of the spells. His grandfather clock tolled 6:00 and Lars decided that he really had to get ready for dinner. He decided to dress casually in dress khakis, a button down polo shirt and a black leather trench coat. He also grabbed a backpack from his office and stuffed several items that he was likely to need if the apparition's prediction was true. He stuffed in the Liber Vitae, a couple of notebooks (one can never be prepared enough for writing things down), pens, pencils, a slide rule, a calculator, and a couple of apples, just in case he got hungry after dinner. He hoped the restaurant took plastic; he didn't have cash. He then decided that the practical thing to do would be to hit a teller machine on the way to the restaurant. He rechecked the contents of his backpack, got his keys, and headed for the door.

On the way to the restaurant he turned on the radio and heard the news complaining that the crime rate was rising and that there seemed to be two different mass murderers loose in the city. One of them was just cutting off peoples' heads and then leaving them there and the other one was dismembering and vivisecting his victims. People were being warned to stay indoors at night.

'Wow this guy moves fast,' Lars thought. 'Supposedly he's only been here 24 hours and already he had run up an impressive body count. Since I am the last of my brethren in the city I had better stay very alert.'

He looked out at the traffic and noticed that it had come to a standstill. While this was not unusual in rush hour, it should have been over half an hour ago. He tuned into the AM band and listened for the traffic report, but there didn't seem to be any major delays. As he thought, 'What in the heck is going on here?' he caught a glimpse of something very fast moving by his car. The next thing he noticed was a tearing sound, like metal tearing through metal. He looked up and suddenly there was light in his car. Something had managed to cleanly slice through the top of the car! He looked around and noticed a giant of a man standing out in the middle of the freeway looking right at him.

"Good afternoon, Priest, hope you are prepared to meet your maker." He casually held a sword that looked like it came from the middle ages; the darn thing had to be at least five feet long. Of course, it looked puny on him as he strolled to the car. This giant warrior was dressed in what looked like red leather armor. Lars got out of his car on the passenger side and said, "Hey, you gonna pay for the repairs to my car?"

"What, this infernal machine? Of course not, you pompous ignorant coward of a priest." With that he heaved a mighty stroke with the sword and sliced cleanly through the engine compartment of his car.

'This overgrown refugee from a barbarian movie is going to pay for that,' Lars thought angrily, 'He is going to pay big time.' Lars shrugged out of his leather jacket so it would not hinder his movements. He had to give this guy some room; that pig sticker that he was carrying could easily make short work of him. Lars didn't want to kick his ass too quickly. He wanted to make him pay for the indignity of making him late and killing his car!

"Are you ready to die yet, priest? I hope you put up more of a fight than the rest of your 'brothers'. They were all pantywaists and didn't put up much of a fight. By the way, Kerrigan sends his regards and his regrets that he didn't get to meet you in person. Goodbye."

Lars was expecting something along these lines. His sensei had said that one could see an attack coming by watching the way the opponent's body moved. This mountain sized oaf's body had screamed that he was going attack as soon as he was finished running his mouth. He swung at Lars, and Lars ducked his first swing, trying to place which style he was using and to gauge his reactions and speed. It was always wise to gauge an opponent before committing oneself to an attack. He caught his swing, twisted his wrists and reversed the direction of his swing, forcing Lars to roll to one side to evade the cut.

"Quit moving around, you little priest! Quit trying to prolong the inevitable! I haven't lost a fight in centuries! I am not going to now on this miserable little world!"

"I hope you can fight better than you can make insults, jerk," Lars said.

He lunged at Lars, trying to skewer him on the point of his sword. Lars moved to the side and let it pass harmlessly to his right, then moved in for a stiff arm to the solar plexus. The warrior blocked and redirected the blow to his left and drew back his sword for a lunge. Lars used his right hand to dislocate his opponent's arm at the elbow, knowing the added benefit was a nerve block on the entire arm.

His adversary screamed in agony. "Agghh! You miserable puppy!"

"Youch! That leather is hard," Lars said at the same time. "Guess you won't be throwing any sidearm pitches anytime soon, hey pin head?"

With almost nerveless fingers he switched his sword from the right to the left hand. 'It figures,' Lars thought, 'Jerky boy is ambidextrous. Just my luck.'

"I underestimated you, Priest. I won't make that same mistake again," he said. He kept his sword in low-guard position. Lars noted this, and thought, 'Any fool that has at least thirty minutes of sword play knows that the low-guard position is a sign of weakness. He's begging me to attack. Too bad I don't have a sword.'

Lars started to slowly circle around his opponent in an effort to get the oaf to look at him silhouetted by the setting sun. The giant started making slow and deliberate circles with his weapon and looked like he was in severe pain. Lars knew that the nerve block would be wearing off soon. The only good thing about that was that there would be an immense amount of pain as feeling returned to the lower arm, almost like that tingly feeling when an arm or leg has gone to sleep. All he had to do was look for that telltale sign.

"Enough of this!" bellowed the warrior, "Since you won't come to me, I will come to you! You insufferable little priest, I will take great pleasure in gutting you like the pig that all of your kind are." He swung at Lars' head in an attempt to behead him, while simultaneously using his right arm as a club to knock him off balance.

Lars leaned back and evaded both attacks. After the sword had passed in front of his face, he folded at his waist and used a spinning right heel kick to knock the sword out of his grip and break several of his fingers. He screamed in agony as Lars heard the distinctive crunch of breaking bone as his foot connected.

"Had enough dim-wit? My faith won't allow me to kill you out of hand, but I hope you have a lot of money or something on your person to pay for the repairs to my car!"

The oaf screamed in pain again. "You little coward, I will be back and the next time I will have my due." He started mouthing off in a strange language like none Lars had ever heard. It had liquid sounding consonants and vowels that seemed to flow together. Realizing that the mental midget was using magic to try and get away or to do something just as nasty to his likable person, Lars rushed him and delivered a sitting drop kick right in the mouth. Just as his feet were connecting to the massive head, the warrior seemed to finish his incantation. Lars heard the sickening crunch as his two hundred and fifty pounds snapped the guy's neck like a stack of dimes, but it didn't stop the spell.

He looked up just as giant black rolling thunderheads rolled in fast from the horizon and the smell of ozone thickened. Within seconds of his completion of the incantation, a hurricane-like wind popped up from nowhere and it started to rain cats and dogs, like someone had unzipped the sky.

Lars had a sinking feeling in the pit of his stomach that said he was in trouble. Lightning flickers were racing in the thunderheads and with a great clap of thunder a tremendous bolt of lightning landed less than five feet away from him. Several smaller bolts landed anywhere from twenty to one hundred feet away. It sounded like the greatest of all symphonies were raging and the percussion section was centered on Lars and the corpse. His head was ringing from all of the massed thunderclaps that happened in such close proximity to his suddenly very frail self.

After ten lightning bolts had connected closely to his proximity, it suddenly started to clear up as fast as it had started. The only thing that remained to prove that there had been an intense rainstorm was water all over the ground and several scorch marks from the lightning strokes dotting the area. He looked down at his playmate and saw that by the angle of his head that he was dead. He rifled through his pockets to see if jerky boy had any type of identification on him, but all he found was a small leather pouch that appeared to contain money, his sword, and the body. He pocketed the pouch, picked up the sword, and went over to his car. He slid the sword into the trunk and waited for the state police to arrive.

He looked at his watch and noticed that it was 6:45; he was going to be late for his dinner date with the Ryans.

He pulled out his cellular phone and dialed the number for the restaurant, glad once again for his eidetic memory.

"Hello. O'Bannion's. How may we help you?" the voice on the other end answered.

"Hello, this is Lars Jorgensson. Has a Mr. Ryan arrived yet?"

"No sir, he hasn't arrived yet. Would you like to leave a message for him?"

"Yes, I would. Please tell him that I have been delayed and that I will see him and his wife soon. Ask him not to leave; I will be there shortly. Tell him it's my treat. If he has any questions he has my cell phone number. Thank you."

"Thank you, Mr. Jorgensson. I will see to it personally. We look forward to your arrival." With that the line went dead.

Looking at the wreckage strewn about the highway, Lars noticed a couple of things. First, all of the onlookers who had dared to stay and watch remained in their cars. He didn't really blame them. Second, the lightning show hadn't started any fires. This was a good thing; the last thing this area needed was a wildfire. He turned around and looked at the dead body. He appeared normal, if you dress up as a Halloween reject and attack someone with a five-foot blade of steel, and when you are losing, summon up a lightning storm to obliterate your enemies. "Well, the angelic apparition said that Kerrigan was wasting all of my brothers. Obviously he didn't know that it was one of his henchman that is doing the killing," he said aloud to the dead body.

He called his insurance agent, Marty, and tried to explain to him what had happened. Marty's terse reply was, "Stay right there. This I have to see for myself. I'm in my car right now and heading in your direction. Where exactly are you, anyway?"

"On Route 19 heading into the city. You can't miss me; I'll be the one with all of the state police clustered around. I am going to be late for dinner. After the cops have finished taking my statement, can you give me a lift to O'Bannion's?"

Just then, two state police troopers drove up. They turned on their lights and the first officer got out of his car and started to direct traffic. The second one got out of his car and said, "Hello, Mr...?"

"Jorgensson, Lars Jorgensson."

"What seems to be the problem here, sir? I am hoping that you have an explanation for the body over there and why your car seems to be beside itself."

"Why, yes, officer, I do. You see, I was driving down the road, minding my own business, when out of nowhere, jerky boy over there sliced the roof of my car off. See? It's just sitting there on my trunk, upside down and filled with rain. When I got out and asked him if he was going to pay for the repairs, he said no and chopped it right in half!"

"He chopped it in half, Mr. Jorgensson? With what, a switchblade?"

"Ha ha, very funny, sir! I like law enforcement officials with a sense of humor! No, sir, he had a sword. It's in what's left of my car. I didn't know if you would need it for evidence and I didn't want it ruined in the rain."

"I see. He just cut through your engine block with a sword. Must have been pretty sharp."

"I imagine it was. Luckily I didn't find out first hand. He tried to kill me with it. Fortunately, I've had some martial arts training."

"Any idea why he wanted to kill you?"

Lars paused as if in thought. "No, none that I can think of. He kept calling me a priest, I guess he didn't like my tattoo."

"And are you a priest?"

"Not in the sense you're thinking. I'm not ordained or Catholic or anything. I'm just very devout, that's all."

"So you killed him in self defense?"

"No, actually it was accidental, I'm afraid. I tried to drop kick him in the chest, and he slipped in the rain. I got his chin instead. I'm not being charged with anything, am I?"

"No, Mr. Jorgensson, at least not yet. I just need to get some personal information about you, and please don't leave town for a while. We may have a few more questions."

Lars supplied the officer with his address and phone number and surrendered the sword just as Marty pulled up. "Would you please excuse me, Officer?"

Not waiting to hear the response Lars walked over to Marty and said, "Can I put some stuff in your car, Marty? My car is ruined and I am going to be needing some of my items from my wreck."

"Sure thing, Lars. I have got to hear how this happened. Besides if you think that this is going to be covered under your comprehensive plan, you have another thing coming!"

The officers were starting to question some of the other folks who witnessed the fight. Another squad car pulled up. An officer got out of his cruiser and walked over to the first officer and started to talk to him. Marty looked over at him and his face, which was normally a shade of light brown and gave away his Asian descent, turned slightly gray as the second officer moved towards them. "Don't look now, but your day is about to get worse," Marty said just as the officer met the two of them alongside the road.

"Good afternoon, Mr. Jorgensson. My name is Lieutenant Anderson. I was just wondering how many people you have aggravated enough to wipe you from the face of the earth. According to the patrolman you just spoke to, you were just driving down the highway minding your own business and the man who is now dead just up and attacked you. He cut off the top of your car, sliced open the engine compartment, and then had a fight with you, which he lost, since his body is now cooling over there on the grass." Just then there was another wail of a siren as an ambulance pulled up and went over to the body on the ground.

"Good afternoon, Sergeant Anderson." Lars hated overgrown puffed up supercilious idiots who thought that they were the law. Didn't they know? HE *was* the law and he was the one who enforced it, not these *people* who thought that they did. "Yes, that's right. That refugee from a Halloween carnival just up and attacked me. He kept calling me priest; maybe he didn't like my tattoo, I don't know. Well anyway, he just up and attacked my car, tried to kill me with that five-foot long steak knife and all I did was defend myself with my martial arts training. I was going to drop kick him in the chest when he slipped on the grass and my feet connected with his chin and snapped his neck like a dry stick. The lightning and stuff was weird but then it isn't unusual this time of year given the right conditions now is it, Officer? Are you going to charge me with anything, because if you are then this line of questioning is over unless my attorney is present. And just for your information, Corporal, the name is Doctor Lars Jorgensson. Do please make a note of it. If you have no other questions and since my car is a mess, I would like to make arrangements to get into town. I have a dinner date with some of my other colleagues. If you will excuse me?"

****

Lars walked into O'Bannion's exactly one hour and forty minutes late. He spotted Lilly at a corner table and walked past the hostess to join them.

"Lars, what a surprise," said Lilly. "I didn't expect to see you tonight."

Lars took a seat. "You look lovely tonight as always, Lilly. Didn't your husband tell you I'd be here?"

"Yes, he did," answered Lilly as she picked up her wine glass. "I'd just given up hope."

Mike chuckled. "Is everything all right, Lars?"

"No," said Lars sadly. "My car is dead."

"Dead? Define 'dead'."

"It's dead. No hope of resurrection or repair. Some freak accosted me on the highway and killed it with a five-foot sword."

"Well! The nerve!" exclaimed Lilly. She leaned closer to Mike and said quietly, "Sounds as if I'm not the only one who's had a nip of something tonight."

Lars snorted in mock indignation. "Don't I wish! Don't worry; I'm sure it will be on the news at some point or another. I think it has something to do with what I wanted to talk to you two about."

Mike leaned forward. "And that would be what?"

"Well, I've been getting some really weird vibes lately, and I've had three visitations in two days."

"Visitations?" asked Lilly. "Like religious fanatics wanting to talk to you about God?"

"NO! They don't come around anymore since I told them more than they wanted to know! Like messengers, from Him," answered Lars, pointing toward the ceiling. "The one yesterday said that there would be two evils fighting for a prize. If the lesser evil one won, everything would be copasetic. If the greater evil won, all hell would break loose here and in some other world, too. Given the fact that we've worked together on, umm, *interesting* things before, I thought maybe between us we could figure out what is going on."

Mike leaned back as the waitress approached to take their orders. After she left he said, "I'm not sure I like the sound of this. Why do I smell Nyakas?"

"Because you're paranoid," said Lars. "I'm not even sure he's involved in it. It seems that the greater evil is some bad dude named Kerrigan."

Lilly looked blankly at Lars. "The name's not ringing a bell. What else do you know?"

"Well, I know that his friends have been killing my brethren, but they've also been killing bad guys too. You know those murders that are all over the news? I think it's them. Based on what I've been told, it fits. My brethren are just beheaded; the bad guys are, well, mangled. I won't go into detail since we're about to eat. The last of my kind who was murdered showed up in the High Court with a message, something about he will decimate all who stand between him and the prize. Apparently, my new mission in life is to protect the prize from Kerrigan. Trouble is, I don't know for sure what the prize is or who the lesser evil is."

"Sounds like an odd puzzle, Lars," said Mike. "Why would they tell you to protect something and not tell you what it is?"

The waitress came back with their drinks. After she walked away, Lars answered, "I have no idea. The only thing I know for sure is that Kerrigan's henchmen are after me, and one of them killed my car. I do, however, have a theory. Have I told you that Robyn Smith was in one of my classes last term?"

Mike's chin hit the table. "Robyn Smith? Impossible! She's in the realm of Nyakas."

"That's what I thought, too, but it's her. I've had the opportunity to talk to her. Seems she's a junior here at the university. Her parents are Kevin and Gina Smith, and they live in upstate New York. Sound familiar?"

Mike closed his mouth and nodded numbly. "How?"

"Well, I was curious, so I did a little traveling and snooping over the Christmas break. Robyn was banished from the Realm of Nyakas. Her father-in-law used some sort of spell to have her transported to her own alternate timeline, and apparently her memories of Nyakas were banished as well."

"Are you sure she was banished?" asked Lilly. "It could have been an escape attempt that didn't go quite right. After working that mission with her, that wouldn't surprise me in the least."

"I'm sure," said Lars. "From what I gathered, at least from eavesdropping on conversations, she was happy there. It was Nyakas' father who was unhappy with the arrangement. Besides, if she'd just escaped, she'd be in her 30's by now. I checked her records; she's 19. That fits with my research on the time space continuum."

"So what's the theory?"

"First the facts, at least as we know them. One, Robyn was happy with Nyakas. Two, she was banished. Three, she's living here. Four, she is younger now than she was when she went on the mission. Five, she appears to have no memory of her former life. Six, Kerrigan and some other bozo are looking for a prize, and Kerrigan is the greater evil. Seven, the clown who killed my car looked like he'd stepped out of a Mummers Parade. Now the theory. The lesser evil is, as Mike suggested, Nyakas, and the prize is Robyn."

Lilly traced the edge of her wine glass with the tip of her index finger. "Not bad, but what would Kerrigan want with Robyn?"

"Don't know," answered Lars. "It's the only logical explanation I can come up with."

"I think it's reasonable," said Mike, "but I think that I'd feel a lot better if I had some confirmation. I hate working with theory rather than concrete fact."

Their food arrived and they changed the subject while they ate, each pondering the situation in their own way. After coffee and dessert, Mike and Lilly offered Lars a ride home. During the drive, Lars said, "I found two things on jerky boy. One was a sword and the other was a leather pouch. I assumed it had money in it, but I didn't check."

Lars reached into a pocket of his leather coat, pulled out the pouch, and spilled the contents into his hand. Several coins that appeared to be gold spilled out, along with a small fortune in gems. Lars picked out several diamonds, rubies and emeralds. The smallest was the size of his little fingernail and the largest was the size of his thumb. He estimated that he held a quarter of a trillion dollars in his hands. He had hardly expected a ruffian in leather armor to be carrying around a pouch with several jewels as casually as Lars would carry a wallet.

"Hey, Mike! Pull over for a minute! You have to see this!"

"The middle of the highway is not exactly a point where one can stop. Give me a minute and we will see what you have."

Lilly turned around and said, "Let's see what you've got, Lars."

Lars raised his hand. Lilly turned on the vanity light and peered at the fortune in Lars' hand. "Wow, that was one bloody rich guy to be carrying around that much in jewels. I see several the size of the crown jewels of Britain! What else did that bloke have? Did he happen to have an ingot of gold stuffed up his arse for me to have?"

"I didn't examine the body that closely, Lilly. The only other thing he had was his sword. I'd show it to you, but the police thought it was evidence. Mike, are you ever going to turn off the road?"

"It will only be a couple of minutes. There is a church that isn't too far away from here. After all that I have heard and experienced over the last several years, I suddenly feel that I must unburden myself to a priest. Hopefully we can get in to see him before Kerrigan sends any of his troops our way. Of course, we will be on holy ground."

Lars pouted in the back seat. "What does that make me, chopped liver? I'm a priest!"

"No, Lars, I mean an ordained priest. The kind who wears a clerical collar, not a tattoo."

"So I'm not ordained by the Church! That doesn't make me any less a priest."

"Except for the fact that an ordained priest can't be made by law to tell anyone what I tell him."

"Well, at least I've known you long enough to actually believe your silly stories."

"Look at it this way, Lars," added Lilly cheerily. "Maybe while we're in church we'll have a visitation!"

Lars snorted. "You don't have to be in church to have a visitation! If you want a visitation, come to my house!"

Mike continued to drive at what, for him, was sedate pace onto First Street and parked in front of the church. As they got out there was a shifting of the light coming from the street lamps and an unnatural purplish light appeared in front of them. Kerrigan stepped out from the vortex, dressed in red leather and carrying a sword across his back, and said, "Greetings and goodbye, Lars. You will not get a chance to be a thorn in my side." He waved his hand and there was a reddish flash from it. It struck the pavement; the concrete curdled and started to boil.

"Hah! You missed, ugly!" Lars said.

"Have I? Just wait, he'll be here to squash you like the bug you are. Just so you know, I personally ordered the destruction of your pathetic order. I was personally responsible for destroying those who, like me, serve a darker purpose. I know that they at least put a better fight than your order did."

"We do fine when we are out numbered, but one on one we are a little rusty. I, however, do not suffer from this handicap. Come on over and let's dance, you insignificant coward! Let's see if you can do the dirty work that you send other men to do for you! Do you always hide behind your hired underlings' skirts? Oh, I am truly sorry, you are dressed in red, and perhaps your armor should have been painted yellow to match the stripe running down your back. Oh and by the way, one of your little flunkies has already met his match. I must presume that you are Kerrigan?"

Just then a loud roaring filled the square of concrete as a shape rose up out of the ground. It rose for a minute or so and when it stopped expanding it was the height of a very large man. It had a humanoid shape, in that it had a head, two arms, two legs, and a main torso, but that was where all resemblance to human stopped. It looked like it had come from the center of the earth and picked up bits and pieces from the surrounding rock as it rose. This creature appeared to be radiating heat and a sort of elemental fury that couldn't be denied. It looked like something out of a B-rated monster movie, like maybe Magma man, with bits of molten rock jutting out at strange places. It looked unerringly at Lars and moaned. Lars felt an unknown source try to grip him in something but it slid right past him like skates on an ice pond.

"Be gone, vile beast of the netherworld!" Lars shouted at it and raised his holy cross that Saul had given him. This didn't seem to have any effect on the monster; however, it did make Kerrigan flinch.

Lars saw that Mike was advancing with a sword in his hand. 'Wait a minute,' Lars thought, 'Where did he get a sword?' Lars hadn't heard a trunk opening or any other sound except for his words and this thing appearing. Mike wasn't even wearing a trench coat where he could have hidden a sword that darn long. It looked like a katana, the Japanese long sword.

Mike had undergone some sort of transformation. It looked like he had some new kind of focus to him. He was concentrating on Kerrigan.

Lars said, "Lord, if you have anointed me, I need some help now." No sooner were the words out of his mouth than a pencil thin ray of light speared down from the heavens. It struck Lars on the head and the accumulated knowledge of every master swordsman of the ancient world was given to him. A sword had appeared along with the light and was buried to the hilt in the pavement; Lars had been too stunned with his newfound knowledge to grab it when it appeared.

He looked over at Kerrigan and saw that he also was speared in a ray of light and a voice from above said, "You also will stay. The odds are now even and my instrument will fight you here and now. If they win you will be banished for a brief time and you will not be able to interfere here in this dimension. And just to make sure that you won't be able to leave prematurely, another will be here to make sure that the fight will stay fair. Are we agreed, Mistoph?"

With another puff of smoke and brimstone the demon that had talked to Lars earlier appeared and said to Kerrigan, "Hey pretty boy, looks like the odds are now turned, huh? According to my master you will be detained until the fight is over. By the way, do you have your life insurance paid up? We are hoping that Mike will cut you up into little pieces so we can mail them back from whence you came."

Kerrigan looked over at Mike and Lars and shot them a look of pure evil, and said, "I have razed entire armies and have all that I need right here. I am not afraid of priest or your lackey. He will go the way of the wild kazmodro of my world. I have forgotten more swordplay than your underling could personally learn in his short life. My 'friend' will make short work of you, priest, almost as fast as I cut down your subordinate." With that he reached behind his shoulder and slid a sword that looked remarkably like Mike's, except that it was longer and looked razor sharp on both sides.

During this time Mike had been rapidly closing the distance between him and Kerrigan and without a second's hesitation launched a blindingly fast head cut at Kerrigan. Kerrigan managed to get his sword up in the nick of time. Kerrigan looked at Mike and sneered, "Is that the best that you can do?"

Mike looked at him and said, "Of course not! You didn't think that I would let you get away without having a little bit of sport, did you? You might have learned more of the sword than I have in your so-called life, but I wouldn't count on it. I have been trained by the best from sixteen different worlds. So do you have any more people to call in before I play with you some? One on one isn't exactly fair. Hey, Mistoph!" Mike called over to the demon that was waiting with an evil grin on his ugly face. "Do you think that your master and the Almighty would let putz-boy here have some more playmates? He has gone to such trouble to make your ranks on both sides thinner. Don't you think that we should thin his some?"

Mistoph looked over at Kerrigan, grinned hideously with glee, and said, "Hold on a sec, I'll check."

Kerrigan wasted no time and launched a series of head- and straight-arm cuts meant to wound and possibly kill Mike. Mike parried all of these cuts with ease, and he laughed contemptuously at Kerrigan and threw Kerrigan's words back at him. "Is that the best you can do?"

Lars didn't have any time for the drama unfolding just fifty feet away. His focus was on the molten magma man in front of him. "Man, this thing sure is ugly. I hate ugly. I wonder if this would do any great harm to him?" He said a series of words, which he had learned from the Libre Vitae. A small thundercloud was rapidly growing over the thing's head and was spreading out to encompass the entire street, shading it in the half-light normally associated with thunderstorms. The lighting on the street started to dim and he saw miniature lightning flashes in the thunderhead.

The magma man looked at Lars and reached up his hand like he was getting ready to throw something. As his arm reached the point where someone would throw a ball, the end of his hand came off and flew right at Lars.

Lars dropped to the ground, rolled out of the way, and just barely managed to evade the magma ball that had been thrown at him. His leather trench coat wasn't so lucky. It scorched and started to burn from the intense heat that passed within millimeters of it. Small pieces of magma had trailed behind the ball and landed on his coat. He rolled again to crush the embers and quickly kicked up to his feet, expecting to see another of those balls being winged at him. He stopped and looked on in amazement and horror; the original magma thingy had shrunk a little bit and at the edge of his peripheral vision he saw another fire start and another one of the magma creatures getting to its feet.

"Oh great!" Lars exclaimed, "NOW there are two of them! How come the Evil One's play toys have such great abilities?"

"That is because I rely on quality rather than quantity Lars, remember?" A voice inside Lars' head said. "To you will be given much, but also much is expected. Always remember that I will be with you. Use all that you have been taught and you will triumph." The voice cut off and from the thin air the same voice said, "Mistoph, your master and I have agreed. Kerrigan will be able to call in more of his minions. If they break off from their fight you and yours will be able to do with them as you see fit. This fight will stay in this street so that no other of our sons and daughters need get involved. The only observers to this conflict will be Lilly, Mistoph and my envoy." With those words reverberating in the air, another figure began to coalesce from the muted street lamps. Another of the angels who had visited Lars manifested and walked over to Mistoph and silently began to watch.

Mike looked over at Kerrigan and said, "Gonna call up some more of your 'army of evil,' jerk? You've got clearance from both sides to call for back up. I will just step over here and let you have a couple of moments to do so. You also might want to change your breeches; I can smell your stink over here. You reek of fear. Remember all of the people that you have massacred over the years. I want you to feel all of their pain, before I cut you up into nice bite sized chunks that I can feed to the fish in my lake!"

The thunderstorm that Lars had summoned had been building and was now ready to rain. With a look at the magma man and a shout to the heavens Lars said, "Let there be rain!" With a mighty thunderclap and stroke of lightning that split the magma man thingy in two, it started to rain. The raindrops started to sizzle, slowly at first then with a sound like the buzzing of a large swarm of bees as the water came down in a torrent. With a shriek of agony which sounded like a steam whistle, the thing started to dissolve and melt. Lars turned his attention just in time to notice that the other magma creature had come up closer than he had realized and took a slow swing at Lars. Lars interposed his sword and cleanly sliced its arm with minimal resistance as it cut through a harder exterior shell.

"Great," thought Lars. "This thing learns from its mother's mistakes! I won't be able to dissolve this one as I did the other one." Lars backed off and looked at the second one and realized that the arm he had sliced off had started to bubble and was burning the pavement; it looked like another one was trying to form! Lars backed off another ten feet. The heat that was emanating from these things was like a blast furnace. He looked at his sword and saw that the top third had been melted off when it had contacted the creature. "Great, not only do I get to fight something that continually makes more of itself, and learns how to defeat my attacks, it also melts the only weapon that I have!"

Lars glanced quickly around at his surroundings and noticed the church, complete with archaic trappings such as gargoyles, stained glass, flying arches and buttresses. It would have been quite pretty if the circumstances weren't so dire. In the stained glass window, a warrior who stood poised for battle with his sword resting point first on the ground and was dressed in plate mail and a shield looked down on him. In contrast, a wicked looking gargoyle, complete with wings, a wicked looking smile and a face that would have done a twisted Renaissance period master proud, also looked down on him with a sneer on its face. Lars thought, "Maybe that spell could be used on those two objects. I could use the reinforcements and neither of those two things are affected by the heat!"

He looked over at the magma man, which had begun to moan in a very minor key. This moan started out slowly and was building into a crescendo. Lars recited some more words that he learned from the text of the book that he was given. He shouted these words up into the very heavens and pointed at the stained glass warrior and the gargoyle, finished off the incantation and pointed at the magma things. He had to struggle to be heard; the magma man's moan became deafening and every window on the street was blown outwards in an explosion of sympathetic harmony. The stained glass warrior was unaffected by the scream. He looked down on the scene and replied, "Master, what you have commanded so shall I obey. Your enemies are my enemies." With that he leaped down and landed on the pavement with the sound of ringing glass between Lars and the first magma man. The gargoyle was starting to move. It looked unerringly at Lars and asked, "Master, who do you want me to kill?"

"Destroy the molten pile of rocks over there." Lars pointed at the second rock man. The gargoyle leaped off of the cathedral and landed right in front of the second creature. The magma men were continuing to advance and paid no attention to the two warriors that now stood between them and their prey. The glass warrior raised his sword and advanced on the first one. The gargoyle was more direct; it jumped and landed on the first magma man, squishing him like a grape. There were pieces everywhere, and each of them in turn started to make another duplicate of itself. The gargoyle looked over at Lars and said, "My job is done. Release me, Master."

Lars looked over at the gargoyle and pointed at the creatures that were now about two feet high and growing very fast and said, "After you have vanquished my foe, then and only then will I release you."

The first warrior seemed to be doing much better and was holding off all of the attacks of the magma man that had finally taken notice of him. The magma man wasn't losing any bits of himself, but it wasn't doing any damage to the warrior either.

Lars surveyed the fight and thought very fast. "How can I destroy these things without making them divide into many, many more of these monstrosities? How do you smother a fire very quickly but not with water?"

Lars looked at the battlefield. His warriors now faced fifteen magma men. He began to chant in Latin, slowly at first but with gathering volume and tempo. An inrushing of air started to scream with increasing speed and violence. Lars changed the chant ever so slightly and the scream stopped with knife-edge suddenness. Lars continued his chant and noticed that the magma men were starting to move slower and slower. His warriors were unaffected and continued the fight. His gargoyle was starting to look charred around the wings, hands and feet. His glass warrior had his lost his shield sometime while Lars was thinking and chanting.

"See if you can survive in a vacuum you burning pile of rock!" Lars yelled at the magma men. The magma men were starting to dim but were still going strong. Lars yelled to his two warriors, "Beat them into smaller pieces! Make them divide!"

His warriors heard his voice and waded into the fight. As the magma men tried to reform, the golems pounded them into smaller and smaller pieces. The vacuum was drawing away all of their heat and the oxygen that fed them.

The last two magma men tried to make one large body; but the two golems got there just as they merged. The gargoyle leaped up into the magma man's chest and with both hands ripped his head off its shoulders. Simultaneously, the glass warrior used its sword in a great horizontal stroke that cleaved it in half at the waist. With a scream that was audible even in the vacuum, the big magma man burst apart in thousands of small fragments.

The two golems turned, looked at Lars and walked through the barrier. They said together, "Master, your enemies have been vanquished, we wish to rest. Release us."

Lars looked at his warriors and said, "You have fought well and valiantly. You have my thanks and the thanks of the Most Holy One. I release you to go back to your own time and place."

As Lars' voice was starting to fade a twinkling sound began and rapidly built to a crescendo. The light that was in the glass warrior's eyes faded and it seemed to implode. The gargoyle crumbled into a small pile of rock at Lars feet.

As Lars took care of the magma creatures, Mike waited for Kerrigan to summon more warriors. Kerrigan started to chant a spell in a language that Mike did not know. The spell started to form and then fizzled with a loud disastrous pop and some fireworks.

Mistoph looked over at Kerrigan and said, "That won't work, dumb ass. You can only bring people in; you can't go anywhere! Care to try again? I see that Mike is getting a little antsy and might decide to start cutting you up into worm food before too very long, so you might want to get a move on if you're calling up reinforcements!"

Mike pushed off from the building that he had been lounging against for the last several minutes while Kerrigan had been casting his spell. "C'mon, the high and mighty Kerrigan is so scared of me that he decided to run off and doesn't want to play?" Mike drawled in a voice dripping with contempt and scorn.

Kerrigan looked up just as he was completing his incantation and a strange light came into his eyes. The look of hunger was in his eyes. Another purplish vortex of light started to coalesce and people started to come out of it. "You wanted some play things, fool? Well, here are the best of my army that I could easily call in. Hope you have fun with them. I will enjoy watching them breaking you into many, many, tiny pieces," Kerrigan said.

Six warriors rushed him from the vortex and the first launched a thrust designed to pierce his heart. Mike easily slid to the left of the thrust and with a backhanded cut casually cut off his head. He continued his sideways movement, reversed his cut, and parried another cut that was aimed at his head. The other five warriors circled him warily. They had seen what he had done to the first warrior and were none too eager to meet a man who made that look easy.

Mike rushed one of the five remaining warriors and swerved to the right at the last second. He dropped to the ground and made a fast sliding cut at his opponent's knees and removed his left leg at the knee. The man went down screaming and the other four warriors saw their opening. They started to move toward Mike when they saw their opening vanish before their eyes. With the speed of an adder, Mike rolled back to his feet and looked at them with his sword held easily in one hand.

The four warriors looked at one another and with an attack that bespoke years of harsh intense training started to advance on Mike with their swords moving in complex patterns of steel. These men spread out in a diamond around Mike trying to get him boxed in amongst them. Mike was having none of it as he moved to meet the spearhead of the diamond and feinted with a straight cut to the arm. The man moved to parry it and Mike moved his cut up and casually sliced his head from his shoulders. He continued the cut and brought it down behind his back to intercept the cut from the man on the right who had tried to cut off his head from behind while he was occupied with the man in front. With a loud clang of metal on metal the two swords met behind Mike's back, Mike flexed his arms and his opponent's sword was shoved back. Mike spun around and said to him, "Now that wasn't very nice, was it? I really don't like to play with people who don't play fair."

The three remaining warriors looked at Mike and advanced in a 'V' formation with the open side pointed at Mike. The two warriors who made up the wings seemed to be more proficient with their weapons as they interlocked the cuts to provide the most amount of protection for them and to do the most amount of damage to their opponent. They wove a complex dance of death that Mike walked into, confident in his ability. Mike parried the first three cuts that were aimed at his head, gut, and groin and made a lightning fast stop-thrust that punched a hole through his enemy's breastplate. At the same time he reached out with his left hand and casually grabbed his other enemy's sword hand. He pulled out his sword and pivoted on his left foot and turned his back to his enemy's arm, which it put the last man in a difficult position, as he couldn't directly attack Mike without putting the other guy at risk.

With a shove in the back of his playmate hard enough to make him stumble, Mike asked the two men, "Have you guys had enough? Three of your comrades are dead; one might as well be dead from blood loss. Are you people so eager to die?"

The two remaining men looked at each other with fear their eyes. Kerrigan was looking on and yelled out to them, "Either go down fighting or I will kill you myself!"

At that moment he heard a great inrushing of air. Kerrigan turned to look for the source of the sound and saw Lars' warriors beating his magma man down. Kerrigan screamed towards Lars, "You insignificant puppy of a priest. Nobody has ever beaten my magma man!"

The two remaining warriors looked over at Mike with despair on their faces, and charged him. Mike saw that the left one was slightly faster and moved to meet him. As the three men met in a clash of steel, Kerrigan's warriors mumbled, "Lord, we are sinners and we repent of our sins."

Mike moved toward the left. The warrior wasn't making any effort to protect himself. Mike cleanly removed his head from his shoulders. The one on the right slid to a halt, dropped to his knees and said, "Strike cleanly, milord, and do it fast before Kerrigan kills me."

With a look of compassion on his face Mike calmly drew back his sword and punched it right through the warrior's breastplate and out his back. With blood spurting out of his lips, he said with the remaining breath he had, "May the Most High have mercy on my soul and may you vanquish Kerrigan. Thank you, milord." The light went out of his eyes and he slid backward off of Mike's sword.

Mike looked over at Kerrigan and said, "Were those the best warriors you have, Kerrigan? You miserable excuse for a warlord! Without an army at your back you are nothing but a bully whose time to die has come." Before he could do anything more, Kerrigan disappeared.

The shields that surrounded Lilly, Mistoph, and the angel disappeared. The envoy vanished with a wide grin, and Mistoph kicked a rock dejectedly.

"I know it's for the best," he said grumpily, "but I hate it when the good guys win!" He kicked another rock and then disappeared.

There were sirens blaring mere blocks away and getting closer. They got into the car quickly, and Lilly slid behind the wheel. She started the car and shifted into gear, pealing out of the church parking lot before Lars even had his door shut. She turned onto several side streets, putting as much distance between them and the church as quickly as possible. She drove through the nearest suburb to the interstate and then to Lars' house. When they arrived, Lars took out the bag of jewels and showed Mike the contents. As they studied them, the envoy that had witnessed the event appeared.

"Greetings, oh victorious ones!" He exclaimed with a wide grin. "The Most High is pleased with your performance. We have taken the liberty of removing your presence from the scene. No one will know you were there, and the earthly authorities will be most disturbed! You will have a period of time to plan for upcoming contingencies and rest. Use the time wisely. Lars, your speculation is correct. Be on guard and watch the prize." He shimmered and disappeared.

Lars turned to look at Mike and Lilly. "See? I told you! If you want a visitation, come to my house!"

Chapter 35

Kerrigan stood on the battlements, watching the trees burn and listening to the screams of the children in chains. It was music to his ears, yet he was still not content. He'd gone to great lengths to find Robyn since Malitor's spell had jerked him back from Hell. Not that he minded slaughtering villages in the process; he rather enjoyed that. But as much as he delighted in torturing peasants and extracting their lives from their pathetic bodies, his prize eluded him. Malitor was impatient for him to find his daughter-in-law and finish her off once and for all, and he was having a difficult time coming up with excuses that would appease him.

Latos approached from the behind him. He was a short half bald man with putrid burn marks upon his face, wearing clothes that only partially covered his body. He looked a 2,000-year-old corpse with a heartbeat. His arms dangled from his thin, malnourished body and ended with hands that looked as if a rabid dog had ripped off a few of the fingers. His torso was thin with ribs protruding outward as though ready to break through the flesh. Frail legs bowed inward and seemed ready to break at any time. His voice was raspy. "Lord, the peasants have been questioned and the men seem to be satisfied. The girl you seek was not found. What should we do?"

Kerrigan smiled. "Burn it." He returned his attention to carnage and destruction he had caused. 'Soon, my child, we'll be together.'

A few minutes later, Latos hobbled to Kerrigan's side. "The fire has been started," he said with great excitement in his dead eyes.

"Good, very good. Gather the others and tell them to meet me on earth."

"Earth, my lord?"

"Yes, tell them to meet me in Madrid, Spain."

"Lord, can you be sure the child is there?"

"Oh, she's there," he paused and looked around. "Yes, Latos, go, ride, gather the others."

He heard Latos hobble away and a moment later there was a familiar voice from behind him.

"Kerrigan, have you tracked them down yet?"

He turned and bowed slightly. "Lord Malitor, how good of you to join me. Of course, my lord, I travel soon to collect the prize."

Malitor moved closer to Kerrigan. "I'm very glad to hear that. And what of Nyakas and Gravity?"

"They are no concern to us. I believe they have traveled to the realm where the girl lives."

"And why are they there and you are not?" Lord Malitor sounded irritated.

"Don't worry, my lord, my men are on their way. Nyakas and Gravity wouldn't have the first idea how to move around on that plane, they'll be lost. Have no worries, my lord, I'll take of the problem."

"Be sure you do, and don't underestimate their abilities or the girl. She might not know what her part is, but it won't take long for her to find out, especially if they get to her before you do. Be sure you don't fail me."

Chapter 36

Gina sat on the deck with her coffee mug cradled in her hands and watched the sun rise. Kevin and Robyn were still sleeping, and unable to sleep, she decided to get up. 'Robyn leaves again tomorrow,' she mused, 'I thought this was supposed to get easier, but every year before she goes off to school I sit on the deck and watch the sun rise because I can't sleep. My baby is a senior in college already! It seems like just yesterday she learned to walk. I wonder if I'll miss her tomorrow night just as much as I did last year.'

She heard the screen door open and light footsteps behind her. She smelled fresh coffee and didn't have to turn to know it was Robyn, who came to sit beside her on the swing.

"Couldn't sleep again this year, Mom?"

Gina smiled. She knew Robyn better than anyone. Unfortunately, Robyn knew her almost as well. "Nope, I'm four for four. Have you got your stuff packed? You won't have time to do much today."

"Yeah, it's done except the essentials." Robyn put her head on her mother's shoulder. "Why do you do this, Mom? I'm a grown-up now. You can stop worrying."

"It's not that easy, dear. In my head I know you're 21. I've baked you 21 birthday cakes, bought you at least a hundred and fifty birthday presents, watched you go to the prom, graduate from high school, and move on to college. Unfortunately, in my heart, you're still a baby. I hate it for you, honey, but you always will be, so you might as well face the fact that I'm not going to stop worrying."

"Did Grandma worry about you when you went into the Army?"

Gina laughed. "Are you kidding? She was hysterical! She and your Grandpa drove me to the bus station and she cried all the way there and all the way home! I know how you feel, Robyn, because I felt the same way. She worried about me until the day she died, and for all I know, she's still worrying in Heaven and still driving your Grandpa crazy doing it!"

"Tell me again about when you told her about Dad." Robyn loved this story. More importantly, it always made her mother laugh, and Robyn knew it would get her mind off tomorrow, even if it was just for a minute.

"When I met your Dad we were both stationed at Fort Hood, and I knew right away that he was the guy for me, but I didn't let him know I knew. I let him chase me until I finally caught him six months later. When I called home to tell my parents I was getting married, my Dad was in Oklahoma City on business, and I knew right then that I should wait until he got back to say anything. But Mama knew something was up, she could hear it in my voice all the way from Oklahoma. So I told her, and at first I thought she was happy. Then the questions started. 'What does he do? Where is he from? Does he want children? Is he going to stay in the Army? How will he support my grandbabies if he doesn't have a job? You don't know he can get a job if he gets out of the Army! He's a soldier, for Heaven's sake! What's he going to do outside the Army? How are you going to support my grandbabies if he stays in the Army and has to go to war?' The more I tried to explain, the more hysterical she got. So finally I told her that she didn't have to like it, I was going to marry him and that was that! Then it got really quiet, and I knew I'd messed up, and she said, in her calmest voice, 'Gina Marie, don't you ever speak to your mother like that again!' And she hung up the phone. Well, by that time I was madder than a wet hen and crying and your Dad was sitting there trying to get me to calm down when the phone rang. Turns out she'd hung up on me and called my Daddy in Oklahoma City! He said to me, 'Gina, I hope you know what you're doing, girl. I hope this man of yours is worth it because your Mama's riled up good. Don't you be rushing into anything, now. You got plenty of time. And don't you think about eloping or your Mama will never forgive you. You get yourself back here to Tulsa and have a church wedding and then she'll accept it.' So that's what we did. We went to Tulsa, and we weren't there a day before Mama thought your Dad was the best thing since sliced bread. The three of us went into town a couple days before the wedding, and she was introducing him to everyone she knew as her son-to-be. So you see, my dear, the worrying starts from the minute you find out you're pregnant, and it doesn't ever stop."

"She's right about that one, kid." Kevin had been listening at the door and waited until the right time to come out. As usual he was wearing the robe Robyn had given him for Father's Day two years ago, had his long sandy brown hair pulled back in a ponytail, and was drinking a Pepsi. He hated coffee. He fit his large frame into a rocking chair and watched as the sun came over the horizon. "The worrying never stops, even though we both wish it would. Trust me, it bugs me almost as much as it bugs you! We have a busy day ahead, Squirt, but if we get moving soon we can get a good workout in before class. I'll try to cut you loose early and you can go shopping with your Mom before dinner."

"OK, Dad." Robyn got up and went in the house to get dressed. As she went up the stairs, she reflected on her father's life. After he'd finished his four years in the Army, he enrolled in a wrestling school in upstate New York. Gina had completed her enlistment and joined him shortly after the professionals had discovered him.

By the time Robyn was born, he was well known as "Brick Barabas." Her earliest memories were of playing with gentle giants in hotels and locker rooms while her father wrestled with his friends, whom he publicly hated. When she was old enough to notice this, she asked her mother about it, and Gina explained to her three-year-old daughter that Daddy didn't really hate them, it was just pretend. From that day on, when Gina and Robyn went to wrestling events, Robyn followed her father's lead. If he 'pretended' not to like someone, so did she. As a result, Robyn soon had a reputation with the fans as a precocious Daddy's Girl.

One day when Robyn was ten she got up for school and found her mother packing her suitcase. Dad was on the road, and Robyn asked her mother if they were going to be with him for a while. Gina looked at Robyn and began to cry. She told Robyn that her Dad had been hurt the night before and was in the hospital. His opponent had miscalculated a jump and accidentally broken his back. They got on a plane that morning, and a week later they came home without him. It was another two weeks before he came home in a wheelchair and began his rehabilitation at a nearby hospital. A few months later, the doctors told him that he should consider a career change; another break like that could well paralyze him for life. So he decided to do the next best thing and opened a wrestling school. It had a slow start, but his wrestling buddies sent people who they thought had potential and business slowly picked up. Within a few years he had a handful of additional trainers and the school was a booming success. He taught Robyn everything she wanted to learn and during her summer breaks she helped train. There were more and more women coming to his school, and not very many women to train them.

Today was her last day of work at her father's wrestling school and she tried not to think about it. Soon she was back downstairs refilling her coffee cup and trying to hear through the open window what her parents were talking about. They weren't talking at all. Dad had moved to share the swing with Mom, and he had his arm around her. Robyn knew it was hard on them to let her go. It was hard for her to go, but she couldn't make her own way in the world if she stayed and worked for Dad the rest of her life. She grabbed a tray from the cupboard over the refrigerator and put her cup on it, along with the coffee pot and a cold Pepsi. She took the tray outside, gave the Pepsi to her father, refilled her mother's cup, and sat down with her own cup in the rocking chair her father had abandoned. The three of them sat quietly until Gina announced that she was starving and suggested that they have breakfast before they ran off to the gym. An hour later, Robyn was in the car with her Dad, going to work.

They began working out as soon as they turned on the lights, and soon other people arrived. Robyn had just finished her workout when she heard her name. She turned to see Steve Mason, also known as Rico Suave`, one of her favorite students. He had short black hair and a great tan, but he was short for a wrestler, only about 5'10". He'd worked up to 210 pounds and would be a leading cruiserweight wrestler when he got a contract. Some of her dad's friends had their eye on him, so she didn't think it would be long before that happened. She'd seen it happen before.

He walked over and hugged her. "It isn't true, is it?"

"Absolutely not," Robyn said, smiling, "What are we talking about?"

"I heard you're leaving us," Steve said sadly.

"I leave every year at this time, babe. I have to get back to school."

"Yeah, but you came back before. You aren't really going to leave for good, are you?"

"Of course not! I'll be back to visit."

"And you'll be back to train next summer, right?"

"No, not next summer. I'm going to be working on my internship."

"But who's going to train?"

"My dad and the other trainers! It's not like you'll be here next summer anyway. You'll probably be on the road wrestling and making far more money than I will be. Really, Steve, it isn't as if you're never going to see me again!"

"Oh, sure, you say that now. You'll get back to school and forget all about me," he pouted.

"How could I forget you? We have too much fun making your girlfriend jealous!"

Steve laughed, "Yeah, we do, don't we? Will you still e-mail?"

"Try and stop me! Now get to work!"

"Yes, ma'am!"

****

It had been a good day. Robyn stuffed the contents of her locker into her gym bag and slammed the door. She walked out of the ladies' locker room and was greeted by balloons and cheering. She stopped in her tracks and looked at the staff and students standing in front of her. There was a banner over the ring that said, "We'll miss you Robyn" in big red letters. A very tall clown with a red nose and fuzzy purple hair came from the center of the crowd to hand her a big bouquet of magician's flowers and kiss her cheek. She looked at the clown and laughed. "Thanks, Dad. Was this your idea?"

"Not all of it," he answered, "The party was your Mom's idea. You can blame her!
I just contributed the clown."

She was ushered to the center of the ring where her Mom stood with the biggest
sheet cake Robyn had ever seen. The students began to chant, "Speech! Speech!
Speech!" A microphone was placed in her hand. She didn't need it, but wrestlers don't
speak in the ring without a microphone, so she spoke into it. Her voice boomed through
the school.

"I really don't know what to say. You all know I love surprises, and this is definitely
a big one. I want to thank my parents for everything they've put up with in the last 21
years, and I want to thank all of you for your support and hard work this summer. I'm
going to miss working with you guys, but I don't doubt that we'll all meet again. There
is a lot of talent in this room right now, and a lot of you are going to be very successful.
I'll be more than happy to see any of you in the squared circle and be able to say, 'I had
something to do with that!' By the way, Dad will keep my address on file here, so if you
want to spread the wealth my way, feel free! Whatever you do, in the ring or out, do it to
the best of your ability, and you'll be a superstar."

The ring shook with thunderous applause as her friends poured in. The cake was cut,
pictures were taken, and Robyn was hugged until she thought there was no one left in the
county who hadn't come to her party.

****

The next day, she stood in the middle of the room, looking at all the boxes she had
just moved in. She wasn't looking forward to unpacking, but she was glad to have a
bigger room. She had almost twice as much space as she had the year before, and her
mother had a wonderful time seeing that it would be filled. It had taken her car and her
dad's truck to get it all to the campus.

She walked to her bed and fished a bandana out of her suitcase. Pulling her short
wavy blond hair away from her face and untucking her plain white T-shirt, she picked a
box at random and turned to her daunting task. Soon she was kneeling in the middle of
the floor pulling linens out of a box when there was a knock at the door.

"Who is it?" she called, not wanting to get up if she didn't have to.

"It's a cute guy looking for a pretty Physics Major. Anyone there fit that
description?"

Smiling, she got up and opened the door to find her best friend, Brett Masters,
standing on the other side. "Yes, as a matter of fact there is. Where's the cute guy?"
She stepped aside as he took as swing at her shoulder and connected with the door.

Laughing, she pulled him into her new room and hugged him. They were the same height, 5'9", and both worked out in the weight room regularly, but that was where the similarities ended. His hair was dark brown and neatly cut, while her blond waves tumbled wherever they pleased. His eyes were brown and hers were deep blue. He was told from time to time that he looked like John F. Kennedy, Junior. Robyn was never mistaken for anyone, not even someone's sister's best friend from Kansas. She looked at his casual khaki slacks and sweater, and felt like a homeless waif compared to him, in her faded jeans and hiking boots.

He surveyed the boxes and said, "Mom and Dad had a good time, huh?"

"Yeah! Well, Mom and I had a good time. All I had to do was mention that I was looking for a few things to fill the extra space in my new room. Dad told us to have fun and paid the bill, and you see what I got."

"No, I see boxes. Any cool stuff in them?"

They began opening boxes and pulling things out, and in a short time the room was in a state of total chaos. They decided to get the boxes out, and soon they were trudging down the stairs to the dumpster, arms loaded. As she turned the last corner, she ran into something. Peeking around her load, she saw that she had walked right into Jack Armstrong, the quarterback for the football team. She'd only seen him up close a couple times, and he always struck her as ruggedly handsome. He had sandy brown hair and hazel eyes and was built like a brick wall. Brett was already out the door. 'Thanks, Brett,' she thought.

"Sorry! I couldn't see you around all these boxes."

"That's OK." he answered, "Do you need some help?"

"If you could just open the door for me, that would be great."

He opened the door, and as she stepped through, the toe of her boot caught on the threshold, and she stumbled, sending boxes tumbling everywhere. Jack caught her and kept her on her feet, and she blushed in embarrassment.

"Thanks," she said, "my Dad doesn't call me Grace for nothing!" She stepped away and began picking up boxes. He walked out and started helping her.

"So your name is Grace?"

She laughed. "No, it's Robyn. My father is the only one who gets away with calling me Grace, and he's bigger than you, so don't even think about it!"

"OK! I won't! Are you new here?"

"Heck no! This is my fourth year. I just never got noticed by anyone on the football team before!"

"I can't see why not. You should be a cheerleader. You're pretty enough."

"Are you kidding?" She laughed again. "I'd kill myself! I'd fall off the top of the pyramid at the tryouts!" This wasn't entirely true. She was agile and athletic and would probably make the squad if she tried out, but she never did because she couldn't stand the thought of hanging around with a bunch of narcissistic airheads. "Besides, I have too much to do. My class load this semester is going to be enough to handle by itself."

"What's your major?" he asked as they walked to the dumpster.

"Physics, with a minor in Earth and Space Sciences."

"Wow! What are you going to do when you finish?"

"Meteorological research. I want to figure out how to predict earthquakes and stuff like that. Eventually, I'd also like to work with NASA on the next space shuttle design," she said as they put the boxes in to dumpster.

"That sounds cool. I hope you won't be too busy to go out once in a while."

"Why?" she asked cautiously.

"I was thinking maybe we could go have dinner or something. Have you been to Henry's?"

"Yeah, I love Henry's!"

"He's got some new stuff I wanted to try out. Are you busy tonight?"

"Tonight isn't really a good night. I have to get my room in order before my roommate comes in tomorrow." While this was partly true, she didn't want to tell him that she and Brett had decided to go out and catch up on summer vacation.

"How about tomorrow night?"

"I'll let you know. Do you have a number where I can reach you?"

They exchanged phone numbers and he walked her back to the door, and then went off toward the fraternity houses.

She went back in to find Brett sitting on the stairs waiting for her. "What was that all about?"

"When you ran off and left me all alone, I walked into Jack Armstrong."

"Oof!" Brett laughed, "I don't see any wounds, so I guess he didn't hit you or anything."

Robyn started up the steps. "No, actually he held the door so I could go out, but I tripped and dropped all my boxes." Brett started laughing, but Robyn ignored him. "HE was gentleman enough to help me get them to the dumpster."

"Pish posh," Brett replied. "I bet he asked you out, too. Are you ditching me tonight, Ms. Popularity?"

"No, I'm not ditching you tonight," she replied, matching his tone. "I'm ditching you tomorrow night. Tonight you're stuck with all the gory details of my final summer vacation, such as it was."

They walked back into her room and began putting things away. A couple hours later, they moved to his room and got it straight. Since it was late in the afternoon, they decided to get cleaned up and meet for dinner. Robyn went back to her room and checked the answering machine. There was a message from her roommate, Stephanie. This was their third year living together, and Stephanie wanted to know what the room was like. Robyn called her back, and Stephanie's mother answered the phone.

"Mrs. Antipolis? This is Robyn. Is Stephanie there?"

"Yes, Robyn. Just a second."

She heard the phone being passed and then, "It's about time you called back!"

"Sorry," Robyn laughed, "but I have better things to do than sit by the phone waiting for you to call!"

"I'm hurt, Robyn. What's our new pad like?"

"A lot bigger than last year. We actually have room to breathe!"

"Cool. I was afraid they'd mess it up and put us in a mouse hole like last year."

"You were afraid? I mentioned that my room this year was supposed to be bigger, and Mom took me shopping!"

"Oh, no, is there any space left for me?" They both laughed. Stephanie had gone shopping with Robyn and her mother before, so she could only imagine the chaos that awaited her.

"Of course! I would NEVER infringe on your space!"

"Yeah, well, we'll see. I'll be in tomorrow afternoon. See ya then!"

"OK, Steph. 'Bye!"

She hung up the phone and headed for the shower. When Brett knocked at her door a half hour later, she was already dressed in a cream sweater and short brown wool skirt with matching opaque tights and penny loafers. Her makeup (what little she wore) was on, and she was almost finished drying her hair. She let him in without shutting off the hair dryer. He sat down and turned on the TV until she was finished. He had changed clothes, too, but was still dressed in the same style as before. He was comfortable in preppy clothes and only owned one pair of jeans. When she questioned him about this early in their friendship, he explained that he'd gotten used to dressing that way because of all the time he'd spent on the golf course. He was on the top man on the college team and, in addition to finishing his degree in Golf Management, was taking steps to get into professional golfing.

She finished getting ready and they left. Traffic was light and the drive to their favorite deli in Pittsburgh only took twenty minutes. Since they were driving Robyn's car, she put in her current favorite compact disc.

"This is cool," said Brett. "Who is it? And when did you start listening to the Blues?"

"I've liked the Blues since I was little. My Dad listens to it sometimes, especially when he's trying to bug my Mom. Her name is Valerie Jenkins and she's a friend of my Dad's. This is her first release, and it's really climbing the charts. She's kicking off a tour the day after Christmas in Washington DC."

"Is that the woman you went to see at that club?"

"Yeah, she's been singing at 'Blues' for about six months now, and she really put it on the map. It was a nice club before she got there, but now you need reservations!"

They listened to a couple songs when suddenly Brett exclaimed, "Hey, I've heard this one on the radio! This is an awesome song! What's it called?"

"'Paradox.' She wrote it right before she started at 'Blues.' That's where she debuted it. It was awesome; I was there when she sang it the first time. She was doing a charity gig, and everything she made that night, salary, tips, everything went to a dojo where they work with underprivileged kids. The owner of the club, Frank, invited a lot of his rich friends, and of course my Dad and some of his friends were there, so she donated almost a hundred-thousand dollars."

Brett's jaw dropped. "American dollars?"

Robyn laughed. "Yes, American dollars!"

"She's that good?"

"She's a real entertainer. Ever since that night 'Blues' has been standing room only. It didn't take long for word to travel about her! You know what's funny? Frank set her up with a record producer back in February, and she didn't decide to do the album until almost May. Once she started it, she worked her butt off and had the whole thing finished by the first of July. We're talking writing new songs, recording, mixing, everything."

"What was she waiting for?" Brett asked.

"I asked her the same thing. She said she wasn't singing to be famous, she was just singing because that's what she was made to do. She didn't want fame to get in the way of what she loved. Finally, Frank told her to do one recording and one tour, and if the fame got in the way, she could sing in "Blues" for the rest of her life!"

They pulled into the parking lot and went inside. They ordered sandwiches and sodas, and sat down in the deli.

"So," Brett said, "What are these gory details about summer vacation?"

"Well, it really wasn't all that exciting. I just worked for Dad."

"Doing what?"

"He had a bunch of new students come in, and almost a quarter of them were women, so he needed someone female to help with the classes. Since he's been teaching me wrestling moves since I could walk, I was pretty busy! A couple of them told me I should go into wrestling myself. If I weren't so busy already I'd think about it. You can make great money getting beat up every night!"

"Why would you want to get beat up? I'm telling you, you should just come out and caddie for me. We could have a blast!"

Robyn laughed. "If I hang around with you on the golf course, everyone will think we're dating and then all those eligible attorneys and doctors won't ask me out. I'll just stay in the gallery and watch. How was the game this summer?"

"Good! I knocked about ten strokes off. My Dad actually pulled himself out of the office to come play a few rounds. Scott and I met in Myrtle Beach for a week and played a bunch of the courses there."

"Wow! Myrtle Beach is the golf capital of the universe! You should get Scott to caddie for you." Scott, Brett's younger brother, was in the Air Force and trying to decide whether or not to reenlist. "He'd be better than me, and maybe we could all get a date. Did you catch a glimpse of the ocean while you were there?"

"Oh, yeah! Bikinis everywhere! We had a ball! Thank goodness for Dad's credit card. If Dad hadn't been paying for it we'd have been sleeping on the beach, and forget all the golf we played!"

They laughed and talked over dinner, then went to a movie. They drove home in companionable silence. They had started out dating three years earlier and soon discovered that they were better off as friends. Since then, Brett had become like a brother to Robyn, and although she loved him, it wasn't the romantic love she craved. He was her best friend, and that's all he'd ever be. They both liked it that way. When they got back to campus, he walked her to her room, gave her a hug, and went upstairs to his own room.

Robyn went in and changed into her pajamas. She turned on the TV and wandered around the room a little bit, getting used to her new surroundings. When she felt she had prowled enough, she turned off the TV, crawled into bed and fell asleep.

Out of the darkness of her slumber, a man approached. He had long black hair and olive skin and was dressed all in black with a long cloak. He walked to her, put his arms around her, and enfolded her in his cloak. She hugged him back, feeling safe. He kissed the top of her head, and then took a half step back. They walked arm in arm across a small field to a big lake. They sat on the bank, Robyn in front of Nyakas, with his arms around her. She looked down at his strong arms and ran a fingernail up his arm against the dark hairs. His skin puckered in goose bumps. He slapped playfully at her hand and told her to stop. Laughing, she leaned her head back against his shoulder, but the temptation was too great. She ran her fingernail up his arm more quickly, and he shivered, laughed, and told her to stop again. She laughed with him and ran her fingernail up his other arm.

"Robyn, stop it!"

"Why?"

"Because if you don't, you'll regret it!"

"Ooh, big man!" She reached under the cuff of his pant leg and ran her finger up his shin. He moved like lightning, pushing her to the ground, and rolling her onto her back. He held both her wrists with one large hand and tickled her ribs with the other. She shrieked with laughter, squirming to avoid his hand. He relaxed his grip on her wrists slightly, and she was able to free one hand and tickle him back. He jerked back in surprise, tried to catch her hand, and lost his grip on her other hand. She went on the offensive, tickling as quickly as she could. He tried to catch her hands but was laughing too hard, so he did the only thing he could think to do. He lay down flat on top of her, pinning her hands between them. They laughed together and he kissed her, twining a large hand into her blonde waves, then pulled her head to his shoulder, holding her close.

She laughed, kissed his neck, and said, "I love you, Puff."

"And I love you, Buzz."

Chapter 37

Jack called Robyn the next day. She had told Stephanie about the incident, and was told under no circumstances was she to turn down a date if he called. Unwilling to abandon her friend on her first night back, she agreed that she would meet him at Henry's only if he brought a friend for Stephanie. Both Jack and Stephanie agreed to this arrangement. At 6:00 sharp, Robyn and Stephanie walked in the door and looked around. The guys hadn't arrived, so they sat at the end of the bar where they could see the door. Steve, Robyn's favorite bartender and asker of philosophical questions, came to take their drink orders and inquire about their summer vacations.

"Robyn, I have a question that I know you can answer," Steve said.

"And what would that be?" she asked with a smile.

"Why does the first bug to hit a clean windshield always impact directly in front of the driver?"

"It's the way cars are designed. The Big Three auto makers get kick-backs from the people who make windshield solvent."

"Then how come if my Dad is driving his truck, the bug impacts directly in the center of his field of vision, but if I'm driving his truck, it impacts directly in the center of my vision, given the fact the fact that he's two inches shorter than me?"

"Extraordinary aim," Robyn answered seriously. "If I was a bug on course to a clean windshield, I'd want to hit where it would be least convenient. The really smart ones, like butterflies, can actually maneuver so that they start in the center of vision and roll up to the top of the windshield, thus leaving a trail."

They laughed as he poured draft beers for them and pushed a bowl of popcorn in their direction, then went back to work. Jack and his friend, Tom Mahoney, who was the kicker on the team, arrived a few minutes later. They moved to a table and ordered nachos and beer. They talked about the classes they would be enrolling in the next day and how grueling football practice had been. Robyn and Stephanie glanced at each other across the table and pretended to be sympathetic. They'd had late night discussions about the mentality and egotism of football players. Robyn concluded that they had been partially right. These two had huge egos, but they seemed to be fairly intelligent.

They stayed at Henry's until almost 11:00, and then Robyn and Stephanie went home. They stayed up late, talking in the dark about how maybe it wouldn't be so bad to date a football player. Both men had promised to call their respective dates. They would see.

Chapter 38

Robyn walked to the Physics building for her last class of the week. She'd just spent two hours in the library gathering references for a term paper on Mars, and her backpack weighed about thirty pounds. After class she had about three hours of studying ahead, and she knew Jack would probably call in the middle of it and try to take her out. They'd seen each other a few times since their first date. Stephanie had gone out with Tom every weekend, and they really seemed to be hitting it off.

"Robyn!"

She turned around and saw Jack jogging toward her. "What's up, babe?"

She smiled. "Not much. Going to class."

"With half the library? Here, let me take that." He took her backpack from her and slung it over his shoulder. "Jeez, Robyn, you shouldn't be carrying this. You could hurt your back."

"It's fine, Jack. I'm stronger than I look. Besides, this is my last class, and when I get back to my room most of that weight will be on my desk."

"What time is your class over?"

"We usually get out of there about 2:30, but we may run over to 2:45 today. We have a lab."

"Good! I don't have practice until 3:30. I'll meet you back here then and carry this to your room for you. You might be stronger than you look, but I don't think it's worth the chance, do you?"

"Really, Jack, you don't have to do that. I can get it home just fine; it's not really all that heavy and it will be a good workout for me. I've had to deal with a lot worse, trust me."

"Really? They make shopping bags this heavy?"

"What do shopping bags have to do with it?"

"I figured they were the 'a lot worse' you were talking about."

Robyn laughed. "No, the 'a lot worse' would be getting up from a suplex only to have your opponent jump from the top rope and land on your back!"

Jack looked at her like she was speaking a foreign language, and she laughed again. "You don't watch wrestling, do you?"

"Yeah, I do. I didn't know you did. Most of the women I know can't stand it."

"I grew up around it. My father was in the business when I was little."

"Really? Who's your father?"

"Does the name Brick Barabas ring a bell, or was that before your time?"

"Brick Barabas? He's incredible! I've seen the footage of him in the ring. Man, that guy was so agile for his size! He's really your dad?"

"Yeah. He started teaching me wrestling moves about the same time I started walking. After he got hurt he opened a wrestling school. I help him train beginners in the summer."

"That's amazing! You actually do that stuff yourself?"

"Yeah. I'm not professional caliber by any means, but I do all right most of the time. If nothing else, I'm a good 'red shirt' for the girls to practice with! I'd tell you all about it, but I've got to get to class. I'll see you later, OK?"

"OK! See you later!" He handed her backpack to her, kissed her cheek, and sprinted off toward the gym. Robyn could only imagine the conversations that would take place while she finished her day and wondered if she should have said anything.

'Too late to worry about it now,' she thought, 'I'll just have to deal with it and learn from the mistake.'

She went to class, and when she came out, Jack was waiting for her. He took her backpack and walked her home. He didn't say anything about their earlier conversation, and she waited for the other shoe to drop. Suddenly, from the corner of her eye, she saw someone running toward her. She knew in her gut that this was Jack's idea and that she was being tested. She decided to give them a healthy dose of 'I Told You So.' They had sent Tom after her, so he didn't have as much of a weight advantage as some of the others would have had. She braced herself and waited for him to get to her. As he went to tackle her, she grabbed his shirt, fell and rolled backward, planting her feet squarely in his abdomen and flipping him over her. Quickly, she rolled up and sat on him, punching him in the head a few times. Then she got up, grabbed him by the hair, and pulled him up. She hooked her leg around his and fell backward, using her weight to slam him into the ground while using his body to partially break her fall in a perfect side Russian leg sweep. Like lightning, before he had a chance to recover from the stun, she threw her body sideways over his. She hooked her arm under his leg and pulled it up and used her upper body to hold his down.

"One! Two! Three! Ding ding ding!" she yelled, and got up. She brushed the grass off her clothing as Jack and a few other football players gathered around.

"That was amazing!" Jack exclaimed.

"Thanks," she said, and took her backpack from him. She took about ten steps away from him as if she was trying to walk off the adrenaline rush. Without warning, she turned, dropped the backpack, and sprinted toward him. She leaned forward, building speed and momentum, and as she reached him, she stuck her arm out to her side. As she ran past, her arm caught him in the throat and he fell to the ground. She stopped a few feet past him and turned around to face all of them. She glared at Jack as he got up.

"I don't lie about my abilities. Don't test me again, Jack. Don't any of you test me again." She walked to her backpack, picked it up, and strode angrily to the dorm. She was nearing the door when Brett caught up to her.

"Hey, beautiful!"

"Hey yourself," she answered and jerked the door open.

"Uh oh, why are you mad, and why do you have grass stains on your jeans?"

"I made the mistake of telling Jack who my dad is. He decided it would be fun to test me." She stomped up the stairs.

Brett followed. "What happened?"

She told him what happened. By the time she finished, they were at her door. Her hand shook with anger as she tried to get the key in the lock, and this made her angrier. Brett took her key and opened the door, and Robyn stormed in, threw her backpack on the bed, and began pacing. Brett caught her arms as she walked past him and looked into her eyes. She was really angry and this was the only way to get her to pay attention.

Holding her arms to her sides, he said, "You have five minutes to change. I'm going to my room. Meet me there in five minutes and we're going to the gym."

"Good idea," she agreed, and he let go of her arms. He left the room and shut the door behind him. She changed into shorts and a sports bra. As she laced her sneakers on, the phone rang. Not in the mood to deal with telemarketers, she let the machine pick it up. It clicked, and her outgoing message kicked in. "Hi, you've reached Robyn and Stephanie. We're far too busy studying to talk right now, but if you leave us a message we'll call you back on our next break or when melt-down occurs, whichever comes first. Thanks!"

The machine beeped. "Robyn, this is Jack. I know you're there because I saw you go into the dorm and you haven't come out yet. Please pick up. I just want to apologize. I didn't know it would make you so angry."

She walked over to the phone and picked it up. The answering machine beeped and stopped recording. Then she hung up. She grabbed her sweatshirt, keys, and student ID, and walked out the door. The phone rang again as the door shut. She pulled her sweatshirt over her head as she went toward the stairs and started up to Brett's room. He met her half way, and as they went down the stairs she told him about the phone call. As they walked out the door they saw Jack near the dorm with a cell phone in his hand.

"Hey Jack!" Brett called. Jack looked over, saw Brett and Robyn, and hung up the phone. "She isn't home, man! I wouldn't talk to her right now if she was!" He put his arm around Robyn's shoulders and they walked to the gym. They headed straight for the weight room, and Robyn went through her normal routine twice in an effort to calm herself. Brett stayed nearby but out of the way, watching his friend. He knew that when she got like this she forgot what pain was for and had a tendency to hurt herself. She pushed herself for almost two hours before he stopped her. He steered her out of the gym to his car and drove to Henry's. Fortunately, it was still early and there were plenty of tables. He asked for a quiet one in a corner, sat her down, and ordered spring water. They sipped their drinks and talked about nothing in particular for a while, then ordered soup and salads. They were just getting ready to leave when Tom appeared at their table.

"Robyn, please don't kick my butt again. I just wanted to tell you I'm sorry. I had no idea what Jack was up to. He just bet me twenty bucks that I wouldn't tackle you, and I took him up on it. Sorry."

"It's OK, Tom. Now you know. Don't take bets unless you know the whole story."

"Yeah, no kidding. Is Brick Barabas really your dad?"

Robyn couldn't help but smile. "Yeah, he's really my dad."

"Next time you talk to him, will you tell him he did a great job training you? My ears are still ringing."

This time she laughed out loud. "Sorry! I'll tell him."

"Cool. See you later."

"Hey, Tom," Robyn called after him, "tell Jack he better get his act together if he wants to date the Brick's kid!"

He gave her a thumbs-up, and they got up to leave. As they got back in the car, Brett said, "You're not seriously considering going out with him again, are you?"

"I don't know. He did something really stupid. They're lucky I did know what I was doing or someone could have gotten hurt. But it says something for you when the QB wants to date you."

"Yeah, usually that you're easy! You're going to do what you want anyway, but I don't like it. I don't think he's right for you."

"I may go out with him, I may not. It's not like I'm going to marry him, Brett. He's got a long way to go before I'd even think about anything serious with him."

"Just remember that. I don't want you to get hurt, buddy."

"I know. If it looks like I'm even thinking about getting serious with him, you have my permission to knock some sense into me."

"So you can beat the snot out of me, too? The only way I'd knock some sense into that thick skull of yours is with my nine-iron. If I bend it on your head, you're going to buy me a new one!"

"Deal. You and my dad are the only ones who would get away with that!"

They went home and Robyn went straight to her room to start her paper. Stephanie was sitting at her desk, her long brown hair pulled back in a ponytail. Robyn envied her friend; Stephanie always looked good, even when she rolled out of bed with a hangover. Stephanie looked up when the door opened.

"Thank goodness you're back!"

"You missed me that much? I had no idea!"

Stephanie stuck out her tongue and tossed an eraser at her. Robyn caught it, laughing, and handed it back as Stephanie said, "Will you PLEASE call Jack back? He's called five times in an hour and a half. Did you guys have a fight or something?"

Robyn told her friend what happened, got a glass of water, and went across the room with the phone so she wouldn't disturb Stephanie any further. She sat down on her bed and dialed Jack's phone number. He answered the phone, and without preamble, she said, "OK, Jack, say whatever you have to say to me, and then quit calling because Stephanie and I have work to do."

"Robyn, I'm sorry! It wasn't meant to make you mad. It was a joke. I figured you'd step out of the way or duck behind me."

"Well, you thought wrong. I can take care of myself. Don't underestimate me again."

"I won't. Can I take you out this weekend to make up for it?"

"I'll think about it. If you think just taking me to Henry's is going to make me forget about what happened, think again. You'd better be prepared to do some serious butt kissing before I let this one go." She could hear Stephanie laughing softly.

"I can't think of another butt I'd rather kiss. Are you coming to the game tomorrow?"

"I have to. Stephanie is making me go."

"Cool! My first touchdown is for you, OK?"

"OK. Goodbye." She hung up the phone, looked at Stephanie, and they both exploded in laughter. A few minutes later, the only sounds in the room were of pages being turned and pencils scratching on paper.

Chapter 39

She woke the next morning to the ringing of the phone. Robyn heard Stephanie answer it, and a moment later the phone was placed on her pillow. "It's your dad," Stephanie said, yawning, and went back to bed. Robyn picked it up and answered as she tried to focus her eyes on the clock.

"Wake up, lazy bugger!" Dad had probably been up for hours, so he was bright eyed and bushy tailed.

"Hi, Dad. What's going on?"

"Just checking in. What are you still doing asleep at 9:30 in the morning?"

Robyn groaned. "It's only 9:30? Dad, it's too early! I was up studying until almost three."

"On a Friday night? Are you sure you were studying, and if so, what?"

"Yes, I was studying. I got on a roll doing research for a term paper on Mars for my Astronomy class, and before I knew it I just couldn't stay awake."

"So have you learned a lot about Mars? You're sure it was Mars and not Venus you were studying?"

"Yes, Dad. I really was studying, I promise. I turned down a date to stay home and get some work done."

"You turned down a date? With who? Anyone I know?"

"You haven't met him, but you've seen him. It was Jack Armstrong, our football team's starting quarterback."

"Hallelujah! Hey Gina, Robyn is dating the quarterback! That's my girl! Tell me all about him."

Robyn laughed and sat up in her bed. "You might actually like this one, Dad. He's a Phys. Ed. Major and if a team in the NFL doesn't pick him up he's going into the Army. He's an ROTC captain, so he'll be an officer. He's from Dayton; parents married to each other, two brothers, no sisters. If I could let some of the air out of his ego, he'd have potential for perfection."

"Sounds like a good one. When can I meet him?"

"I won't be able to bring him home until around Christmas time. He's got a game or practice every weekend between now and winter break. If you want to meet him between now and then, you'll have to come here."

"I'll see what I can do. Let me know when your home games are and maybe we can catch one together."

"Sounds good. I'll e-mail the schedule today. Everything else going OK?"

"Yeah, everyone says hi. The kids at school miss you, but I can't decide if it's the guys or the girls who miss you more!"

She laughed. "Well tell them all I said hi. By the way, our kicker told me to tell you that you did a good job training me."

"Pardon? Dare I ask what it is I trained you in?"

She laughed and said, "I told Jack yesterday that you are my father, and he didn't quite believe me, so he set up a little test. He got the kicker to try to tackle me, and I flipped him and then did a side Russian leg sweep and got a three-count. Then I got up and clotheslined Jack. Needless to say, I was not happy that he didn't take me at my word. But what's funny is that I saw the kicker last night and he told me to tell you that you did a good job training me!"

Kevin laughed. "Way to go, honey! I'm proud of you. Don't let anyone push you around. I'll tell everyone at school. Now get up and get to work!"

"OK, I'm up! Talk to you later. I love you, Dad."

"I love you too, babe."

She rolled out of bed and pulled on her sweats and running shoes. It was almost time for Brett to come down to get her. Maybe she could beat him to the punch for once.

Brett was in his room when his door opened and Robyn jumped in, making a feeble attempt to startle him. He sat motionless at his desk. "I'm studying, Robyn, the thing some of us need to do to stay in school." He turned his black leather chair around to face Robyn, who had appropriated a seat on the edge of his bed.

"It's time to go running, remember?"

"Oh yeah! Hold up a second." Brett threw on his running shoes and they began their usual five-mile run at the library. "So buddy, how's Jack, the football star, the Man, the drunkard who doesn't even deserve anything remotely like you, doing today?"

Robyn replied, "Fine, I guess. Why do you ask?"

"Oh I don't know. I just want to know about his well being."

Robyn glanced at her friend and asked, "Why do you hate him so much?"

Quick to reply, Brett snapped back, "Why do you like him so much? He's a jerk, Robyn."

"You're just jealous."

"Jealous? Of muscle head? Steroid boy? Are you serious?"

Rolling her eyes, she asked sarcastically, "Well, anyway, how's Sarah?"

Brett grinned and enthusiastically said, "She's great! We're going to have dinner at Henry's tonight. I can't wait! So, back to the Jack subject."

"Let's not and say we did."

"Is everything all right with you two or are you still fighting? Robyn, I'm sorry I offended you. I didn't mean it. You know I care about you a lot. I just don't want to see you get hurt."

"I know that, Brett, it's just that I know there's someone else out there."

"So what you're saying is you and Jack are just not made for each other."

She laughed. "No, I don't think we are, that's why it's not serious! It really doesn't have anything to do with Jack. It's just, oh, forget about it."

"No, no, come on! You can tell me."

"All right," she said excitedly, "There's this guy, he's tall, dark, and not handsome." She pulled ahead with a look of knowing something he didn't.

"Hold up!" he called, catching up with her. "Who are you, and what did you do with my friend Robyn? What do you mean, he's not handsome?"

"He's not just handsome, he's gorgeous, he's mysterious, he's strong, he's everything."

They slowed to cool down, Brett, with his famous smile, said, "He sounds great! Where is he?"

Robyn paused with a long face and a deep sigh. "My dreams."

Brett looked at her with a look of question and then put his arm around her and said, "It will be all right. One day he'll come out of nowhere and save you from all of this. I love ya buddy."

"Thanks, Brett," she said, leaning on his shoulder. "I love you, too. I'll race you. Go!"

She raced him back to the dorm, and he won by half a step. She went upstairs and took a shower, then settled onto her bed to read more about Mars. She managed to get a couple more hours of work in before Stephanie informed her that it was time to get ready for the football game. Sighing, she closed her books and changed into warm clothing. Even though it was sunny, it would still be cold in the stands. Soon, she, Stephanie, and Brett were on their way to the game. Robyn knew she'd have a good time, but the price would be studying that night.

Chapter 40

Nyakas and Gravity walked up to a small farmhouse. It appeared to have been abandoned, but still seemed to be in decent shape. There was a large barn nearby, and the only apparent damage was the missing hayloft door. The farm was away from the noise of the city, but not too far.

They went into the house and evicted the rodents who had taken up residence. By evening the place was livable. Nyakas stepped outside onto the porch, looking at the city lights on the horizon. He knew that somewhere close by, he'd find Robyn. What worried him was that he didn't know whether she would remember him. He decided to go to the campus and look around.

****

'This is sad,' Robyn thought. 'Here I am on a Saturday night, and I'm studying. I'm dating the quarterback on one of the greatest teams in the league right now, and I'm stuck with my books. Why wasn't college this hard the past three years? College seniors are supposed to have fun, not be stuck inside all the time.'

The phone rang, snapping Robyn out of her reverie. 'Now what?' she thought as she answered the phone.

"Robyn! What are you doing?"

She smiled when she recognized Jack's voice. "Hi, Jack. Not much, just fighting brain rot." She could hear the music in the background. There was a party starting.

"Physics?"

"Quantum Mechanics."

"Yuck! Well, why don't you take a break and come over? We decided to have a little party since you turned down our date for tonight, but I still want to see you."

"OK, but just for a little while. I'll be there soon." She hung up the phone and went to her closet, glad for once to have an excuse to leave. Stephanie had gone to dinner with Tom, but she'd be home early. Stephanie hated fraternity parties. She claimed there was too much smoke to irritate her contact lenses, and the drunks always got out of line. Robyn agreed with her to a point, but when she was invited to them, she usually went and left when she'd had enough. She changed into a clean pair of jeans and a sweater, touched up the tiny bit of make-up she was wearing and brushed her hair. Then she went back to the desk, scribbled a note for Stephanie, grabbed her keys and jacket, and left.

Jack's fraternity house was only a few blocks away, and she had a good idea of what the parking would be like, so she walked past her car and headed over on foot. She heard the "little party" well before she saw it, and knew that the football team was effectively inviting everyone within a quarter mile radius to join the merriment. They had played their best game of the season that afternoon, and were now headed for the finals, which was not a big surprise. Their team always went to the finals.

She let herself into the fraternity house and wove her way through the crowd to the cooler corner, where she was sure she'd find Jack. Sure enough, there he was.

"Robyn! How are you, babe?" He hugged her and pressed a beer into her hand.

"Hanging in there," she answered, leaning past him to exchange the beer for a diet soda. 'Funny,' she thought, 'he didn't sound that drunk on the phone. Big surprise!' She talked with him for a while, and then the rest of the football team came over and started rehashing the game again. She slipped away and started mingling with drunks. She pretended to be interested in hearing about the game again, when suddenly there was a hand on her arm. She turned to see Jack with another beer in his hand.

"Let's go out on the porch, Rob. It's getting a little smoky in here." It was, in fact, getting very smoky. He led her out to the porch swing and they started making out. Since he had been drinking, he progressed a bit faster than she intended. When it got out of her comfort zone, she pulled back and told him to stop. In his intoxicated state, he forgot what the word meant, and within moments, Robyn was trying to get away.

"Jack, stop!" He pushed her back to the corner of the swing. "I said stop! I don't want to do this, Jack!" There was nothing nearby for her to wrap her leg around to increase her leverage, so she tried punching him in the head. He grabbed her wrists in one hand and held them behind her head, pushed her back, and sat on her legs.

"Fire! Help, fire!" She yelled, trying to get some attention, but no one answered, and he kissed her to keep her from yelling again. She twisted, trying to force him off the swing as he began to fumble with her belt.

Suddenly, he was gone! She looked up to see a man she didn't know standing over Jack, who was sprawled on the floor.

"She said stop!" the stranger growled. Even in the dim light she could see that he had a great tan and was incredibly handsome. He was wearing a black cloak with a hood pushed back. She couldn't help thinking that she'd seen him somewhere before.

Jack got up and tried to tackle the man, but he stepped out of the way, and Jack's momentum carried him off the porch and almost into the giant oak tree in the yard. At that point, three of Jack's teammates came out, saw what happened, and jumped toward the black-cloaked stranger. She watched in amazement as he sidestepped Jeff, who also went off the porch. He grabbed Dan, the full back, and twisted his arm around his back.

He then took a half step to the left, just in time to shove Dan into Marc, the halfback who was rushing him. There was a loud thunk as the two semi-empty heads made contact and the two men fell. Robyn gasped as Jack and Jeff rushed past her to attack from the rear. In one fluid move, a leg appeared from under the black cloak, and the foot connected with Jeff's temple. Jeff fell, and Jack tripped on his fallen comrade. He got back up and grabbed for the feet he now knew were under the cloak. There was one foot on the ground, and one on course to Jack's forehead. It connected, and Jack fell.

The man looked around, and then stepped over Jack and Jeff to Robyn. He took her hand and helped her to her feet. He was tall and it was obvious that he worked out a lot. With a shock, she realized that he looked incredibly like a man she'd been dreaming about since she was seventeen. He was still holding her hand, and his was very warm. She had a sudden urge to put her arms around his waist and let him enfold her in his cloak. She heard a noise, and realized he'd spoken.

"Pardon?" she asked, feeling stupid.

"You might want to leave. Can you get home OK on your own?"

"Yes, thank you."

He kissed her hand then let it go, half-bowed, and swept off the porch. His cloak trailed him and a gust of wind made it sweep up and around him. She blinked and he was gone, leaving her there alone. She stared stupidly after him for what may have been a second or an eternity, until Dan started to wake up. She looked at the four football players who had been defeated easily by one man, then turned and sprinted off the porch. She ran all the way home, and didn't stop until she had locked her door behind her.

Stephanie looked up, startled. "Robyn, what's wrong?"

"I just went over to Jack's for a while, and he was drunk. When he got a little too romantic I got scared and ran home. Really adult, huh?"

"I'd call it smart. Are you OK? He didn't hurt you, did he?"

"No, I'm fine. I got away before he could really do anything." She got a wine cooler from the refrigerator and sipped on it while she pretended to study. Then she changed into her pajamas and went to bed. She curled up thinking about her rescuer. She knew she'd seen him somewhere before, but she couldn't place him. Where had he learned the moves that allowed him to win easily against four to one odds? Granted they had been drunk, but it had seemed as if it had been easy for him. He wasn't even breathing heavily when he helped her up. She tossed and turned, and when she finally slept, she dreamed, as usual, about a man named Nyakas, who wore a black cloak.

****

Nyakas walked into the small farmhouse and hung his cloak on a peg near the door. Gravity, was sitting in front of the fireplace. "Did you see her?"

"Yes. Now all we have to do is get her to come with us. I'm not sure how to do that. She's changed some, and I'm sure she doesn't remember me."

"She will. How will you approach her?"

"I'm not sure, but I'll come up with something. I didn't think it was possible, but she's more beautiful than when she was taken from me." From the corner of his eye he could see Gravity shake his head. Nyakas knew he was being pitiable, but he couldn't help it. "Maybe I should ask her out. What are the customs for that here?"

"Typically you just ask. It's called a date, and to be safe, for the first one, try dinner and a movie. I'll help you pick one. I do think that you should choose a name more fitting this society. If you tell her your name is Nyakas she might remember too quickly and be frightened away. You know how she was with things she didn't understand."

"Yes, you're right. People here seem to have two names. It's very odd. It's as if by carrying one name in a group of people, they are somehow connected. I suppose I should decide on two names. Any suggestions?"

"It's up to you, but the second name should be something fairly common so it doesn't attract attention."

"How about Stevens?"

"Fine. First name?"

"Alexander, for Alexander the Great."

"Alexander Stevens. I don't think anyone will question that."

"Good. Thank you, Gravity. I don't know how I could do all this without your help."

"Anything to help, my lord."

Nyakas smiled. That was Gravity's way of saying that he hoped the situation would be resolved soon. This culture was entirely too greedy and materialistic for their taste. He stood up and got his cloak. "I'm going out to get comfortable, Gravity."

"Yes, my lord. Don't be too long."

Chapter 41

The following afternoon Robyn was coming out of the gym when Jack walked in.

"Hi, Robyn," he said, "How are you?"

She glared at him and tried to brush past him, but he grabbed her arm. "What's wrong?" he asked.

"What's wrong? What do you mean, what's wrong? Don't you remember last night?"

"I remember going out on the back porch and making out, then waking up under the swing. Did I pass out on you? If I did, I'm sorry!"

"No, Jack. You didn't pass out. You were knocked out. You tried to rape me, and some guy came and pulled you off me. You tried to fight him and he knocked you out. Now if you'll excuse me, I have some things to take care of."

"Come on, Robyn, I wouldn't hurt you. Why would you think I was trying to rape you?"

"Oh, maybe the fact that you pinned me down on the swing and started unbuckling my belt."

"Why didn't you just tell me to stop?"

"I did! I told you and you didn't listen! I yelled for help, but the music was too loud for any of your drunk friends to hear me!"

"Robyn, I'm sorry! I was drunk! I didn't mean to scare you. Hell, you must have wanted it if you let me go that far. Just decided you couldn't handle it, huh? Come on, babe, it's OK. Sweet old Jack won't hurt you."

"Leave me alone, Jack. Don't call me, don't talk to me, and don't even look at me. I didn't want to have sex with you last night, and now it will be a cold day in hell before I even go out with you again." She walked back to the dorm, but went past her floor to Brett's. She knocked on his door, and he opened it with the phone in his hand. He motioned for her to come in while he finished his conversation. She sat down on his couch, and then got up to stand by the window. She could see Jack outside, talking to someone. The girl turned and Robyn could see it was one of the cheerleaders, Susan Cashwell. She watched as he moved to stand closer to her. They laughed about something, then he put his arm around her and they walked away. Robyn watched, angry tears springing to her eyes. She turned her back to Brett, who was pacing as he talked to his mother, and brushed away the tears as they spilled over. She tried to stop, but for some reason they just kept coming. Brett didn't seem to notice, and she was grateful to have a few moments to pull herself together. A few minutes later he started to wrap up his conversation. She felt calmer and she sat back down on the couch. One glance at her face told him she'd been crying, and he knew her well enough to know that didn't happen often. She was about the toughest woman he knew besides her mother.

He hung up the phone, sat down beside her, and put his arm around her. "What's wrong?"

She leaned her head on his shoulder. "You were right about Jack."

"Of course I was! I'm right about almost everything! What did he do to prove my point?"

"I went to the party at the frat house last night and he got a little too romantic on the back porch swing. Just when I thought he was going to rape me some guy in a black cloak got him off me and I got away."

He interrupted her. "He tried to rape you? Robyn, why didn't you tell someone? Why didn't you come get me? He shouldn't be out walking around, he should be in jail for assault!"

"Brett," she said, her voice cracking again, "I can't talk to anyone else about this. Not now."

"Robyn, he tried to rape you! The guy who saved you could testify to it."

"If I tell the authorities and he gets arrested, then I'll have some big trial to deal with and when people find out I'm still a virgin, they'll all think that I was going along with it and just got scared, and that's not what happened at all! I did get scared, but I had no intention of having sex with him!"

"Who cares what everyone else thinks? You never have before!"

"It matters now!" She started crying again, and turned away.

He turned her back and pressed her face into his shoulder, holding her firmly, and let her cry. "OK, I'm sorry. There's more to it, isn't there?"

"A little while ago he saw me coming out of the gym and I told him I didn't want to see him anymore, and just a minute ago I saw him getting all cuddly with Susan Cashwell. He didn't care about me, he just wanted to use me."

"I'm sorry, buddy. He's a jerk, and you're too good for him. Tell me about this guy in the black cloak. Do you know who he was?"

She sat back and dragged her sleeve across her eyes. "I've never seen him before. He was a real looker, but his cloak caught my attention. It was the same kind of cloak as the one Nyakas wears in my dreams."

"Are you sure you were seeing right? It must have been pretty dark."

"I saw him clearly. I also saw him take down four football players without breaking a sweat."

"Four? Come on, Robyn."

"I'm serious. He took out Jack, Jeff, Dan, and Marc. Granted, they'd all been drinking, but you know how they get. Marc is downright mean when he's been drinking."

"Marc is just downright mean, drinking or not. Wow, he must be quite a fighter."

"Yeah. I wish I knew who he was so I could thank him."

"Me too. He saved me from having to kill the QB for hurting my best friend. I wish you'd reconsider going to the cops. The next girl may not have a guy in a black cloak to save her."

"I'll think about it. I wrote it all down last night, as much to get it off my chest as to keep the facts straight in case something else happens."

"Good. When you decide to go, tell me and I'll go with you."

"Thanks."

"Come on, let's knock off studying and go get some dinner."

"Sounds like a plan. Let me get a shower and change. Steph has a date tonight, so at least I won't be alone, and I know I'll be safe with you."

"I'll be down in a half hour."

"I'll be ready. Thanks, pal."

"You betcha." He smiled at her and she went to her room to get ready.

Chapter 42

Brett was finishing his workout at the gym the next day when he saw Jack come in. He was with Susan, and from their behavior, it looked to Brett liked they'd already gotten sweaty together. He was livid about what Jack had done to Robyn, so he wiped the weight bench off with his towel and walked over to Jack.

"Jack, can I have a word with you?" he asked politely.

Jack looked surprised that Brett would even approach him, but said, "Sure. I'll be back, Sue."

They walked to a corner, and Jack said, "OK, Ace, what's so important?"

"I need a favor Jack, and only you can do this."

"I'm a busy guy, bud."

"Brett. The name is Brett. The favor is that you steer clear of Robyn Smith. She told me what you did, and I don't want you anywhere near her. Just stick with your little friend over there and leave Robyn alone!"

"Whoa, 'Brett,' I don't know who you think you are, telling me who I can and can't see. Robyn's a little upset with me right now. She'll come around."

"I don't think so, but if you want to delude yourself, you go right ahead. Keep waiting for her to call you; that sounds like a good plan. Just know that she's special to me, and if you lay a hand on her again I'll see to it that you pay dearly. I don't let people hurt my friends."

"Yeah, whatever. Tell your 'special friend' I said hi. Hey, if she won't put out for me, at least someone is getting some."

He turned to walk away, and Brett grabbed his shoulder, spun him back around and grabbed the front of his shirt. He was easily four inches shorter than Jack, but he yanked him down so they were nose to nose. "Don't you ever talk like that about Robyn."

He shoved Jack away and stalked out of the gym, and started running. There wasn't a damn thing he could do about Jack now, but he'd be watching, waiting for him to make a move on Robyn or any other girl. Nobody deserved to be treated the way he'd treated her. He decided that the minute he saw Jack take advantage of another girl, he'd tell Robyn and try to convince her to go to the campus police. At the very least it would get Jack suspended from the football team. Then his scholarship would be revoked and he'd either have to pay out-of-pocket or leave. Unfortunately, he also knew Jack was a little too smart to do something like that. Jack would be on his best behavior for a while, or he'd keep dating girls like Susan. Robyn was too special to be with scum like him. She deserved the best, and he'd see to it that she didn't settle for less.

He slowed to a walk and thought about his first date with Robyn. He'd been captivated with her and for a while he thought he was falling in love with her. But every time he thought about progressing past friendship, something stopped him. They had fun together, and there were definitely feelings between them. But he didn't love her in the way she deserved to be loved, and he knew she felt the same way. So he looked after her with a brotherly affection, made sure she didn't study too hard, and treasured her as a friend. He walked back to the dorm and took a shower. Then he called Robyn and announced that she needed to get ready; they were going to the mall.

Chapter 43

Stephanie came in and plunked her library books on her desk. "I love this Indian summer! Hopefully it will last through the weekend. But since today is Thursday and I have exams all day tomorrow, it will probably rain on Saturday." She reached into the refrigerator for a soda.

"Probably," Robyn said, not looking up from her notes, "but that's OK, I'll probably sleep most of Saturday. Do we have any coffee left? I'll need it tonight."

"Yeah, there's enough to get us through until we can get to the store this weekend. Man, I saw a guy at the library a while ago. He was a real hunk, but he was wearing a black cloak, and it's almost eighty degrees out there! The librarian almost kicked him out because he brought a wineglass in with him, but when he started reading War and Peace, she let him stay. So much for no food or drink in the library. What's wrong, Robyn?"

"Nothing. He was wearing a black cloak?"

"Yeah. Do you know him? If you're going for him, you better tell me now, because if you don't, I will! Just don't tell Tom, OK? He'll find out and probably get mad, but it will keep him on his toes! Plus, it will serve him right for flirting with the cheerleaders, the little snot."

Robyn glanced around the room and spotted a library book on her desk. "Oh, shoot! This book is due today!" She grabbed it before Stephanie could look at the due date, which was almost a week away.

Stephanie laughed, and said, "OK, you're going for him. I'll make sure I tell Tom so Jack will hear about it! He's such a jerk; I can't believe he treated you like he did. Go turn in your book, but you might want to change first."

Robyn looked at her jeans and baggy T-shirt. "Do you think so?"

"He's gorgeous, Robyn."

"Good point." She pulled off her clothes and put on her favorite denim mini-dress. She slipped on a pair of sandals, grabbed her book and backpack, and headed to the library.

It was a short walk, and upon entering, she saw the same man in the same cloak that had saved her from being raped. Suddenly, her mouth went dry and her hands began shaking. Steph was right; he was gorgeous. He sat at a table by himself, reading "War and Peace" with a wineglass in front of him. It looked familiar. It was a rather large glass goblet with a silver dragon entwined around it. He turned the page, then absently ran his finger along the dragon's tail. She couldn't help feeling like she had seen him do that a hundred times before and knew it was something he did when he was concentrating.

'That's dumb, Robyn. How can you know that? You don't even know him.'

He seemed intent on the book, his handsome tanned face passive, only his eyes moving as he read. His black hair hung loose around his shoulders and over the back of his cloak. He was more than handsome; he was beautiful.

'What is it about him? Why do I feel like I know him as well as I know myself? I don't even know his name!'

"Hi, Robyn!"

She jumped and looked around. Christina, one of her classmates, was standing beside her. "Hi, Christina. How are you?"

"Exhausted. I had to finish a term paper and study for exams. Are you OK?"

Her heart pounded as if she had almost been run over by a truck. "Yeah, fine. I have a term paper too. Excuse me, I have to turn this in."

"OK, see you later."

Christina walked away, and Robyn walked toward her mysterious hero. As she approached, she realized that she couldn't think of anything to say, so she did the only thing she could think to do. Just as she was about to walk past him she dropped her book. He looked at the book on the floor and leaned down to pick it up. From where she stood it looked as if the book had a magnet that was attracted to his hand, because as he reached for it, it seemed to elevate into his hand. He looked up at her and said, "Here, you dropped this."

She took it and thanked him, feeling lost in his eyes. They were dark, almost black, and seemed to shine with a recognition that he wasn't quite ready to acknowledge. He smiled, and then returned to his book. She took the book to the return counter, and started wandering around, pretending to look for another book, but watching him, hoping he'd take his book and wineglass and leave. Then she could follow him and accidentally bump into him again. If he seemed nice she would ask him out, if he didn't ask her first. She smiled at a sudden mental picture of this man meeting her father. He wouldn't be intimidated by Dad like a lot of other guys were. Not that it was without reason. He had a habit of cleaning his shotgun whenever she had a new guy coming to pick her up. He'd really try to intimidate this guy, too. He'd be a challenge to Dad, but she couldn't say for sure why that was.

She watched a little while longer and pretended to browse through some encyclopedias, but he showed no inclination toward leaving. She knew she couldn't lurk in the library all day. After all, tomorrow might be Friday, but she had her last mid-term exam to study for. She didn't want to take the chance of failing Quantum Mechanics this early in the game. It was one of those classes: if you fell behind, you stayed behind. She tried to think of something to say. It had to be something witty that didn't sound stupid. After all, he was reading "War and Peace", not a comic book. A number of pick-up lines popped into her head, but she knew they would never work. She thought about the direct approach and just thanking him, but she really wanted to go out with him too. As hard as she tried, she couldn't think of anything, so she decided to resort to another tactic. Reaching into her backpack, she pulled out a piece of notebook paper and a pen. She wrote her name and phone number, and then folded it into a square that would fit in her hand. Her heart pounded as she walked toward him, 'accidentally' bumped into him and dropped it in his lap.

"Excuse me, but I think this is yours," he called after her.

She turned to see him open it. He read it, looked up, and said, "I don't have a phone."

"Not a problem." She reached into the pocket of her backpack and flipped him a quarter, flashed her famous million-dollar smile, and left.

She went straight home and tried to study, but she was far too edgy. When the phone rang an hour later, she nearly jumped out of her skin and was immediately grateful that Stephanie was out.

"Hello?"

"Hi." The voice was familiar, and she knew who it was.

"Hi. You found a phone."

"Yes. Why did you give me your number? And why were you watching me in the library?"

Wondering how he knew she'd been watching him, she answered, "I couldn't think of a way to thank you for saving me two weeks ago."

"Ah, from the football players."

"Yeah. You do remember me then." His voice was deep and mesmerizing. She felt as though she was entranced in some magic spell.

"I could never forget such beauty, Robyn."

The spell broke. "How do you know my name?"

"You gave it to me."

"Oh yeah. Duh!"

He laughed. "I also heard your boyfriend use it."

"He isn't my boyfriend. Not anymore."

"Why?"

"The status of dating the quarterback isn't worth it. I dropped him like a bad habit. I deserve better than to be attacked every time he gets drunk. So, you have an advantage over me. You know my name."

"You're right. My name is Alexander Stevens. So you wanted to thank me?"

"Um, yeah, exactly, Alexander. So, why don't you let me take you to dinner? Or can you think of a better way for me to say thank you?"

She could hear the smile in his voice as he said, "You already have."

Her heart melted and dropped at the same time. "So you don't want to go out?"

"Did I say that? You don't have to take me out to thank me. But I would like to take you out."

"Well, that sounds like an offer I can't turn down. When?" She was rather pleased with herself for not sounding too excited, even though her mind was screaming, 'Now! Right now!'

"Tomorrow night? How about dinner and a movie? I'll be ready to relax after my exam tomorrow."

"I know what you mean. I have a Quantum Mechanics exam. What do you have?"

"US Economic History. Not my strong subject."

"I loved that class! Dr. Huffington was great, except when he ditched class once to go to a concert and wouldn't take the rest of us. Do you need any help?"

"You can try, but I don't think there's any hope for this test. You know it will be tough when you read "War and Peace" to take a break! I'm glad it's only a mid-term. Besides, I don't want to take you away from your studying."

"True. I do need to review some stuff. I'll be glad to help you with what comes after the mid-term, if you want me to."

"Of course you will; dinner and a movie. What do you say?"

"Yeah, that sounds great, but I meant I'll help you study for your history class."

"Maybe next week. I'd love to converse, but I have about four chapters to read. See you tomorrow about 6:00?"

"Sure. Do you want to meet somewhere?"

"How about the library?"

"See you then and there!"

"Good night, Robyn."

"Good night, Alexander."

Chapter 44

Somehow she got through her exam. That was the good news. The bad news was she finished it at 9:30 in the morning. There were still eight and a half hours until her date. She puttered around her room, straightening up. Then she went for a long walk and tried to keep her mind off the impending evening. She was enjoying the crisp fall air and the red maple leaves when she heard her name. Turning, she saw Jack jogging toward her. She turned and walked back toward the dorm, but he overtook her quickly.

"You don't talk to old friends any more, Robyn?" he asked sarcastically.

"Sure, I talk to old friends. You don't qualify."

"Still pining for me, huh?"

Robyn laughed. "Pining? Sure, Jack."

He smiled. "I knew it. What are you doing tonight? Studying again? You do that a lot."

"I have my priorities straight. Survival first. My parents will kill me if I fail a class at this point."

"So you are going to study."

"I have a date, nosey."

"A date? No way! You can't have a date because I'm going out with Susan."

She laughed, astounded at his arrogance. "She deserves you. OK, you caught me. I'm going to study. Goodbye, Jack." She turned off the path quickly and went into the dorm, laughing to herself.

Returning to her room, she checked the answering machine and discovered a message from her father. She picked up the phone and hit the speed dial button for his private line at work. It rang twice.

"Kevin's Pool Hall. You want balls, we got 'em!"

"Cute one, Dad. I'll have to remember that one."

"Hey, kid. Haven't heard from you in a while. How were the exams?"

"I lived through them, but I don't know how I did. I think I bombed my Electronics exam; might only get a C."

"Only a C! Oh, no!" He laughed. "How's Jack? Are you still bringing him home for Christmas break?"

"No, we broke up. I deserve better."

"Better??! Robyn, come on! He's the quarterback AND in ROTC, for Pete's sake! He's almost perfect!"

"Sorry, Dad. He is also incredibly arrogant, drinks too much, and he tried to take advantage of me at a party after a football game. Still think he's almost perfect?"

"He tried what? You didn't just say he tried to take advantage of you, did you? If he did I'll just have to fly up there and shoot him. I'll have to make him a little less perfect. Does he still plan join the Army after college?"

"Yes."

"Damn! Can't shoot him in the knee caps!"

"Don't worry, Dad. I took care of it. I don't need him. Besides, you and Mom are always telling me I'm way too young to settle down! I have too much to do to be stuck with him!"

"That's my girl! I heard from Jessica today. She told me to ask you if you're ready to be her tag partner yet!"

Robyn laughed. "No, I'm too busy. Tell her she's doing great on her own, she doesn't need me. I don't think the wrestling world is quite ready for a female tag team. Getting too many women into the sport would spoil it somehow."

"How did you come up with that conclusion?"

"Wrestling is just a soap opera with testosterone, Dad. I know that better than most people. I've seen you come out of the ring after beating the snot out of someone and buy him a beer!"

"True. I agree with you, but don't tell your Mom, OK?"

"How much do you love me, Daddy?" Robyn was teasing. She was Daddy's girl to the core and would not even think of telling her mother.

"Brat," was the answer, but he was laughing. "Anything new there?"

"No, just studying."

"OK, kiddo. Keep in touch and let us know when you'll be home."

"OK. Tell everyone I said hi. Love ya Dad!"

"Same here, kid. Talk to you later."

She hung up the phone with a grin. Grabbing her robe, she went to the bathroom, and took a long hot bath. She took her time getting dressed, and when she looked at the clock it was 5:30. Checking the mirror one final time, she was satisfied with what she saw, at least as satisfied as she could be. She'd picked a dress her mother had given her for Christmas. Conservative but cute, it was blue, two shades darker than her eyes, with little black flowers. It stretched almost all the way to the toes of her favorite black ankle boots (an idea she got from a fashion catalog and had used with some success), with short sleeves, a scoop neck, and buttons the length of the front. She wore it with a simple gold necklace.

'Not much I can do about my hair,' she thought, trying in vain to straighten the soft blond waves that surrounded her face and refused to do what she wanted it to. 'Oh well, it works for Meg Ryan.'

At 5:45 she grabbed her purse, tossed in her keys and checked her wallet for cash, just in case Mr. Wonderful wasn't so wonderful. Tossing her short black lambskin jacket over her shoulder, she left her room for the short walk to the library. She was there in ten minutes flat, and he arrived a minute later. He was wearing black jeans, a black silk shirt with a leather vest, and boots. His black hair was restrained in a braid and hanging down his back. She felt a rush of something familiar that she couldn't quite pinpoint and shrank into a shadow to watch him for a minute and to allow the déjà vu to pass. He strolled casually to the place where she stood, mostly hidden by shadows and bushes, took her hand and kissed it softly.

"Good evening, my lady," he said, looking into her eyes.

"Hi, Alexander," she stammered. 'My lady?? What's THAT all about?' Coming from anyone else, it would have sounded corny. With him, it was somehow familiar.

Without another word, he led her to a black, late model BMW and opened her door. The interior smelled like a leather store, and she could tell it was kept immaculately.

"Nice," she said as he got in, "but what's the fascination with black?"

He grinned sheepishly. "Easy. It matches everything."

"Can't argue with that one. How was your exam?"

"Hell on earth. Yours?"

"Piece of cake, but I finished it too quickly. I didn't plan to get out of there before 10:15, and I was done at 9:30."

"Hate when that happens," he laughed.

"Me too! I didn't quite know what to do with myself! Where are we going?"

"Do you have a preference?"

"Depends on if you want to take the chance of causing a scene."

"What kind of scene, good or bad?"

"Well, my favorite restaurant is Henry's. I love going there, the trouble is, so does Jack. He always goes there when he has a date."

He mulled this over for a second. "I assume he has a date tonight? Do you want to go to Henry's or avoid it? Personally, I love the place too. That's where I was planning to go, but if you don't want to run into Jack, we'll go somewhere else."

"No, actually I do want to go to Henry's. I want Jack to see me."

Alexander shot an unmistakable look of confusion at the beautiful girl sitting beside him. She laughed and told him about meeting Jack on campus earlier in the day, and about her conversation later with her father. A few minutes later, they strolled into Henry's. It was busy, as it usually was on a Friday evening, so they waited at the bar for their table. They sipped beer from frosted mugs and talked about school. Suddenly, Alexander glanced past her and slipped an arm around her shoulders. He pulled her closer to him and whispered, "Your buddy just came in."

"Jack?"

"Yes."

She laughed as if he'd said something cute and asked, "Is he with someone?"

He nuzzled her hair and she shivered unconsciously. "Susan Cashwell, I think."

She looked back over her shoulder and, sure enough, there were Jack and Susan. There was no doubt that Jack had seen them because he was coming to claim a couple stools right next to them. He sat right beside her and ordered beers for Susan and himself.

"Hi, Robyn. I didn't expect to see you here."

"I told you I had a date, Jack. You didn't believe me."

"Is it my fault I thought you were kidding?"

She countered quickly. "Is it my fault you didn't take me at my word again?"

Robyn smiled and turned back to Alexander. She did her best to ignore the fact that, while Jack had his arm around Susan, he was steadily moving closer to her. She shifted discreetly toward Alexander, hoping that Jack was not actually trying to crowd her, but knowing at the same time that it was not accidental.

"So Robyn," Susan said, "what are you up to these days?"

Robyn turned and answered, "Just working on getting through my senior year and getting enrolled in my Master's program."

"So you aren't going to go get a job after graduation?" Susan asked. She was the daughter of a wealthy family and tolerated working class people only because she had to. Robyn had wanted to tell her more than once that her family was a lot better off than Susan's, but her father didn't like it to be public knowledge, so Robyn merely treated Susan like the airhead cheerleader that she was.

"I have a job, Susan. I'll be working this summer and part time while I go to school next fall."

"Really?" Alexander jumped in, trying to save her. "Where are you going to work, Robyn?"

"I'm going to help out in the weather department over at WPIT. It will fulfill my master's internship requirement and provide some on-the-job training. Plus I'll get to play with the radar!"

Susan smiled and said, "Have you decided what you're going to do with all of this when you grow up?"

"Well, Susan, I thought maybe I'd be a weather girl. All I'd have to do is pretend to be you and I'd have the perky dumb blond routine down cold."

"Hey, Robyn, your table is ready. Rachel will walk over with you." It was Steve. He was looking at Robyn, imploring her with his eyes not to start a brawl in his bar, even though in this case he thought it was justified. He shot a warning look at Jack and went back to work.

Robyn and Alexander got up, took their mugs and followed Rachel to their table. Robyn chose the chair that had its back to the bar and hoped that Jack's table wouldn't be in front of her. Alexander held her chair while she sat, then casually took the chair across from her and started looking at the menu. Robyn didn't bother with picking it up. She was too irritated, and she knew what she wanted, which was really for Jack and Susan to marry each other and move to North Dakota. Robyn figured it was a safe bet that she would never have occasion to spend more than a week there, so the chances of running into them would be minimal. She wiped the condensation off her mug with one finger, slowly tracing stripes from the top to the bottom. Alexander watched her over the top of his menu.

"Is he always like that?"

Robyn looked up in surprise. She had been deep in concentration, and had almost forgotten where she was. She sat back and smiled. "Yes. So is she. I don't know why I let them get to me. I guess it's just because they think they're so much better than anyone else. Luckily, most of us know the truth! I can't believe I was dumb enough to date him!"

Alexander grinned. "We all have lapses in good judgment once in a while!"

"Well, mine is sitting at the bar. I can't believe my Dad liked him! Well, he never actually met him, so maybe he really wouldn't have. He just liked him because he's a football player and in ROTC. If he had met him, he might not have liked him after all. So, what are you getting?" She knew she was babbling, but she didn't try to curtail it too quickly.

Alexander sat patiently until she took a breath, laughing quietly. She was cute when she did that, and he just watched. "I'm not sure. What about you?"

"They have a killer new steak sandwich here. It's kind of a Philly, but with a Mexican twist. I've wanted one for days, I just haven't had the time to get one, and I haven't been able to convince Henry to start a delivery service. He says he'd have to hire a bunch of new people and it wouldn't be cost effective, plus people come here 'for the atmosphere as well as the food.' Anyway, the steak sandwich is really good. Of course, so is the manicotti. What are you laughing about?"

"Just listening to you switch subjects back and forth. Do you have conversations with yourself when no one else is around?"

Robyn stuck her tongue out at him and picked up a menu. She tried to smack him in the head with it, but he caught it quickly and pulled it out of her hand. She didn't realize it until she saw it in his hand and found herself looking stupidly at her own. He laughed out loud then, a contagious, rumbling belly laugh, and she and several people around them were soon laughing with him without really knowing why. As she laughed, Robyn seemed to hear her voice, as if from a distant memory, saying, "I love you, Puff." Having no idea where it came from, she tried to shake it off, but the déjà vu was so strong that she suddenly felt sad, as if she had lost something very important.

"Anything wrong?" Alexander asked.

She picked up her purse and fumbled through it as if she were looking for something. What she was really trying to do was avoid looking at him. She wondered if this was what it was like to have amnesia. Her dreams about Nyakas had become much more vivid since she'd met Alexander, and she was having flashbacks about something she couldn't remember but knew she should. Flustered, she stammered something about everything being fine and excused herself to the ladies room.

Henry believed that atmosphere was as important as product and service, and the ladies room reflected this. It was decorated like lady's sitting room in Renaissance England, with red velvet chairs, marble fixtures, and gilt mirrors. His only concession to the modern era was the plumbing, and that was only because he had building codes to comply with. It was softly lit with the barest minimum of fluorescent lighting and electric candles in sconces all around the walls.

Robyn went to the nearest mirror and dug her brush out of her purse. She looked in the mirror and suddenly felt as if she was looking at herself in another time and place. Another wave of déjà vu passed over her, and she sat down in one of the red velvet chairs. In her mind, she could see a lake with fish that she knew were the best she had ever caught, but couldn't name. She was fishing and laughing with Nyakas, who was teasing her. Robyn shook her head hard, banishing what seemed to be a vivid memory. 'OK, Robyn. It's the lighting. Alexander is really affecting you. He called you 'my lady' and it went to your head, right along with the beer. What is it about him? I can't possibly know him that well; we only just met. Just pull it together, babe. You've been studying too hard. You'll be OK in a few days. Go have another beer and get the manicotti. That will soak up the alcohol better.'

She went back out and sat down. Again, Alexander asked if everything was OK. She smiled and said, "Yeah, everything's fine. I guess I'm a little more fried from exams than I thought."

"If you want to do this another time, I'll understand."

"No, really, I'm OK. Being out tonight is just what the doctor ordered. I've been spending far too much time in my room studying. Jack didn't believe I had a date tonight, and I can see why! It's time to at least pretend I have a life!"

Connie, their waitress, came to take their orders, and Alexander looked at Robyn with surprise when she ordered the manicotti and another beer, but he didn't say anything. They talked through dinner, then he paid the bill and they went to see what movies were playing. Not really finding anything they wanted to see, they decided to sit by the duck pond on campus. When they got there, Robyn thought about the lake with the fish. Banishing the thought quickly as folly and wishful thinking, she made a joke about needing her fishing pole. He took her home after a couple hours and walked her to the door. He kissed her hand, promised to call her soon, and swept back down the hall. Robyn watched him leave, then went inside to bed. She dreamed, of course, about fishing in a lake with Nyakas, who teased her, made her laugh, and loved her more than life.

****

Gravity sat in the barn alone. He heard a noise and slowly drew his sword from the sheath on his back.

"It's just me," Nyakas said, walking past his friend.

Gravity let out a sigh of relief. "Where have you been?"

Nyakas grinned. "We went to dinner and sat by the pond and talked. It was all I could do not to take her in my arms and tell her everything!"

"All right, all right, slow down! Tell me what happened!"

"I'm sorry. We met at the library and she got there before I did. When I got there she was standing in a shadow watching me, as beautiful as the day I laid eyes on her."

"Maybe she's starting to remember some things about you."

"I think you're right. She acted a little strangely before dinner, but she said she'd just been studying too much. She doesn't know that I know her better than that."

"What happened to make her act strange?"

"She was rambling, like she used to when she was nervous. You remember; she would just keep talking. I teased her about it, and she tried to hit me in the head with a menu, so I grabbed it from her hand, and the look on her face was so priceless that I had to laugh. She laughed, too, but then she looked sad. I think that's when she started to remember something, but then she got up and went to the ladies room. It was like she had to have a little time to make sense of it. How are we going to do this, Gravity? We don't have much time left, and she'll need to be trained again."

"I know. I'm worried about it, too. You'll need to try getting her to remember who you are without frightening her. Did you kiss her?"

"No. Well, yes. I kissed her hand."

"Well, she used to go on at great length about how you kissed her. I always told her I didn't want to know, and she did it to get on my nerves, but you might want to try that."

"Perhaps you're right. I really wanted to, but I didn't want to push too hard. She's been pushed recently, and I don't want to scare her off. Not after finding her again."

"Well, I would suggest that tomorrow morning you get one of those portable phone contraptions so that she can get in touch with you."

"You're right. I'll go check into it tomorrow morning."

"Good. Well, now that you're back, I can go to bed. I can't believe you stayed out so late, but I'm glad you had a good time. Did she say anything about her mother?"

"Not specifically, but I can tell you that she's married to Robyn's father and apparently was when Robyn was born."

"You're kidding! But when she was with us before her father hadn't known about her until she was eight!"

"I know. She told me the night she drank too much Ambush that she always wished that her father had been there when she was little, and then a page came and told me that Stephan was there. I guess Vermeer heard about it somehow, or my father had another spy on my staff. Not much point in worrying about it now."

"Yes, don't worry, we'll figure something out. Let's get some sleep and tomorrow morning we'll get your phone and decide what to do next."

"Yes. Good night, Gravity."

"Good night, my friend."

Chapter 45

Robyn rolled over in bed and opened one eye. When she focused on the clock, it said 12:32. A glance at the closed curtains revealed sunlight seeping through, and Stephanie's bed was made. She sat up and groaned as her head began to throb. Rolling out of bed, she stumbled across the room to turn on the coffee maker she'd had the foresight to set up the night before, and then crawled back into bed to wait for the coffee to brew. When it was done, she stumbled back and poured herself a cup, splashed in a little milk, then sat down on the couch and turned on the TV. As she drank her coffee and half-watched cartoons, her headache began to subside. Half way through her second cup, it was nearly gone, and she put it down and took a shower. She came out feeling nearly human. She put on her jeans and a sweatshirt and called Brett.

"Brett's room!"

"Hi! What are you doing?"

"Good grief, she lives! I came by your room this morning, and Stephanie told me under no circumstances was I to wake you up. Are you just getting out of bed?"

"No, I've been up long enough to drink two cups of coffee and get a shower. Now I'm starving. Have you eaten?"

"Yes, twice as a matter of fact. But I have a surprise for you. Stay there, pour me some coffee, and I'll be right down."

True to his word, there was a knock at the door a minute later. She had unlocked it and called him to come in. He entered with a big grin and one hand behind his back.

"Hi, sleepy head!"

"Hi! What did you bring me?"

"Not so fast! Coffee?"

She handed him a cup. "Just the way you like it, white and sweet, just like you. Now what did you bring me?"

"How much do you love me?"

She stomped her foot in playful exasperation. "Almost as much as I love my Dad! Come ON, Brett!"

He laughed and handed her a bag. She peeked inside to find a large chocolate éclair. She looked up at him, and then threw her arms around his neck. "I do love you, Brett!"

He laughed again as she sat down on the couch and pulled the pastry out of the bag. She was like a child, sitting Indian-style on the couch and savoring each bite, then licking her fingers. He knew what she'd want next, and he was ready with a cold glass of milk. She accepted with a smile. "You're too good to me, Brett."

"I know. I'm spoiling you. Now, tell me all about your date."

"So THAT'S what this is all about!"

"Yeah, of course! Had to butter you up so I could get all the juicy details before Stephanie!"

She laughed, drank her milk, and put the glass on the coffee table. "Well, we had a really nice time. We went to Henry's for dinner, and of course, Jack and Susan showed up. They tried to give me a hard time, but I had fun in spite of them."

"Good. Don't let them get one over on you."

"You'd have loved it! Susan asked me what I plan to do with my amassed knowledge 'when I grow up' and I told her that I was going to be a weather girl, and I'd be great because I'd just pretend to be her and everyone would think I was really a dumb blond!"

He laughed loudly. "Oh, Robyn! Brutal!"

"I know, isn't it great? So then we got to our table and we were talking, or rather I was talking. You know how I get when I'm flustered, I just go on and on."

"You? I've never noticed that!" She pushed his shoulder and he laughed. "Then what?"

"He asked me if I have conversations with myself when no one else is around."

"And do you?" Brett asked playfully, laughing.

"You've already talked to him, haven't you? Are you trying to get my side of the story, or are you just trying to get on my nerves?"

"Yes, I want your side and I am trying to get on your nerves, and no I haven't talked to him. I don't know him from Adam. What did you say?"

"Nothing. I tried to smack him in the head with a menu and he grabbed it out of my hand before I realized it. I must have looked like an idiot because he started laughing, and I couldn't help but laugh too. But then, you know how something triggers a memory of something you'd forgotten about?" He nodded. "Well, I 'remembered' myself saying 'I love you, Puff.' I don't know anyone named Puff, and there's certainly nothing 'puffy' about him!"

"Puff? Like powder puff?"

"Beats me. I don't know where it came from, but it was so weird that I couldn't shake it. So I went to the ladies' room to pull it together, and when I looked in the mirror the lighting must have been funky because it was like I was looking at myself, but not myself. Like it was a different time or something."

"That's strange. Hell of a first date, Rob, I'll give you that!"

"But that's not all! It was so strange that I sat down and I guess I remembered something I must have dreamed. I was fishing in a beautiful lake, and Nyakas was sitting beside me. He was teasing me about something and we were laughing, and he sounded exactly like Alexander when he laughed. It was like this loud, boisterous belly laugh, like you hear in comedy clubs all the time."

"Well, that must be it then! When he laughed it made you think about something you dreamed, and that's where that déjà vu came from! A lot of people laugh like that. Between that and the cloak, that has to be it."

"I bet you're right! You're so smart, Brett. What would I ever do without you?"

"Get your own éclairs, for starters!"

"Right again! What's it like outside?"

"Gorgeous. You'll roast in that sweatshirt. We should go do something totally unrelated to school."

"Well, I have to get groceries. It's my turn to buy them and you're drinking the last of my coffee. How about we go to the mall for a while, then to the grocery store, and we can decide what to do after that."

"You're right, you do need groceries. You just drank the last of your milk. Where's Stephanie?"

"She was gone when I woke up. Probably out with Tom, getting the details of my date third hand. I'm sure Jack told everyone at the fraternity all about what he saw." She grabbed a T-shirt and went into the bathroom to change. Then she laced on her hiking boots, grabbed her purse, and they left.

Since Robyn's car was a little bigger, they decided that she should drive. They went to the mall in pursuit of whatever they could find. Their search landed a copy of Valerie Jenkins' "Paradox" compact disc for Brett and new socks for Robyn. As was their tradition, they went to the food court next, and Robyn bought the ice cream. It was her turn because compact discs were definitely cooler than socks, and the person who bought the uncool stuff had to buy the ice cream.

After they finished they left the mall and continued their mission at the grocery store. Robyn wandered through the store picking up the things that she and Stephanie needed, and Brett followed her, being a pest. He loved going grocery shopping with her. His favorite game was to see how many things he could sneak into the cart without her noticing. His record was nineteen. Today he started with a lemon, a bag of candy corn (which she hated), and a box of animal crackers. Next were English tea bags, a can of tuna, and a can of oven cleaner (she didn't have an oven). She pretended not to notice his antics until he got to the condoms, and then he was reprimanded and sent to put back all of his previous treasures. He pouted and put them back but still managed to slip in a quart of chocolate milk and a candy bar at the register. She was in a good mood, so she bought those, too, and handed him half of his candy bar in the car.

"Hey!" he exclaimed, "What happened to the rest?"

She smiled at him and took a bite of the other half. Laughing, she started the car and drove back to the dorm. It was a short drive and in a few minutes they were carrying bags up the stairs to her room. She unlocked the door and they went in just in time to hear Stephanie say, "Oh, hang on, she just walked in. Rob, it's for you."

Robyn took the phone as Stephanie grinned, winked, and went back to the movie she and Tom were watching.

"Hello?" she said as she grabbed the milk to put in the refrigerator.

"Hi, Robyn."

"Alexander?" Brett looked at her in surprise and went to watch the movie with the others. "Hi! Did you find another quarter?"

He laughed. "No, I got a cell phone. I figured it was about time. How are you?"

"Fine! What are you up to today?"

"Not much. I was going to try to study, but I haven't been able to bring myself to look at my books. What have you been doing?"

"Oh, I slept late and went shopping."

"Did you buy anything good?"

"Nope! Socks and groceries. Nothing exciting."

"I'd have to agree with you on that one. I hope you had a good time last night."

"Are you kidding? I had a ball, and you inspired a chocolate éclair this morning!"

"How did I do that?"

"My friend, Brett, wanted to hear about our date before anyone else, so he brought me an éclair to bribe me into telling him!"

Stephanie looked up in surprise, and then smacked Brett in the arm. "You cheated, you little shit!"

Brett smacked her back. "Did not! It was fair and legal. If you'd been here you could have heard it too!"

Robyn laughed and said, "All right, children, that's enough! I'm on the phone here!"

"What am I missing?"

"Stephanie and Brett are fighting again. I guess Steph wanted to hear all the details too! I don't get out much, so when I do, it's a big deal to my friends! It looks like they're watching "Mother's Deception" on video here. Have you seen it?"

"No. Have you?"

"Oh, yeah. It's really good. Why don't you come over?"

"It sounds good, but I don't want to intrude."

"Intrude? No way! OK, hang on a second." She held the phone out so he could hear her friends and said, "Hey, guys, what if we rewind the movie and wait for Alexander. He's a Mother's Deception virgin, and I can tell you about our date until he gets here."

She was answered with a loud affirmative response, and she said, "Alexander, I think they want you to come over."

He laughed and said, "I think they just want to hear about our date, but if you want me to come over, I'll be there soon. 'Bye, Robyn."

He hung up, and she turned back to the groceries. She heard the TV shut off and the tape rewinding, then Stephanie was taking the coffee out of her hand.

"Well, come on, you told Brett about it, now spill it! Was he a keeper or a loser?"

"If I wanted to lose him, why would I invite him over here to watch the movie?"

Brett piped up. "Because he's a Mom's Deception virgin, and we can't have that!"

They all laughed, and Tom said, "Well, whether you had a good time or not, I saw Jack this morning and he was not in a good mood. I didn't get the whole story, but apparently he and Sue had a fight about you last night and she dumped him."

Robyn stared in disbelief. "You're kidding! What did she do, step on a worm and steal its brain?" She couldn't help but laugh, and she didn't laugh alone long.

"Come on, Robyn," Stephanie said, "You're going to have to tell me about it sooner or later. Or I can just accost him for details when he gets here."

"No, that's OK. We had a really good time. We went to Henry's for dinner, and then we went down to the duck pond and talked for a couple hours. He's very intelligent, and it was great to actually have a date with someone who was interested in talking to me instead of trying to cut to the chase. Then he brought me home."

Stephanie leaned closer. "He brought you home? And??"

"And what, Steph?"

"Did he kiss you?"

Tom and Brett groaned, and Tom said, "You know, women always talk about how they want us to talk to them, get to know them before we go any further, and what's the first thing she wants to know?" He matched Stephanie's tone. "Did he kiss you?"

Brett and Robyn were near tears with laughter, and Stephanie said, "Shut up, Tom! I didn't ask if he asked her to go to bed with him! The way a guy leaves you on the first date says a lot about him, and frankly, you're lucky to be here right now. Spill it, woman!"

Robyn wiped the tears away from her eyes and composed herself. "Yes, Steph, he walked me to the door and kissed me. On the hand."

"On the hand?!" Brett and Tom exclaimed in unison.

Stephanie waved her hand to silence them. "Where on the hand? The back, palm, or fingers?"

"The back," Robyn answered.

"Wow!"

The others waited for her to say more. When a few seconds passed and she didn't say anything, they all exclaimed, "What?"

"Well, my grandmother used to tell me stories about her grandmother, who was apprenticed to matchmaker in Greece. She was really good at it, but she couldn't find the right man for herself. One day she was in the marketplace and someone bumped into her and she dropped her packages. She started to pick them up and came face to face with a guy she didn't know. He handed her stuff back to her and apologized for bumping into her. Then they introduced themselves and he asked her if she would have dinner with him. She accepted, and he kissed the back of her hand. Grandma said that's how she knew he was the right man for her, and sure enough, they ended up getting married and were happy together for 57 years!"

Brett was the first to speak after a few seconds of stunned silence as they each digested the story. "Cool! Hey, Rob, maybe there's hope! How did he know to kiss her hand?"

"Grandma said she asked him the same thing. He said he didn't know, it just seemed like the thing to do."

There was a knock at the door and they all looked at it, then at each other. Robyn went to open it, then turned back to them with her hand on the doorknob. "Be nice!" she mouthed to her friends, then opened the door to let Alexander in.

"Hi, Robyn," he said as he came in. He handed her a bag. "Since you invited me to watch a movie, I figured the least I could do was bring the popcorn."

"All right!" Brett and Tom exchanged high fives, and Tom said, "He's a keeper, Rob!"

"A keeper?" asked Alexander, "A keeper of what?"

"Never mind," she answered and stuck a bag of popcorn into the microwave. "They're just giving me a hard time. Do you know my friends?"

"No, but I think that's about to change."

"Yeah. That's Brett Masters in the chair, my roommate Stephanie Antipolis on the couch, and Tom Mahoney, in his rightful place on the floor at Stephanie's feet. Guys, this is the now-infamous Alexander Stevens."

He was greeted politely and Robyn tried not to look surprised. Stephanie moved to the far end of the couch so Alexander could sit down, which he did. Robyn took the popcorn out of the microwave and dumped it into a big bowl, which was placed within reach of everyone. She sat down on the couch between Alexander and Stephanie, propped her left foot on Tom's right shoulder, and started the movie.

Everyone but Alexander had seen the movie several times, and they all laughed when they all quoted the same part at the same time and Alexander chimed in with, "In stereo, where available!" Robyn watched him covertly, and a couple times managed to reach for a handful of popcorn at the same time he did so she could "accidentally" touch his hand.

After the movie, he asked her if she'd like to take a walk, and she quickly accepted. Grabbing a light jacket, she said good-bye to her friends, and they walked out of the dorm together. It was beginning to get dark, and the sky was painted with the last bit of a spectacular sunset.

"Thank you for inviting me to watch the movie with you," Alexander said.

"You're welcome! I hope you liked it."

"Yes, I did like it."

"Good," she said. Suddenly she wasn't quite sure what to say, so she fell back on small talk. "It's a nice sunset, isn't it?"

"Indeed. Quite lovely."

"You aren't from around here, are you?"

"No. I've moved around quite a bit. I lived in Madrid longer than anywhere."

"Madrid? Wow! I've never even been out of the country, unless you count the Canadian side of Niagara Falls. What is Spain like?"

"It's a beautiful country. The people are as nice as you'd ever want to meet."

"Wow. I really feel like a country bumpkin now," she said wistfully.

"Why?"

"You've lived in places that I've only read about. You must have experienced things that can never be experienced here in Pennsylvania. I did a good bit of traveling around the country with my Dad, but he stopped going on the road when I was still a little kid. I must seem kind of, I don't know, uncultured to you."

He casually took her hand. "No," he answered, "I find you intriguing and beautiful. I'm beginning to think that I can't spend enough time with you. I have traveled a lot, and I've known a lot of people, but none interest me as you do."

"Me?" Her voiced squeaked, and she cleared her throat. "How am I interesting? I'm just a workaholic college student."

"I think there is a lot more to you than you give yourself credit for."

"Maybe. I guess nobody has ever said I'm interesting before, so I never gave it much thought."

"Well, you are interesting, Robyn. Interesting, beautiful, and complex. One minute you're a sophisticated woman, the next moment you are a child at play. I never know quite what to expect from you."

"You sound like you've known me for years!"

"I feel as if I've known you my whole life."

She didn't know how to respond to that. She felt a connection with him that she was ready to neither acknowledge nor explain, even to herself. She would admit to herself that holding his hand felt very nice, and that her night would be made if he kissed her.

They walked a bit longer as the sun set and the moon rose. Soon it grew chilly, and Alexander steered her back toward her dorm.

"I had a wonderful time tonight, Robyn. Again, thank you for inviting me."

"It was my pleasure. I had fun too. I hope we can get together again soon."

"I'd be honored. Shall I call you?"

"I hope you will."

They arrived at the outside of her dorm and he stepped to the door to open it for her. Their eyes met as she walked through the door, and she felt lost in his gaze. He walked in behind her, and put his hand on her face. Her eyes drifted shut as they moved toward each other. His kiss was light, almost teasing. She put her arms around his neck, and he put his around her waist. The kiss deepened slightly before he moved back. Her knees were weak as he took her hand and led her up the stairs. He saw her safely to the door, then kissed her again.

"I'll call you soon," he said as her door opened. He glanced at Brett, standing in the doorway. "It was nice to meet you, Brett."

"Same here, man," Brett replied. He watched Robyn as she watched Alexander walk back down the hall.

"Robyn," he said softly. She didn't reply. She just watched Alexander.

"Robyn!" He said a little louder.

"Hmm?"

Brett grinned and cupped his hands around his mouth. "Earth to Robyn! Come in, Robyn! The Spaceship Alexander has departed the planet, it's time to come home!"

Robyn glanced at him and stuck out her tongue, then brushed past him. Tom and Stephanie were getting ready to go out, and Robyn walked casually to the window.

"I'll be back later, Robyn," Stephanie said.

"OK. 'Bye." She looked out the window and was delighted to find that Alexander's car was in plain sight. She heard the door shut, and seconds later she saw Alexander walk to his car. She folded her arms across her ribs, remembering his kiss as she watched him start the car and drive away.

"Oh, this is priceless!"

She jumped, startled. She'd assumed that Brett had left with Tom and Stephanie. Instead, he was standing right behind her.

"Brett! I thought you'd left."

"Oh, no, buddy! Not a chance! Oh, man, he could have you wrapped around his little finger in a nanosecond if he wanted to!"

Robyn blushed and went to get a glass of water.

"So," Brett said, following her, "what did you two talk about?"

"Nothing important," she said evasively.

"Nothing important, or nothing?"

"Nothing important," she said, a bit more adamantly. "He thinks I'm interesting."

Brett laughed out loud. "Interesting? That's a new one! Judging by the results, I should give it a shot!"

Robyn was blushing furiously and having a difficult time looking at him, so she said, "I'll give you a shot, right in the teeth, if you don't shut up!"

"Ooh! Oh, looks like I hit a nerve! What's wrong, Robyn? Got the hots for your knight in shining armor?"

"Brett! Give me a break! Look, I really need to study for a while."

"No you don't. It's Saturday night, and you're already acing all of your classes but one. OK, we won't talk about him anymore. Besides, I don't think your face could get any redder."

She gave him her best wounded look and pointedly turned her back to him. She sat down on the couch and turned on the TV. Grinning, he sat down beside her and put his arm around her shoulder. She moved away from him, and he moved closer. She got up and sat in the chair, crossing her arms and blatantly ignoring him. He got up and sat on her lap.

"Brett, get off me!" She shoved him off her lap, and he allowed himself to fall on the floor.

He sat up beside her legs and tilted his head back until it rested in her lap. He looked at her and said, "You know you love me."

"Only because you bring me éclairs."

He laughed, and they settled back to watch television.

Chapter 46

Alexander called the next afternoon while Robyn was out. When she got back and heard his voice on the answering machine, she listened intently to the message, then rewound it and listened to it several more times, savoring the sound of his voice. He'd left a number for her to call. She was disappointed to get his voice mail, but she left a message anyway.

"Hi, Alexander. It's me, Robyn. I got your message. Sorry I missed you. I'll be in most of the night. I have a lot of studying to do. Hope to talk to you soon. 'Bye."

She hung up the phone, then listened to his message again. Sighing, she sat down at her desk and tried to study, but her thoughts were on him. After catching herself daydreaming for the fourth time, she closed her books and went running. When she got back there was a new message and she eagerly pressed the play button.

"Hi, Squirt. Sorry I missed you. Just wanted to check in since you haven't called your old man this week. Call me when you get back. Love ya' babe!"

Disappointed, she dialed the number, surprised when her mother answered the phone.

"Hi, Mom. Dad left a message on my machine. Is everything all right?"

"Oh, sure, honey, everything is fine. You know how he is. He gets antsy when he doesn't talk to you for a while. How is everything there?"

"Fine. I'm working hard. Quantum Mechanics is kicking my tail."

"Well, hang in there, honey. You'll get through it."

They talked a while longer, and her mother promised to let her father know that she was fine. After she hung up, she went back to her books, then went to bed early.

A couple of days passed without incident, and without word from Alexander. Tuesday afternoon she went to the library to start research for a paper. She began with the reference books, which sat on low shelves. The tops of the shelves were about four feet high and cleared so that the heavy books could be placed on them and read.

Robyn found the book she needed, plopped her book bag on the floor at her feet, and put the book on top of the shelf. She leaned her elbow on the bookcase, resting her chin on her fist as she pored over the book. She was so engrossed in her reading that she didn't hear the footsteps behind her.

Suddenly, there were arms around her waist. Startled, she instinctively drove her elbow into the ribcage behind her. The arms dropped away and she spun around. She was aghast to see Alexander holding his ribs.

"Alexander! I'm sorry! I didn't know it was you! I thought it was Jack! I'm so sorry, I didn't really hurt you, did I?"

He straightened and took a deep breath. "I'm all right."

"Are you sure? I'm so sorry, let me see." She reached for his shirt, and he stepped back.

"Really, Robyn, I'm all right. Really. Please stop apologizing. I'm fine."

"Are you sure?"

"Yes, perfectly."

"I'm sorry," she said contritely.

He chuckled. "It's OK. What are you doing?"

"Research. Nothing very interesting."

"Would you like to get an early dinner?"

"Only if you let me buy. I'm so sorry."

He laughed and picked up her book bag. He reached for her hand and said, "Don't hit me, OK?"

She blushed and said, "I'm really, really sorry. Are you sure you're OK?"

He turned to her and took her face in his hands. Her knees turned to water and her heart jumped into her throat as he lightly kissed her forehead and said, "I'm fine! I promise!"

They went to his car and drove to Henry's. Robyn apologized all the way there, and he kept telling her that he was fine, although he knew that there would soon be a small round bruise on his torso. She was much stronger than he remembered. Gravity would be glad to know this.

Chapter 47

Robyn was just stepping out of the shower Friday night when her phone rang. She threw on her robe and ran out of the bathroom to grab the cordless phone from the coffee table.

"Hello?"

"Hi!"

"Hey, Dad! What's up? I haven't heard from you in a few days, is everything all right?"

"Yeah, everything is fine, Robyn. I just wanted to let you know we finally broke ground on the new gym. Should be done by the middle of the summer. How is everything there?"

"Everything is fine, Dad. I can tell there's something else. What is it?"

"Umm, well, nothing much."

"Dad, spill it!"

"Your mom and I went to the store today to get groceries and, as usual, I was the pack horse. By the way, I tried to pull a 'Masters' but I failed. Brett will have to teach me how to be a little more smooth about doing that."

"Dad, Mom is too good to fall for those tricks! She taught me to do them!"

"Well anyway, we were walking down the baby food aisle and I thought, 'Oh, no! Here she goes about Robyn again!' She started grabbing diapers and formula, so I stopped her and she told her I didn't think you would eat that kind of stuff anymore, and I wasn't quite ready to be a grandpa yet. She just looked at me and smiled and then said, 'Well that's good, because I'm sure Robyn's younger brother or sister will use these up before Robyn's child needs them.' I, of course, stood there in the middle of the store staring at her like an idiot."

Robyn screamed, "Yes, yes! Someone else for Mom to worry about! Dad, I owe you my life! How can I ever thank you?"

"Hey, I was shocked when she said it, especially standing right in the middle of Herrigans. I guess she wanted to wait but she couldn't resist one-upping my smart-ass comment."

"I'm so happy," Robyn replied, "I'm going to be a sister, that's so cool, I can't wait to tell Brett!"

"So what are you and Brett doing tonight?"

"We're going to 316's with some friends."

"Well you know to be careful and no drinking and driving; that goes for all of you." Kevin always gave the same 'briefing,' as he liked to call it, before she went out, and it was exactly the same every time.

"I know, Dad! I've got to get rolling. I'm not even dressed yet!"

"OK, babe, I won't hold you guys up. I love you, sweetie."

"I love you too, Dad."

Robyn hit the off button, laid the phone down and screamed with excitement just in time for Brett come through the door.

"Hello to you, too! Is it my new cologne, or just my electrifying personality?" Brett asked.

"No, no, my mom is pregnant! I just talked to my dad, I'm going to be a sister!" She yelled excitedly, speaking loud enough for the bottom and top floor to hear her.

"Hold on, I don't think you woke the people on the other side of town yet! You, a sister? I feel bad for the poor kid already!"

"Shut up," Robyn replied with a smile.

"Well, are you ready?" Brett asked.

"Nope, but I will be in a few minutes."

As usual Brett was dressed in khaki pants and a cardigan sweater with a white T-shirt underneath. His brown dress shoes were shined and his was hair slicked back. Robyn finished dressing quickly, and soon her wavy blonde hair hung loosely around her beautiful face. Her blue jeans were snug around her small waist, and she wore a white t-shirt and a lightweight, forest green sweater.

As they walked from Robyn's room, Brett seemed to notice there was something different about Robyn ever since she had started dating Alexander. She was always beautiful, but she seemed to have more assurance about herself. She seemed more confident and a little less worried about her grades. She was smart and often she actually hurt herself by studying too hard. Her grades couldn't get any better and seeing her smile more made Brett a whole lot happier.

"Is Alexander going to meet us at 316's?"

"No," Robyn pouted, "he had something he had to take care of tonight."

They got into Brett's car and went to Henry's to eat as they usually did before going out on the town. They talked about Robyn being a sister soon and Brett's offers from some people to play on the PGA tour, which made Robyn very excited.

Henry's was packed, as it usually was on a Friday night. They waited for a table and their favorite waitress came to their aid.

"Good evening, Robyn and Brett, the usual table?"

"Yes, please," Brett answered.

"Follow me!"

She sat them at a corner table, and took their drink orders and gave them menus. It wasn't like they needed them; they already knew what they were going to eat, but they took them and looked them over anyway.

"Brett, look who's here," Robyn said.

Brett looked up to see Jack. "Great! Numb nuts graces us with his presence, I'm so overjoyed I could spit." He raised the menu up a bit to hide behind and bellowed, "Old Smiling Jerk is in the house!" It echoed through Henry's and everyone stared at Jack.

Jack's face twisted in scorn and he walked over to their table. "Problem?"

"No, no problem," Brett replied with a smile, "By the way, Jack how's your love life going? I saw Jessica Hartley leave your frat house today, and she just didn't look satisfied. Oh yeah, I forgot, I'm sorry. You big football star, must take steroids, make big muscles. Too bad about the side effects." Jack grabbed Brett from his chair and lifted him to his feet. Brett quickly grabbed the big man by his collar. "Now do yourself a favor and just go away."

Jack smiled as he pulled himself away from Brett's reach. "Don't turn your back, Masters, don't turn it for a second." Jack walked away to go sit with his friends at another table. People laughed and joked that the golfer had just humiliated the football star.

Robyn laughed. "Are you nuts? He'll crush you like a pimple!"

Brett smiled brightly and replied, "No way! He's never met my 9 iron! With that I'll change his religion and sex!"

Robyn laughed and they sipped their drinks as they waited for their food. They sat and talked about nothing in particular. Their food arrived, as it always did, with great speed and quality. They ate and then went to the bowling alley to meet with Tom and Stephanie. In the car they saw some other friends at a stoplight.

"Hey, Chauncey! What's up brother," Brett yelled.

"Hey what's going on man," Chauncey replied.

"We're going bowling with some friends at 316's in a few minutes!"

"Sounds cool, we'll be there."

They entered 316's about 10:00 to find that it was cosmic bowling night. The owner of 316's was a man who had once wrestled with Robyn's Dad, and it had photos of a lot of wrestlers she knew. There were television sets mounted to walls and suspended from ceilings. On the nights when there was no wrestling on TV, they showed videos of past matches. This place got a lot of business, especially because upstairs was a dance club and bar which stayed open until three o'clock in the morning when most places closed at one or two. They got their bowling shoes and lane twenty, Brett's favorite number. He said it was his Dad's football number when he had played. Brett was always good at any sport he played; he was just naturally gifted as far as athletics was concerned. When he got older and wanted to continue playing ball his father recommended against it; Brett wasn't very big at all. He decided to play a sport that didn't require pads and mouthpieces, only a collared shirt and golf clubs.

Tom and Stephanie came in right behind them, and soon Chauncey joined them. "What's up guys?" Chauncey said loudly. He was tall and thin with light brown skin and short hair. His brown eyes always twinkled mischievously as if he were up to no good. He was with an attractive young woman with long brown hair.

"What's up, man?" Brett extended his hand to his friend.

Robyn, Tom, and Stephanie greeted Chauncey, and he said, "Guys, this is Jeannie."

"Hi, Jeannie!" they said in unison and then they all talked for a few minutes before the games began. Bowling was competitive at 316's. The teams were determined by who you were with that evening. Brett decided it was good thing he'd brought Robyn because she was a much better bowler than Sarah. The bowling alley was packed, especially since a lot of people were walking back and forth between the bowling alley and the club upstairs. As usual, they began teasing each other in an effort to keep their opponents' scores lower than their own.

Brett took his position and began his approach. "Tom, keep your eyes open this shot, because I'm going to set you back about a touchdown."

Halfway through Brett's approach Tom said, "Brett, tie your shoe before you slice it into the next lane!"

Brett laughed and the ball found its place in the gutter. The group laughed hysterically as Brett and Robyn played another of their games: Unknowing Fashion Show Winners. They secretly chose people from the crowd to win in various categories from Sexiest to Freakiest. The night's Sexiest winner was a girl in a white see-through mini-dress with nothing underneath except a white bra and panty. The Freakiest was a guy who had both ears lined with earrings, as well as piercings in his nose, lip, eyebrow, and who knew where else, wearing jeans that were ripped and torn to nothing but threads and a collared shirt that Brett thought he could wear on tour.

They talked and bowled until about 1:30, and then went upstairs. The club was rowdy as it usually was on a Friday night. Robyn and Brett made their way through the crowd, greeting those they knew on their way to the bar. This was one of Robyn's favorite places because it reminded her a lot of her Dad, who had taken great pride in being a wrestler. Neon raced up the walls of the entire club. The pictures of some of the greatest wrestlers, including Brick Barabas, at past wrestling events hung on the walls, and life-size cardboard cutouts stood vigil in strategic spots. The owner had a tendency to rotate them, even going so far as to put them in dark corners and rest rooms. The hardwood floor was always polished to a shine. The bar wrapped around almost the entire perimeter of the club.

"Robyn, your boy is here," Brett said sarcastically.

Robyn glanced in the direction Brett was looking and saw Jack. She waved with a fake smile. "Yeah, great, glad to see him. It doesn't matter anyway; he decided to do something stupid and lost the best thing that could have happened to him. Now he's got no one and I've got Alexander. I think I'm a lot better off."

"You got it bad on Alexander, huh?"

"What do you mean, got it bad?" Robyn said with a self-confident smile.

"I mean, you almost look like you're walking on air sometimes, like after he kissed you the day we watched Mom's Deception."

"So he kissed me," Robyn replied. "Are you jealous?"

"Jealous! Yeah, right! Concerned maybe. He just seems to have such a hold on you. Don't get me wrong, I'm glad to see you happy with someone else besides me."

"A little arrogant aren't you, Brett?"

Brett smiled. "No! You misinterpreted what I said! I'm just glad to see that you've finally hooked up with someone who treats you right. I just wish I knew him better. You and I will have fun together no matter what we do."

"Yeah, you're right." For a second she looked as though she felt sad and didn't understand why.

"What is it?"

"Nothing much, there's just something familiar about him. I feel like I've known him forever."

As Brett and Robyn took to the dance floor, evil entered the club. Kerrigan strolled in arrogantly, taking full look at what he called heaven. He looked intently at the crowded club and smiled with joy, thinking, 'This area could be a holocaust of death! All these people! I could burn this place to the ground and while some stampeded one another I could watch the rest burn. The lucky ones who would make it out I could slaughter at my leisure! My sword is hungry for blood!'

He walked across the floor confidently, and people seemed to move as he got close to them without knowing why. He strode across the floor to sit at a seat on the banister across from the bar and fell in love with the realm that was known for being corrupted by greed and technology. As he watched the young people dance, he enjoyed himself so much that he almost lost sight of why he was truly there in the first place. He soon saw his prize, and his smile reached from ear to ear on his chiseled face. He stood up slowly and began to stalk his prey, paying no mind to those who stood in his way, just brushing past as though they never touched him. His eyes were locked on the pretty girl he had been dreaming about, the one who had killed him so long ago, the one he would vanquish. He was but a few steps from the thing he wanted so much when another figure walked up to his prize. Unperturbed, he continued walking to the bar to watch.

"May I have this dance?" said the now-familiar voice from behind Robyn. Her heart skipped a beat and she turned quickly to find Alexander standing behind her in black jeans, soft black leather boots, and a black collared shirt. His hair was finely braided and lay neatly down the middle of his back. His eyes met hers as he told her he had requested a song for them. Brett welcomed Alexander with a handshake and returned to the bar to get drinks. Alexander led Robyn to the middle of the dance floor and his arms wrapped around her waist. Her left arm found its way to his shoulder and she played with his braid, and her right hand gently rested on his heart. They danced silently through the song just staring at each other, each with something their hearts that neither quite had the courage to say. They moved gracefully around the floor as though they had danced often before. He leaned his face down to hers and their eyes closed. Their lips almost met when suddenly he sensed an evil presence. Without looking around, he knew Kerrigan was at the club and that he would target Robyn. Instinctively, he lightly picked her up and moved her to the opposite side from where he knew Kerrigan was, placing himself between his love and the one who hunted her.

"I'm sorry," Alexander said with an embarrassed smile on his face.

"Don't be. It's all right," Robyn replied, knowing at that moment that he was the one she had been dreaming about. She kissed him lightly as the song ended.

Smiling, Alexander said, "Why don't we go have a seat? I see your friend Brett found a table with some of your friends."

Robyn was lost in his eyes, not knowing that his real name was Nyakas and how he longed to tell her the truth. "OK," she said, and led Alexander to the table where her friends sat. There was only one chair left at the table, and Alexander motioned for Robyn to have a seat. He was still a little unsure of himself when the others were around, although when they were alone he was more relaxed.

Robyn, still standing beside him, looked at him innocently. "No, that's OK. You go ahead."

"No, I can't let you stand!"

"I'd rather stand, really. Have a seat." He looked at her sheepishly and sat down, and she promptly plopped into his lap and wrapped her right arm around his neck. The startled look on his face caused gales of laughter, but he put his arms around her waist and made no attempt to move.

As everyone chatted casually, Robyn turned to face Alexander. "I didn't expect to see you here."

"I finished early, so I decided to see if I could come find you."

"You came all the way out here to see me?"

"Of course. You said you were coming here, and I wanted to see you."

"Really? I'm glad." She smiled and kissed him.

"I'm glad you're glad," he said, "but why are you glad?"

She laughed. "Obviously you haven't had as much beer as I have since you can say that! I'm glad because I wanted to see you, too. I missed you."

He smiled and pulled her closer, lightly kissing her neck. She relaxed in his arms, feeling as if there were no other place on earth more perfect for her to be. As the conversation continued he leaned forward to speak softly in her ear. "If I tell you something, will you give me an honest reaction?"

"You know I will."

"I love you."

She turned quickly to face him. "What did you say?"

"I said I love you."

"That's what I thought you said. Wow, that's pretty amazing. I was just thinking that same thing."

"Really? You love you too?"

She laughed. "Well, yeah, but I also love you."

He smiled and kissed her. Everything around her seemed to fade out and she was conscious only of him.

Across the room, Mike, Lars, and Lilly made their entrance into the smoke-filled club. Lilly was dressed in a revealing black dress, cut low to show more of her cleavage than most husbands would allow and with a slit up her right leg that would have only been inches away from showing her panties if she had bothered to wear any. She wore this with a pair of black shoes that had four-inch silver stiletto heels, which drew even more attention to her because of the added height. Her long brown hair had been coerced into a French twist. If there was any doubt as to the gender of this huge person, they were quickly put to rest.

Mike wore blue jeans and a black sweatshirt, knowing that everyone would be so busy looking at Lilly that they wouldn't pay any attention to him. His steps were soft and quiet, and made even Lars wary of his unassuming friend.

Lars wore khakis, a white collared shirt, and his black trench coat. He walked with his friends past a few people who stood at the top of the short staircase that led to the floor area and the bar. Lars passed a man and had the feeling of impending danger. He turned to find Gravity standing quietly at the top of the stairs, and just looking at the man gave him an uneasy feeling. Their eyes locked for a moment as Gravity nodded to acknowledge Lars' presence, then continued to watch for Kerrigan, whom he knew was here. Although Lars could sense evil in Gravity, he knew there was more ahead, and it was much bigger. Lars crept quietly behind Mike and Lilly, knowing there was more to be seen.

Mike had caught sight of Robyn and a few of her friends and led Lilly that way, speaking quietly to her. Lars, not knowing where he was being led, followed. As Mike drew closer, so did Kerrigan.

Lars shivered. He knew that evil was in front as well as behind at this point, and suddenly all the gibberish about 'the lesser evil' and 'the greater evil' made perfect sense. The lesser evil was behind him, the greater evil ahead of him, and the knowledge made him a bit edgy.

Mike went up to Robyn, who was sitting on Nyakas' lap talking to her friends and laughing out loud at a joke Brett had just cracked. Nyakas suddenly felt the presence of Kerrigan nearby. With one fluid motion he picked up Robyn and stood her up on her feet. She was startled at first, then she saw Mike, and then Mike saw Nyakas. The hatred these two had for one another ran deeply although they had not seen one another in a very long time.

Robyn said, "Hey, Dr. Jorgensson! Funny meeting you here!"

"Hi, Robyn," Lars replied. He leaned toward Mike and Lilly. "This is the student I've been telling you about."

Lilly stepped forward gracefully. Her Welsh accent was less pronounced since she had been living in New England for so long but it was still unmistakable. "Robyn, what a pleasure to finally meet you. Why don't you come buy me a drink? I would like to talk to you about Dr. Jorgensson. I'm told he has a small reputation challenge with some students and I would love your input." Lilly took Robyn's arm lightly and led her to the bar. Robyn followed, not even realizing what had happened.

Nyakas looked to see that Kerrigan had appeared to the left of Mike and Lars, and their eyes met as well. Nyakas was suddenly very angry, and he slowly reached for the blade that was snuggled at his back. He felt a hand from out of nowhere grab his hand.

"Not here, not now," Gravity said from behind him, and Mike and Lars backed up, wondering where he had materialized from.

Nyakas' anger subsided slightly as he realized that the two people he wished most to defeat stood in front of him. He also knew that if he did what he wanted to do here, in this place, Robyn would witness all of it and hate him before he could explain. They all stood in a half-circle as though they were the only ones in the club. Nyakas slowly looked at Mike, Kerrigan and Lars, and said, "Three quarters of a mile south of here is an opening in the road. Meet me there, all of you, in a half hour." He quickly turned around and walked briskly to the steps, and Gravity backed out, following his friend without turning his back on his soon-to-be opponents. Kerrigan quickly disappeared into the rest of the crowd, and Mike stood and almost seemed to wait for something.

Lars looked at his friend and said, "Those are the two evils, and it is quite clear what will be done in the next half hour."

Mike said nothing; he just walked down the stairs and out to his car with Lars quickly following behind him. Mike got to his car and said, "You don't have to go if you don't want to, Lars."

Lars feigned a look of surprise and said, "And miss out on the fun while you get all the credit? Who knows, it was probably one of those idiots that ruined my Porsche. If I find him, so help me, I don't know what I'll do, but I'll be miffed!"

Mike chuckled and said, "OK, get in."

Mike and Lars were silent as they drove to the opening in the road. Mike saw the clearing, and parked on the shoulder, and they walked to the clearing in the pines. The first thing they saw was a stockpile of wood in the middle of the clearing in the shape of a teepee. The grass was short, the night air crisp and cold, and the moon full and illuminating. They walked around the left side of the woodpile and about forty yards beyond it as Kerrigan came from the opposite side of the field.

He was in armor, awaiting the war that was about to begin. He wore his swords on his sides, smiling in anticipation of his chance to annihilate these people. As the three waited, the woodpile spontaneously erupted into flames. Kerrigan almost seemed startled and then he realized their third party had just arrived.

Nyakas and Gravity made their way through the opening in the trees as though in slow motion, their steps methodical and sure. They were men on a mission and no one could stop them. Their eyes assessed their opponents and the world stood still for a moment as all their eyes met. The fire burned high and bright, and all five men moved toward it. Mike and Gravity drew their steel and walked as if anticipating the others' moves.

Suddenly, four other men, all wearing armor like his, joined Kerrigan. Three of them made their way toward the rest as fast as they could; the fourth remained at his master's side.

The first one brought his blade above his head and swung at Lars in a downward motion, as if to drive him into the ground. Lars lunged deftly to the left. His opponent's sword sliced cleanly through the air and sliced the turf where Lars had been standing. As he jerked the sword from the sod, Lars delivered a solid roundhouse kick to the back of his head. The man staggered forward and turned unsteadily to regard Lars with a glazed look. Lars was ready with a snap kick to the groin, a roundhouse to the face, and a punch, which landed with a solid thunk on the top of his enemy's head. The man fell dazed to the ground and Lars swept in and deftly grabbed his sword. With one solid stroke, he took the man's head.

Meanwhile, Gravity wasted no time in getting face to face with Kerrigan's other two warriors. The first attempted to take off Gravity's head, but Gravity's blade was much quicker than his. It rose from its place at his side as if of its own volition and sliced through his opponent's torso like butter. The other came from behind him, attempting a sneak attack. Unfortunately for him, Gravity knew he was there, and although it was not his first choice for positions, he knew the man would try to cause him harm and fail. With his wakasazi in his left hand, he spun around and found the man's eye. The blood streaked as the wound was opened, and Gravity's next blow was through the throat of his enemy. Kerrigan found quickly that his plan to let three of his four warriors try to halt the opposition wasn't going to work. As soon as the third warrior fell, he and his last warrior melted into the shadows and disappeared.

While Lars and Gravity wasted no time with their adversaries, Mike and Nyakas stood motionless, sizing each other up. They began to slowly circle the fire; it seemed the only thing they could agree on was which side of the fire on which to meet. They met with a clanging of steel on the south side of the flames. Nyakas struck for Mike's head. Mike parried easily with his wakasazi and simultaneously struck for Nyakas' midsection with his katana. Nyakas danced quickly out of the way, realizing that he wouldn't last long with his one sword against Mike and his two. Suddenly he remembered something he had seen Robyn do centuries before. When Mike spun on the ball of his foot to strike again, Nyakas dropped quickly to the ground and kicked Mike's left wrist. Reflexively, Mike dropped the wakasazi and Nyakas wasted no time kicking it away before he could retrieve it. Unfortunately his aim was off; he had intended to kick it away from Mike to a place where he could retrieve it himself, but he kicked it too hard and it slid into the fire. Mike was caught off guard by the extreme move but with uncanny speed reversed his cut and swung sideways to take off Nyakas' head.

Nyakas blocked the blow with his short sword, pushed hard and sent Mike backwards. Mike's balance was good but he had never guessed that Nyakas was so strong. He stumbled back a few feet before catching his footing and rushed forward as Nyakas rose quickly to his feet. Their blades locked as the two men met face to face. They began pushing with all their might against the other until Mike dropped in a crouched position, pulled Nyakas' legs out from under him and sent him sprawling onto his back. Nyakas lay dazed for a second and then saw Mike bringing his blade again. Before Mike could connect, Nyakas kicked Mike in the stomach and sent Mike to the ground. Quickly they both rolled to their feet and rushed at one another again. Suddenly a thunderous clap ripped though the night and sent both men backwards in a tornado like spin. They were momentarily stunned. As the shock wore off, they looked to see Gravity's hands coming back to his sides where they had been in the air only seconds before. Mike noted absently that all of their other adversaries were gone.

Gravity's eyes opened and Nyakas realized what had happened. It was Gravity's spell that had stopped their fight. He didn't like it though he knew why and that it was for the best. Nyakas got to his feet and began walking in Gravity's direction. He nodded, and Gravity knew his friend was irritated that he had stopped the battle. Nyakas brushed by him quickly and headed towards the opening in the woods. Lars strolled unassumingly toward Mike, who held his steel ready in his hand, awaiting Gravity's advance. Gravity stood motionless, his cloak blowing softly in the night wind for a moment before he walked towards Mike and Lars. He sheathed his swords as a gesture of good will, and they did the same.

"We are taking Robyn to our realm. Either you are with us or against us. I hope you're with us, for your sake," Gravity said as he turned away from them and began to follow Nyakas back through the opening in the woods.

Mike quickly replied, "Over my dead body! You're not taking her anywhere!"

"I'm sorry you feel this way," Gravity replied, turning back with a normal non-expression look on his face. "Mike, I remember we did this once before and all it led to was you and my friend developing that professional hatred for one another. Let it go, if not for me, then for the girl you try so hard to protect. Neither Nyakas nor I will hurt her, but Kerrigan will."

At the mention of the enemy's name, Lars jumped as if he'd been shot and exclaimed, "Mike, this man is right. His soul speaks truth. Nyakas is the lesser of two evils and wishes only good for the child."

Mike looked at Lars, and said "I guess I have no choice, then."

Gravity replied, "No, not really, Mike. You of all people know the lengths Nyakas went to get Robyn, and what he will do to keep her safe." He nodded to Mike and Lars, then walked past them and got into Nyakas' car to go find his friend.

Nyakas, meanwhile, had walked back to the club and found Robyn just before she left for the evening. She saw Nyakas and ran to him. Just before she reached him, she jumped, and he caught her. "Hi! What happened to you? I came back from the bar with Mrs. Ryan and you were gone!"

"I had something to attend to. I have to talk to you about something. Can you come back to my place?" As he spoke, Gravity pulled the car into a parking space and got out.

"OK, just let me tell Brett." She went to Brett and said, "Hey, buddy, I'm going to go back with Alexander. He said he has something to talk to me about."

"Uh huh, and you're buying that 'talking' excuse?"

"Brett, come on."

"Hey, just calling them like I see them, buddy. I saw you playing tonsil hockey with him earlier. Here, take this, just in case." He pressed something into her hand, and she looked to see a condom.

"Brett!"

"Just looking out for my best girl! Now scoot!"

"All right, all right! But I will give this back to you in the morning."

"Nope, don't want it back, especially if you wind up doing what I think you will. Yuck!! See you tomorrow, and hey! Be careful!" He got into his car with an impish grin, and she stuck her tongue out at him. As she walked back to Alexander's car she nonchalantly put the condom in her pocket.

He opened the door for her and said, "Is everything OK?"

"Yes, he's just giving me a hard time as usual."

She got into Alexander's car and saw someone in the back seat. As he got in, Nyakas motioned to the figure in the dark and said, "Robyn, this is my friend, Gravity."

"Oh," she said, "nice to meet you."

"And you, my lady," Gravity answered. He was familiar to Robyn, but she couldn't say why, nor could she understand why he was making her nervous. She fought the urge to turn around and watch him to be sure he didn't try anything funny. Nyakas drove out of the city, and they didn't talk much as they drove to a small farm. He parked in front of the house and they got out of the car.

"You live out here?"

"Yes," he answered, "I'm more comfortable away from the city." He led her inside. It was dimly lit and there was a fire in the fireplace. She was still nervous and instinctively looked around for a secondary escape route in case she needed it. She made a mental note of a door on the other side of the small house, and heartily hoped it wasn't a closet.

Gravity went to the fireplace and added a log to the fire. "I'll leave you two alone, Nyakas. She doesn't remember me, and I'm making her nervous." He took a cloak off a peg on the wall, walked out the door Robyn had noticed, and shut it behind him.

Alexander turned to her. "Please, come and sit with me." He led her to the chairs in front of the fireplace. "There are some things I need to explain to you."

"I'd have to agree with you there. Maybe you could start with your name."

"My real name is Nyakas."

"Then why did you tell me it was Alexander Stevens?"

"Because I didn't want you to remember too quickly."

"Remember what?"

"You have had strange dreams for a few years, haven't you? Recurring dreams about a place and people you don't remember."

"Yes."

"Those weren't dreams, Robyn. They are memories. They really happened. Let me start at the beginning. About eight years ago in your time you were in the Army."

"I couldn't have been! I was fourteen!"

"It was an alternate timeline. I know it sounds strange, just please let me explain." She nodded, and he continued. "You were a Major, and you were looking for some people who were missing. You and your team tracked them to a place called Area 51, and Romithian slave traders captured you. I happened to be in the market when your team was put up for auction, and as soon as I saw you I knew you were the woman I'd been seeking for so long. So I bought your group and set them all free on the condition that you stay and be my wife. You agreed, but it was only to ransom your friends. You weren't very happy at first, but you began training in swordplay with Gravity. In time, you came to love me as I loved you, and never were there two people who were happier. This made my father very angry. He felt that I was foolish for marrying you, and so he decided to separate us. He sent Kerrigan after you, and you killed him. We thought that everything would be fine after that. We even had a child together. Then my father made a deal with some powerful people and they took you and our son from me. They sent you back to the life you remember and repressed your memories as best they could. Our son has been with my father. I've spent the last seven hundred years in my time searching for you."

"Why? You didn't think that I'd be dead after seven hundred years?"

"Time is different in every dimension. It passes more quickly in my realm than in yours."

"So that makes you how old?"

"In my dimension, about 1,900."

"You're kidding, right? You missed Halloween, so you're trying to frighten me with this weird story and the dark house and the fireplace. You're waiting for me to get jumpy and clingy, right?"

"No, Robyn. I know this sounds bizarre to you, but all of it is true. I've been looking for you for two reasons. The first is purely selfish. I love you, and I've missed you, and I want you in my life. The second is to protect you and your loved ones from Kerrigan. Part of the deal my father made included his resurrection so that he could avenge his own death. My father knew that the most expedient way to see that you stayed out of my life forever was for Kerrigan to find you first and kill you. He is totally ruthless and not at all happy that a woman bested him with a sword. He's been on a rampage since he was resurrected trying to find you, and he's slaughtered whole villages in the process. At this point, I don't think he will bother your friends or family. As long as he knows where you are, he won't have a reason to. But he will use them to get to you if he has to."

"Oh. So how do I fix this?"

"Come home with me and train again. The only thing you can do is face him with your blade and kill him again."

"But if I do that, your father will just have him resurrected again."

"No, he can't. The others agreed to help him only on the condition that they would only do it once. It took a considerable amount of combined power to accomplish what they did, and none of them are willing to do it again, especially after they've seen what Kerrigan has done in the past seven hundred years. If you can defeat him again, there won't be anything my father can do to us."

"Why does your father hate me so much?"

"Because you're mortal, and he thinks you don't deserve to be with me."

"I'm mortal? He's not?"

"No. He's a minor god, and I was to succeed him. He is an evil, power hungry man who is accustomed to getting what he wants."

"So you couldn't succeed him if you were married to a mortal woman."

"It's not a widely accepted custom among my brethren."

"Your brethren? Are you one of those immortals, like in the movies?"

"Not exactly. I'm a dragon."

"A what?"

"A dragon. Think, Robyn. Do you remember a lake? It had wooded hills and a mountain behind it. You used to fish there. You said the fish you caught there were the best you'd ever had. Do you remember?"

She looked at the flames and remembered the flashback she'd had at Henry's. "I think so."

"The first time you went fishing in that lake, you saw a dragon. He flew from beyond the mountain, then dove into the lake. He washed some of the fish onto the shore, and you and Gravity picked them up just as the dragon flew out of the water."

"That was you?"

"Yes, that was I. My father cannot accept the fact that you are the other half of my being. Living without you these seven hundred years has been more difficult than anything I've ever done. I have told him that I will succeed him only with you at my side."

"How do we get to your home?"

"Gravity will open a dimensional portal."

"How long will it take to do all of this?"

"I'm not sure. You learned your skills quickly the last time, but you'd had considerable physical training before you came to us. Of course, you'd never handled a sword before. It may only take a few months, it could take longer, depending upon how fast it comes back to you."

"Months? But I still have school! I only have a few months left before I graduate! Can't we do it here so I can finish school?"

"Robyn, don't forget that time travels much slower here. A few months in my home will be a matter of days here. It is entirely possible that you could come back and defeat Kerrigan, then come back here and less than a week will have passed. Remember, for you we were separated five years. For me, it was seven hundred. Besides, you'll be safer at my castle, and it will lure Kerrigan away from you friends and family."

"What if I don't defeat him? What if he kills me? How will my family find out what happened to me?"

"He won't kill you. You defeated him once. You can do it again. If it will ease your mind, I promise to come back here and tell them myself if something does happen to you, but it won't because I won't let it."

"What if I don't go?"

"Then he will kill your friends, then your family, and when they are all dead, he will kill you."

"So the only way to save them and myself is to come back with you and learn how to kill him before he can kill me. Is that it?"

"Yes."

She looked at the flames. "Do you know how incredible all of this sounds?"

"Yes, I know."

"I'm supposed to just believe everything you're telling me?"

"I wouldn't lie to you, Robyn."

"But you already have! You lied to me about your name, where you're from, and I bet you aren't even enrolled in the college! Why should I believe you now?"

"Because I'm trying to protect you, Robyn. I had to have a cover story so I wouldn't frighten you away on our first date! Tell the truth. If I'd told you all of this over dinner at Henry's you wouldn't have had anything else to do with me, right?"

"Probably."

"All right, then! I was hoping you'd remember some of this on your own so it wouldn't sound so strange when I told you the whole story, but unfortunately Kerrigan forced my hand."

"How much longer did you plan to wait? Until I was so hopelessly in love with you that I'd take everything you said at face value?"

"Robyn, damn it, by then you would have remembered. You were starting to already. Don't accuse me of trying to play on your emotions when I was doing nothing of the sort!"

"Yes, you were, Puff!"

"What?"

"You were trying to play on my emotions!"

"No, you called me Puff."

"Stop trying to change to damn subject!"

"Robyn, listen to me for a minute! Why did you call me Puff?"

"I didn't, Alexander! Nyakas! Whoever you are!"

He got out of his chair and knelt before her on the floor. He took her face in his hands, looked into her eyes, and softly said, "Buzz, you called me Puff."

His voice made her think of a dream she'd had. They were snuggling in bed, and he said 'I won't use your nickname around other people either, Buzz.' She looked at him, shocked, not knowing what to say.

"You remember, don't you?"

She nodded, stood and walked away from the fire. She turned away from him and put one hand on her hip and the other on her forehead, trying to made sense of it all. It was cooler away from the fire, and she felt lightheaded as memories flooded back to her. She remembered being captured, getting married, the first night she and Nyakas were together, the birth of her son.

"Oh, no, he's got Marcus!" She turned back to him as tears filled her eyes, and she felt as if her heart was breaking. "Your father has Marcus?"

He came to hold her. "Yes, my love. I tried to get him back, but he's hidden him away."

As she wept helplessly, part of her wondered why she would be so sad over losing a child she couldn't really remember and if there was anything that could be done to get him back. When she composed herself, she asked the question.

Nyakas held her closely as he said, "I don't know. Maybe, after Kerrigan is dead, we can find him, but by now my father has probably got him totally corrupted. I'm sorry, Robyn. I wish I could be more helpful, but I know how influential my father can be, and Marcus was a new hatchling when he was taken. If anything can be done to fix this, I promise, it will be done. For now, you need to come with me and begin your training again."

"When?"

"As soon as possible."

"Can I go home and at least tell Brett and my parents?"

"Are you sure it's a good idea to tell them what you're doing?"

"I won't tell them everything, but I need to let them know I'll be gone for a little while so they won't worry."

"All right. It's going to be dawn soon. Why don't you lie down on the bed over there and get a little sleep. When you wake up I'll take you back to the campus and you can take care of your loose ends, and then we'll go. Is that acceptable?"

"Yes. Are you going to sleep too?"

"I'll sleep later. I'm going to stay awake to protect you."

"OK." She went to the bed in the corner, dropped her boots onto the floor, lay down, and promptly fell asleep.

Chapter 48

As Brett made his way back to the campus, he smiled, thinking of how happy he was that his friend finally had someone that treated her the way she needed to be treated. He drove to the dorm parking lot, grabbed his golf bag out of the trunk, and went inside. The golf bag was propped in the corner and he pulled out his nine-iron out, swinging it softly on the carpet to practicing chipping. There was a knock at the door and he stopped, trying to figure out who would be knocking at such a late hour. He put his golf club down, walked nonchalantly to the door and opened it wide to see a very large man.

"Sorry, don't need a roommate. Don't want one either. Take it easy," Brett said, and began to slowly close the door. The large man kicked the door and knocked Brett back. He slid down the wall, feeling every inch on the way down, and slowly got to all fours. He saw the large man enter the room with another man he hadn't seen. The large man was menacing; his bald head gleamed like a shined sterling silver ball. He walked into the room with pure hatred in his eyes.

The other man was wearing a long robe that covered his entire body. As he came in, Brett saw that he was leading Stephanie. She said nothing because she was gagged with what looked to be a rag of some sort. Her hands were tied around her back and tears flowed from her eyes. Brett could already see that she had been beaten. As Brett got to his feet, the large man watched in amazement, astounded that the young man would be dumb enough to get up and face him. Brett picked up his nine-iron and backed up just a little to put a fair amount of distance between him and his opponent.

"All right, steroid boy, it's my turn! 'Fore'!" Brett exclaimed as he swung for the head of this massive man. Instead of ducking out of the way, the man took the swing from Brett. The golf club met his face and zipped across his cheek, and the man's head turned. At that point, Brett realized he had just made a vital mistake.

The man backhanded Brett in the cheek and sent him back to the floor. Blood trickled from the corner of his mouth and the whole side of his face was bruised. His knees were weak as he got back to his feet and he began to stagger. The man took a shot at the other side of Brett's face. The backhand seemed to be more painful than the last; it sent Brett spinning and he crashed to the floor. His left eye was cut deep at the corner and the blood from his mouth still dripped. He felt dizzy but made his way to his feet and looked at the large individual. The man then sent a lightning-fast spinning roundhouse kick to Brett's chest that sent him to his black leather chair. Brett's momentum and weight sent the chair crashing backward onto the floor. Brett felt pain in his ribs and he knew that they had to have been broken. He began coughing up blood and lay on the ground as the large man began his walk around the room. The man in the robe tossed Stephanie on the couch and the tall man walked over to where Brett lay.

"So, you're Robyn's friend. It's such a pleasure to finally meet you, Mr. Masters. My name is Kerrigan."

Brett looked at the man for a second and said, "The pleasure is all mine. You mind helping me up so I can kick your ass?"

"You can't even walk, Mr. Masters. What makes you think you can take me?"

"Because, you enormous piece of trash, I fight dirty," Brett replied. He coughed up blood uncontrollably.

"All you have to do is tell me where Robyn's parents live and I will let you and your friend over there live. Do it not and you both will die."

"You go to hell!"

"Mr. Masters, you really don't want to see your friend die now do you?"

"You're going to kill us anyway. I don't know who you are or where you come from but I'm going to send you back there right now."

Brett quickly tried to get to his feet although the damage had been done. As he was close to getting to his feet Kerrigan quickly swept his legs out from under him, sending Brett back the carpet. Brett made a small thud on the carpet and blood came from his mouth. Kerrigan picked him up by the back of his khakis and set Brett's chair back on its legs, then deposited Brett in it. As Brett lay in the chair, barely able to keep himself from sliding out, Kerrigan's assistant took tie straps and tied Brett's arms to the arms of the chair. Brett watched as Kerrigan walked around his room. He looked at the pictures on Brett's desk of Robyn and him together and smiling, and then dropped them one by one on the floor. Brett's anger flared, his face red, but he said nothing because he didn't want anything to happen to Stephanie. He watched as Kerrigan went over to Stephanie lying on the couch and wiped her hair away from her face. He was gazing at her beautiful face and admiring the carnage and pain he knew he was inflicting.

"Mr. Masters you surely don't want this beautiful girl to die, now do you?" Kerrigan asked.

Brett began to cry as he studied Stephanie and tried to make the right decision. She looked back at him and shook her head, but Brett wasn't sure if she meant not to tell this maniac anything, or don't let him kill her.

"Mr. Masters, I'm talking to you! Hello! Hello, is anyone home?" Kerrigan demanded impatiently.

Brett slowly looked deep into Kerrigan's eyes. "You'll pay for this! I swear as long as I walk this earth you'll never be safe!"

"What are you going to do? You're all tied up with no place to go."

"Well, untie me and we'll see what happens then! What do you want with Robyn anyway?"

"It's personal. I want her to die in a loud grotesque manner. She took my life once and now I go to take hers. When I kill her I will be a god amongst my peers and I will be granted absolute power!"

"Well, I would love to know where it is you're from if they make you a god for beating a girl," Brett said sarcastically.

Kerrigan made his way around the rest of the room surveying everything. He stopped in the middle of the room and stared at both Brett and Stephanie.

He then motioned to his assistant to cut one of Brett's hands loose. As he did so Brett pulled it quickly from his grasp and spit in his assistant's face.

Kerrigan laid a piece of paper on the desk and moved Brett toward it. "I'm going to give you a chance to say something to Robyn before I decide what I'm going to do about the two of you."

Brett took the pen and sat for a second and began to write a letter to his friend. His eyes filled with tears as he wrote. He found it hard to think of what to say, so he made it short and sweet. He folded it neatly as neatly as he could with one hand, laid it on the desk, and sat silently.

Kerrigan turned Brett around to face him. He then went to the couch and lifted Stephanie up to her feet. Brett could hear Stephanie trying to scream and when Brett got ready to scream Kerrigan's assistant went behind him and held his mouth closed. Kerrigan brought Stephanie to stand directly in front of her friend. He took a knife from inside his long flowing robe. He stood behind Stephanie and ran the flat of the blade across her lips. Brett could see her whole body shake with fear. The blade was shiny and Kerrigan placed the blade so Stephanie could look at herself. Brett struggled to free himself and scream for help.

Kerrigan took a long look at Brett, smiled amicably then with cat-like reflexes he drew the blade across Stephanie's neck. Blood sprayed across Brett's face. His cry of horror was muffled and tears ran down his face as Stephanie's body fell to the floor in a clump and her blood soaked the carpet. Kerrigan motioned to his assistant to release Brett. Brett lay back in his chair, his tears still flowing freely. He looked at Stephanie on the floor and softly said, "I'm so sorry, Stephanie."

Kerrigan watched Brett's agony and smiled. The assistant went to Brett's side and cut the other strap. Brett did not attempt to run or scream; he just stood up. His legs were weak because of the injuries he had already suffered, and his face was covered in blood and tears. He could only stare into the eyes of his captor.

"Anything you would like to me to tell Robyn when I see her?" Kerrigan asked as he reached for his sword.

"Only one thing I need you to tell her," Brett said as he paused and looked at his hands. "Tell her to whoop your ass!"

Kerrigan quickly pulled his blade from a sheath at his side and Brett closed his eyes. Kerrigan's blade was quick and precise as it cleanly took Brett's head off his shoulders. Kerrigan watched as the body fell to the floor, blood pouring out of the wound he had just inflicted. He walked around the body and chuckled. He picked Brett's body up and walked to the wall, then took a few knives from a pouch he had inside his robe and drove the blades through Brett's body to pin it to the wall. He put Brett's nine-iron in his right hand. He then took the blood from the floor and wrote 'Fore' over his right shoulder. After looking at what he considered a work of art he gently kicked Brett's head to a far corner of the room. He picked up the note Brett had written, added his own post-script in blood, then folded it and gently placed it in Brett's pants pocket. Kerrigan stood in the middle of the room and his assistant at the doorway.

Kerrigan said, "She will come to me now. She has no choice, and when she does I will give her what I gave her friend." He grinned with menace and walked out the door, closing it gently behind him.

Chapter 49

It seemed like mere minutes later when Robyn heard voices. She opened her eyes to find that it was daylight. Nyakas was sitting in front of the hearth talking, and she assumed it was with Gravity. Their voices were low, and she couldn't hear what they were saying. She sat up and looked at her watch. It was 7:00, and she wondered if they'd been up all night. The fire was still burning, warding off the autumn chill.

The house looked different in daylight. It was very small. The bed she sat on was on the south side of the house; the doors faced east and west. The fireplace was actually in the middle, providing not only heat to the small house, but also a wall that separated the sleeping quarters from the living quarters. There were two beds in this room and a door that stood open and led to what appeared to be the bathroom. On the other side of the fireplace were a wooden table with two chairs, a small couch, a pair of wingback chairs in front of the fireplace, and a microscopic kitchen. She got up and wandered into the bathroom, as much to announce that she was awake as to answer nature's call. She managed to make herself somewhat presentable, washing off what was left of the make-up she had worn the night before and raking her fingers through her hair. Her clothes were a little rumpled, but no more than usual. She came out and stopped at the side of the bed long enough to grab her boots and carry them to the other room.

"Good morning, gentlemen," she said, plopping down on the hearth to put on her boots. They glanced at each other and returned her greeting.

"It's nice to meet you again, Gravity. I'm sorry if I was rude last night." She extended her hand to him and he shook it. His grip was like iron and his hand was callused from years of swordplay.

"Think nothing of it, my lady," Gravity said.

Robyn chuckled and shook her head. "I do have a name, Gravity. It's Robyn, in case you've forgotten."

The two men looked at each other. She saw the look between them and asked, "What?"

"Nothing, my lady," Gravity said, standing up, "You just used to say that all the time. If you will excuse me, I'm going to start preparing for our journey."

"Yes, we're going to do the same. Thank you, Gravity," answered Nyakas. He turned to Robyn as Gravity left the house. "Did you sleep well?"

"I guess I must have. I shut my eyes, and the next thing I knew it was daylight."

"You had a long, busy night. I thought we'd get some breakfast first, then go back to the campus, unless you'd rather go home and change first."

"No, that's fine. People around here are used to seeing me look like hell on Saturday morning."

"You could never look like hell. I've been there, you don't look a thing like it!"

Robyn chuckled. "You know what I mean."

"No," he said nonchalantly, "actually I don't. You always look beautiful to me. Are you ready?"

"Yes."

They got in his car and drove toward the campus. On the way he stopped at a small coffee shop that Robyn frequented and they ordered breakfast. Since it was still early, their food came quickly. Robyn noted with a bit of amusement that they'd beaten all the regulars except the die-hard hunters.

"Can I ask you a question?" Nyakas said.

Robyn picked up her coffee cup and said, "You just did."

He rolled his eyes and clenched his jaw. Robyn grinned; she loved it when he did that, so she provoked it as often as possible.

"I'm trying to be serious, and you're cracking jokes," he said.

"That wasn't a joke, it was a statement of fact," she countered quickly.

"It must be Brett's influence," he muttered. "You weren't like this before."

"Hey, welcome to the new improved me!"

"That remains to be seen."

She tossed a sugar packet at him and picked up her fork. "Here, eat that. It may sweeten you up a little. What's the next question?"

He put the sugar packet back with the others and said, "When you said you loved me at the club last night, was that you talking, or the beer?"

She put the fork back down on the plate. "Wow," she said around a mouthful of scrambled eggs. "Serious conversation over breakfast. I guess we must be moving to the next level in our relationship. That was me, but you were Alexander. Are you still him, or was it all just part of the cover story?"

"I am essentially still the same person. Very little of what you knew of me before last night was a cover story. I had the fake name, I never actually lived in Madrid, and I'm not a student. What I feel for you has remained the same, and I have made no attempt to keep that from you."

"I meant what I said last night. In the harsh light of day, your story still sounds bizarre, but some things make a little more sense now. I trust you not to kidnap me. If it turns out that you've fed me a bunch of bullshit, and I wind up in a Kansas cornfield, there will be hell to pay."

He smiled. "What about an Iowa cornfield?"

"Now who's cracking jokes?"

"I know, I'm sorry. I just couldn't resist getting one up on you. We used to do that a lot."

"That was then, this is now. Welcome to the real world. What else do I need to know? Do I need to pack anything to take?"

"No, everything you need is already there, and most of what you have won't cross the dimension."

"Are you really a dragon?"

"Yes."

"Are you same as the ones in the fairy tales? The ones who eat virgins?"

He smiled. "No, we stopped sacrificing virgins years ago. They were becoming too scarce." He was teasing her, and he winked at her so she'd know it. "Why do you ask?"

"Because if you are the virgin-eating variety, then I'm not one!"

"What if I only eat women who aren't virgins?"

"Then I am a virgin."

"I see. So you're just trying to see which side of the fifty-fifty shot you fall under."

"Something like that."

"I won't eat you. Well, I hope to eventually, but you liked it before."

She blushed crimson and picked up her coffee cup, and he chuckled. "Are you ready?"

"Yes," she answered as she looked around, trying to memorize one of her favorite haunts. She waited as Nyakas paid the bill, then they left to go back to campus. On the way, she used Nyakas' cell phone to call Brett.

His answering machine picked up on the third ring. She waited for the outgoing message to finish and left a message. "Wake up, sleepy head! I'm on my way over there, so get decent! You have about ten minutes. I'm in the car. I'll even be nice and bring breakfast with me. Make sure you're wearing more than your tighty whitey's."

She saw Brett's favorite coffee shop and directed Nyakas into the proper parking lot. He parked the car, then looked at her questioningly. "Tighty whiteys?"

"Yeah, you know, briefs, not boxers. Don't they have underwear in Oz?"

"Well, not exactly. And it isn't Oz, it's Temeer."

"Pardon me!" She grinned and reached for the door handle, but he grabbed her other arm and pulled her toward him. He put his other hand in her hair to pull her closer and kissed her. She leaned on the console between them and put her arm around his shoulders.

As he moved back, she opened her eyes and looked into his. "It makes sense now."

"What does?"

"I've been waiting for you to find me without even knowing it. That's why it feels like you're touching my soul every time you kiss me."

"You are the only woman I've ever loved, Robyn. When you were taken away I felt like half of me was missing and I didn't feel whole again until I saw you on the back porch of the fraternity house fighting off Jack Armstrong. I never want to be away from you again."

She smiled slightly and touched his face. "Well, then, you'd better shut the car off and come inside while I get Brett's coffee."

He grinned and shut the car off. She dropped a small kiss on his lips and got out of the car. Inside, she bought the biggest cup of Kenyan AA coffee she could get and a lemon muffin, along with a box of Stephanie's favorite tea and a caraway seed bagel. Back in the car, she called Stephanie to let her know she was on her way and got the answering machine.

'Hmm, that's strange. Maybe she's in the shower,' she thought as she waited for her outgoing message to finish. "Steph, if you're still asleep, you might want to get decent. I'm with Alexander, and we're headed back that way. I have to pick some stuff up, and I have breakfast for you. If you want to call me back, we've got his cell phone, and we'll be in Brett's room in about five minutes. See you in a little while."

She handed the phone back to him, and he said, "That was fast."

"I got the answering machine. She must be in the shower. I'll stop in my room first and drop this off for her, then we can go see Brett."

"Maybe you should tell them both."

"Good idea. We'll drag her wet little butt upstairs with us."

He chuckled, took her hand and kissed it. He pulled into the dorm parking lot a few minutes later and parked. Robyn took the food she had bought and went to her room. Stephanie wasn't there, and her bed hadn't been slept in. Everything was as she had left it the night before.

"That's really strange. Maybe she stayed at Tom's last night," she said, turning on her computer. "I'll just e-mail Mom and Dad, then we'll go see Brett. If push comes to shove, I can write Stephanie a note and ask him to give it to her." She opened up her e-mail and wrote, 'Dear Mom and Dad. Hope everything there is going well. I have some stuff out of town to take care of for my Masters program and I'll be in and out of touch for a while, maybe up to a month. I just didn't want you to worry if you couldn't get up with me. It all came up pretty suddenly and I want to go ahead and get it taken care of. Between internship interviews and school I'll be hard to reach. I'll talk to you soon. Take care of my baby brother or sister! Love you both, Robyn.' She clicked 'Send' and shut the computer off, took the bagel and tea out of the bag, and left them on Stephanie's desk. Then she and Nyakas headed for Brett's room. As they neared his room, Nyakas slowed his walk and pulled Robyn behind him.

Puzzled, she asked, "What's wrong?"

"I don't know, but whatever it is, it isn't good."

He led her down the hall and she could see Brett's door partially open. He looked in first and she saw a look of shock, then anger on his face. He looked at her and the anger turned to compassion.

He took her shoulders and said, "You don't want to see this."

"What? What is it?"

"Robyn, please. This is very bad."

Dread curled in her stomach. She called Brett's name, but there was no answer. She shrugged out of Nyakas' grasp and went through the door. Brett's breakfast fell from her hand. There was blood everywhere, splattered on the walls and the floor, staining Brett's favorite leather chair. Directly across from the door, next to the window, Brett's headless body hung on the wall, his 9-iron in his hand. Over his right shoulder, someone had written 'Fore!' in blood. He seemed to be fastened there with knives. There was a piece of paper in his pocket. As her eyes filled with tears, she walked as gingerly across the room as possible, trying to avoid the blood on the floor, took out the paper, and read it.

'Dear Robyn, I don't know who this nut case is, but he's looking for you and I don't know why. Watch your back, pal, because I got a feeling that Steph and I won't be around to do it anymore. Just remember the good times, Rob, and remember that I love you. Tell Alexander he's a lucky guy. One other thing. Take my box and don't let anyone else have it. It's yours now. I love you buddy. Brett.

PS Soon, my pretty. Regards, Kerrigan'

She opened his top dresser drawer and took out a small wooden box, trying not to look at the body on the wall. As she turned around, another horror greeted her.

"No!" She cried as she saw Stephanie's body on the floor. Her throat had been cut, and she lay in an unreal amount of blood. Robyn burst into tears and walked quickly toward the door. As she approached, she saw Brett's head behind the door. It looked as if it had been kicked across the room. Robyn's stomach turned and for a moment, instinct prevailed. She grabbed the nearest trashcan and vomited. Nyakas came to her side and rubbed her back as her breakfast returned, and when she finished he took the trashcan from her and steered her, sobbing, from the room. He hurried her back to the car, and then called 911 to report the murders, cautioning the operator to send only officers with a strong constitution. He shut the cell phone off and drove back to the farm.

Robyn wept as they drove into the country. The beautiful foliage passed unnoticed. She held the small box in her lap, tracing the edge with her finger. It contained Brett's personal treasures, and she was the only person who understood what the contents meant to him. She opened the lid and was surprised to find a piece of paper folded and tucked underneath his other things. She opened the paper to find it was a note that Brett had written to her three years earlier but for some reason had never given to her.

'Dear Robyn,

> Well, I guess this dating thing isn't going to work out for us. I admit, you are one of the most attractive women here, and I really do care about you a lot. I really want to love you, but somehow it just doesn't seem right. I don't think I deserve you right now. Besides, right now we both need to concentrate on school, and I need to concentrate on my game. I guess you're right. We should just be friends. It's funny, from anyone else that would have been a brush-off! Anyway, always remember and never forget that no matter what happens or where I am, you'll always be my best friend and I'll always be around to look after you. I love you buddy. Brett'

Robyn folded the paper and placed it reverently back in the box, sobbing. She shut the lid gently and hugged it to her chest. Nyakas drove in silence, and Robyn was too wrapped up in her own grief to notice the tears that ran down his face. She didn't notice when they arrived at the farm until he opened her car door and led her into the barn. Gravity was there and he seemed shocked to see them.

"Back already, Nyakas?"

"Yes. Kerrigan got to her friends already. We have to go."

"You're right. I'm very sorry for your loss, my lady."

Robyn managed a nod as she wept, and Gravity said, "She'll need to change clothes. Why don't you take her in the house and let her do that. I'm almost ready."

"Of course," Nyakas answered. He took her back to the house and handed her a pair of soft brown leather pants with a matching tunic, a wool cloak that matched his, a pair of wool socks, and soft brown leather boots. "Here. Go put these on. We'll be leaving soon. Don't worry, you'll be safe."

Numb with shock, she went to the bedroom, took off her clothes, and put on what he'd given her. When she came out he handed her a steaming cup and led her to the hearth. He sat in a chair and pulled her down onto his lap. She sat there, huddled against him, sipping her tea with Brett's box in her lap.

"What's in the box, love?"

"It's Brett's treasure box," she answered, opening the box. "There really isn't anything of value, just stuff that had sentimental value. See, he kept the ticket stubs from when I made him go a foreign film to remind him never to get roped into going to see a movie with subtitles again. This is the golf ball that he was using when he made his first hole-in-one. His first girlfriend gave him this necklace. He hates wearing jewelry. This is the key to his parents' house, and this one goes to his grandparents' house. This was his lucky glove; he always wears it for tournaments. Here is the removable tattoo he bought when we went to see wrestling. They had a live event at the college and I dragged him along. They had just finished the second match when he realized he'd forgotten it. This is the spare key to his brother's ex-truck. He came home on leave last year, and it died on his way back to North Carolina, so he traded it in. The rest is mostly letters and ticket stubs from movies and concerts he went to."

Somehow, recounting these treasures of Brett's temporarily kept the reality of his death at bay. She gently shut the box, and he held her until Gravity came in.

"I'm ready, Nyakas. Are you?"

Nyakas looked at Robyn's tear-stained face and said, "Yes. Let's go." He took the mug from her hand and placed it on the hearth, as if he'd be back later to wash it. She got up, and he led her to the barn. Gravity closed the door behind them and went to stand in the middle of the floor. The lighting was dim. The missing top door in the hayloft let in cold air and sunlight. Dust motes danced in the light before Robyn's glazed eyes, making the moment seem even more surreal.

Gravity stood still and seemed to go into a trance. His hands fluttered mysteriously and he uttered something Robyn couldn't comprehend. Suddenly, blue light appeared from nowhere directly in front of him. As he continued, the light widened into a large circle, and elongated into a large oval door. Nyakas took Robyn's hand and walked through. She followed, and Gravity walked through behind her. The blue light disappeared and she found herself in a forest clearing feeling slightly disoriented. They had somehow passed from late autumn to early spring in one step. The new leaves had just emerged from their buds, and the new grass smelled fresh and clean. The breeze was balmy, but with a bit of a chill.

There were two men waiting, and they had five horses. Nyakas helped her onto the smallest one and she shifted in the saddle, trying to get comfortable and settle the box in her lap so it wouldn't fall.

Nyakas rode his horse to her side and said, "Why don't you let me hold that for you? I have a pocket inside my cloak that is big enough."

Silently she surrendered the box to him and watched as he slid it into a large inside pocket. Then they rode from the clearing. They passed a few farmhouses. Soon the houses began to be closer together and the scattered farms became a village. There seemed to be several villages surrounding a large castle in the distance. People began lining the street, shouting excitedly that the queen had returned. They rode through the streets to the castle with Nyakas' subjects cheering and throwing flowers in the road as they passed. The clamor subsided somewhat as they rode through the castle wall.

They dismounted and the horses were taken to the stable. Robyn looked around, trying to see anything that looked familiar. She felt as if she were in a dream. Everything was vaguely familiar, but she couldn't say why or where she had seen any of it.

It was getting dark, and Nyakas led her through a walled courtyard with a hedgerow and into the castle. Robyn seemed to remember that the hedges had been shorter, about four feet tall. They nearly reached the top of the wall now, although they were neatly trimmed. They walked down a narrow hall and up a staircase. He paused at the top of the stairs, and she automatically turned right and proceeded down the hall. It seemed familiar, but she wasn't sure which door was right.

He led her to a room and she looked around. A chill ran up her spine, and she thought about her eighteenth birthday. She'd asked to have her bedroom remodeled as her gift, and her father had taken her shopping to pick out what she wanted. The bed at her parent's house was a twin-sized version of this large, four-poster bed. The desk in front of the far window was a smaller version of hers. At the time she didn't know why she picked those pieces; her father had been dumbfounded, but he bought them for her anyway. It made sense now, and Robyn wondered if she would ever be able to show him this room. As tears gathered in her throat, Nyakas gently placed Brett's wooden box on the desk, then put his hand on her shoulder.

"I'll leave you to settle in, my lady. Is there anything you need?"

"Please don't leave me," she answered softly. "I don't want to be alone right now."

"Are you sure you want me to stay? I could get Betty for you."

"I want you to stay, if that's all right."

"Of course it is. I'd be glad to keep you company, but I need to step out for a few minutes. There are a couple things I need to take care of so you can start training tomorrow, and then I will return. Is that OK?"

"Yes."

He touched her face, and then swept from the room. She sat down on the couch in front of the large fireplace. There was a fire crackling, and somehow she knew that this was the only heat source for the room. Unable to stop them, the tears that had been gathering in her throat began to flow down her cheeks. It was all too much, finding out that she was married, a queen, and had a child, and then discovering the gruesome scene in Brett's room. Yesterday she'd just been Robyn, an average woman in college. Now she was the Queen of Nyakas' kingdom and her two best friends were dead. Everything around her seemed familiar, but strange at the same time. Tomorrow she'd have to start training to use a weapon she couldn't remember ever using with a man who intimidated her, something that rarely happened. She felt like a homesick child and wondered if she'd ever get home again.

The door opened and Nyakas entered. He came to sit beside her, put his arms around her shoulders, and pulled her close. "My love," he said, "what is it?"

"I'm afraid," she sobbed into his chest.

"Afraid of what?"

"I'm afraid that Kerrigan will hurt my family and I'll never see them again. I couldn't stand it if he did to them what he did to Brett and Stephanie! I'm afraid of training with Gravity, afraid that Kerrigan will come after me before I'm ready and kill me, or that he'll wait until I am ready but I'll freeze and I won't be able to kill him again. I'm afraid of running into your father, and that he'll try to separate us again and that we'll just spend all of eternity in this vicious cycle. I'm afraid that I'll never get to see my son, or worse, that I will and he'll hate me. I'm afraid of being a wife and a mother and a queen when I don't have the foggiest notion of what I'm doing!"

"Robyn," he said, holding her tighter, "I'm not going to let anyone hurt you. I will protect you, and so will Gravity, until you are ready to begin protecting yourself. I will die before I let anything happen to you, whether it is by the hand of Kerrigan, my father, or anyone else. As soon as this situation is resolved I will take you back to see your family, and if you don't love me as you did, I will leave you there. Please understand that I want you to stay. We were so happy before you were taken, and I want that again for both of us. But if you aren't happy with me, I will take you back to your home and leave you alone as soon as you are safe. I won't be happy living without you, but I'd rather live without you than have you miserable with me. If you do decide to stay, I won't keep you from your family. I will do everything in my power to see to it that you stay in touch with them and visit as much as possible."

"Thank you. That helps a lot." She relaxed in his arms slightly and listened to his heartbeat. "So I'm really going to start training tomorrow?"

"Yes. I've already spoken with Gravity and I told him to take it a little easy on you for a few days so you'll have a chance to readjust. He has a tendency to be a little overzealous, which is fine for the squires and knights who have always been here and know him. But you don't remember how it was with you two. When he trained you the first time he was very hard on you, but you'd had a lot more training in the Army and you never broke. You were like a sponge; you just soaked up all his abuse and let it flow back out through your blade. I remember a few nights when he came to dinner looking like he'd been through the wringer, and you floated in a short time later looking absolutely radiant. Of course, I was biased then, as I am now, but the look on his face was priceless! The thought cheers me to this day!"

"Are you sure I'll be OK with him training me now? I really don't think he likes me."

"You'll be fine, I promise. Don't tell him I told you, but he does like you. He is very selective about his friends, and he does not show his feelings often. It wasn't only loyalty to me that kept him by my side while we searched for you. He was just as worried about you as I was. Just keep in mind that he's hard on you because he wants you to be able to defend yourself against any attacker. When you were taken away, you had just bested me and were very close to defeating him."

"I beat you in a sword fight?"

"Yes. I intended to fight at what I thought was your level and let you gain an advantage before defeating you, but you closed quickly before I had a chance to, and soon I was almost fighting for my life! Luckily for me, we were only fencing. I shudder to think what might have happened if you'd been angry at me!"

"That'll teach you to underestimate me!"

He laughed softly and stroked her hair. "True enough! I had just never met a woman so skilled with a sword, and whenever I asked Gravity how you were progressing, he would give me evasive answers like, 'Oh, she's coming along.' He didn't tell me that you'd already defeated all of my knights! I should have known he was judging you by his own standards, which are almost impossibly high, even for him."

"Well, now you have a chance to do it differently. Maybe this time you'll come and watch for yourself when I defeat your knights!"

He kissed her hair. "That's the spirit. You really haven't changed much; I can still see my Robyn. Are you tired?"

"A little."

"Then here," he said. He got up and went to the bed to retrieve the muslin nightgown and wool robe that had been laid out. "You can put these on behind the screen."

She took them and went to put them on. It was cold in the corner and she shivered as she came out. She sat down beside him again and was soon warmed with his body heat. Betty came in and brought them each a cup of tea, and soon she was dozing in his arms. He lifted her gently and put her in bed, then moved the desk chair to the bedside and sat down. She curled under the heavy quilt and soon her breathing was even. She stirred in her sleep, reaching for something beside her, and got his pillow. She hugged it close and smiled slightly. His heart swelled and before he could stop himself he reached out and brushed her hair off her face. She sighed and hugged the pillow tighter. He watched her in the dying firelight. 'Finally,' he thought, 'I have her back. I thought this day would never come. Please, Robyn, love me as you did then so I never have to live without you again.'

Chapter 50

Robyn was sitting by the lake. It was warm and sunny and the water was so calm it looked like a mirror. She heard an approaching horse and turned to see someone riding toward her from the woods on what looked like a very large palomino horse. As they drew closer she looked at the man. He was bigger than her father and bald, and his clothing looked expensive, even from a distance. He wore a white cloak that billowed behind him as his horse galloped toward her. She stood as they approached and barely hid her shock, first when she realized that the horse had red eyes, and second, that the man who was dismounting was Kerrigan.

The man walked toward her. "Good morning, my lady. I can't tell you how glad I am to see you here. Do you remember me?"

She straightened her back and looked him in the eye. "Yes. I saw you at 316's. You followed me around until my boyfriend showed up."

He laughed. "So, that's all you remember? Good, very good," he purred. He started walking around her in circles. "It's so good of you to come back here to my turf, Pretty." He leaned close as he walked behind her and spoke softly in her ear. "I have the home field advantage, now, my dear child. I do appreciate your returning so I can avenge my own death in front of all of my subjects and Lord Malitor. I'm sure Vaytawn will like to watch too." He was in front of her now, and she did her best not to show her fear. "Unfortunately, they aren't here right now, so I can't just have done with it." He paused, as if listening to something. "Then again, maybe I won't wait for them!" Like lightning, he drew his sword and swung it at her neck.

She froze in fear and yelled, "No!" Suddenly she found herself sitting up in her bed. Nyakas was sitting in front of her, holding her arms. Disoriented, she tried to pull away, not realizing who it was. "No, let me go!"

"Robyn! It's me! It's OK, I'm right here! It was a dream!"

She stopped struggling and looked at him. "A dream? Is it really you?"

"Yes, it's really me." He pulled her to his chest. "You're shaking. What were you dreaming about?"

"Kerrigan rode up to me at the lake and he was going to kill me."

She felt him stiffen and knew this was not a good thing. "What did he say, Robyn?"

"Um, he said it was nice of me to come back here so he could avenge his death in front of his subjects, Lord Malitor and Vaytawn. He said he had the home field advantage."

"Did he call you by name?"

"No, he called me a dear child."

"Good. That's good. Don't worry. You're safe. He can't get to you here. Just don't leave the castle grounds without Gravity, or me all right? Don't go through the wall with anyone but one of us."

"I won't. Will I ever stop being afraid?"

"You can stop being afraid right now. I'm here and I'm going to protect you."

"When I stopped being afraid I had the nightmare."

"He's communicating with you through dreams because he isn't here. If he were back in this dimension he'd be outside the castle walls yelling your name. You don't have to worry about the dreams too much unless he uses your name. When he does that, it means he's back here and we'll have to watch for his tricks."

"Like what?"

"He's very deceptive. He can shape-shift to look like anybody."

"Even you and Gravity?"

"Yes, he can shape-shift to look like you if he wants to."

"Then how will I know if I'm walking down to the lake with you, or it's him trying to lure me out?"

"Good point. Don't go out with anyone who doesn't call you Buzz. I'll tell Gravity in the morning."

"OK. Will you stay here with me?"

"I'm not going anywhere. Are you all right now?"

"I think so."

"Good. Try to get some more sleep." He pulled the quilt back over her and sat back down in the chair.

She tossed and turned, but she couldn't get the dream out of her mind. Finally, she turned to him. "Why are you sitting over there?"

"So I can watch over you and protect you."

"Way over there?"

"Do you have a better idea?"

"This bed is big enough for both of us. You can come snuggle with me. If you want to, I mean. You don't have to if you don't want to."

He smiled, thinking, 'So you are a virgin this time. Interesting turn of the tables. Last time it was me.' He pulled off his boots and got into the bed beside her.

She curled into his arms, resting her head on his shoulder. She was still jumpy from the dream, so she tried to calm her nerves by listening to his heartbeat. It felt very strange to be lying in bed with a man, but what made it even stranger was that she was not uncomfortable. She'd fallen asleep with Brett one time when they were watching movies, and when she woke up she felt like she'd been caught naked by a bunch of strangers.

He began to hum softly. He'd sung to her before when they were alone, but he'd never sung this one, at least not that she could remember. Soon she fell into a deep sleep.

Nyakas held her as she slept. He'd forgotten how sweet it was to hold his sleeping wife. He thought about their first night together and how nervous he'd been. She'd taken charge of the situation, urging but not pushing. She was patient, but didn't back off and didn't allow him to, either. It had been the sweetest night of his life, and he knew now that he could return the favor. 'At least one good thing will come of all of this,' he thought with a smile. All he had to do was wait for the right time. He hoped that her first time would bind her to him forever.

Chapter 51

Robyn started to drift toward consciousness. She was warm, and her bed felt more cozy than usual. Her mind started to wake up, and she tried to remember what day it was so she could figure out what class she had first. Someone behind her kissed her shoulder and she smiled and hugged the arms that enfolded her, one around her waist, and the other around her shoulders. She sighed with contentment, and then realized with a jolt that somebody was in bed with her. She sat up quickly and looked around, disoriented. It looked similar to her room at home, but her mind rejected that thought quickly.

Nyakas propped up on one elbow. "Good morning. I didn't mean to startle you."

Robyn put her hand to her chest, trying to keep her heart in place. She remembered where she was and why he was there, now all she had to do was get her heart rate back down. "It's OK," she answered, "I just forgot where I was for a minute."

"Understandable. Did you sleep well?"

"Yes. Did you?"

"No, I stayed awake. I'll take a nap while you train."

"Why did you stay up?"

"Because I'm not going to take the chance of anything happening. Until Kerrigan is eliminated, you might as well get used to being within sight of somebody at all times."

"Hmm, I'm going to be living in a fish bowl. Sounds like fun," she said wryly. She yawned and ruffled her hair, then fell back down on his chest. He grunted, and then chuckled. He started rubbing her back and she sighed and moved closer, wrapping her arm around his waist.

"I'd love to stay here all day, my love," Nyakas said, "but you need to get dressed."

"No!"

He chuckled and said, "Yes. Betty will be here soon with breakfast, and Gravity will be waiting for you in the courtyard."

She groaned. "Do I have to? Can't we just go fishing today?"

"Sorry, dear. We have to get you started. Would you like me to stay and watch today?"

"No, that's OK. I don't need any witnesses to my first humiliation."

He laughed. "It won't be that bad! Today will probably be primarily physical training so he can see how much endurance and stamina you have. You might not even pick up a sword."

"Well, then maybe it won't be too bad. I've tried to stay in pretty good shape, if for no other reason than to be able to out-run my Dad when I go home on vacation. All right, if I have to do this, I might as well get it over with."

She rolled out of bed, scooped up her clothing, and went to dress behind the screen. She could hear Nyakas moving around. There was a bright light and warmth on the other side of the screen and Robyn peeked around to see him adding wood to the fire. Then the door opened and a woman entered with a small tray. She was petite with long blond hair and sparkling blue eyes. The corners of her mouth always tilted upward in a slight smile, and she seemed to radiate sunshine. Robyn couldn't tell how old she was; she guessed she was slightly older than her mother.

"Good morning, Betty," Nyakas said.

"Good morning, Majesty," she answered with a soft brogue. "Lord Gravity has sent word through the servants that he wishes to speak to you as soon as possible."

Robyn emerged from behind the screen. "Good," she said. "Keep him busy a while, will you please? Maybe he'll forget all about me."

Nyakas chuckled and kissed her cheek. "I doubt that! How could anyone forget you? Have some breakfast, I'll be back soon." He touched her face and left the room.

Betty placed the breakfast tray on the table and poured Robyn a cup of coffee, then moved to the other side of the room to open the curtains and make the bed. Robyn sipped the coffee, then helped herself to a roll and a bit of cheese. Betty finished her duties and asked Robyn if there was anything she required.

"I don't think so, but I do have a question," Robyn answered.

"And what might that be?"

"Did I know you when I was here before?"

Betty laughed. "Oh, no, my lady! I was but a glimmer in me Da's eye when you were so cruelly taken."

"So you weren't the one who looked after me before?"

"No, my lady, but I am honored to serve the queen my mother held so dear."

"Your mother was my servant?"

"Aye, my lady. Do you not remember Gwyneth?"

"I don't remember a lot of things about when I was here. How is she?"

"Mum died about two years ago."

"Oh, I'm sorry."

"Y' did not know, and she's with me Da now. She's happier there, I'm sure. She told me every day from my first that if you did not return during her lifetime that I would

be the one to serve you, and she trained me well. If there is anything I can do to ease
your new transition, please let me know." Betty excused herself and left the room.

Robyn sat in front of the fire sipping her coffee. She knew she'd have to work hard
to learn what was necessary to defeat Kerrigan. Suddenly there was nothing more
important than doing just that. She resolved that even if she had to walk through fire,
she'd defeat Kerrigan and avenge Brett and Stephanie. She placed her cup on the table,
rose from her seat, and was putting on her cloak when Nyakas walked in.

He looked like something was troubling him, and he walked to her and put his arms
around her. "How would you like to go fishing?"

"After I finish with Gravity? Sounds great!"

"You won't be training today. We have the day to ourselves."

"Did something else come up? I'd really like to get started."

"You'll get started tomorrow. That's what Gravity wanted to talk to me about."

"Why tomorrow? I've given it some thought, and I really want to get going on this."

"Gravity is going to take you on a trip tomorrow, and you'll do your training away
from the distractions of court life."

"Away from the distractions of court life, or away from you?"

"Both, actually."

"But I don't want to leave you. Why can't I train here?"

"Because there isn't enough time for you to train here. Out there your training will
be more intense because you will be Gravity's only student. You'll learn more quickly,
and that's what is important right now. Believe me, Robyn, I don't want you to go. I
want you here by my side. But as much as I dislike it, his logic is sound."

"But why is it so important that I learn quickly?"

"Because my father won't allow us the time we need this time to get you trained
properly. He'll know soon enough that you are back in my realm and so will Kerrigan.
You need to be able to face him as soon as possible. The more quickly you face him, the
less likely it will be that he will hurt your family or friends, and if you are away, it will be
harder for him to find you."

"Oh, all right. When do I go?"

"Tomorrow morning."

"Can you go with us?"

"I'm afraid not."

"Will you stay with me today?"

"Nothing could keep me from your side. Come, the fish await you."

Chapter 52

Nyakas stood outside the castle walls at false dawn, looking out toward the forest and mountains. He struggled with his mixed emotions. He could not feel more content knowing Robyn had come back with him. She had started to remember things he thought would never come back to her. Her remembrance of 'Puff' and 'Buzz' gave him hope. It was a private matter that always stayed in the back of her mind and he was pleased she had remembered it. His contentment was mingled with sorrow, because she and Gravity would be leaving soon, and he hated the thought of being away from her. He worried about what could happen with no one out there but Gravity to watch over her. He had the utmost confidence in Gravity's abilities, but what would happen to her if something happened to him?

As if in answer to his thoughts, Gravity walked slowly behind his king so as not to disturb him while he was concentrating.

"Gravity, good morning," Nyakas said without a backward glance.

"Hello, my lord," Gravity replied.

"Fine morning, is it not?"

Gravity knew he was making small talk. "Yes, lord, fine morning it is. Nyakas, I know you don't like this at all and I can understand why, but it's best this way."

"Gravity, I do understand. But I just got her back, and now the two people I care about most are leaving. Call me selfish but that's how I feel," Nyakas snapped. Gravity put his hand on Nyakas' shoulder, then turned and walked toward the stable.

Nyakas' eyes filled with tears of fear of what could happen while she was out in territory she still had yet to remember. He walked back inside the castle and found himself on the battlements.

His transformation from his human form to dragon was quick, but no less spectacular for the speed. His black scales lined his one hundred thirty yard body. His talons looked like solid gold, as did his tail. There were three long horns on the middle of his very large head, and smaller ones running down his spine from the back of his head to the end of his tail. He rested his mass as though he were going to lie down and sift around his gold. There was no gold on the battlements so he lay curled until he knew it was time for Robyn to leave.

Robyn found her way to the battlements where she had remembered always coming to think, and there for the first time she laid eyes on the dragon she had seen as Puff. She stared in amazement at the beautiful sight of this phenomenal creature she had loved for so long.

Without warning, Nyakas said, "You're leaving soon, I know."

She was so completely taken with the sight of him that she didn't realize at first what he'd said. "Pardon?"

"I said you're leaving soon." He did not attempt to hide the sorrow in his voice, which was so deep it echoed across the land.

"Yes, I'm leaving soon," she said with sorrow that matched his own. She came to get a better view of the magnificence she had long forgotten. She smiled and lay in the arms that were crossed over one another to stay warm in the chilly weather. She could still feel his heartbeat.

"I'll miss you, my love," Nyakas said.

"And I you, Puff."

"Be careful out there, both of you, do you hear?"

She touched the huge face and said, "You can't lose me. I love you, Nyakas."

"I can't tell you how much it means to hear you say that. I love you, more than I can even say."

They sat for a while as the sun crested the hills, and then Nyakas turned back to his human form so as not to alarm any of his subjects so early in the morning. They wandered slowly to the courtyard where Gravity waited. Gravity mounted his black horse and held the reigns of Robyn's. She mounted the horse warily, remembering it would take time for her to remember everything. She took the reigns and look down as Nyakas kissed the back of her hand.

"Return home soon. You too, old friend."

Gravity half-bowed, then he turned his horse towards the woods and started at an easy walk to make it easy for her to keep up. Nyakas watched as she rode into the woods, then returned quickly to his chambers.

Gravity and Robyn rode quietly into the woods. Robyn tried to remember this man who made her feel uncomfortable and intimidated, yet somehow she knew he wouldn't hurt her. As she rode just behind Gravity, she noticed his swords. One lay across his back and the other along his right pant leg. His cloak was black and bore the same markings he wore on his face, neck and arms. "The markings, the tattoos, where did you get them?"

Gravity's voice flat as he answered, "The one who grants me power gave them to me."

She was confused and frightened by his answer and wondered what kind of power he spoke of. She said nothing else as they moved silently through the woods. They rode steadily through the day, taking only short breaks to eat and allow the horses to graze. It was late in the afternoon when Gravity halted and announced that they had reached their first destination. They dismounted and set up camp for the night. Gravity had some wood in his bedroll, which he set up tee pee style. With a flick of his wrist the fire appeared. Robyn was amazed at the magic but said nothing, not wishing to offend him. He stood away from the fire looking out into the forest as though he could see for miles. She took out her bedroll and laid it down on the ground near the fire. She took her blanket and curled into a ball to keep warm, and before she could stop herself, fell asleep.

Gravity sat as the fire began to subside. He watched as his friend lie down to rest and could feel pain in his heart, because he knew what had to be done to have her properly trained. He watched as she slept throughout the chilly spring night.

The next morning she awoke to the sound of a sword cutting quickly through the air. She rose from her bed and watched the magnificence of this swordsman, wondering if she had once been that fast. She dismissed the thought quickly since she couldn't remember ever having picked up a sword. As he finished he drew his swords back into their sheaths, and stood motionless.

"Good morning, your majesty. Did you sleep well?"

"Yes, I did, thank you. Did you?"

"I did not sleep at all. I watched as you slept. Nyakas said you were having nightmares."

"Only one so far."

"We must get started," he said, stripping the ring mail shirt he wore. He ran past her and she assumed she was to follow. They ran about three miles, and she thought that it shouldn't be that bad. She ran past him, knowing where they would stop, and smiled as he came to meet her. She was somewhat out of breath from running full stride the last one hundred yards. He came to where she was and was not short of breath at all. Without a word, he dropped down and began doing pushups. She followed suit and after a hundred she could feel the burning in her arms. She knew then she should have paced herself better. The pushups were followed by sit-ups, and then Gravity found a branch and began to do pull ups. She pushed her way through them, and when she dropped from the branch, she silently congratulated herself for doing so well. Her pride was short-lived because he began to run again, and she knew she had to follow. 'This is going to be hell,' she thought as she did the running and exercise routine twice more. When he finally allowed her to stop, she was exhausted and could not lift her arms. He, on the other hand, looked as though he hadn't broken a sweat. His facial expressions never changed; he was quiet the whole time during the exercises. She took out her water skin and sipped, careful not over water herself as she knew the day was far from over. Gravity waited for Robyn to get to her feet and handed her a wooden sword. She looked oddly at the weapon he had given her.

"Now, Robyn, this is where your training will begin," Gravity said with the usual lack of expression.

"All right, what do I do?"

He stood behind her and showed her first how to hold the weapon, and moved slowly along with basic defenses and strikes. She listened attentively to his teachings. She also got sore knuckles from her first day of training as he slapped her knuckles with his wooden sword whenever she made a mistake. She quickly made it a point not to make the same mistakes twice.

The weeks went along quickly. One evening, as the sun slowly set in the west, Robyn sat, exhausted from the day's workout, near the teepee of wood that was set in the middle of their little campsite. Gravity stood at the edge of the forest looking out for what seemed to be miles until the sun finally set.

Robyn wore her deerskin pants and her half shirt of chain mail with what had once been a white tunic but was now a dingy brown. Her leather boots were worn and dirty. She sipped water from her water skin and ate the meat and bread she had gratefully accepted from Gravity.

Robyn watched as Gravity made his way back to their small site. His muscle structure was still amazing to Robyn because the clothing Gravity usually wore made him very unassuming. In reality, he was huge, muscles sculpted and hard as rock. His black cloak hung loosely around his neck and his ring mail clinked softly. As he slowly walked past the wood, it burst into flames. His deerskin pants were dirty and his white tunic was as dingy as hers. However, his black leather boots looked like they had just been polished, something Robyn just couldn't understand. He sat down Indian style at the other side of the fire and said nothing. Robyn studied his face, assuming that he would not notice.

"Is there a problem, your majesty?"

Robyn, lost for words, stammered, "No, no, of course not. I was just, umm, wondering what you thought about my training today."

"You still need much work and it will come easier as the months go on."

"You don't like me, do you?"

"I never remember myself saying or even thinking that."

She said nothing and it was quiet as Gravity pondered her words and let them take effect. "Are you all right?"

"No," she answered quietly. Tears filled her eyes as she gazed angrily at the fire, but she seemed determined to hold whatever it was that bothered her inside.

"What is it?"

"Why did Kerrigan do what he did to my friends? They didn't do anything wrong! He took them away from me without any reason. They're dead because of me! I never got to tell Brett how much he meant to me and how much I cherished our friendship. He's gone because of me!" She turned away from the fire and sobbed.

Gravity moved to sit beside her and placed his hand to her shoulder. She didn't see the tears that filled his eyes but did not fall. Robyn sat with her head in her hands and cried as if her heart would never mend. Soon, she composed herself, laid her hand upon Gravity's, and said, "Thank you."

"You're welcome. There was nothing you could have done to save them. He would have gotten you, too, if you had been there. That is why we are here."

"Now what, Gravity? What's next for me to learn?" She turned back to face him, wiping the tears away with her hand.

"Well, your majesty, do you like your sword?"

"You mean this piece of firewood with a handle? No."

"Would you like a real sword?"

"Well, yeah, of course I would. The only way I am to defeat Kerrigan is with a blade."

"You can have one if you want one, but it is purely up to you."

"Well, where do I get one?"

Gravity looked up at the sky and Robyn slowly did as well, keeping Gravity in her peripheral vision. Gravity stared at the sky for a second; he raised his finger and pointed to his chest. Robyn looked at his chest, trying to figure out what it was he was trying to tell her.

"Robyn, it is here in your heart you'll find the place from which to bring the sword."

"May I ask how on the earth I am supposed to get a sword from my chest?"

"Anything you wish for or believe in can happen. Heart is the strongest thing in your life. It may not always be the smartest, but it is truly the strongest."

Robyn looked at him confused for a second. "So you're saying that all I need is heart to defeat Kerrigan? Gravity, do you really believe that heart will be able to conquer?"

"Yes, of course. It worked the last time you killed him."

Robyn's voice quivered as she said, "Brett had the biggest heart I ever knew other than my father, and look where he is."

"Your friend had no idea what it was that came through the door, so he had no chance."

Robyn stood and walked around for a while. When she returned Gravity was sitting in front of a fire, staring into the flames as though he was meditating. Robyn took her seat and looked at Gravity, and then began to concentrate herself. She closed her eyes and an overwhelming feeling took over. Her mind and body seemed to separate as she remembered a few incidents when she and Gravity first met. He had given her a beautiful sword once her training was complete, and the animosity between them died. She felt at peace for the first time without Nyakas near. Her hand began to shake and she felt something large, cold, and hard in her grip.

She opened her eyes to see a sword. She took it out of its leather sheath to examine it. It was three and a half feet long and a blue light seemed to glow along its entire length. The handle was ivory and had leaves of gold wrapped around the finely sculpted blade. Two dragons wrapped themselves around the outer portion of the handle and along the hilt. The blade was as light as a feather. Robyn remembered this sword clearly and could feel it move with her. The sword seemed to do more than anticipate Robyn's moves; it actually led her into them. Robyn sat down, amazed at this newfound sword that had materialized in her hands. She stared at it, studying its entire length, like a child with a new toy.

"Robyn, this is your sword. I gave it to you seven centuries ago."

"Why did it just appear out of no where? Why did it just come to my hand?"

"Your concentration and heart made it appear. Your willpower made it come back to you. Now, you must sleep. You have a big day ahead of you tomorrow and you will need rest."

Robyn laid the sword beside her bed and drifted off to sleep, remembering Gravity's words. She had heard her dad tell wrestling students hundreds of times that heart is what inspires the best to dig down deeper than the rest to win. She slept through the night, and didn't wake until the sun rose. She felt different than she had and wondered why. She watched as Gravity practiced, then picked up her sword. Gravity stopped, but Robyn didn't notice. She was alone with her sword. He watched with amazement as her face changed. Her innocence seemed to drain away to be replaced with stony determination. A chill ran down his spine as he realized that he hadn't seen her face like that in over seven hundred years. He knew then she was ready to go to any length to defeat Kerrigan. She took her stance, looked into the blade and without pausing she planted her left leg far to her left. Her right was bent and she moved it forward. She struck the air quickly with the blade in her right hand, keeping her left in a guard position. Only then did she realize that Gravity was watching, and she stopped, a bit embarrassed.

"No, no, go on. You're doing fine. You just need to spread a bit more," he said with what sounded to be almost pride in his voice.

"I'm sorry, was I supposed to do that? I didn't realize where that came from."

"It is an advanced move that I taught you after you were well trained. It is accompanied by quite a flurry of other moves, but you've almost got the last move down already."

If Robyn thought for even a minute that Gravity would take it easy on her because she remembered a move, she quickly found out how mistaken she was. He was harder on her that day, and became increasingly demanding each day. As her training progressed, she started to remember what a formidable team they had once been. She could remember picking on him and how uncomfortable it sometimes made him feel. She always wished she could see him smile but she could not recall him doing it. She wondered why she didn't know more about her very secretive friend. She knew that this training was far from over, that the next few months would be grueling and that she would be truly tested, mentally as well as physically.

The training got tougher as they moved week after week to a different place, first to the mountains, then the plains, and finally wastelands. Every day the only things Gravity talked of were her training and the mistakes she made. As she progressed, she began to notice things about him that she hadn't before. She caught him a few times gripping his fist as though he was proud because she had done well that day. Every night before they went to bed he would tell her what she had done wrong, and she could never go to sleep without the knowledge of a mistake.

Finally, he told her that they would be going home, and that she had come a long way. Now, he said, it was up to her to see if she was ready to face the evil that had sought her for so long. Robyn was apprehensive but Gravity reminded her that she had defeated the man before and that he believed she could do it again. She felt as though she had finally connected with him although he still never showed any emotion or spoke of himself.

That night, she dreamed of the time she had spent with Nyakas in the Great Hall, dancing the night away, but she could see Gravity watching with a look off absolute sorrow, and it seemed as though all he wanted was release from this torturous life.

She woke the next morning feeling refreshed and longed for the enticing foods that awaited them at the castle, and the first night she could spend with Nyakas. As they rode back to the castle, silence rose from the woods and Robyn could see it made Gravity feel uneasy.

"Stop!" He said with a quick halt of his horse.

"What is it, Gravity?"

"We're not alone," Gravity said as he looked from side to side.

They dismounted. Gravity's cloak flowed with the morning breeze over his black ring mail and his black deerskin pants. His eyes were like a hawk's awaiting prey, his swords in his hands. He stood motionless, not taking a stance yet. Robyn pulled her sword and awaited her opponent. Her deerskin pants were loosely fitted for better maneuverability, her tunic was open at the neck, and her cloak flowed with the breeze. She stood with a look of determination and waited for the opposition.

They both heard footsteps about thirty yards away. A man in a crimson cloak walked through the trees and smiled at them with his swords in hand. His half suit of chain mail hung loosely around him over his brown tunic, his pants loosely fitted for the same maneuverability as Robyn's. He stared arrogantly at his opponents.

Fourteen men came from behind Robyn and Gravity. Gravity turned to face them to keep them from advancing any further. They stopped, not because of Gravity, but because Kerrigan motioned to them. They stood steadfast, not fighting until they were told to do so.

Robyn looked into the eyes of the man she had once defeated and the stare down began as the others moved to surround them. Gravity knew his young knight was ready for battle, but not against fourteen opponents. He repositioned himself to stand back to back with her, and readied his mind and magic.

"Welcome, Robyn, I'm so glad to finally see you get the training you needed," Kerrigan said with an arrogant look on his well-chiseled face.

Gravity half-turned to watch both the men behind them and Kerrigan. He replied, "Kerrigan, it's always a pleasure to see you. Are you that worried that it takes fourteen of your underlings to subdue the two of us, or are you just scared?"

Kerrigan looked at Gravity with disgust on his face and answered, "No, Gravity I just want to see nothing but blood soak this ground. I hope you trained her well, my friend."

"I'm not your friend."

Kerrigan raised his hand to the others to attack them and they did so without hesitation. The first came at Robyn with an overhead blow. Robyn lunged quickly and skewered her opponent, who fell to the ground in a hump. Gravity faced two as one came for his head and the other for his legs. With lightning-fast reflexes he brought his blades to meet theirs and quickly spun out of their reach to give himself more room. Gravity quickly sent his opponents to the hard ground with quick blows and waited for them to give up, but they didn't want to cooperate. He wished to let them live to see the ruination of their master, but since they insisted on fighting back, he had no choice but to kill them.

Four more came from the direction where Kerrigan was standing. Robyn was the first to see them and quickly went to meet them before they made their way to where she stood. She quickly ran at the first one as he attempted the same maneuver his friend had used. As he made his overhead swing, Robyn sliced through his torso and tore him open as he fell head first to the ground. The second came swinging his blade in a circular motion to try to get her to back up. Instead, she stood toe to toe and as he came for a quick side shot to lop off her head, his own came off with her quickly moving blade. He fell as his head rolled towards Kerrigan's feet. Her adrenaline surged as Kerrigan kicked the head away, and she began to fight more fiercely. As she fought her way through the battle, the repressed memories of her former training started to flood her memory, along with the vivid memory of how Brett and Stephanie had died.

Gravity was making short work of his opponents. His blade moved briskly and he quickly disposed of seven. As his blade spun, he spoke ancient words. The forest seemed to shake with a thunderous clap and three more were stunned. He shot fire from his hand at one who had climbed a tree to attack from above and set the man ablaze. Gravity rolled out of the way to avoid his blade as he fell, screaming, from his perch. He stepped over the fallen bodies of eight opponents to face the last six.

Robyn, meanwhile, took advantage of her last opponent's mistake and lunged for his throat. Blood from his wound sprayed across her face and tunic, and she hesitated, shocked as the warm sticky liquid struck her. In her state of disarray, Kerrigan took advantage and kicked her in the back. She made a solid thud as she hit the ground hard.

He advanced on her quickly and kicked her several times while she lay on the ground. The cracking of her ribs was the only sound she could hear.

Another eight soldiers who had emerged from the woods surrounded Gravity. He fought tirelessly to get free to see how Robyn was doing. Robyn lay on the ground, aware of nothing but the pain in her ribs. She thought it was over until his boot made contact with her head in a stepping motion, and with that a quick splitting headache overcame the already immense pain in her ribs.

"You are weak, my pretty. You should have not come back." He pulled Robyn up by her hair and looked at her face, which now was bloody from a split lip and a cut just above her eye.

Gravity used his magic to create a circle of lightning that crackled around him and then struck out at his opponents. Four found themselves stunned on the ground and the other four felt the wrath of Gravity. As he once again spoke ancient words, their souls seemed to release from their bodies and find their eternal resting place in his body. Those who had been stunned came to their senses long enough to look in amazement as Gravity took one strong blow and swiped their heads off cleanly. He looked around to see Robyn lying helplessly on the ground at Kerrigan's feet.

"Say hello to your friend Brett, my pretty," Kerrigan said with arrogance in his voice.

Robyn lay helplessly on the ground awaiting her impending death, but a sudden jolt flung Kerrigan forward and his sword dropped to the ground. Robyn dragged herself away and Gravity picked her up. She watched a young man who looked vaguely familiar fight boldly, buying time for Gravity to get her a safe distance away. Kerrigan's blade was much faster than the boy's, who appeared to in his late teens. He fought Kerrigan as though he knew he could win, striking with all his might, but Kerrigan easily blocked his blows. The boy found an opening and cut the cheek of the demonic warrior, and for a second the fighting halted. Kerrigan looked shocked as the boy tried to catch his breath. Kerrigan went to work with increased vigor and the boy quickened his defense. Gravity made sure Robyn would be all right, then made his way back to the fight. At that very moment Kerrigan had found the boy's opening and made a quick slice up the length of his body. The boy's armor was no match for Kerrigan's blade. His blood slowly dripped from the length of the wound and the boy stood as his nerves would not let him fall, his sword still in hand. As he tried to lift it, Kerrigan laughed in amusement, "Boy, I can see you're a lot like her! You're weak!"

Gravity watched as his young student's knees buckled and he fell to the ground. With a scream that could make the hair on any man's neck stand on end, Gravity ran as fast as he could at Kerrigan, but Kerrigan disappeared as Gravity closed the distance. He tried to grab him, but he was too late.

Robyn watched as Gravity walked in slow motion, leaned down at the boy's side and held him in his arms. Gravity's armor was torn yet there wasn't a mark on his skin. He had taken down about twenty men as far as Robyn could see. She watched her teacher as he knelt beside the boy and it almost seemed to her that something had dropped from his face. She thought it might actually be a tear although she couldn't tell. She struggled to her feet and waited as Gravity picked up the boy and laid him over his horse. Gravity turned to Robyn and placed his hands upon her ribs and with his ancient words, she felt the pain disappear as a gold light appeared from his hands, and a short pain came with it, though it was gone after his hands left her side. She followed her teacher's lead as they mounted their horses and rode back to the castle.

Nyakas was in his chambers when he heard commotion outside. He went to his balcony first to see if she had arrived and from his vantage point he could see that she had, but he saw the unexpected as well. His heart sank as he saw Liam, the grandson of William, Robyn's favorite squire, laid across the back of his horse. He hurried down to be with Robyn and his friend.

As Robyn rode into the courtyard, she looked for Nyakas in the crowd. She saw him standing alone at the back of the crowd. Her heart leaped as their eyes met and she slid from her horse. She ran and dove into his arms, and her tears fell like rain.

"I'm so glad to see you and to be home," she sobbed into his chest.

"It's all right, Robyn, everything is all right now, no one is going to hurt you," he said, holding her tighter. "What happened?"

She took a deep breath and said, "Kerrigan showed up with a lot of friends. Gravity took care of most of them, and I took care of some, but when I met Kerrigan, I was no match. The boy came from nowhere to knock him away from me so Gravity could get me clear of the danger. He fought so hard, but before Gravity could get back to him, the damage had already been done."

"It'll be all right," he said. His arms around her were tight, and she couldn't see his face contorted in rage.

The council watched Gravity, waiting to see what he might do. They said nothing, not wanting to disturb him so soon after battle. His armor was shredded, but he had no injuries. Nyakas watched his friend stand alone in the middle of the courtyard watching the other knights and squires take young Liam's body to the storage area.

Gravity stood motionless as people started to disperse from the courtyard as Nyakas and Robyn watched. Gravity tore off the remnant of his armor he wore and stormed to the salle. Nyakas told Robyn to wait for him in the courtyard and followed Gravity. The arms master behind the counter where armor and weapons were stored stood still as Gravity stalked in.

"May, I help you, General?" he asked, his voice shaking.

"Yes. I want a half suit of ring mail." Gravity's voice revealed his anger.

The arms master quickly retrieved the armor and handed it to Gravity. Gravity left the salle, putting it on as he walked toward his horse.

"Gravity," Nyakas said running up to his horse and grabbing the reins. "Where are you going in such a rush?"

"I'm going to pay my respects to someone," Gravity said curtly.

"Gravity, please give it until tomorrow," Nyakas said still sounding concerned.

"I'll be back tomorrow. Do not worry my lord. I will not do anything that will endanger me, Robyn, you, or anyone else who stays within the confines of these castle walls." He nodded and rode towards the woods. Nyakas wanted to say something else but Gravity had gone. He watched as his friend rode out of sight. 'I feel the same as you, my friend, the same as you,' he thought and then returned to Robyn, knowing there was nothing more he could do.

Gravity's horse galloped through the woods. As he rode, he thought of the times he had watched young Liam. Nobility did not impress Gravity, but the tenacity of the young lad had impressed him very much. He had seen knights weep in fear just before battle, and he had seen young squires and farmers walk tall and proud, ready to defend what little was rightfully theirs. People who were ambitious but not of noble birth truly impressed Gravity. They possessed less than some knights yet they fought for what they believed in and for what was theirs. Gravity felt there was no better fight than to fight for those you care about and for your beliefs. He'd die for his king if necessary because he was his friend.

Gravity neared the cathedral, like an amphitheater made of hard stone and well constructed. Statues of dragons climbed the wall around the entire circumference of the cathedral, looking like they were trying to make it to the top where seven other statues stood. The statues at the top were the gods of Dragon Lord and the dragons that climbed the wall were the ones who would someday succeed the others who were at the top. The ones at the top stood proudly and were life size, ranging from one hundred to three hundred yards in length.

The double doors to the cathedral were open and guarded by what looked to be demons of some sort. They wore full suits of chain mail. Both were about six feet tall and three hundred pounds of fat. Their faces were red and scorched, and their hands and feet were disproportionately large. They had no hair, just the rough skin that looked charred from years of continuous heat.

Gravity waited until he was approximately fifty yards away before dismounting. He still wore his swords, but they were hidden underneath his long black cloak. His new armor was menacing and his hood was pulled over his head. He stalked to the double doors and as he approached the two guards crossed their pole arms to prevent Gravity from passing.

They spoke in unison, their voices raspy. "Who goes there?"

"Gravity, General of the Armies of King Nyakas. I wish an audience with Lord Malitor."

The pole arms were moved back and he was allowed passage. He walked slowly and others moved out of his way as he made his way to the Great Hall where Malitor presided. Followers wore black in respect to Lord Malitor. Cells containing various beings for sacrifice lined the circumference of the cathedral. Although the evil dragons of Dragon Lord liked to have virgins sacrificed to them, the good dragons preferred animals or great warriors who found it an honor to be sacrificed.

As people watched Gravity walk slowly through the Great Hall, Malitor wondered what the right hand man of Nyakas would do. Most were more scared of Nyakas than some other gods. Everyone knew the power of Malitor but could only wonder about his son and why his father had once imprisoned him. They all wondered why their god would put him there unless he was afraid that his son could actually defeat him.

Gravity found himself now at the feet of Malitor and respectfully bowed. Malitor glared down as Gravity bowed and then a smile came across his face.

"Good to see you, Gravity. I was wondering when you would come to see me," Malitor said confidently.

"My lord, I come to seek Kerrigan. Do you know where I might find him?"

"Why, he is not here. Why do you seek him? Maybe I can assist you in some way."

As Malitor spoke, Gravity saw a young man in silver and black plated armor come from behind the throne and stand to the left of Malitor. Gravity had to look closely, but he knew full well it was Nyakas and Robyn's son who stood motionless at Malitor's side.

The young boy's long black hair was braided. His dark blue eyes matched his mother's perfectly. Gravity could easily see the eyes of a dragon and the heart of a mortal. Gravity's ability to see into another's heart showed him that the boy hurt, and that he knew that this man knew his father and mother well. The boy said nothing as he stood his rightful place at his grandfather's side, but he seemed to be sad without knowing why.

Gravity shifted his attention from the boy back to Malitor and said, "Well, my lord, Kerrigan killed one of my young squires. I must ask, was it you who knew where I was when I took Robyn to train?"

"I can see you're still not going to bend from my son and be one of the elite," Malitor said with anger in his voice.

"I'm sorry, my lord, I cannot. I will not, ever. Your son is my friend and I cannot to do that to him," Gravity replied in the same tone.

"You are evil like the rest of us. Why is it you care to help him when even you know it is forbidden for a dragon to take a human bride?"

"It is only forbidden because you say it is forbidden. Who ever said your rules were Nyakas'? The heart is blind to such matters."

"You sorely test my patience, Gravity. I was hoping you were a little smarter than that," Malitor said, with a bit more calm to avoid looking like he was losing control.

"Marcus, what do you say? You surely have an opinion on the matter."

Marcus looked stunned that someone would ask his opinion on a matter, especially one that involved his mother and father, whom he only vaguely remembered. He stood silent looking at his grandfather for help but yet Malitor watched Gravity.

"I am only allowed to speak with permission. I'm sorry," Marcus said softly. He wanted to see his parents so badly that he could taste it. He had heard the stories of his father's earlier days as a great protector and hero. He longed to meet his mother and hear her tell him the story of how she went to war with what seemed to be an unstoppable opponent and won. This time it would be even harder. Kerrigan was resurrected and given more power than he first had. He would be a very deadly adversary this time with the help of Malitor and his elder son, Vaytawn.

"Please let him speak, Malitor. It is only fair to hear his opinion on a matter that involves his mother and father," Gravity said with his usual non-expression on his face.

Malitor knew he had something up his sleeve, but he smiled and said, "Sure, why not? Go ahead, Marcus tell him what you think about the whole situation."

"I can't say much, other than my father and mother gave up on me and now they make no attempt to come and see me."

"How is it that you know this, if may I ask? Is it because your grandfather and your uncle tell you?" Gravity asked.

"Well, Grandfather sends a messenger to my father sometimes, asking him when he is going to come and see his son, yet he never comes."

"Marcus, I am Nyakas' friend and general of his armies. If there were a messenger sent I would be the first to know, and I would personally take the messenger to your father. Your grandfather has never sent a messenger to the kingdom of Nyakas. Your grandfather hates your father and deliberately separates you from him so that he can eliminate your mother."

"Grandson, he speaks nothing but lies and cannot be trusted," Malitor snapped, trying not to sound concerned.

Marcus looked confused for a moment as he watched Gravity's face while the germ of truth began to settle in his head. He stared at Gravity wondering why it was that what he was saying seemed true, and why his Grandfather always talked so bitterly about Nyakas, who was once a great protector and warrior.

"Marcus, I speak truth. Your father and mother wish for you to be with them but must first stop the thing that is trying to tear you away from them. They will continue to fight until they get you back."

Malitor was no longer able to stay calm. "Be quiet, Gravity! You are nothing more than a witch and a stealer of souls! You make deals with demons and you know nothing of love or heart! You don't even have a soul!"

"I asked where Kerrigan was and you said he was not here, so I guess you have already answered my question. Thank you for your time. Good day, Lord Malitor, Marcus." As he turned to walk away, he looked back at Marcus and Marcus returned his gaze. Gravity silently exited the cathedral, and people moved to the sides, afraid to stand in his way. Reaching his steed, he mounted, grabbed the reins and took one final look at the cathedral, his anger still not yet subdued after the death of Liam. He then turned to the woods and rode quickly back to the castle.

Chapter 53

After Gravity's hasty departure from the salle, Nyakas took Robyn to their chamber where a hot bath awaited her. He waited on the balcony while she stripped off her clothing and slipped into the bubble bath. She soaked in the hot water, glad to be home with the man with whom she had fallen in love for a second time. Nyakas knelt behind the tub with his shirt off, and Robyn's hands rubbed his chest while Nyakas fed her some grapes and rubbed her aching shoulders.

"I missed you while you were gone," Nyakas said.

"And I missed you, my lord."

Robyn still felt the affects of the battle. Gravity had healed her ribs, but her torso still bore the bruises Kerrigan had inflicted, and her face still throbbed a little. The war scars would heal, but she felt responsible for the boy's death, and she couldn't help but think that if she hadn't frozen up when she realized whom Kerrigan was, maybe she could have defeated him.

"What is it, Robyn?" Nyakas asked, as he rubbed harder to get the stiffness out.

"I feel responsible for what happened to that boy. I just wish I could have done more."

"He made his choice—no one forced him to fight."

"I know, but he fought for me. I can't understand it," she said, tears building up in her eyes again.

"When you were here before, there was a young squire named William. He was not highborn. In fact it was only his talent with a sword that won him a place among the squires in the first place. He had admired you from the first day he met you. He saw how you handled Gravity, and how you kept a confident smile and carried yourself with assurance, as if Gravity could not to get to you. He wanted to be as good as you, he wanted to be able to sit at our table and talk to you, and get to know you. He was mature for his age. He lost his parents early in life, and Gravity had kind of adopted him and tried to make him into a good knight. When you were taken, William was devastated, but eventually he married and had a family. He told all of his children and grandchildren about you. One of those grandsons was Liam, the boy who saved you today. I have no doubt that Liam died a happy young man to have saved the life of his grandfather's beloved queen." He leaned forward to kiss her cheek, then helped her as she climbed out of the tub. She found her robe waiting for her in Nyakas' hands. He wrapped her in it, then picked her up and carried her to the bed where he laid her down softly.

Before he could even lay her flat she had already fallen into a deep sleep in his arms and he covered her with her favorite blanket. He pulled his chair up to the edge of the bed, brushed the hair away from her brow and watched his beautiful wife as she slept. He noticed she had built some muscle in the past months, and he smiled slightly. Her hair had grown past her shoulders. Earlier it had been braided and tied with a leather thong. Now it fell in soft damp waves around her face. As he brushed it away he looked out the window of their chamber as if he were looking for a sign, though none ever came.

She slept for a couple of hours before Nyakas woke her up. Betty came and helped Robyn dress, and then she and Nyakas went to the Great Hall for dinner. Conversation was subdued and many of the knights welcomed her back warmly. She didn't notice that much of the council was absent, but Nyakas did. They did not linger over dinner as they normally would have, but instead ate quietly and left.

As they approached their chamber, Nyakas noticed that the council was waiting for them at their door and they did not look at all pleased. Nyakas looked at all of them and stopped, then turned to Robyn and said, "I'll be right back, Robyn; I have to take care of some business." His voice was soft and sent a warm sensation through Robyn's body.

"Don't be long, please. I need you right now, Nyakas."

"I won't," Nyakas replied with a smile.

He shut the door behind her and went to the council chamber to listen to whatever it was that precipitated this emergency meeting. The council chamber was a large circular room. It had ten chairs around a rectangular table. Nyakas' seat was at the head and the rest of the council sat along the sides. The chairs had high backs that were smooth and finely finished, and the arms were ornately detailed dragonheads. There were six openings in the castle walls allow sunlight into the room, and six iron sconces with candles for evening meetings such as this. The sun had just set, and a page circled the room lighting the candles. Only Gravity's place was empty as Nyakas and then the rest seated themselves. Nyakas looked at his friend's chair and wished he were there to help him since it was obvious that he was outnumbered. The council was silent, waiting for Nyakas to speak. "Whatever business we have, let's finish it quickly."

"Nyakas, we wished to speak with you about some matters," said Sir Robert, a council member. "We mean no disrespect my lord, but the Queen you take is mortal and we know all about the story surrounding that personal subject. We wish you to try something else. If she stays here we all might be the next to be taken out by your father and brother. The boy would have made a good knight and we know his death was a great loss to you. We're sorry, but he died because of the queen. You must start to think about the rest of your kingdom."

"Liam died protecting the queen, as he would have to protect me. He would not want me to put her aside because of the current circumstances, and I refuse to do so."

"But my lord, your father is ruthless, as is your brother. They will stop at nothing until she is out of the picture. They will see how this has hurt your kingdom and will come to destroy it," another council member said sounding irritated.

"I'm the king and no one, not my father or brother or anyone else will take my kingdom or my wife away from me!" Nyakas stood and hit the table, breaking it in two.

The council members sat frozen in their chairs, not knowing what to say. Nyakas stopped and looked at the table he had just destroyed, his eyes filled with anger. He paced the room to collect his thoughts. The council sat silently as Nyakas stopped at the head of the table and sat back down saying nothing, just leaning forward as he looked out amongst his council. He could see the fear in their eyes as he looked at each of them; they looked away as Nyakas' eyes came to rest upon them.

"You may all take your leave now," Nyakas said with a note of finality; although he had more to say he dared not speak in anger.

They all rose from their chairs and left the room. Nyakas remained to compose himself. He thought of the amount of time he had spent to find Robyn and remembered back to the night he lost her. He loved her strength and courage, and remembered how he could always read her emotions on her face. He always knew when she was angry with him, when she was teasing, and when she was struck again with the magnitude of her love for him. He loved the way she would wink at him from time to time when they were not alone to let him know she loved him. He was amazed at how she always knew when he'd had a bad day, and she would sit with his head in her lap and run her hands through his hair.

He pulled himself out of his reverie and went back to his chamber. Robyn sat at his desk in her muslin gown, curled up with a mug of hot tea. He watched her as she stared out at the stars. Her legs were tucked primly underneath her. A cold breeze blew in the open window, and he smiled as her toes curled up. Her hair blew softly, and it had been centuries since he'd seen a more beautiful sight. She slowly glanced around to see Nyakas watching her.

"Is everything all right, Nyakas? You look like you had a rough meeting."

"Everything is fine, Robyn. I was just taken in by the beauty I have missed for so long," he replied. He avoided telling her about the meeting, knowing it would only add to her anxiety. "You are beautiful, Robyn."

Robyn sat up straight, putting her feet on the thick carpet and the mug on the desk. She smiled, but her face was questioning. "Are you sure everything is all right?"

"The council had some minor matters for me to deal with. Everything is fine now that you're back, " he said as he looked deeply into her eyes and walked to her. She stood up and he put his arms around her waist. She put her arms around his neck, stared back into his eyes, and smiled as she remembered the dragon she had loved so much. They kissed, moved to the bed and lay down. Robyn laid her head on Nyakas' broad chest and slowly fell asleep. Nyakas held her close and his eyes wandered the room as he listened to her even breathing.

After a half candle had passed, Nyakas couldn't fall asleep. He sat up and looked at Robyn, moving her as gently as possible from his chest to her pillow and brushing her hair away from her eyes. He quietly pulled on his brown leather boots and moved silently across the room. Moments later he stepped onto the battlements to look out beyond the stars. He stood envisioning the time when his family would be whole again when he heard Gravity coming up the stairs.

"Is everything all right, my lord?"

"Yes. Where did you run off to in such a hurry?"

"I went to Dragon Lord to see if I could find Kerrigan."

"Did you see my son?" Nyakas asked with loss in his voice.

"Yes, my lord. I looked into his heart and saw he wishes for the day that he can be back with you," Gravity said. He allowed a hint of joy to creep into voice since he knew it would give Nyakas hope.

"How does he look?" Nyakas asked as he turned around to look at his friend.

"He is the image of both his mother and father. He has the power of a dragon with the feelings of a human."

"What did my father say? Did he let Marcus speak, or was he only allowed to speak when given permission?"

"He followed your father's wishes. Malitor has brainwashed him, of course, and told him that you and Robyn don't want to see him. Apparently, Malitor invents a messenger every now and again to ask you when you will come to see your son, but you never do. Don't worry; I set him straight on that count. That was when your father told him to be quiet and told me to quit saying such things, and so I did, but I continued to search his soul. He knew it and opened up to me, and I could see he longs to be with his parents."

"You could see him for what he truly was? So what is he? Is he a dragon, a mortal, what?"

"He is both. I know this sounds strange. He can turn into a dragon but he is hindered. He has been forced to learn all the traits that are inherent to all other dragons. He does not mature quite as quickly as a dragon does. He is still a child and he has much to learn. He has a huge heart like both his parents, and is very mature mentally for his age. You will be with your son soon enough, my lord, I promise you. He will leave Malitor to find you if that is what it takes. It was easy to see that he is disgusted by your father's methods."

Suddenly, Gravity and Nyakas heard footsteps and became silent. They turned to see that it was Robyn slowly walking up the stairs trying not to be heard. As she crept she could see them both talking, but they already knew she was there.

"Good evening, your majesty," Gravity said.

"Good evening, Gravity," she said as she came the rest of the way up, a little disappointed she had been caught.

"What's wrong? Could you not sleep?" Nyakas asked, concerned.

"Well, it's kind of hard not having you by my side," she said with a smile.

He opened his arms and she stepped into his embrace and laid her head on his chest, listening to his heartbeat. Gravity watched for a few seconds before he just slipped away into the shadows and walked back down to his chambers. Robyn and Nyakas stood for a few minutes just holding onto one another and then they slowly came apart and went back down the stairs, where they curled into bed and fell fast asleep.

Chapter 54

After Gravity's departure, Malitor sent Marcus to his chambers so that he could be alone. Marcus did as his grandfather wished, but walked slowly, pondering what Gravity had said to him. He went to his large chamber, took off his armor, and lay on his bed with his head cradled in his arms. Tears rolled from his eyes. He wanted so badly to meet his father and one day fight beside the Protector of the Gate. He quickly fell asleep and dreamed of the day when he would be reunited with his parents.

Malitor sat on his throne, ill tempered at the words that had been said by Gravity. He pondered the loyalty of his own minions, wondering if they were taking Nyakas, Robyn, and Gravity seriously, or trying to toy with them. As he sat silently Kerrigan strode down the hallway to meet Malitor, oozing arrogance. Kerrigan bowed and a smile gleamed across his face. Malitor could see blood on the front of his cloak and armor and a smile reached his face as well.

"Kerrigan, I take it you have good news for me," he said with a smile.

"Yes, my lord. Robyn will be no match. She is far from ready and one of Nyakas' lies six feet under thanks to me," he replied with a grin.

Malitor looked a bit confused for a second, and wondered who would have been with Gravity and Robyn that he could have killed.

"Really? Who?" Malitor asked with confusion in his voice.

"A young lad who was a favorite of your son and Gravity."

"Well, that is all good, but what about Robyn? If she isn't prepared, then why didn't you take her out, too?"

Kerrigan stiffened. This was the question he'd hoped to avoid. "Well, my lord, the boy got in the way and before I could destroy her Gravity pulled her out of harm's way."

"Than why didn't you kill Gravity? If he was the problem, the solution is simple enough! If it's in your way, get rid of it! You and Vaytawn said that Gravity is not to be feared, yet you had a chance to destroy her and you didn't!" Malitor's face began to turn red and the scales of a dragon began to show through his human facade. Kerrigan wisely backed up a few steps, knowing that Malitor was rarely angry enough for his face to alter.

Malitor looked past Kerrigan to see his son Vaytawn walking down the hallway. He calmed himself for his son's arrival. Vaytawn bowed before his father and a smile reached his face.

"Good news, I hope, son. I've been waiting all day for good news. I'm sure you can find something to tell me that will brighten this day."

"Father, how good to see you. Yes, news, of course. My spies tell me that the kingdom of Nyakas is in turmoil after what happened today. All of the council except Gravity are saying that the king is putting them all in danger, risking his kingdom and its people for love, and that he is going to have their ruination if he doesn't stop at the rate he is going," Vaytawn said gleefully.

"Very good, my son. So Kerrigan, you actually made a wise decision with your actions."

"Lord Malitor, don't worry. Robyn can't think with a clear head. Before I left earth, I murdered her two friends, and I'm sure revenge is on her mind. She can't fight--her mind is being torn up. She'll freeze in battle, you can count on that."

"Excellent. Now, I want you to go to earth and seek out the others who wish to aid her."

"They will not all work together. Mike Ryan despises your son, and the other I'm sure is not quite sure of him or Gravity either," Kerrigan said. "Their hatred for one another runs deep and I can assure you they will kill each other rather than join forces."

"I hope you're right for your sake, Kerrigan. Sometimes two enemies who are after the same goal can put their differences aside to fight along side one another until the goal is reached." Malitor sat back in his throne, knowing now that sooner or later he would have his son back in line.

Chapter 55

Robyn walked down the hall to Brett's room. It was foggy, and she could see that Brett's door was open. She walked in and saw his body hanging on the wall. The room smelled like fresh blood and fear. She stared at the scene, aghast at the carnage, when a noise distracted her. She followed the sound and discovered Stephanie lying in a pool of blood, calling her name.

"Robyn," Stephanie said, "Why did he do this? He said he was looking for you, and he wouldn't believe us when we said we didn't know where you were."

"I'm sorry, Stephanie," Robyn answered, weeping, "I didn't know he was looking for me. I would never have put you in this position if I'd known something like this would happen."

"It's OK, buddy," said a voice behind her. She turned to see Brett's head on the floor. "We're OK now. We're in a better place with no exams. We still love you."

"Please, my lady," said another voice coming from near the door, "do not blame yourself. You knew not what that demon-man was capable of."

She turned to see Liam. "Oh, Liam, why did you interfere? Was I worth your sacrifice?"

"Yes, my lady, and more. I am but a poor farm boy. You are the queen, and when I began my training, it was with the understanding that I would use my training to defend my liege."

"But you could have been the greatest knight in the kingdom."

"For a moment, I was, my lady. It is more important that you live now."

"Yes, Robyn," said Stephanie, "You didn't know at first, but now you do, so now you can keep him from doing this to anyone else. Don't let our deaths be in vain."

She awoke with a jolt and sat up. The dream had been different this time. Why did she keep having this dream? Disoriented, she looked around. Nyakas was sleeping soundly beside her. Not wanting to disturb him, she slipped out of bed and put on her robe, then slipped on her cloak and boots and went to the battlements. She saw Gravity standing in his favorite spot and went to stand beside him.

"Still couldn't sleep, my lady?"

"No. Rough day, huh?"

"Indeed."

"I bet right now you're wishing we hadn't come back today."

"Not at all. Kerrigan would have attacked us regardless of our destination. If Liam hadn't been out, you would probably be dead now."

"I'm sorry, Gravity. You must be disappointed in me."

"Not at all. You did very well, right up to the point when Kerrigan overwhelmed you."

"Gravity, why is it that you are so distant with everyone except Nyakas? We just spent months alone in the wilderness, and I still hardly know anything about you."

"Your majesty, my job as General of Nyakas' armies and his first knight keep me rather busy. I must go now, my lady. There is much to do tomorrow."

"Wait, Gravity!" Robyn said quickly, "Why don't you ever tell me anything about yourself? Is your past so bad that the only person you can confide in is Nyakas? There was a lot of animosity between us when we first started, but I have seen past that and have waited for you to open up to me like a friend and you never do. Why?"

"It's not quite that easy, Robyn," Gravity said slowly, turning to face her.

"I thought we were friends, Gravity."

His reply was terse and harsh. "I can't afford to be friends with you, because if I start to care, I can't do my job to protect the queen and the king. I will not be able to sleep at night if anything happened to either of you, and that's something I will have to deal with it." He turned to leave.

"So that's it, huh?" Robyn said to his back, "I guess they were all right."

Gravity stopped and waited. "About what?"

Robyn fought against the tears in her eyes. Her voice was thick as she said, "You're truly a man without a heart. You have no feelings." She walked briskly past him to her chamber.

Gravity stared at the ground for a while, pondering what Robyn had said. His eyes filled with what appeared to be tears, yet none ever fell to the ground. He looked up at the stars, then swallowed deeply and walked back down to his chamber.

He sat there the rest of the evening, remembering his past as though it were yesterday. He had been a child when his mother told him about his father, who was a king found sleeping with her, a peasant woman. All the king could do to save his royal status was leave her and their unborn child. Periodically a man in brown riding leathers would come to the house and drop off a small bag of gold, but that was the only contact he ever made.

Gravity vowed revenge and went to extreme lengths to make sure he had it. He started sword fighting at a young age. He was taught by a clan of samurais for many years and became one of the most feared swordsmen in the land. However, he did not live by the code of his brethren. He became a pirate and assassin for hire. His life was built around the obsession of the day when he would get a chance to meet his father and take what he believed was rightfully his. He went on to learn about how magic could help him to be even more powerful in his chosen occupations. He made deals with demons, devils, and other entities that had absolute power, and it was granted to him in exchange for services he provided to them. He was called a witch and was a stealer of souls and was the most feared person in the land until the return of Nyakas.

Nyakas met Gravity one fine morning and demanded payment for being within the vicinity of the Great Nyakas. Outraged by the dragon's insolence, Gravity drew his steel and went to work on the formidable opponent. The seven-hour-long battle ended in a stalemate; Gravity's skill exceeded Nyakas', but dragons heal more quickly than witches. Nyakas respected his adversary for standing strongly against an opponent who could best him and asked Gravity to be his first knight. Gravity accepted with no small amount of confusion. Together, they built a strong kingdom. They became friends as they battled with all who dared to challenge the kingdom of Nyakas. One day, Gravity found his father, deep beneath the ground. Although he was outraged by many years of hatred, he was finally able to forgive his father and paid respect to him once a year. His mother died a few years later. He buried her beside his father and fenced the two in with a four-foot high fence.

His ability to not have a heart was something Gravity himself tried to understand, yet couldn't figure out. He admired Robyn, tried to help her to be the best, and wished her well with the man with whom she had found love. He watched his friend and sometimes dreamed that maybe one day he would also have someone who loved him as she did Nyakas. He resolved to stand steadfast behind his student and friend, and then blew out the candle and turned in for the night.

Chapter 56

Robyn went back to her chamber and stood on the balcony, crying. A few minutes later, Nyakas came out and put his arms around her shoulders. She turned around and put her arms around his waist.

"What is it, love?"

"I couldn't sleep, so I went to the battlements and Gravity was there. I asked him why he never talks about himself, and he told me on no uncertain terms that he was not my friend and could not be because it would hamper his ability to do his job."

"He didn't mean to hurt you. He just refuses to allow anyone to get close to him. I think in some strange way, he is afraid to let anyone in. There are things about him that I don't even know. But there is nobody besides me who would protect you the way he would."

"I know. I just thought we were friends. I've lost two today, now."

"No, you didn't. You didn't lose Gravity. He won't admit being your friend because he doesn't see friendship the way you do. He expresses his feelings in terms of duty and honor, and those bind him to us. Have no fear, he won't leave you."

"I know. I guess I'm just sad. I really miss my parents."

"Then you must work hard to eliminate Kerrigan so you can go see them. Have you given any thought as to what you will do after you take care of him?"

"Yes. Party like crazy."

Nyakas laughed, and then asked the question that had been burning inside him for months. "What about after that? Will you stay, or go home?"

"I don't have much waiting for me at home anymore. I could go to work for my father, but that's really about it. I can't go back to school, not after what happened. I don't ever want to step foot on that campus again."

"I don't blame you."

Robyn hesitated, searching for the proper words. "I can't remember our wedding, but I'm sure there was something in the vows about staying with you until death parts us, right?"

"Yes."

"Then I have to stay with you. I can't break that vow. My heart won't let me. I need you, I can't live without you. It would be easier for me to give up oxygen than to leave you."

Nyakas sighed with relief as he took her in his arms. "I can't tell you how I've longed to hear that from you. It was hard for you before, to be away from your home. I promise I will make it worth your sacrifice to stay with me."

"It's not a sacrifice. I want to be right here, in your arms, for the rest of my life." She kissed the side of his neck lightly and he lowered his head to kiss her lips gently.

She smiled as the kiss ended and looked into his eyes. "I was thinking earlier that Kerrigan actually did me a favor by attacking us this afternoon."

"How is that?"

"Now I've had actual combat experience. I know what it's like to stab someone with my sword and have his blood gush in my face, so next time I'll be ready. Not only that, but I've seen his face in that situation. That's one reason I froze up. When I realized who he was, I got scared and I couldn't remember what I was supposed to do."

"In that aspect, yes, he did you a favor. Do you think you'll be able to face him again?"

"I have to. There are too many people who love me who don't even know about him, and I have to protect them."

"Good girl! That's what I wanted to hear. Now, come back to bed. You have a busy day tomorrow, and you need to rest."

"OK," Robyn said. He led her back inside and she curled into the bed. Nyakas blew out the candles, then came back and stretched out beside her on top of the quilt. As he brushed the hair away from her face, she took his hand and kissed it. He smiled, leaned over, and kissed her temple.

"I love you, Robyn. I always have, and I always will."

"I love you, too. We belong together. I missed you so much while I was away. I dreamed about you every night. Now that I'm home, I don't want to be away from you ever again."

"Then it shall be as my lady wishes. Now sleep, my love."

Robyn smiled at him, then closed her eyes. When she opened them, the sun was beginning its ascent. Nyakas sat beside the French doors, going over some paperwork. Beside him on the floor sat a stack of papers. She rolled over and yawned, and he looked up.

"Good morning, my love," he said. "Did you sleep well?"

"Yes," she answered, getting out of bed. She scooped up her clothing and paused to kiss him. She had meant it to be a light peck, but he put his arms around her and pulled her down on his lap. Startled, she dropped her clothes, and his paper landed on top of them.

She giggled as they kissed, and when it ended she said, "You didn't miss me, did you?"

"Of course I missed you!"

She touched his face. "I was only kidding! I missed you, too. It's wonderful to start the day in your arms, but I have a lot of work to do today, and from the look of it, so do you."

"Not really, I'm almost finished. I will get a bite to eat and get a little sleep, though."

"You know, you don't really have to stay awake now. I can defend myself if something happens, and it's not as if you wouldn't wake up."

"You may be right. I'll give it some thought."

"OK. I'd better get moving."

"Yes, do that, so you can come back up here more quickly."

She smiled and kissed him again, then went behind the screen to dress so she wouldn't distract him. She finished dressing and sat on the couch to put on her boots when there was a tap at the door. Betty entered with a tray and said, "Good morning, Majesty. And to you, milady."

"Good morning, Betty," said Nyakas absently.

"Good morning," said Robyn as she tied her boot.

"Can you pause for a bit of breakfast, milady?"

"I'm afraid not, but thank you. I've become accustomed to fasting before I work out."

"Very well, milady," said Betty.

"I hope you didn't go to all that trouble on my account."

"No, darling," said Nyakas, grinning, "she went to all that trouble on my account."

"Good," said Robyn brightly, "then it won't go to waste! Well, it will, but it will be your waist, not mine! See you later, dear!" She grabbed her cloak and swept out the door. A few minutes later she trotted into the courtyard, stretched, and began running. During her time with Gravity, she had tripled the distance she could run, and doubled the calisthenics. She went through her normal routine, ending in the salle instead of the courtyard. Gravity looked up as she came in the door.

"Good morning, my lady," he said, "I didn't expect to see you quite so early."

"Why not? I'm actually running a little late."

"I thought maybe you'd go soft when we got home. A rich meal, a soft bed, and someone to share it with does that to some people."

"Well," she said, drawing her sword, "I'm not some people. I have a lot of work to do, and not a lot of time to do it. Shall we?"

He moved into position and attacked, as usual, and she defended. When she saw an opening, she went on the offensive, and so they went, back and forth. Suddenly there was a noise behind her. A quick glance revealed a second opponent, one of the knights she had met briefly. His name escaped her, and she didn't have time to try to think of it as she ducked out of the way of his blade. She adjusted her position so that her back was away from both opponents, but they didn't make it easy. They advanced aggressively, and she defended desperately, using everything she could think to use. The second man advanced past Gravity and slashed downward in an attempt to slice from her right shoulder through her midsection. She stepped back quickly and parried a blow from Gravity, then switched her sword to her left hand and clothes lined the second man, catching him neatly across the throat and sending him sprawling onto the sawdust. She quickly slapped his neck with the flat of her blade, simulating a cut to the carotid artery the way she'd been taught and turned back to Gravity. As she began to gain an advantage with him, another of the knights joined the fray and she was forced to defend again, two against one. On and on it went. Her breathing became labored after nearly an hour, and she began to fall back on simple wrestling moves as the fighting intensified. Then, out of nowhere, a blade struck her full in the back. She'd been hit with the flat so it hurt but did no permanent damage. The fight was over and she turned to see who had struck her down. It was the first knight, who had been "resurrected" to rejoin the battle. He'd changed his leather jerkin to simulate a new attacker. Gravity stood about three feet away, watching critically.

"Thank you, gentlemen," he said, "that will be all for now." The two men bowed to her, then turned and left the salle. Robyn sheathed her sword and stood where she was, trying to catch her breath. Gravity handed her a water skin and she sipped from it, waiting for his critique.

"You lasted longer than I thought you would," he said.

"Thank you," she answered simply, taking the veiled compliment for what it was.

"We'll need to work more with multiple attackers. You can expect that from Kerrigan. The other moves were interesting. When did you pick those up?"

"I was raised on them. My father was a professional wrestler, but it wasn't the sort of wrestling they do here. It's purely for entertainment, but the moves are effective in other situations."

"So I see. Perhaps, when you have more time, you could teach some of them to the knights."

"Certainly," she said, a little surprised. "Now, tell me what did I do wrong so we can fix it."

He launched into a dissertation about her strategic and tactical errors, then they got the knights, Jude and Darven, back and they began again. By mid-day, she was tired and hungry, and Gravity told her to take the rest of the day off. They both knew why; it wasn't that he was being generous. There was other business to attend to that neither of them wanted to discuss.

Robyn walked back through the courtyard and into the castle. She stopped a page as she entered and asked where Betty was, and was told that she was in the royal chamber. Robyn went up to find Nyakas asleep and Betty pouring steaming water into the bathtub. There was food on the table, and she sat down to nibble while she waited for Betty to finish, then gratefully slid into the hot water. She soaked off the worst of the sweat and dirt, then vigorously scrubbed off the rest. When she finished, Betty was waiting with her gown and helped her dress. Nyakas woke as Betty was getting the last of the buttons in the back of Robyn's black velvet gown. She finished quickly and left. Robyn went to the bed and curled up beside him. He held her close, as if she were a shield against what they had to do that afternoon. They lay together for several minutes, neither of them speaking. Finally, he kissed her hair and got up to dress.

Robyn went to stand on the balcony. The day had started sunny, but it was now overcast and gray, as if the weather knew what would be happening later. She looked at the beautiful view and wondered if Liam could see it from above. The mountains had their snowcaps on, and the lake was slate gray. Most of the trees were bare, and the ones that weren't had dried, brown leaves hanging limply from their branches. She was sure she hadn't stood there long enough when Nyakas came out, put his arms around her waist, and said, "It's time to go." Her heart sank, but she followed him from the room to say good-bye to a young man who could have been a very good friend if time had permitted them to become so.

They walked, hand in hand, to a field. Liam's body lay on a funeral pyre, and the wood was stacked neatly beneath it. It looked to Robyn like almost the entire kingdom had come as she and Nyakas walked through the crowd to stand beside Gravity at the front.

Liam was dressed in what he dreamed of wearing, the uniform and armor for knights of the Kingdom of Nyakas. The black plate mail armor was almost form fitting and a gold cloak had a black dragon's head in the middle. His sword rested at his side, and his hands were placed upon his chest. He looked at peace, and Gravity placed his hand on the young boy's chest as if he were trying to will his heart to start beating again.

Nyakas started to walk back into the castle. Robyn looked confused as he left her side and she whispered to Gravity, "Where is Nyakas going?"

"Don't worry, your majesty, he's not going far," Gravity replied.

Within moments, there was a large whoosh. The people stared and pointed at the spectacle on the mountain. It was Nyakas, and he sat on the mountain breathing fire to show that a great warrior was being laid to rest. The belief was that if a dragon flew overhead during a funeral or happened to be within the vicinity of a person who died, that the person who died would be allowed to sit with the gods, which was the greatest honor. The dragon, the most feared and admired creature in all dimensions, was a good omen, and the family of the boy would have no need to worry about where he would spend eternity. Nyakas stood proudly on top of the mountain breathing enormous flames into the air, and those gathered around the funeral pyre watched breathlessly as the magnificent creature flew around the body of the vanquished warrior. Then everyone knew it was time.

As Nyakas circled, Gravity produced flames from his fingertips and lit the wood. The fire was small and then began to rise higher and higher. That, too was a good omen; the higher the fire was, the closer Liam was to being at the side of his own god, and the better his chances of being a personal instrument in his god's army. Gravity stood at the side of Liam's body and remembered his first days of training with the boy. Liam had a tenacious spirit that would not allow him to give up. He always came back for more. When training ended each day, the boy would stand in the courtyard for the last few minutes of day and practice on the mistakes he had made. Gravity felt even though he was not of noble blood, his efforts made him one. The boy never allowed himself to be pampered after a day's work, although there were probably a few times he may have needed it. Gravity knew he was hard on his students, but they knew that when he gave them one hundred percent of himself, he expected nothing less of them in return. He could never live with anything less; he couldn't bear the heartache it would cause if one of them died in combat because of a deficiency in their training. He couldn't help but think that if he had trained him a bit harder that he would still be around. But he realized that no matter how hard he was on his knights, sometimes training wasn't enough.

The crowd began to drift away slowly. Soon, no one was left to watch the flames consume Liam's body with his family except Robyn, Nyakas, Gravity, and a handful of men who would bury the ashes when it was done.

The sun set and the flames began to die down. When it started to get cold, Nyakas led Robyn gently back to their chamber. She went to the window behind the desk and could still see what was left of the funeral pyre and Gravity silhouetted by the dying flames. The sight saddened her more than the funeral had, and she started to cry again.

Nyakas put his arms around her and turned her away from the window. She cried on his chest until she couldn't cry anymore, and only then did he break the silence.

"Betty left us some food. Come eat something."

"I'm not hungry."

"Then at least come and drink some tea. There isn't anything you can do for Gravity except work harder and learn more, and you can't do that if you're exhausted and starved." He led her to the couch and handed her a cup of tea. She sipped it, and was soon persuaded to nibble on a piece of fresh bread and some apple slices.

When he couldn't coax her to eat any more, he pulled her close and held her. They sat together in silence in front of the fire. She held on to him for dear life, wanting to feel anything except the sorrow in her heart. He kissed her hair, and she looked up and kissed him back. Their kiss deepened and her knees turned to water the way they had when he'd kissed her before, only this time he didn't stop.

She broke the kiss and said, "Nyakas, we are still married, aren't we?"

"Of course we are, my love. Why would you wonder?"

"Well, because back home a marriage can be dissolved after a certain length of time if one of the spouses abandons the other. I didn't know if you do that here."

"Why would I have our marriage dissolved, Robyn? You didn't abandon me, you were banished."

"Doesn't matter. After a person disappears, they can be declared dead after a few years to allow the other person to get on with their life."

"You are my life, Robyn. I would never put you aside for any reason. Why are you bringing this up now?"

"Well," she said, studying her fingernails intently, "I was saving myself for my husband." She could feel her face turning scarlet, and her fingernails were infinitely interesting to her since they gave her something to look at besides him.

Nyakas smiled and lifted her face up with his finger under her chin. He'd never known her to be embarrassed about anything, especially sex, and he found it rather amusing. He kissed her lightly and said, "So that's what this is about. Robyn, if you aren't ready to make love, that's all right. I've waited seven hundred years, it's not going to hurt me to wait a little longer."

"But I do want to," she said, looking at her fingernails again. She sounded like a little girl, and Nyakas had to smile. "I want to be with you, Nyakas. I'm just a little scared."

He pulled her to his chest and cradled her in his arms. "I understand, darling. I'll never forget my first time. At first I suffered from what you called performance anxiety, but you made it the most incredible night of my life. I always regretted a little that I couldn't do the same for you. Now I have the chance, and there is nothing to be afraid of. You just let me know when you are ready."

"I think I am, but I don't really know. All I know is that I want to feel something besides sad, and when you kiss me all the bad things go away. I'm starting to feel like Typhoid Mary; my friends are dropping like flies."

"Your friends' dropping like flies is not your fault. That's Kerrigan's fault, and we can thank my father for that. Don't worry about that right now. When you take care of Kerrigan, Gravity and I will take care of Vaytawn and my father. But it won't be tonight, and it probably won't be this week."

"I know," she said. She put her arms around his waist, snuggled her head into his neck, and sighed as he pulled her closer. His gentle kisses fell on her face, and when he got to her lips she returned the kiss. She ran her hands across his back and he ran his fingers through her hair. He shifted his kisses from her face to her neck and over her chest. His hands moved gently over her body, and he let the velvet of her gown carry the motion of his hands. He lightly stroked her back, neck, breasts, and waist. She moved her hands to his hair, running her fingers through his lush black locks. His hair came loose from its bonds, and fell around his face and over his broad shoulders to land on her chest. She kissed him passionately, clinging to him as if she could not get close enough.

He began unbuttoning the back of her gown, kissing her shoulders as he pulled the cloth away. He watched her closely, looking for her reactions. He expected to see some fear as he undressed her, but saw nothing but desire. She pulled her arms out of the long sleeves quickly, turning them inside out, and the bodice of gown fell into her lap. She began to unbutton his tunic. He took her hands in his, kissed each finger in turn, and pulled his tunic over his head. He stood up and helped her to her feet, and her gown fell into a soft pool of black velvet. He lifted her gently, carried her to the bed, and laid her on top of the quilt. He sat beside her, brushed her hair away from her face, and said, "Are you sure you want to do this?"

Robyn put her hand on the back of his neck, pulling him toward her, and said, "Yes. Please, chase away the monsters."

He kissed her gently, then more deeply, running his hands over her body. It had been so long since he'd been with her that part of him wanted to make love to her immediately, but he reminded himself that, at least emotionally, she was a virgin. He remembered his first time with her, and that bolstered his self-control. He was determined to make this as special for her as he could. He stroked her soft body and kissed her until she whimpered softly; only then did he allow himself to taste the pleasure he'd missed for so long. He took her gently, and her body arched toward his. They moved together gently in their sensual dance, and he used every ounce of control to see that her ecstasy was spent before his.

Voluntary thought ceased for what may have been seconds or hours, Robyn didn't know for sure. When she opened her eyes he was preparing to move away, but she held him close. She was still floating in a sea of contentment and couldn't bear to be away from him.

"Don't leave me yet," she said.

"I wasn't going far," he answered with a lazy smile.

"If it was more than a few inches, it was too far. Stay with me."

He held her for a few minutes before he got up. As the cold air hit the glaze of sweat on her body she whimpered and gathered the quilt around her. He went to the fireplace and added a log, then came back to the bed.

"Here," he said, offering her a glass. "Have a drink."

She hadn't realized that she was thirsty until he mentioned it, so she took the glass. The water was cold, and she didn't think she'd tasted anything so good before. He got back into bed while she drank, then took the empty glass from her hand and put it on the bedside table. She immediately curled into his arms and rested her head on his chest. His heartbeat was steady and his body was warm. Contentment flooded her, and she realized that for a little while, she hadn't been sad. He kissed her hair, and she looked up at him in the firelight.

"Did I do OK?"

Nyakas laughed. "Of course, my love."

"Was it like the old times?"

"Not quite, but that doesn't matter. What matters is that we're together. I don't ever want to lose you again."

"I'm not going anywhere. Are you?"

He chuckled. "Not for the foreseeable future."

"Tell me what it was like before."

"It was a real-life fairy story. We were so happy together. We worked hard to keep the kingdom prospering, and everyone knew it. The happier we were, the more everyone prospered. Sometimes we would take an afternoon off together and go to the lake. You loved to fish, and you usually caught at least a couple. If you caught two or three small ones, we'd skip formal dinner and eat them up here. Occasionally you'd catch several big ones, and you could feed the whole court. Of course, that always sent the kitchen staff scrambling. They'd have to stop the preparations they'd already begun and start over. I think you got more enjoyment out of that than the fishing, but you'd never admit to it. Every day had the perfect start and the perfect ending, because I always fell asleep beside you, and I always woke up with you in my arms. Whatever happened during the day, I always knew that it would end well. We had it all, and then it was gone."

"Well," she said, hugging his waist, "now it's back. I'm going to work as hard as I can to see that nobody tears us apart again. I'm not going to let anyone get between us."

"I'm also taking measures to see that it doesn't happen again. I'll never forgive Malitor for what he did, and I will see to it that he pays for all the anguish he caused, not just to us, but also to the hundreds of innocents Kerrigan killed in his quest to beat me to you."

"Did he really kill whole villages looking for me?"

"Yes. I saw some of the carnage he caused. Simple beheading is too good for that monster."

"Well, I'm sorry, darling. I'll do what I can to toy with him, but I think I'd rather just kill him quickly so I don't lose the advantage."

"I'm inclined to agree. Underestimation is his downfall. I was thinking earlier that since he's seen you freeze up in battle, he'd probably underestimate you when you do face him again. It might be good to fumble around a little to reinforce that, and then go in for the kill."

"I was thinking the same thing. I want to test it on some of the knights before I do it for real, though."

"Oh, I'm sure you'll have the opportunity to do so. Expect Gravity to push harder now."

"Expect me to push harder now. I have an axe to grind."

"I know him, my dearest. He'll push hard enough for both of you."

"Then I'll just have to push back a little so he'll know I'm determined. I want to get this over as quickly as possible so we can get back to what we had before."

"What about your family?"

Her heart jumped into her throat as she thought about her parents. She didn't know how much time had passed at home, but she knew they were probably worried about her by now, especially after what had happened to Brett and Stephanie. Her heart began to ache as she realized how long it had been since she'd seen them, and she was vaguely surprised as tears she thought she'd already spent began to gather again. She pressed her face into Nyakas' chest, unable to speak.

Nyakas tightened his hold on her, immediately sorry for bringing up the subject. He'd thought she was over her homesickness. Apparently she had a stronger bond with her parents this time. He hadn't counted on his father being so thorough. He comforted her as she wept, apologizing repeatedly.

A few minutes later, she pulled away from him and sat up. She wiped her eyes on the corner of the sheet and took a deep breath. "Is there a way to get a message to them?"

"Yes, but it will have to be done very carefully. Kerrigan will be watching closely, hoping you will lead him to them."

"I need to let them know that I'm still alive and well. They'll be going crazy trying to find me after what he did to Brett and Stephanie."

"I'll make some arrangements in the morning. I have a reliable messenger who I'm sure will be able to handle it. Don't worry, Robyn, we'll let them know you're safe."

"Is it possible to bring them here?"

"I'm not sure that's such a good idea right now. If they are here, Kerrigan will delight in laying siege to the castle. Having the people you love most in one place right now could be disastrous. Don't worry, we have people who Gravity considers competent watching over them, so even if Kerrigan does find them, he'll have to think twice before he does anything. He may be a cold-hearted killer, but he is not stupid."

"I know," she said, lying back down on his chest, "that's part of what scares me."

"Fear is a good thing as long as you don't let it control you. It's late, love. You should try to get some sleep. You'll need it tomorrow."

"I don't know if I can sleep."

"Well, then just lie here in my arms and rest. Don't trouble yourself over something you can't do anything about right now. We'll fix it, I promise."

She rested in his arms but didn't sleep very much. She thought about what she had to do to accomplish her mission. She knew that Gravity was angry over Liam's death and he would probably be more of a taskmaster than ever. Her job would be to take that anger from him and channel it into learning as much as she possibly could. She didn't know if she would ever measure up to what Liam could have been, but she had to try, and she had to defeat Kerrigan. She had to face him, and the sooner that happened, the better. In the end, she had to be victorious. Her family would no longer be threatened whether she won or not, but if Kerrigan lived there was no telling how many more innocent lives would be lost.

When the sky outside the window began to lighten, she slipped out of bed and dressed quietly. Nyakas had fallen asleep, so she dropped a light kiss on his face and brushed a lock of hair off his brow, and then took her boots and cloak into the hallway. She shut the door quietly and put them on, then began her usual routine. She had been alternating running with calisthenics and doing the routine twice, but today she did it three times. It was just past dawn when she entered the salle. It was still empty, and although the windows had been shut, it was cold. She drew her sword and began to practice. It wasn't long before she heard a familiar voice behind her.

"You should have done your exercising first."

"I already did," she answered without stopping. "Three today instead of two."

"You expect me to believe you've done the run and the exercises three times already, and it's only dawn?"

"I couldn't sleep, so I decided to get some work done."

"I see. Why this sudden need to be an iron woman?"

"I have an axe to grind. I'm working my way to the sharpening wheel."

"So you think that if you work hard enough, you can replace my best student."

She stopped and turned to face him angrily. "I can't bring Liam back. If I could, it would have been done already. I know you're angry, so go ahead and do your worst. You won't break me because I'll be damned if I'll let you win! If I can beat you, I can damn sure beat the son of a bitch who killed my friends! I just have one question."

His eyes were like steel. "What?"

"How does it feel to have your heart break when you don't have one?"

He glared at her. "Bitch. Get out of my salle and go run."

She sheathed her sword and left the salle. She ran the circuit twice without stopping to do the calisthenics, then went back to the salle. Gravity wasn't there, but Jude and Darven were waiting for her, and they engaged her immediately as she entered. She defended against them and lost. She got up and began again, and again she lost. Undaunted, she kept working until she could barely stand. She hadn't eaten, had barely slept the night before, but she didn't stop. Finally, they beat her again, and she didn't get up. She lay in the sawdust trying to breathe, and they helped her up and took her to a bench to sit down. She leaned weakly against the wall and the salle seemed to spin around her. Darven and Jude exchanged a glance, and Jude left the salle.

"My lady," said Darven, "what hast thou had eaten today?"

"Nothing," answered Robyn.

"Prithee, what hast thou done this morn?"

"I got up at false dawn, did my exercise routine three times, two katas, ran twice more, and worked out with you two."

"Thy constitution is not so sturdy that thou canst work so without food. Come, my lady. Thou must break thy fast."

"Whatever you say." Robyn stood up and swayed. Darven put his arm around her waist and helped her out of the salle. The sun had already passed its zenith, and there was a lot of activity. She pulled away from Darven, determined to get into the castle on her own. She refused to let any of her subjects see her weakness, but Darven hovered closely with his hand resting lightly at the small of her back, and they were entering the courtyard when Gravity met them.

"What the hell are you doing, Robyn?" demanded Gravity.

"I'm going to get some lunch, and then I'll be back," she answered evenly.

"Like hell you will," he countered.

"Like hell yourself. I'm going to eat."

"Yes, you are. And then you will take the afternoon off."

"No. I have too much to do."

"Killing yourself the first day back won't accomplish anything except getting me in trouble with your husband. Get inside and eat, and don't let me catch you anywhere near the salle this afternoon." He brushed past her and walked out of the courtyard.

Robyn shook her head as she went inside. Darven escorted her to the Great Hall and seated her at the table as Jude came in with a serving maid. She placed a plate in front of her that was piled high with meat, bread, boiled potatoes, and steamed vegetables. Jude and Darven sat, one on each side of her.

"Now, my lady," Jude said gently. "What were you hoping to accomplish by working like that with no food?"

"I thought I could take it," she answered around a mouthful of potatoes. "When Gravity and I were out there training we really didn't eat very much."

"But did you train so hard?"

"Well, I think so, but maybe not. It was always one on one. Sorry. I won't do it again. Now, since I can't go to the salle, where will we work this afternoon?"

"This afternoon?" Darven asked. "Surely thou art not considering defying Lord Gravity's command."

"Considering? No. Decided? Yes. I'll take a break after lunch so I can digest, but then I'm going back to work."

"Milady, such a decision could be detrimental. My humble suggestion would be to discuss the matter with thy husband the King before rushing headlong."

"You may be right. I'll do that. But I'm not going to sit around all afternoon. I have too much to do."

"Yes, my lady," said Jude, "starting with lunch."

Robyn grinned and did her best to finish what she'd been given, but there was far more food than she was used to. When she couldn't eat another bite, she pushed away from the table, promised her companions that she wouldn't do anything rash, and went to her chamber. It was empty when she got there, so she wandered down to Nyakas' office. He was sitting behind the desk and seemed to be doing paperwork again. She tapped on the door and he looked up.

"Robyn! Come in!"

"Hi. What are you doing?"

"Nothing important. Come, sit." He motioned to a pair of wingback chairs in front of the fireplace. "So, what have you been doing today?"

"Working myself to near exhaustion. I need your advice about something."

"Tell me about this near exhaustion first."

Robyn sat down and rolled her eyes as he took the other chair. "It's really no big deal. I forgot to eat breakfast and I got on a roll when I was working out. I got a little woozy, but I ate lunch, and now I'm fine."

"A little woozy? Define 'a little woozy.'"

"I got a little shaky. You know how you get when you haven't eaten."

"But you're all right now?"

"Yes, I'm fine, I feel just like new. Now I'm ready to go back to work, but Gravity was livid with me because I was working too hard and told me not to come back."

"Gravity got angry at you for working too hard? That doesn't sound like him."

"Well, we sort of got into a little argument earlier, and then Jude and Darven and I worked like the dickens all morning without him. When I got woozy, Jude went to get him. I guess he was still a feeling a little hostile because he demanded that I take the afternoon off, like I'd done something wrong. Anyway, I don't know if I should work where he can't see me, or go back to work where he can see me. Darven told me I should discuss it with you."

"Why don't you just take the afternoon off?"

"Because I have too much work to do. I can't sit on my laurels hoping to get better."

"I understand. Do you want me to talk to Gravity?"

"Talk to me about what, my lord?" The familiar voice came from the open door, and Robyn cringed.

"Come in, Gravity," said Nyakas.

Robyn slid off her chair to perch on the hearth. "Hi, Gravity. Have a seat!" She was trying to sound cheery, but she had the sinking feeling that she was going to get yelled at after they left.

Gravity sat in the chair and said, "Thank you, my lady. What do you want to talk to me about, Nyakas?"

"Is there any reason Robyn can't train this afternoon?"

"It depends on how quickly she wants to burn herself out. You didn't see her an hour ago, Nyakas. She was pale, shaking, and could barely walk on her own."

"Is this true, Robyn?"

"Well, yes, but I feel fine now."

"Irrelevant," said Gravity. "If you continue to push yourself in such a manner you won't be in any condition to fight when the time comes."

"But I didn't do anything we didn't do together in the wilderness! We didn't eat until mid-day, we always ran and worked out, and we didn't sleep as much. What did I do wrong?"

"There is one thing you didn't know about. When we were out there, I supplemented your energy with mine to speed your training. We got the worst of it out of the way in a short time, now it just needs fine-tuning. I'm not going to supplement your energy any more because you need to finish on your own. I won't be close enough to help you when you face Kerrigan."

"Why didn't you tell me?"

"I didn't think you would do this when we got back. I didn't expect you to be so driven, and so I didn't think you would notice."

"Gravity, I still have a lot of work to do. How do I proceed?"

"You start by listening to me and doing as I say, just as you did when we began your training. For today, if you are so determined to work, we will go to the salle, but when I tell you to stop, you stop. Understood?"

"Yes," Robyn said meekly.

"Good. Will you excuse us, Nyakas?"

"Of course, but I need a word with you when you finish. I'll see you later, love."

"OK," she said, kissing him lightly. She followed Gravity out the door and down the hall. A page and a maid passed them, and when they were out of earshot, Gravity stopped her.

"There is one other thing you'd do well to remember," he said.

"What?"

"I will work you as hard or as easily as I see fit. If you have a problem with my demeanor or tactics, keep it to yourself until you are the teacher."

"I'll do that if you'll quit accusing me of trying to take Liam's place. I knew he was your favorite, but that didn't stop me from trying to out-do him, myself, and you."

"I apologize for that comment. It was uncalled for."

"It's OK. I'm sorry I said what I did. I guess we were both angry."

"Yes. Let's get to work."

They went back to the salle and he immediately engaged her. She defended against his fierce attack, careful to keep her guard up so he wouldn't have an opening to use against her. He backed off marginally and she advanced, taking advantage of what looked like an opening. It turned out to be a diversion, because as she advanced, Jude attacked from behind. She scrambled to defend against two attackers who refused to let her turn her back away from them. She parried blows furiously. She didn't know how much time passed when Darven took Jude's place, and it seemed like an eternity when Jude took Gravity's place. They rotated for what seemed like forever, although in reality it was slightly less than two hours before they let up. When they finally did stop and Gravity again banished her from the salle, she walked stiffly to the castle.

Chapter 57

Gravity dismissed Darven and Jude and went to Nyakas' office. The door was open and Nyakas sat at the desk. Gravity tapped lightly on the door and Nyakas looked up.

"Gravity, come in. Are you finished with Robyn?"

"Yes, my lord," answered Gravity as he entered and shut the door. "What did you wish to see me about?"

"I need to get a message to Robyn's parents. She's concerned that they are worried about her."

"It will have to be handled very carefully, Nyakas. You know that Kerrigan will use them to get to her."

"Yes, I know. That's what I'm worried about."

"I'll handle it. I know someone who can deliver the message and keep watch over them."

"Good. Thank you, Gravity. Was my wife sufficiently tortured?"

Gravity grinned slightly. "I don't think she expected to work so hard this afternoon. Jude and Darven got a good workout."

Nyakas laughed. "Well, then, I'll let you take care of your little task and I'll go see to my wife."

"I don't want to know, Nyakas. Just remember that."

They rose simultaneously and left the office, each going a different way. Gravity went to the arch outside the castle grounds and began to chant. When his portal opened he stepped through and found himself near the campus where Robyn had gone to school. He looked around to get his bearings, and set out to visit one of her professors.

A short time later he tapped at the door of a modest Victorian house. The door opened and Lars stood in the doorway.

"Uh oh. Whatever it is, I didn't do it, OK? Really!"

"I need to speak with you," Gravity said shortly.

"Answer a question for me first."

"What? I haven't got all day."

"Did you have anything to do with two murders that took place on campus two weeks ago?"

"Only two weeks? Good. No, I didn't kill Robyn's friends, but I know who did. It's one of the reasons I'm here."

Lars stood aside to let Gravity enter. "What did you mean, only two weeks?"

Gravity turned to face Lars, glancing around to familiarize himself with his surroundings. "Time is different in my dimension. It passes more quickly than here. I need you to do something to help Robyn. She's worried about her parents. I need you to go to her home, let them know she's safe, and watch them from a distance. This is very important."

"Why is it important? And why me?"

"Because Kerrigan killed her friends. If he finds out where her parents are, he'll try to kill them, too. You can defend them if the need arises."

Lars nodded. "I thought he was the one responsible. I am due to take a sabbatical. Consider it done, but Kerrigan will recognize me. It will have to be done carefully."

"Can you handle it?"

"Yes, I believe I can. Tell Nyakas he came to the right man. It's good to know he's finally realized he can't fight evil with evil."

Gravity stared in disbelief. "Do you always say exactly what you think? You'd do well to overcome that bad habit, whelp. Do I have your assurance for Robyn?"

"Um, yes," stammered Lars.

"Good," said Gravity. "I'll be in touch." He turned and walked out the door and back to his portal.

Chapter 58

Robyn headed for her chamber and intercepted a page in the passage to find Betty. She was half way to her destination when Betty caught up with her.

"My lady," said Betty, "what is it that I can do for you?"

"I need a bath, Betty. How long would that take?"

"Not long to put together, my lady. I can have it ready for you in a quarter candle."

"Please do."

"Yes, my lady." Betty turned and walked back down the hall, and Robyn went to her chamber and flopped down on the couch. She shut her eyes, and a moment later she heard the door open.

"Not a moment too soon," she said, not opening her eyes.

"I'm glad to see you, too, my love," answered Nyakas.

Robyn opened her eyes in surprise. "Oh, hello. I thought you were Betty."

"Tiring of me already? I see, you had your way with me, and now you're thinking of branching out."

Robyn blushed and said, "No, it's just that Betty is going to put a bath together for me. I really need it."

"Good cover story. When is she coming up?"

"Less than a quarter candle, however long that is."

"Damn, not enough time."

"Time for what?"

"This." He knelt beside her and kissed her.

As he pulled away she said, "I don't think I'd be very good right now anyway."

"Why?" He moved to the other end of the couch to take off her boots for her.

"Because I'm too stiff to move!"

"Oh, poor dear. Did you work hard this afternoon?"

"Yes," she whimpered, "Gravity, Jude, and Darven had me going non-stop for over two hours."

"Aw, poor thing. Roll over." She stiffly rolled onto her stomach, and he slid his hands under her tunic and started to massage her back. She sighed in contentment as his warm hands worked the stiffness out of her sore muscles. A moment later, there was a tap at the door and Betty came in.

"Oh!" she exclaimed, "My apologies, Majesty! I shall return."

"No, Betty," Nyakas said, "It's fine, come in."

"Aye, my lord." Betty came in followed by six men who carried a bronze tub and buckets of steaming water. They placed the tub near the fireplace and poured the water into it, then the men left the room. Betty hung Robyn's robe and a towel in front of the fire, and said, "Is there anything further you require?"

"No, thank you, Betty," said Nyakas. Betty curtsied and left the room.

Robyn got up stiffly and began to undress, dropping a trail of clothing between the couch and the tub. She slid into the steaming water with a gasp. "Shit! It's hot!"

Nyakas laughed. "Yes, love, that's why it's steaming!"

"Hush, Einstein," she said. "Give me a few minutes to get the grime and sawdust off, and then we can do what you suggested. I think we'll have time between now and dinner."

"Oh? Which suggestion would that be?"

She blushed and said, "You know."

Grinning, he sat back on the couch, put up his feet, and crossed his arms. "No, dear, I'm not sure which suggestion you're referring to."

"Yes, you do. You came up here all ready to seduce me, and now you're playing hard to get," she answered, scrubbing at the dirt intently to avoid looking at him.

"I'm doing no such thing," he answered. "I just want to hear you say it."

"Say what?"

"That you want to make love."

"OK. Fine. I do." She quickly sank down into the water under the pretense of getting the sawdust out of her hair. When she came up and opened her eyes, he wasn't on the couch. She started to look around when there was a soft kiss on the back of her neck. She reached behind her head to twine her fingers into his hair as he kissed neck her softly. He moved slowly from behind her, kissing his way around her neck and across her jaw to her lips. She returned his kiss hungrily, then slowly rose from the water.

He reached for the towel and ran it over her body, getting the worst of the water off her, then scooped her up and carried her to the bed. He trailed kisses over her body but teasingly avoided the spots he knew were most sensitive. It appeared to him that those spots were essentially the same as before; the kiss on the back of her neck had been an experiment that seemed to be working.

It didn't take long to drive her to exasperation, and she said, "Would you please stop teasing me?"

"I'm not teasing you, love," he said to her left arm.

"Yes, you are, and you know it."

"Is there something you'd rather I do?"

"Yes! Stop teasing me!"

"I'm not teasing, Robyn. If you want me to do something else, all you have to do is say so."

"I did say so!"

"You told me to stop. If that's what you want me to do, I guess I can try." He sat up and partially turned away, hiding a grin.

"Nyakas! Damn it! Why are you doing this?"

"Doing what, my dearest?" His tone was innocent, and he turned back to look at her. She seemed genuinely embarrassed as she got up, stomped across the room, and put on the robe that was still hanging in front of the fire. This surprised him; he'd thought she'd overcome her inhibitions after the first time, just as he had.

She stood in front of the fire, unsure of what to do next. She didn't want to go back to the bed, but flopping back down on the couch might look like she was pouting, and she was far beyond that. She was bordering on angry, but she wasn't sure why. After a moment's thought, she perched on the edge of the hearth, as if she were trying to dry her hair. She really didn't care what her hair looked like at the point, but it was important to keep up appearances. Sitting in front of the fire had the added benefit of an easy explanation of why her face was red.

Nyakas let her sit for a moment, the got up and went to sit behind her. He put his arms around her waist and pulled her back against his chest. He dropped a light kiss on her cheek and said, "I'm sorry."

"Sorry? Sorry for what?" She sounded angry, and he laughed inwardly.

"For embarrassing you," he said as sincerely as he could manage. "I overcame my inhibitions almost immediately after we made love the first time. I assumed that you had, too."

"Of course you did! You're male! I don't know any guys over the age of 12 who are embarrassed about sex!"

"Well, I was until you got a hold of me. If I'd had my way, we might have still been sleeping in separate rooms when you were taken."

"Yeah, well, it didn't take much for you to get over that, did it?"

"No, just one night with you."

"Women are different."

"Yes," he said seductively nuzzling her ear, "I know."

"Not just physically! See, guys spend a lot of time trying to get into girls' pants. Those of us girls who are waiting for somebody special spend a lot of time telling them no. After a while it becomes automatic to resist, and when the special somebody comes along, it takes time to get out of that mode."

"I see. How much time?"

"I don't know! I've never done this before!"

He chuckled. "We still have plenty of time before dinner. Do you want to make love? A simple yes or no will suffice."

"Yes."

"Come back to bed, then. I promise I won't tease you this time."

"So you were teasing!"

"Yes, but only because I wanted to hear you say you wanted me."

"I want you," she said, blushing yet again.

He smiled, led her back to the bed, and did as he promised.

Chapter 59

Vaytawn sat in his office. From his window he could see his daughter, Parek, training in the courtyard. The child was really quite talented with a sword, and she was her father's daughter through and through. Of course, that was as it should be. He stroked his chin thoughtfully; he could see Parek's mother only in the girl's eyes. It had been a shame that he'd had to kill Delaria; she'd been such fun to play with. But it would never have done to have her influence on the child. Delaria had come from good breeding, but she was far too softhearted.

Nyakas had no idea what he'd given up when he told Malitor to give his concubine to Vaytawn. Delaria had been skilled in many things, the most important of which were her submissive nature and her skill abed. Of course, Nyakas would not have liked Delaria's submissiveness; he had that odd taste for strength in his women. Vaytawn could not understand that, but it little mattered now.

Nyakas had committed a grave mistake. He'd gone looking for precious little Robyn and brought her back. Now they would both pay; Vaytawn would see to that.

Chapter 60

An hour later, Robyn lay contentedly in Nyakas' arms. She yawned and said, "Do we REALLY have to go down to dinner tonight?"

"I'm afraid so, my love," he answered.

"But why? I don't want to move, let alone dress."

He smiled and started stroking her hair. "I know. But everyone is expecting us, and the men will want to see the Queen."

"Can't we just say that I worked too hard today and fell asleep?"

"That wouldn't excuse me."

"Oh. Well, you're the king! Why do you need an excuse? Aren't they all supposed to just take your word for it? Please, Nyakas, just this once? Next time I'll know not to do this before dinner."

"Well, my darling," he countered, "the fact that you need to eat still remains. You did work hard today, and going to bed without dinner won't help you tomorrow, especially given your tendency to skip breakfast."

"Can't we just have it brought up?"

He laughed. "All right! All right, but just this one time." He pulled the bell cord to summon a page, then got out of bed and shrugged into his robe. There was a tap at the door as he tied the sash and he went to answer it as Robyn pulled the quilt up to her chin and tried to hide.

Nyakas opened the door and said, "Ah, Evan. I might have known you would be the one to answer. Please send word to Kelvin that the queen and I will be taking dinner in our chamber this evening, and ask Betty to bring it up."

"Yes, Majesty. I hope all is well."

"Yes. The queen overexerted herself today," he glanced over his shoulder as Robyn giggled at his choice of words, "and she's not up to court tonight."

"Yes, Majesty. I'll see to it right away," answered Evan with a straight face.

"My lord," said a familiar voice from the hallway, "did I hear you say that the Queen is unwell?"

Robyn cringed and slowly pulled the covers over her head as Nyakas answered, "Well, not exactly, Gravity. She's just, umm, tired."

"I see. I trust you'll be able to take care of this on your own?"

Robyn could hear the grin in Nyakas' voice. "Oh, I'm sure I can."

"Good. Robyn," he said loudly enough for her to hear, "you might want to actually get some rest tonight. There's work to be done tomorrow, and we'll need to start early."

She peeked out from under the covers and waved shyly. "OK, Gravity. I'll do that."

Gravity turned back to Nyakas with a half-smile. "Wake her up early enough to eat something. Food, I mean." Nyakas laughed as Gravity walked away, and he shut the door.

Robyn pulled the covers back over her head to hide her burning face, and Nyakas came to sit on the bed. He peeked under and saw her snugly wrapped in the sheet. Smiling gently, he kissed her forehead and got up. She was glad to be alone for a moment. She was sure Gravity hadn't meant it, but his comment had embarrassed her more than she cared to admit. She knew that legally she was married, but she also knew that if her father came into the room, she'd be scrambling to hide, and she wasn't doing anything wrong now!

There was a tap at the door a few minutes later and Nyakas opened it to let Betty in. Whatever she had on her tray smelled wonderful, and Robyn was suddenly ravenous. She waited until she heard Betty leave and Nyakas said, "She's gone. You can come out now." She peeked out and saw that they were, indeed, alone. Nyakas had exchanged his robe for a pair of silk pants and a tunic. She started to get out of bed, and then realized she was still naked, and her robe was on the floor on the other side of the bed. Modesty hadn't been much of a problem the last few months, but suddenly she felt very self-conscious.

Nyakas noticed this surreptitiously, but he pretended not to. He wanted to see what she would do. She slid across the bed under the covers, then stretched down to reach the robe. Unfortunately, it was a little out of range, and she stretched a little too far. She overbalanced and didn't quite recover quickly enough. With a yelp, she tumbled out of the bed onto the floor. She snatched her robe and struggled into it as Nyakas stifled a laugh.

He pretended to look up and notice her, saying, "Are you all right, darling?"

"Fine," she said, "just fine."

He chuckled a bit, trying to contain himself. She stood up gracefully as if nothing was wrong, and he began to laugh out loud. He tried to stop, but she walked over, looking at him as if she knew nothing about what was amusing him, and that made him laugh harder. She looked down her nose at him in a familiar gesture he liked to call "the plebian look," and he collapsed into gales of helpless laughter.

Indignantly, she grabbed a roll off the tray and took it out to the balcony. A minute later she heard the hysterics subside, and then he was standing behind her, putting his arms around her waist.

"Sorry," he said, trying not to start laughing again. She tried to shrug away from him, and that made him laugh again, but he wouldn't let her go. Instead, he pulled her closer and turned her around to face him. She slapped his shoulder weakly, but his laughter was contagious, and she couldn't help but laugh, too. He pulled her head into his chest and held her close as they laughed.

They went back inside and ate dinner. He urged her to eat as much as she could, offering new treats until she flatly refused to eat anything else. Only then did he recline on the couch and pull her to his side.

Her robe shifted as she settled against him and she adjusted it. He chuckled and said, "You know, darling, this modesty is charming, but it could get to be rather inconvenient."

"Inconvenient?"

"Well, yes. I mean, what will you do if you fall out of bed reaching for your robe again and break your arm?"

She feigned outrage and playfully punched his ribs. "Sorry! I don't really know why I'm behaving this way. I thought I left all of my modesty in the woods when I was out with Gravity. I guess it's just because all of this is new to me."

"That's all right," he said. "I love you more than life, and I wouldn't trade the last twenty-four hours for anything."

"Are you sure?"

"Of course I'm sure. Why would I?"

"Well, I mean, I'm not really, you know, experienced. I just thought maybe I could do better if I knew what I was doing. It's great for me! I just want it to be for you, too."

"It is, love. Having you back in my arms, and in my bed, is more than I could ask for. This new innocence is more alluring than you know."

"You're kidding!"

"No, I'm not! You were experienced before, and it was really good, but now I get to teach you as you taught me, and it's incredibly gratifying."

"If you say so."

"I do. Now come to bed so we can practice." He kissed her gently as she smiled.

She put her arms around his waist and snuggled closer. The kiss deepened and she felt as if she were being swept out to sea with high tide. She felt herself lifted from the couch as Nyakas picked her up and carried her to the bed. He lay beside her and she began to loosen his tunic. She felt certain that she could not get close enough to him; even skin-to-skin was not close enough.

Suddenly, there was a loud knock on the door. A voice said, "My lord, come quickly!" The voice sounded frightened, and Nyakas lifted away from Robyn and out of the bed. He tucked his tunic back in and Robyn gathered her open robe around herself and sat up. Nyakas glanced at her as reached for the door.

"I love you, Robyn. I'll be right back," he said.

Robyn looked at him and smiled. "I love you too, and you better hurry."

Nyakas stepped out the door to find one of his knights in armor. "What is it?"

"My lord, there are men at the gate," the knight replied as Nyakas shut the door gently.

"How many?" Nyakas asked as they started toward the battlements.

"Lord Gravity is on the wall awaiting your arrival," the knight answered. "He sent me to get you before I could see how many there were."

As Nyakas went to see to the problem, Robyn got out of bed and went to the window. She saw several men on horseback, but the one in front caught her attention. He was a bald man on a large palomino horse. 'Kerrigan!' she thought. Quickly she dressed in her leather pants and tunic and laced on her boots, then went to the battlements.

Gravity was on the battlements when Nyakas arrived. When Nyakas saw that there were archers in place and more men on duty, he knew the company was unwelcome. He went to stand beside Gravity and looked out to see whose presence graced his castle. There were eight men; seven were in long black flowing robes that covered their bodies as well as their faces. They sat on black steeds with glowing yellow eyes, like a cat's. The last man was on a palomino horse. His bald head was shiny as he sat on his horse with his hands across his waist and his horse turned sideways, ready for whatever Gravity might attempt. The man glared at Nyakas and Gravity.

"Where is she, Nyakas? Have you hidden her away from me so that I can't take care of the business I should have taken care of a long time ago?" Kerrigan asked, smiling.

"No, Kerrigan, I haven't hidden her. I'm afraid I put her to sleep, and I don't wish to disturb her. I must say, her stamina has improved, but it is still no match for mine. Sorry, old man," Nyakas replied politely, trying to anger Kerrigan.

"Let's end this now Nyakas, and we can all get on with our lives," Kerrigan replied starting to sound irritated. When he saw that no move was being made to fulfill his request, he added, "Gravity, please go get my prize so I can let you and your king get some sleep."

"As you heard, she is asleep. I won't wake her, nor will anyone else. Be gone, Kerrigan, or I will have to finish what I should have out in the wilderness," Gravity said.

"I have searched long and hard to find her. Nyakas, your father resurrected me so I could avenge my death and now I will."

"You won't get that chance today, so why don't you leave and let us get on with our lives," Gravity said sarcastically to irritate Kerrigan more.

"It's all fine because I made quick work of her friends and of one of your knights," smiled Kerrigan, adding in a whiny voice, "I'm sorry, Gravity, if are you sad."

"No, Kerrigan, I am proud of Liam and I'm proud of Robyn. Robyn can and will defeat you. She is better than Liam and someday will even be better than me, but I know for a fact she'll always be better than you," Gravity replied without expression.

Robyn arrived unnoticed on the battlements just in time to hear Gravity's remark and realized that her teacher did care about her and was her friend, even if he did have an odd way of showing it. His pride in her was the only thing she ever wished to hear out of his mouth. Smiling, she moved to where they were standing. Kerrigan's face lit up, while Nyakas looked surprised and Gravity looked as if he were about to ask her what took so long to get there. She smiled at both Nyakas and Gravity, then turned to her nemesis.

"Hello, Kerrigan," she called, "so I finally get to meet with you. I've waited a long time." She looked at the man she wished most in life to be dead, something she had never wished on anyone.

"Robyn, it is such a pleasure to finally get to meet you face to face rather than kicking you when you're down and slaughtering your friends," Kerrigan replied.

She moved quickly toward the steps, intending to go down and annihilate him, but Gravity and Nyakas grabbed her arms and held her back. She fought against them for a few seconds, and then calmed herself, knowing they were right. Kerrigan smiled as he turned his horse away from the castle and the others followed suit.

"You will meet me at your parents' house," he called over his shoulder. "I hear they need a babysitter so I thought I would volunteer." Robyn's face turned white and her heart dropped in fear, knowing exactly what he meant.

"We must leave now, Nyakas!" she said, turning to face him with tears in her eyes.

"Are you sure your ready for this, Robyn? I can't bear to lose you," Nyakas replied.

"It doesn't matter! I can't let anything happen to my family! I would never forgive myself," Robyn replied.

Nyakas took her hands and then looked at Gravity, who was watching them. Robyn looked to her teacher for some words of wisdom.

"Is she ready, Gravity? Please tell me truthfully."

"She was ready after she got back from the wilderness; the reason we trained back here was to help her control her anger and fear. She knows in her heart how to control them both, that's why I attacked her in her chamber so long ago. That's why I said what I did about Liam; I knew it would enrage her. It wasn't because I was serious, and she handled it well. I'm proud of you, Robyn. You know what must be done. Don't change a thing," Gravity replied with a smile she had waited so long to see.

They saw Kerrigan and his men enter the forest. Robyn turned on her heel and walked quickly to her chamber. She stalked in and began throwing clothing into a bag.

Nyakas came in and said, "Robyn, we're not leaving quite yet."

"Didn't you hear him? He said he is going to go babysit! He's going to try to hurt the baby."

"Your parents have gone on vacation and won't be back for a while."

"What do you mean?" she asked, sounding concerned.

"Gravity went to your home. They just happened to get two tickets in the mail to go on a cruise," Nyakas replied.

"How did you know Kerrigan would come here and then go to my home to fight?" Robyn replied, starting to smile.

"I didn't, but I took the liberty of playing it safe."

Robyn walked slowly over to him and wrapped her arms around his neck. "I love you, Nyakas."

He put his arms around her waist, "And I you, my love. Now let's get back to that practicing thing again."

They went to bed and made love like never before. Afterward, they fell quickly asleep, not knowing what was in store for them in the morning.

Gravity watched from the battlements and smiled slightly. He wondered what would happen when they were rid of Kerrigan and were able to get Marcus back from Malitor. Leaning on the parapet to look at the stars and the moon, Gravity knew the next day they would leave and wouldn't come back until all was well and the mission was accomplished. When he felt certain that there was nothing more he could do, he went to his own chamber and settled in for the night.

****

The next morning Nyakas rose before dawn and dressed quietly in black leather armor, topping it off with a black cloak with the embroidered gold dragon worn by those who were linked to Dragon Lord. His black hair blew softly in the morning breeze as he walked to the stable and asked the stable master to saddle three horses. The stable master was surprised to see him but did as he was asked; he would not question the king about his business. According to protocol, Nyakas could have sent a page, but he felt it necessary to get out of the castle and walk around a bit to steady his nerves, like a general surveying his troops before a battle.

He intended to go back to his chamber to wake Robyn, but as he entered the courtyard the magnificent sunrise caught his attention and he stopped to watch it for a few minutes. A sound from above made him turn and look up. He saw Robyn standing on the balcony watching him. He smiled at her and she blew him a kiss, then turned and walked back into their chamber. A few minutes later she strolled into the courtyard. Her blonde locks were in a ponytail and she wore loose black pants with a green tunic and a black cloak. She stood in front of Nyakas and put her arms around his waist, grinning mischievously. He looked down at her and noticed that her tunic was buttoned just enough to be decent. It was something she had done from time to time in the past just to get a rise out of him, and there was just enough cleavage showing to leave something for his imagination. Her eyes were filled with love as she stared into his, wondering what it was he was thinking. He put his arms around her shoulders and held her close. As she listened to his heartbeat she felt a single tear hit her cheek as it fell from his face.

She looked up at him and asked, "Nyakas, is something wrong?"

"No, not really. I'm just trying not to think about how this might turn out."

"I beat him once. I can do it again. Don't worry, I'm not going to leave you ever, I promise."

"It's not you I'm worried about."

Before she could ask him what he meant, the stable hands were bringing their horses to them. She looked oddly at Nyakas and began to ask were Gravity was. As if on cue Gravity came down the stairs looking more menacing than Robyn or Nyakas had ever seen him look before. His face was determined, as if nothing existed except the task at hand. His hair was pulled into a topknot as usual, except instead of the usual silver ball, it was bound with a gold ball, buffed and shiny and covered with spikes. His ring mail looked snug and he moved as if he wasn't wearing it at all. His eyes were black and seemed to change colors as he walked silently toward them. He seemed to be on a mission, and it didn't matter that he might have to walk through hellfire and brimstone to accomplish his task. His cloak appeared to be the same as Nyakas' but closer examination revealed that it bore Malitor's symbol. As Gravity climbed on his horse Nyakas and Robyn looked at him questioningly.

As always Gravity read their thoughts. "I'm going to bury Kerrigan in it." He guided his horse out of the courtyard without another word.

Robyn looked at Nyakas, as if he hadn't expected Gravity to say that. He smiled at Robyn and shrugged his shoulders, and they mounted horses and followed Gravity. The portal was already open and as Gravity moved toward it, Nyakas told Gravity to stop and wait. Gravity pulled his reins and turned the horse around as Robyn and Nyakas caught up. For a moment no one said anything.

Finally, Nyakas said, "All right, this is it. I want you two both to know I love you very much, so be careful out there! I can't imagine life without you two."

"Don't worry, friend, all will be well," Gravity replied. "She's ready and has been for some time. She just didn't know it."

"Gravity's right. You can't lose us. We'll all be safe and we will all come back together," Robyn replied putting her hand on her husband's.

They all took one last look at one another and headed for the portal. As they approached, they dismounted and turned the horses loose to find their way home. They drew their swords in anticipation of what would be on the other side, walked through and the portal disappeared.

They found themselves on a beach where the sun had already risen. In the distance they could see a large mansion. Nyakas looked at the enormous house and asked, "Gravity, where are we?"

With no expression, Gravity replied, "The house of Mike Ryan."

"You're not serious! This is a joke, right?" Nyakas asked in disbelief.

Robyn answered, "No, he's serious. I just can't understand why he would want to come here."

"Gravity," Nyakas said, trying to sound calm, "he hates us. He'll shoot us both on sight."

"No, he won't. His friend knows why we're here and he will keep Mike from firing any shots in our direction," Gravity stated. He started toward the house.

Nyakas stared at Gravity in disbelief and followed him. Normally, he had complete faith that Gravity knew what he was doing. This time, however, Nyakas had to question his wisdom.

As they approached the house, three people came out the door. Mike, Lars, and Lilly made their way toward them carrying automatic weapons.

Nyakas muttered, "Gravity, remind me when we get home to dock your pay for trying to get us all killed! Great plan, Gravity, great plan!"

"I knew you would like it. I had planned to go and knock on the door; I didn't expect them to come and meet us half way."

"Yeah, Gravity! I bet they just figured they would come out here and greet us with coffee and crumpets! They have semi-automatic weapons and we have swords! This isn't quite balanced," Nyakas replied sarcastically.

"You're losing your touch, old friend. They are just guns. If they wanted us dead they would have already fired by now."

Mike, Lars, and Lilly came within a few feet of their visitors and stopped. Their eyes met one another, and for a moment they tried to stare each other down.

Mike was the first to speak, and he didn't sound amused as he asked, "What are you doing here?"

"We came to ask for you help," said Gravity.

"Why?" asked Lars.

"Kerrigan is here. As a matter of fact, he is very close."

"I knew I smelled something foul," Mike said, glaring at Nyakas.

Nyakas started to move when Gravity put his hand in front of his friend. "Mr. Ryan, we don't need this and I can assure you that you don't want this. I know you two have this impenetrable hatred for one another, but we are fighting the same enemy. If we don't work together, Kerrigan will win and Robyn will die. I'm sorry, I'm not going to watch my best student, my queen," Gravity paused to look at Robyn, "I won't watch my friend die because you two can't get over your differences."

Robyn looked at Gravity and smiled. She had waited a long time to just hear him say those words and now knew that she could beat Kerrigan.

Nyakas knew what it had taken for Gravity to admit to being anyone's friend. "He's right. I'm willing to see past our differences as long as Mike is."

"Go to hell!" Mike replied harshly.

Lilly put her hand on his chest and turned him softly towards her. "Mike, if our son is to be safe then we need to help. These people know we have something to do with this and Kerrigan remembers you and Lars. Don't think he's forgotten. He'll come after our son and us if he isn't stopped. Mike, if you love our son and me as much as you say, you have to do this. We have overcome a lot of things. This is just one more test that we have to face, and we can defeat it as long as we do it together." Lilly looked at all the others. "All of us can beat this if we come together."

"She's right, Doctor Ryan," Robyn replied. "If we don't, your family will be in jeopardy as well as Doctor Jorgenson's and mine and all of our friends. I can beat Kerrigan, I know I can, but we have no idea what he had brought with him to our world. If he didn't bring back-up, that's great, but that doesn't sound like Kerrigan."

Lars said, "Everyone has got a point, Mike. Work together now, and afterwards, if you want to try and cut him limb from limb go ahead, but you'll be doing it alone, I assure you."

Nyakas took Robyn's hand and smiled at her. "I will put my animosity aside to take care of what we came here to take care of."

Mike looked at Lilly, nodded his head in resigned acceptance and told them to come to the house to get what they needed. They gathered their supplies quickly and Lilly talked quietly with the nanny. A short time later they all came back outside, ready for battle. They walked down to the lake and Lars opened a portal to a location near Robyn's house. They walked to the front door and Gravity knocked.

Confused, Robyn whispered, "Gravity, I thought they were on a cruise."

"They are. I'm just letting those inside know that the end is near. I figured I would give them fair warning."

The door opened as if it knew they were there. A smoky haze was all there was to greet them. As Gravity surveyed the room he could feel the presence of Kerrigan's minions nearby and his face became a mask of determination and hatred.

He turned slightly to address Lars, Mike, and Lilly without taking his eyes from the doorway. "There's the first of our opponents and they're all yours. Be careful and good luck. See you when it's over."

Lars and Lilly nodded and went towards the back door to get into position; Mike stared at Nyakas, and Nyakas returned his stare. They nodded at each other. As Mike turned to join Lilly and Lars, Nyakas quietly said, "Good luck, Mike, and thanks."

"Anytime," Mike answered and ran around to the back door.

Gravity and Robyn looked at one another in relief. They turned and walked purposefully down the road to Kevin's new gym.

Chapter 61

Lars, Mike, and Lilly entered the house carefully through the back door. They moved silently through the kitchen to the living room to find their opponents, seven very large figures in full robes with cloaks that concealed their faces. Mike's swords were drawn and Lars took the stance he had been taught early in his martial arts training. Lilly had no stance; she drew the shotgun that was slung on her back. Without a word the barrel exploded and one of the dark cloaked figures was thrown into the wall. Blood sprayed everywhere as the body hit the ground.

The remaining six seemed to be well built and muscular, and they disrobed to give their opponents a shock they would never forget. They were each about 6 foot 3 inches in height and about two hundred pounds of raw muscle. They drew archaic war hammers, swords, pole arms, clubs, and spears. Their eyes were like cats and their hands had three-inch claws. Their heads were covered in fur. Their noses were like a dog's snout and their pointy ears stood straight up. Their legs and upper bodies were as stout as a bull and covered in fine black hair. They snarled and growled at their enemies and advanced quickly.

Mike sliced one across the chest and the creature didn't slow down. Lars grabbed a chair and smashed it over one's back. It turned, looked at Lars, and threw him across the room with one hand. Another of the creatures threw Lilly across the room, and she landed near Lars.

Mike continued to fight against two of the creatures. His blade was much faster than theirs, but although his blade was as sharp as a razor, the wounds he was inflicting seemed to be very shallow. Their tough skin was like steel.

While Mike continued to work on his opponents, Lars tried to roll to his feet. He was met with a large hand, which shoved him in the chest and sent him through the swinging kitchen doors. He flew through the air until his back met the immoveable counter top.

The beast stood over Lilly, assuming she was badly hurt. Lilly allowed him to delude himself. As she played possum, she glanced up. The creature was straddled over her looking up at the ceiling raising his hands as if he had achieved victory. She saw what seemed to be a red gem between the legs of her opposition. Quickly, she pulled her .357 Colt from her side holster and placed the barrel against the gem. The creature's face changed instantly from victory to sheer terror, and his mouth dropped as he looked down at Lilly.

Lilly sneered at the creature and said, "Do I get you all hot?" The barrel of the gun flashed and the creature's body exploded. Its legs fell to each side like logs, and its insides rained down on Lilly. She quickly closed her eyes and mouth and turned her head. When it seemed to stop hitting the side of her face, she yelled, "Their weakness is between their legs!"

Mike piped back, "All right! Must be males!"

Lars was staggering to get back to his feet as another creature was moved quickly toward him with its war hammer raised. It swung down, trying to pound Lars like a nail. Lars ducked quickly out of the way and the war hammer was suddenly embedded in the counter top. The creature seemed to curse in an unknown language and tugged at his weapon. Lars smiled, got directly behind him and kicked as hard as he possibly could between his opponent's legs. The creature stopped, released the hold on his hammer and turned around slowly to find the barrel of a sawed-off shotgun in his chest. It looked extremely angry, but only for a second. Without warning Lars discharged his shotgun at his opponent's face. It exploded and Lars wore the fallout. Disgusted, Lars spat out the remains that had flown into his mouth, made a mental note to keep his mouth shut when shooting demons at point-blank range, and went back to help Lilly up.

Mike was still toying with his opponents, but he looked like he'd had enough fun. He dropped to his knees, and his katana and wakizashi found their marks between the legs of both his opponents and split the red gems that were there. The creatures screamed in pain and imploded as if sucked into a vacuum. Mike turned to the last two monsters. They stood motionless. Lars and Lilly were walking back into the living room and saw Mike stand. The two monsters stood still with their weapons crossed across their chests. They started changing shape and color and seemed to get fatter. Mike looked at Lars and Lilly and all three nodded in silent agreement as they started running for the door. As they did the monsters' bodies exploded and sent them out the door even faster than they anticipated. They found themselves on the ground, their bodies sore from the momentum that had slammed them into the lawn and covered in the pieces of their opponents.

A flash of light made them look up. A portal opened twenty feet in front of them and a very large creature began to emerge. It had the body of a lion with three heads. One was a dragon's head; another was a goat's head while the last one was a lion's head. The tail seemed to end in what looked like a morning star. And to make the creature complete were a set of wings proportioned to its body. The thing had to be nine feet high at the shoulder if it was an inch.

"Bloody hell, what's that thing?" said Lilly.

Lars gulped. "I think it's a Chimera."

The Chimera emerged from the portal, looked over at Lars and reared back onto his hind legs. His wings flapped for balance and the three heads looked at Lars. The lion head roared and a clap of thunder sounded right above their heads. The dragonhead reared back and breathed a cone of fire that was aimed right where Lars was standing. The goat head looked with an evil glint in its eyes; the tingle of electricity was gathering between its horns and then discharged a lightning bolt and shot right toward Lars.

Lars moved forward and to the side to let the fire pass harmlessly, and then he dove into a forward roll so the lightning passed a good distance over his head. Mike moved toward the Chimera's back and Lilly ran back to the house for weapons.

"Hey Lars, are you all right?" called Mike.

"Yeah, I'm fine. This pieced together lion has some very bad breath. Stay away from the business end. It seems to like me right at the moment. I could use some help."

The Chimera turned its goat head to look at Mike and with swung its tail. It anticipated the direction and distance Mike would be knocked and fired a lightning bolt from its horns at that spot.

Mike saw the tail a little too late. It knocked Mike tail over teakettle and directly into the lightning stroke, which hit Mike dead on and lit him up like a set of Christmas tree lights.

Meanwhile the dragon head looked at Lars and breathed another flame blast at him. Lars dove and rolled away from the flame breath. The flame continued into the shrubs in front of the house and they began to burn.

Lars heard the lion head finish a series of liquid syllables. A ball of fire appeared in front of it and grew for a second and shot right at Lars! The Chimera seemed to smile as it said, "Catch!"

Lars hastily prayed and a shield suddenly appeared on his left arm. He used it to block the fireball, which splashed onto the interposed shield and heated it to the melting point. It started to sizzle and droplets of steel landed on the ground in front of Lars.

Mike was screaming, "Yowwwttch. I hate lightning!" He got up to discover that his clothing was scorched and his hair stood on end.

The Chimera turned its lion and dragon heads around, leaving the goat head trained on Lars. The Chimera said to Mike, "Oh? And what do you think about heat?" The dragon head breathed a cone of fire at Mike that was five feet wide as it left its mouth and got bigger as it crossed the distance.

Mike ducked behind the nearest corner of the house, muttering "Oh, shit!"

The flame hit the house and the flame continued blasting upwards and around the corner. Mike looked in amazement and horror as the corners of the bricks began to melt and become rounded and thought 'We have to start getting the upper hand on this thing, make it react to our attacks, not us reacting to its attacks.'

The goat head looked at Lars hungrily as electricity arced between its horns. The lion head had used the time wisely; a transparent bubble surrounded the creature. The lightning bolt shot out from the goat head and hit Lars on the shield, knocking him back almost fifty feet. "Great, now this thing is going to be even harder to destroy. Almighty, how does one kill this thing?" Lars asked to the air.

"You must strike at its back to destroy it Lars. How you get there is your challenge," a voice replied.

'Hmm,' Lars thought, 'I wonder if this would work.' Lars heard liquid syllables coming from the lion's mouth and chanted very rapidly in Latin. He finished his chanting a moment before the lion did and seemed to glow with a white aura. The lion completed its spell and something shot at Lars, who made no move to parry or block the attack. As it came into contact with the white light the attack was turned around and sent back to the lion. It passed through the barrier and completely covered the Chimera's body in a black haze.

It screamed in pain so great that the dragonhead that had begun another attack on Mike missed him completely. The house wasn't so lucky; the breath weapon hit the wall two feet above Mike's head and continued up as the dragon had arched its neck in shock and pain. A line of fire ran up the side of the house and continued to shoot straight up into the empty air. The lion head slumped and the black haze disappeared.

The goat and dragon heads now fixed their gaze on Lars. They combined their attacks to produce an electrified stream of fire. It shot out from the beast's head and horns and combined a few feet after it left the heads.

Lars thought, 'I can repel magic attacks, but I don't want it tested versus electricity or fire,' and ran. The electrified fire attack missed Lars and impacted at the bottom of a large maple tree in the front yard of the now burning house. The tree burst into flames and began a slow descent right at the Chimera, which was looking at Lars and trying to line up another attack on him. It looked up just in time to see the burning tree about to fall on it. It ran and flapped its wings, increasing its speed, and just barely managed to escape.

Mike had been running toward the Chimera when he noticed the tree begin to fall. He changed direction to stay clear for a moment before deciding to go on the offensive.

He jumped at the Chimera, trying to distract it enough to make a mistake. Instead, the dragon head swooped down and caught Mike in its jaws.

Before it could crush him in its powerful jaws, Lilly's voice came from behind it.

"Hey, you overgrown freak show exhibit! Let go of my man!" She aimed the double barrel shot gun she'd rescued from the house at the goat head and fired two shots. One side of the goat's head exploded and she quickly reloaded. She aimed for the dragon's neck, but with two of its heads dead, the Chimera went into shock quickly. It dropped Mike unceremoniously and collapsed slowly to the ground, gasping.

Lilly dropped the gun and ran to Mike, who sat up shakily. "Mike, are you all right?"

"I think so, yes."

"Mike, remind me never to go with you anywhere ever again," Lars grunted, sure that he had a few broken ribs.

"Lars, do me a favor and remember I didn't even want to come out here! It was you and my wife," Mike said as he began to chuckle. "I'm just thankful that we're all still alive."

Lilly helped him to his feet. "I think I'm going to take a vacation. I truly deserve one after that."

"Great idea!" Mike interjected. "Where should we go, dear? Vegas, Miami, England, where would you say?"

"I'd say by myself. Remember, Mike, I have you to thank for all of this, love of my life. If you hadn't tried to face down Nyakas, this would never have happened," Lilly replied, smiling sweetly.

"Oh, come now, darling. You know you'll get bored without me there," Mike said.

****

Gravity, Nyakas, and Robyn stalked towards Kevin's gym. Gravity opened the front double doors with a motion of his hands. They went inside and stood against the walls silently, Nyakas and Robyn on one wall and Gravity on the opposite wall.

"Who's here, Gravity?" asked Nyakas softly.

"Robyn's friend is just down that hallway," Gravity replied.

Nyakas turned to Robyn and looked into her eyes. He cupped her face with his hands then brushed a lock of hair away from her eyes. "I love you Robyn, now and forever more. No matter what might happens here today I will always love you."

"And I you. Nothing is going to keep us apart, not this man, not your father, not anyone, and I am going to see that it stays that way," Robyn replied, lost in his eyes.

Nyakas kissed her softly. When he opened his eyes she had pulled away. He smiled softly and brushed her face one last time before he turned away and left through the door from which he had come. Robyn looked at Gravity. He stared back at her and grinned, and she smiled and pulled her sword.

"You're ready, Robyn. You're the best swordsman I've ever taught. You will win," Gravity whispered.

"I know, Gravity. You know what else? I thank you. I know now all the times you would say hurtful things you were just training me. I just have one question for you before I go. What you said out there with Mike, Lars, Lilly, and Nyakas--"

Gravity interrupted. "That was the truth. What I just said about you being the best is also true. Good luck, friend, I'll see you when it's over."

Robyn smiled and turned toward the gym. Her father had constructed a ramp similar to the ones used by wrestlers when they made the big time. She paused behind the curtain, and Gravity noticed a tape player. The tape inside said 'Brick Barabas' so he pushed the play button. As Robyn started down the ramp she heard her father's old theme music playing. She thought of stopping, but she figured it was Gravity's doing and just smiled slightly as she stalked her prey, her eyes never leaving his. She got inside the ring where she had worked for years. Kerrigan was lounging against the turnbuckle on the other side. He wore black armor that seemed to be form-fitted and his bald head gleamed in the light. His eyes were like ebony, black and mysterious, and his paired swords were already in his hands. He stared at Robyn, and she returned the stare with hatred in her eyes.

Kerrigan observed her entrance coolly. He noted absently that she had built more muscle since the last time he'd tried to kill her. As she got into the ring he commented dryly, "I see that Gravity trained you again, all for nothing I guess."

"Yes, Gravity trained me, but it wasn't anything I didn't know before. It was just something that had to be refreshed," Robyn replied her face expressionless as if it was Gravity himself talking.

A questioning look flashed across Kerrigan's face; he could see there were many changes in his opponent that were just surfacing. With this in mind he quickly went after Robyn, swinging his katana and wakizashi from left to right, trying to back her into a corner. Robyn's blade was as quick as his were and she fended off enough to avoid his strategy.

Robyn advanced toward Kerrigan too quickly. Kerrigan stepped aside to let her pass, leaving her back open. Impatiently he struck for her back, but his blade was not high enough and he drew blood from the back of her thigh.

Pain struck Robyn quickly; she made it to the ropes and held onto them. Kerrigan gloated, but Robyn was quick to recover. She turned around and leaned back against the ropes, glaring at her opposition.

Kerrigan had gained first blood; he ran to skewer her, his swords down like a battering ram. Robyn quickly dropped and pulled the top rope with her. As Kerrigan's legs hit Robyn's shoulder she stood, sending Kerrigan over the top of the rope to the outside of the ring. He grunted as he hit the floor. Robyn slid between the ropes and tried to impale him as she jumped off the apron, but he saw it and quickly rolled out of the way.

As he got to his feet again he realized he only had his katana in his hand. He hadn't even realized he dropped the wakizashi that he'd held in his left hand and now couldn't see it anywhere. He didn't have enough time to look for it. Robyn quickly closed the distance between them again, doing her best to ignore the throbbing in her leg. Her blade was quick as she lunged, and Kerrigan's katana was swift as he blocked the blow. He lunged in return and as he did she grabbed his right wrist with her left hand and jerked him and his blade quickly forward. She brought her right arm straight across his neck and sent Kerrigan up and then down hard. She drew back to give herself distance but Kerrigan was quick to recover and Robyn could tell that he was more powerful than when she faced him the first time.

Robyn began her attack anew and Kerrigan's blade became quicker. This made her nervous and she began backing up. Kerrigan's boot came from the floor and met Robyn's forehead. The stunning blow was not bad, but the spinning roundhouse kick that he followed it with sent her to the ground hard. Robyn tasted blood and the side of her face throbbed. She rolled quickly to her knees when, without warning, Kerrigan's foot came up and met her ribs. The sound it made was like branches being snapped.

"This is ironic, isn't it Robyn? We were in this situation once before but a little boy came to your rescue. Pathetic," Kerrigan said as he grabbed a handful of Robyn's hair and lifted her head up.

Robyn felt the blood drip from her mouth. As she lifted her eyes to look at her opponent, Nyakas flashed through her mind, followed quickly by Marcus, Gravity and her previous training. For a moment she felt utterly helpless, and then she remembered something Gravity had taught her and the pain seemed to stop.

"How are you going to win this time?" Kerrigan asked as his blade rose into the air.

Her voice was harsh and her hand was even harsher as she grabbed Kerrigan's groin and yanked hard. "Heart," was Robyn's reply as she began to get up. Kerrigan's face was red with pain.

Robyn drew back and began pummeling Kerrigan with multiple forearm blows. Kerrigan's head went back and forth with each impact. Kerrigan dropped his sword and Robyn switched from forearms to fists, hitting him in the face and stomach as quickly as she could.

Kerrigan made a last ditch effort to bring his sword magically to his side. The sword moved slowly; the blade rose into the air as if it wanted to go, but the hilt stayed on the floor. The blade shook with the effort Kerrigan expended trying to bring it to his side.

Robyn saw the blade standing straight up. A short kick to Kerrigan's stomach doubled him bent over. As he tried to get his breath Robyn took advantage. She put Kerrigan's head between her legs and grabbed around his waist. With every bit of energy she had left she lifted his body from the ground and swung his body up, then dropped him onto the blade that tried to kill her. The sword ran through Kerrigan's body. He lay motionless for a moment, then he and the blade began to dematerialize. Robyn watched as Kerrigan's body dissolved into mist and dissipated into the air, climbed between the ropes and sat weakly on the ring steps, her victory suddenly overshadowed by pain.

∗∗∗

Gravity left the gym and walked toward a lake that seemed undisturbed. He knew better. Gravity drew his swords and looked around at his surroundings. As he watched the lake he saw Vaytawn come from the wooded area on the other side. He strolled to the edge of the lake, but didn't stop. Instead, he continued to walk on top of the water toward Gravity. His handsome, demonic smile only angered Gravity. His arrogance was hard to miss. He wore a white tunic with teeth of animals as his buttons. His pants were loose fitting like Gravity's, his brown leather boots were finely decorated with lacings and gems. He stood in the middle of the lake staring at Gravity, who still stood on the shore. Gravity's hands went into motion and the wooded area behind Vaytawn erupted into flames and lightning began to crash on the lake and the ground alike. Rain began to pour. The fire continued to burn, undisturbed by it. The thunder that accompanied Gravity's lightning made an eerie sound as if it was something more than thunder. Gravity stepped onto the water toward Vaytawn as the rain ran down his face. His hands gripped tightly around his blades, his black ring mail was beginning to show signs of dampness yet it didn't seem to hinder Gravity's mobility at all.

Vaytawn's smile began to widen as Gravity closed the distance between them. Soon they were face to face. Gravity's eyes began changing colors, flashing gold, green, brown and black. Words seemed meaningless at this point as they stood staring at one another, eyes locked in hatred. They stood and waited as the rain came down even harder, the thunder got louder, and the lightning fell all around them.

Without warning, Vaytawn spun with a lightning fast kick at Gravity's head. Gravity effortlessly moved out of the way and held his swords out to his sides. Vaytawn came quickly at Gravity trying to keep him from using his swords. Gravity waited for his opportunity to use them. He blocked Vaytawn's flurry of kicks and punches.

Vaytawn became irritated when, try as he might, he couldn't land a blow; his opponent had unimaginable endurance. Frustrated, Vaytawn ran at Gravity as if to tackle him. When Vaytawn got close enough Gravity stepped quickly aside, grabbed Vaytawn's head and pulled it to his side, then sent him to the water. There was a small splash as Vaytawn's face hit the water, but instead of going under, he bounced to land on his back. Vaytawn was dazed but struggled back to his feet. His dizziness was far from over. Gravity ran at his opponent, jumped and caught his head between his legs and brought the rest of his body and momentum in another direction and whipped Vaytawn off of his feet and onto his head again.

Vaytawn was now furious. He was still dazed and didn't realize the extent. As he got to his feet his dizziness caught him again and he staggered right into Gravity's clutches again. Gravity picked him up, and flipped him around to position Vaytawn's head between his legs. Vaytawn realized what was about to happen just as Gravity dropped to his knees and the top of Vaytawn's head met the water again. Vaytawn lay motionless, his neck bent in an unnatural position.

Assuming he had defeated his opponent, Gravity began to walk away, but after a few steps he heard a sound and turned to see what he truly had to face. The crimson dragon was as large as Nyakas. His scales were beautiful and covered his entire body. There were no scars, but Gravity wasn't surprised, knowing Vaytawn's vanity. He could see Vaytawn was seriously vexed and understandably so, Gravity thought.

Vaytawn stood and, without warning, shot fireballs from his mouth. They found their mark on Gravity and sent him backwards across the water. Gravity's ring mail was torched and was useless, and he ripped the rest of it off. He tore the shirt he wore under his armor and the tattoos that Gravity's master had blessed him with were exposed.

Gravity's swords were ready and the spiked ball that held his topknot was ready as well if Vaytawn got close enough. He moved toward the dragon, and Vaytawn took flight. With a quick pass he caught Gravity in the chest with his tail and sent him back to the ground. Gravity could see blood trickle from the wound and knew it would heal, but with an opponent like this it wouldn't heal quickly enough. He had to be at his very best to be able to beat this adversary.

Vaytawn quickly landed and moved toward Gravity. As he swiped with his claw it was met with Gravity's blade and Vaytawn yelped as the pain ran through his body. Gravity saw an opportunity to close in, but even he was not quite quick enough. Vaytawn's tail met Gravity's forehead and it was only because of Gravity's quickness that the tail only cut his forehead and did not lop off his head. Gravity hit the ground hard. He could taste his blood as it ran down his face profusely. Gravity thought fleetingly of Nyakas, Robyn, and Stephan and his hands began to clench as Vaytawn laughed, watching Gravity bleed.

Gravity got up and ran at his opponent and Vaytawn, watching in amazement, flicked his tail but it was too late. When Vaytawn's tail began to swat, Gravity leaped. Extraordinary aim and luck left deep cuts on Vaytawn's chest and arms as he passed by.

Gravity landed and began to wield the swords around and around, warning Vaytawn to keep his distance. Vaytawn's arrogance had got the better of him and he leaped for Gravity to crush him like a cockroach. Gravity saw it coming and jumped out of the way, ending up behind Vaytawn.

Vaytawn didn't see him, but he felt pain like never before as Gravity drove his katana deep into Vaytawn's tail. Vaytawn screamed in pain and lifted his tail. Gravity realized he was going for a trip to an unknown location at the moment of liftoff. It was a short flight. He hit the ground hard and his swords fell from his hands. He was quick to recover and picked up his weapons, watching as Vaytawn turned quickly around to see Gravity staring at him.

Vaytawn launched, flying low, and grabbed Gravity in his front claws. The momentum drove Gravity's swords from his hands. Vaytawn quickly gained altitude. He wanted to toy with Gravity before he finished him. Blood still dripped from the cuts already inflicted by Vaytawn as Gravity felt the grip on his body tighten. Vaytawn laughed as Gravity squirmed to get free.

Knowing he had to do something quickly, Gravity spit blood in Vaytawn's face. Vaytawn's grip loosened just enough for Gravity to grab the dagger he had saved specifically for Vaytawn. He flipped the dagger so he had the handle in hand. Vaytawn saw it and his mouth dropped. The dagger was very familiar to Vaytawn; he recognized it as the one he had given Vermeer so many years ago, when he had infiltrated Nyakas' domain. He knew Gravity had killed him with that dagger. What he didn't know about was the enchantment Gravity had placed on it. The dagger glowed red and seemed to get brighter as it got closer to Vaytawn.

"Say hello to your partner in hell! Tell them Gravity sent you," Gravity exclaimed as he brought the dagger to the middle of Vaytawn's chest. The now-enchanted knife ripped through the center of Vaytawn's mass like a chainsaw and Gravity suddenly found himself in thin air. As Gravity fell to the earth the blood from Vaytawn's wound was like a full water tower being emptied. Vaytawn's body seemed to linger in the sky for an instant before falling. As the body fell, the vanquished soul seeped through Gravity's eyes, becoming a permanent part of him and his for the torturing. The body disappeared as it hit the water. The lightning, thunder, and even the fire all subsided and it was peaceful with the sun shining brightly.

As Gravity hit the surface of the lake he realized that his walk on water spell had dissipated. He sank through the water, but rather than swimming, he went to the bottom and began to walk. He could only laugh at what had just happened. He walked out of the lake and looked closely at the world he had hated for so long, and then began walking slowly back to where he had left Robyn.

▪▪▪

Nyakas ran down the dirt road, knowing the presence of his father was nearby. About a mile away he saw his father standing in the middle of the road with Nyakas' son standing beside him. Marcus looked frightened, but without hesitation he ran from his grandfather's side to his father's.

"Go ahead, Marcus. Get as close to your father as you can. He won't be spending any more time with you after this day," Malitor said, smiling.

"No, Father, he comes to my side because he already knows what I'm going to do to you, something I should have done a very long time ago."

"Son, I give you one last chance to join your brother and me to become the most powerful dragons of all time. We could all take over Dragon Lord."

"I wouldn't join you and my brother for tea and crumpets let alone to band together with you two. You're going to die on this day, Father and if you don't it really won't make much difference, because my son will avenge my death," Nyakas replied.

"Alright, Son, I see there's no point in talking to you about this anymore. Looks like I will just have to kill you," Malitor replied as he turned his back to his son and began his metamorphosis.

Marcus intuitively backed away as his father's body began to change as well. Malitor's form seemed to come from his mouth to kill the human disguise he wore. His enormous dragon body stretched at least two-hundred yards. His black scales were like plates of armor and crimson scales wrapped around his neck and the base of his claws. His head bore two large horns that wrapped around to almost touch each other in the middle and two ivory tusks like an elephant.

Nyakas' transformation was much less grotesque. His human disguise seemed to dematerialize as the dragon grew within seconds. His black and gold scales were beautiful, but some of the scales were badly scarred and in a few small spots there were only scars and no scales. His horns stretched straight back from his enormous head, and his body was almost as long as his father's.

The dragons stood staring at one another, daring the other to make the first move. Marcus watched helplessly from the cover of some large trees as his father and grandfather stared each other down.

The two dragons took to flight and Malitor took the offensive by spitting several fireballs. Nyakas flew left to right and dodged out of the way as the fireballs ignited the ground below. Nyakas fired the next volley of fireballs, and Malitor flew down and then quickly ascended. As he passed below Nyakas, Malitor's claw met his son's underbelly and cut Nyakas deeply.

Nyakas screamed in pain as blood sprayed through the sky and flew in right behind his father. He fired fireballs and four of them ignited on Malitor's back.

Malitor growled loudly as the fireballs ignited on his scales. He increased his speed enough to get turned around to go head to head with his son. They flew at one another with great speed, and Malitor ducked at the last minute and hit Nyakas' underbelly again. Nyakas began to fall to the earth, but he caught enough strength to land somewhat clumsily. He flew back into the air and went right at his father again as Malitor laughed at his son's insolence.

Nyakas fired four fireballs without warning. They were right on target and Malitor was dazed. Nyakas' right claw caught the face of his father and raked his eyes.

Malitor was in trouble. Before he had a chance to recover, Nyakas fired lightning bolts from his claws and they found their mark. As the electricity ran through Malitor's body, Nyakas drew his claws close to Malitor's face and fired what looked to be a bolt of black energy. Marcus watched with amazement as the black bolt flew at its opponent, became gold, and encased Malitor. The energy started at his lower talons and quickly moved through his body. Malitor fell. As he impacted the ground the gold encased body shattered and the gold energy bolt flew into the sky. The only sound heard were the last screams of Malitor as they resounded into the air.

Nyakas' body healed as he landed. His wounds slowly closed as his son came to his side to help him. As his wounds healed he changed back to his human form and bent at the waist with his hands on his knees to catch his breath.

****

Gravity arrived at the school just in time to see Mike, Lars, Lilly, and Robyn exiting. They all looked beaten up, but they were alive, so Gravity assumed they must have beaten their opponents.

"You all look terrible," he observed coolly. Mike and Lilly laughed and Lars scowled.

"Thanks, Grav," Robyn said, sitting slowly on the step and holding her ribs.

"Ribs again?" asked Gravity.

"Yeah, he seemed to like them," she grunted. "I hate when that happens."

"Not to worry," said Lilly cheerily, "they've been bandaged, and I found some pain killers for her."

Gravity grunted. "Pain killers don't work as well as magic." He squatted in front of Robyn. "Let me see."

There were three pairs of raised eyebrows as Robyn carefully lifted her tunic up to the bottoms of her breasts, and Gravity placed his hands gently over the bandages. The three spectators realized that they must have done this before, but it certainly did not look right for Gravity's hands to be there. Her torso glowed with a gold light, and then there was a snapping sound as she cried out. Gravity removed his hands and stood up, and Robyn let go of her tunic and slumped forward to rest her forehead on her knees.

A moment later she sat up said, "I'm so glad that bastard is dead. I hate when you have to do that. It almost hurts more than the breaking."

Gravity offered her a hand, which she accepted, and he pulled her to her feet. "Come," he said, "we should go find Nyakas. Hopefully he's finished and we can go home."

****

As Nyakas straightened, he saw the others walking toward him. He looked at Robyn, trying to see if she'd been hurt, then watched as Marcus turned to see what his father was looking at. Robyn paused as Marcus' eyes met hers. Marcus seemed to know instinctively who she was and ran straight to his mother's arms. Robyn caught the hurtling boy and held him in spite of her tender ribs, and they both began to cry.

"I'm sorry, Mother. I love you," Marcus said as his tears fell uncontrollably.

"I love you too, Marcus, and you have no reason to be sorry," Robyn replied.

Mike went to stand in front of Nyakas and extended his hand. Nyakas accepted his hand and shook it. Everyone stopped and watched the two men put their differences aside.

"I was wrong, Nyakas, and I'm sorry," Mike said sincerely.

"Mike, don't apologize. I'm guilty of the same crimes as you. Friends?" Nyakas asked.

"Friends," was Mike's reply as they brought their arms around for a half hug and smiled at one another.

Smiling, Mike went to Lilly's side, and Nyakas went to Robyn and Marcus. Gravity stood a few feet away, observing, uneasy about getting too close.

"Glad you could join us, old friend," Nyakas said.

Gravity said nothing, only giving Nyakas a dark look with a small grin as he was took off what was left of his torn and tattered equipment.

"Where's my brother, Gravity? I would love to see him," Nyakas said as he looked seriously at Gravity.

Gravity looked at Nyakas and replied with an odd little grin, "I'm right here, brother."

Nyakas smiled and said, "Well, where's that guy you went to go see earlier?"

"Oh, he had to split," Gravity said with his famous non-expression.

Nyakas shook his head, grinning, and put his arms around Marcus and Robyn. Marcus looked at Gravity and mouthed the words "thank you" and Gravity smiled slightly and began to open a portal back to home. Mike held Lilly tightly in his arms. Lars stood back and just shook his head trying to make sense of it all. Nyakas, Robyn, and Marcus walked toward Mike, Lars, and Lilly.

Nyakas extended his hand to Lilly and Lars and thanked them both. "We're going back to our home. I would be honored if you would join us for a festival."

Lilly and Lars both looked at Mike, and Mike smiled. "We would be honored."

Gravity waited for everyone as they walked through the portal into the bright sun of a beautiful spring day. As they walked through Stephan and their people met them and cheered for the royal family that was whole for the first time in 700 years. Stephan hugged her brother and Robyn and whispered in their ears how much she missed them and loved them. Marcus was in amazed at how much his father was loved while his grandfather was feared, and decided that it must be much better to be loved than feared.

As the light of the day began to fade, a woman stood on the edge of the forest listening to the party, the celebration of a family brought together and another family destroyed. She was nearly six feet tall with a trim, athletic physic. She wore a crimson tunic and black loosely fitted pants with gems down the length of the thighs. Her boots reached her calves and were laced with gold twining. Her eyes were dark green and had red pupils, her long black hair restrained in a braid which hung over her right shoulder. It was fastened with a simple leather thong and reached nearly to her waist. She wore a black cloak and the hood was on as she watched the festivities. As she watched her eyes never blinked and her body never moved.

"Nyakas, you enjoy the celebration of your new beginning, and I will celebrate your downfall," Parek said softly as she brought her hands together. "My father's death will be avenged, whether it's you first or the rest of those close to you."

As she stood a man on a horse rode up to her side. He was dressed similarly to her except the hood of his cloak concealed his face. His voice was harsh and deep as though possessed by evil as he said, "Lady Parek, should we move to destroy the kingdom?"

Parek's head was slow to turn as she looked at the man. "No. Do no such thing. That's what Gravity and Nyakas expect. This won't happen today. My father and grandfather were too impatient and impulsive. I will not make the same mistake. Take the men back and await my arrival. I will be along shortly." The man bowed in the saddle and jerked the reins to turn the horse sharply. He whistled an order, and there was only a rustle as the twenty men in Parek's standard guard left.

Parek stood a while longer, allowing the anger and hatred to build to an acceptable level while her men left. Finally, she took one last look at the castle and then turned around to walk through the forest to her horse, which she mounted and rode into the gathering gloom.

Inside, the festival had moved into the ballroom where bards were playing and people were dancing. Nyakas and Robyn danced closely together. Marcus watched them as he conversed with Lars and the Ryans. A movement caught his eye and he saw Gravity come down the spiral staircase looking like he hadn't even engaged in battle. Gravity wandered through the crowd to sit by Marcus.

Marcus smiled, seeming a little nervous without knowing why.

"What is it, Marcus?" Gravity asked.

"It's funny. I don't know, I guess there will be no way to ever thank you. This is all so new to me, I just don't want to disappoint them."

"Marcus, you did something only one other person has ever done and that's leave Malitor's side. Your father was the first. I don't think you have to worry about making them proud. They already are proud of you," Gravity replied.

"Thanks, Gravity. You can't understand how much that means to me."

Gravity stood to leave, and as he did a hand grabbed his and pulled him in a different direction. Gravity turned around to see Stephan, dressed in a white and gold gown, smiling at him and holding his hand. Stephan's blonde hair was bound neatly with flowers in a ponytail.

Gravity looked into her eyes, and it seemed as though everyone else had faded away and Gravity was caught in something unfamiliar. Gravity followed her out onto the dance floor and Nyakas and Robyn watched as they danced. Marcus went to the dance floor to join his parents, and they both smiled. Instead of stopping the dance they all locked arms and began to dance together. The family was whole again.

ISBN 1553695410